DOMINION

Novels by Fredrick Huebner

Dominion

Shades of Justice

Methods of Execution

Picture Postcard

Judgment by Fire

The Black Rose

The Joshua Sequence

Praise for the Work of Fredrick Huebner

Judgment by Fire

Nominated for an Edgar Award by the Mystery Writers of America

"*Judgment by Fire* was terrific and *Picture Postcard* is even better."
—*Author Stuart Kaminsky*

Picture Postcard

"Byzantine plot at breakneck speed."—*Booklist*

"The plot is solid…fresh, brisk charm." —*Los Angeles Times*

"Huebner's gift for evoking place has never been better."
—*Seattle Post Intelligencer*

Methods of Execution

"A terrific book…a lawyer's novel in the spirit of the very best of Scott Turow and John Grisham." —*Trial Magazine*

"Forceful prose…well constructed plot…a winner."
—*Library Journal*

"Nail gnawing suspense…Startling and wholly unpredictable."
—*Lexington Herald Leader*

Shades of Justice

"Fascinating." —*The Boston Globe*

"Great Courtroom Drama." —*Los Angeles Times*

"A First Rate Crime Novel." —*Booklist*

"Stands out." —*Houston Chronicle*

Colleen, and the Quantum Entanglement

The powers that be are ordained of God.

Romans 13:1 (King James Version)

Indeed I tremble for my country when I reflect that God is just.

Thomas Jefferson

DOMINION

-By-

Fredrick D. Huebner

Afghanistan

"They're coming," Dane Troyer said softly. The Taliban moved like ghosts down the steep slope through the ragged fringe of the cedar and pine forest, taking what cover they could in their descent.

"How many, Troy?" his Lieutenant, Roy Conover, demanded.

"Shit. Maybe forty, LT."

Troyer and Conover lay on the frozen mud floor of the forward observation post, looking west through a rifle slit in the sand bag wall through night and wind-driven snow to the 11,000 foot north-south ridgeline of the Hindu Kush Mountains. The post was on a triangular spur that extended east from the ridge, overlooking the Pakistan border and the Kunar River canyon a thousand feet below. It had been dug out of a shepherd's mud-walled kraal and reinforced with sand bags and sheet metal, but offered no warmth and little shelter from an RPG or mortar attack. The seven other men and one woman with them comprised A Squad, D Company (Intelligence) 3rd Brigade Special Troops Battalion, 10th Mountain Division. The squad huddled against the cold behind the mud and sandbag walls, M-4 carbines fitted through firing slits, their packs, sleeping bags, and ammunition boxes stuffed between them.

Conover thumbed his JTRS radio headset, simultaneously sending his voice and GPS location data over the military's satellite-enabled encrypted system. "Kamdesh, this is Seneca. Come in." Conover waited nervously for the response, fighting not to show any emotion in front of his troop. He was a handsome, rangy African-American kid in his early twenties, seven months out of West Point.

"Seneca, Kamdesh. Rivas here. What's going on, Lieutenant?"

"We need extraction, sir. Taliban are coming down the ridge above us from the west. We are down four to one, possibly more, and backed up against the canyon. Our medic's been wounded by one of their snipers and needs evac."

"No can do, Seneca. There's a major engagement tonight up valley. I'm going to have to get air support from Bagram. Can you hold out until morning?"

Conover ground his teeth in frustration. "Negative, sir. We'll be overrun." He turned back to his Sergeant. "Are they still moving, Troy?"

"Yes, sir. About 300 yards now. They're coming in slow, not sure what we've got. But they are coming."

"Let's keep them guessing as long as we can. Squad, hold fire until my command! We've got no rounds to waste!"

Conover switched back to his radio mike. "We'll be under fire in five minutes or less, Captain. Are the Apaches flying? We need CAS pretty fast if we're going hold here."

"Understood, Lieutenant. We're going to work the problem, get you what we can. Hang tough. Rivas out."

The Taliban opened scattered fire as their fighters cautiously emerged from the ragged forest into open ground. Red tracers plowed into the post's mud and sandbags. A pair of RPG rounds detonated just short of their position, blasting frozen dirt and snow into the air. Conover waited to a count of ten, and then scrambled over to his rifleman. "Janicki! Can you see them?"

"I've got them," Janicki replied. "Two hundred yards." Janicki was the squad's rifleman, a weightlifter from Irvine, California who could carry the seventeen pound M249 Squad Automatic Weapon in one hand as though it was his sidearm. Janicki had the SAW propped on its folding bipod legs on a sandbag, aimed due west, waiting. At just over a hundred yards, Conover gave the order. "Take them out."

The SAW's 5.56 millimeter bullets quickly cut down the three men at the front of the Taliban line. The trailing fighters dropped flat and returned fire, inching forward. They were well past the tree line now, low but exposed.

"Squad!" Conover shouted. "Open fire! Keep them down!" He picked up his own M4 carbine and began firing. A third RPG blast detonated just outside the bunker and collapsed the mud-brick wall, stunning Conover and showering him with dirt. He sprawled on his back on the floor of the post. As he shook off the impact of the explosion he looked up through a hole torn in their makeshift roof and saw an Apache helicopter fall out of the night sky and spit a stream of fire from its nose mounted 30-mike chain gun, raking the Taliban trapped on open ground. When the chain gun paused the survivors broke and ran for the cover of the ridge. The helicopter followed them as it thundered over the observation post and loosed a barrage of Hydra rockets. White phosphorous explosions dazzled and burned hot in the dark night and wind driven snow as the Apache wheeled around for a second pass at the base of the ridge. The chopper orbited and fired a third and final barrage of Hydras, then raked the ridge with gunfire before descending beside the embattled observation post, exploding loose dust and snow. The pilot cut his engines and the plateau was suddenly silent but for the relentless keening of the mountain winds.

Conover cautiously raised his head and stared at the chopper. It was an AH-64A, the Army's workhorse attack chopper, but was painted flat black with no military markings at all. The hatch door at the front of the tandem cockpit opened and a small man, his face concealed by a flight helmet with night vision goggles, swung easily down the side of the craft. He wore a black flight suit with a single square shoulder patch, a black star on field of light blue. He hustled to the compound, bent low from the waist as he ran, and then vaulted over the low wall, landing in a crouch beside Roy Conover. The man removed his flight helmet and extended his hand.

"Kyle Jackson," he said, grinning. "You're Lieutenant Conover? We picked up your call for CAS, thought we'd see if we could help." Jackson spoke with a soft North Carolina accent.

"That's right." Conover shook the extended hand, looked Jackson over. He saw a very fit man, early in middle age, with a brushy salt and pepper military haircut over a square-jawed, even featured face. "Who the hell are you guys?"

"Private security. We call ourselves Dark/Star."

"Heard of you," Conover replied. "But how in hell did you get yourselves an Apache?"

Jackson's grin widened. "Let's just say it's on extended loan," he replied. "How are your guys? I've got some food and heat packs in the bird, and a pretty good medical kit."

"We could use that. My medic's been hit by sniper."

"Where is he?"

"It's a she. Specialist Carlotta Johnson. Our regular medic lost his mother

and was sent home on a compassionate leave. Johnson volunteered to take his place. This was supposed to be just an observation mission, not combat. I'm going to catch major shit for her being wounded here."

"Maybe I can help. Can Johnson sit up?

"Not sure. We've given her plasma and stopped the bleeding for now, we think, but the pain's got to be getting pretty bad."

Jackson nodded his understanding. "Wait here."

He ran back to the Apache, then returned carrying two duffel bags, a field jacket and an M-4 carbine. He dropped into the post beside Conover and crouched on his heels. "I think between us we've taken out at least two-thirds of the Taliban force. The rest are either holed up on that ridge or retreating back over it. I don't think they'll be back tonight, but best we stay on alert. My pilot will take another pass at the ridgeline with the chain gun as he takes off. He can fly your medic over the hump to Bagram to the field hospital and get their Blackhawks up here to pull you out as soon as the weather clears."

Jackson crawled to the back of the post where Carlotta Johnson lay propped against two kit bags, stirring uneasily. Jackson took her pulse from the artery in her neck, listened to her breathing, and checked the bandage packed against her wounded shoulder. When he was satisfied that she could handle the painkiller without falling into critical hypotension he snapped open a 15 mg morphine injection pen, raised her uniform blouse, and injected her just above her left hip. Conover, Troyer and Jackson then eased Johnson carefully into a sleeping bag and carried her to the Apache. Jackson strapped her into the Apache's co-pilot/gunner seat and leaned in to say a few words, clasping both her hands in his own. He closed the hatch and pounded on the side of the chopper to tell his pilot to raise ship.

At first light the snow stopped falling and the sun broke through the thick storm clouds over the Karakoram Mountains. The distant thunder of helicopters could be heard coming down the river valley. As the relief choppers neared Kyle Jackson gathered Conover and his men into a tight circle in the center of the ruined compound.

"Pray with me," he commanded.

The soldiers knelt with him, joined hands, and prayed.

Chicago

The Major League All Star Game
New Comiskey Park
Chicago, Illinois
Tuesday, July 16, 7:30 P.M. CDT

The Delta-accented bass voice rolled from the announcer's booth behind home plate through Comiskey Park's packed humanity like thunder and glory itself, silencing the excited crowd and filling the clear warm Illinois twilight with joy.

"*Ladees and Gentlemen! This is Reuben Charles, the Voice of Your Chicago White Sox!* And Tonight! Tonight! It is my *great* honor to introduce to you a man that was a *Three-Time Winner* of the Cy Young Award, the man who *led* our Chicago White Sox to be World Series Champions not once but *twice*, our friend, our former Senator from Illinois, and….the *President of these Black and White, these Red And Blue, and Always, Always United States,* Brett Campbell!"

The stadium lights at New Comiskey flared into life, turning the bluegrass turf of the outfield deep green. President Brett Campbell burst out of the White Sox bullpen as he had many times in his nine-year major league baseball career. He was flanked by the red-jacketed all-stars of the National League, Braves and Brewers and Rockies and Giants, and the blue-jacketed players of the American League, Yankees and Orioles and Red Sox and Angels. Campbell ran with an easy loping stride, relaxed and powerful, dressed one more time in White Sox pinstripes, ball held easily in the glove on his right hand, ready to make the ceremonial first pitch with the left arm that had once thrown ninety-six mile per hour fastballs and the nastiest slider in the American League. Campbell had grayed in his three years as President but his shoulders were still strong and wide, waist still narrow. His long dark face bore a genuine smile of pleasure at being home again in Chicago. Campbell waved broadly to the crowd, joshing and elbowing the players running along side of him, some of them once rookies who had played beside him in his final season fifteen years before.

Brett Campbell had been by most accounts a successful President, his accomplishments made larger and his faults made smaller by comparison to his predecessor, a man widely reviled for starting and nearly losing two wars and all but bankrupting the nation in the process. Campbell had campaigned and governed far more from the center than his liberal supporters within the Democratic Party had wanted, choosing a Republican, North Dakota Senator Charles McConnell, as his Vice-President in the first national unity ticket since the Republican Abraham Lincoln had run with Democrat Andrew Johnson in 1864. Campbell inherited an economy flattened by the worst recession since the 1930s, but after three bitterly hard years people were working and shopping and saving money for their kids' futures again. The armed services had killed Bin Laden, degraded the remnants of al Qaida with ruthless drone and Special Forces attacks, and returned home to rebuild. The world showed tentative signs of becoming a quieter, less violent place.

Campbell took the mound and made a show of inspecting it, brushing dust off the rubber, fingering the rosin bag, and flattening an imaginary lump in the dirt with his spikes, the same ritual he had always employed when coming into a game as the White Sox' closer. The crowd fell momentarily silent, then got the joke and roared with laughter as the President looked up and waved, his trademark sudden grin captured by the television cameras and magnified a thousand times as it was flashed to the giant screen above center field. The President shooed away the players standing near him on the mound, placed his heel against the rubber, raised his right leg, wound up and then delivered a sinking fastball straight over the plate, knee high.

The fifty-one thousand fans in New Comiskey cheered so loudly that when the first diversionary explosions came from the stands they were seen and felt more than heard. The cheers turned to screams as the crowd panicked, some trying to force their way up the narrow stairs between sections, others scrambling over the green rows of seats and the backs of those who had fallen before them in a desperate effort to reach the field. Six suicide bombers swarmed over the dugouts and ran on to the field, three from each baseline. Four were gunned down by the Secret Service before they could reach the tight cluster of players and agents that surrounded the President.

Two of the bombers reached the mound and exploded their vests, each loaded with ten pounds of Semtex and steel nails.

One thousand nine hundred eighty nine baseball fans in the stadium died that night, as many from injuries suffered in the desperate attempt to flee as were killed by the bomb blasts themselves. Twenty men and one woman lay dead on the infield turf: five secret service agents, six terrorists, nine baseball All-Stars, and the President of the United States.

Washington

Chapter One

**The White House
Thursday, July 14
10:30 P.M. EDT**

"Paul. Wake up."

Paul Coulter was slumped over his laptop in his cramped five-foot square cubicle. He stirred, opened his eyes reluctantly. "What time is it?" he asked, voice thick with fatigue.

"After ten," Edward Doyle, the deputy White House press secretary responded. "You all right? You look like you haven't slept in days."

"Three days, to be exact. Fuck. I missed a deadline." Coulter tapped keys and pulled up the column he had been editing to email it to PoliticsUSA.com, one of his distributors.

"It can wait," Doyle said impatiently, his nasal accent pure Boston. "The old man wants to see you."

"What?" Coulter twisted around and looked at Doyle incredulously, checked his watch. "He's finally going to give me the interview I asked for six months ago? At ten-thirty on a Thursday night?"

"No. He's in the residence. Says he wants to have a drink with you. Personal. And off the record." Doyle scowled, his thick black brows knitted together with anxiety, certain that any conversation between the President and a reporter was an incipient public relations disaster in the making. Doyle, once a spokesman for a major, now bankrupt, Wall Street investment bank had always counseled his bankers never to speak to the press, especially when being led from their palatial offices in handcuffs. "We're clear on that, Paul? This is strictly off the record?"

"Sure, unless the President says otherwise." Coulter rubbed his dry eyes, looked down at his sweaty, wrinkled white cotton dress shirt and found a new coffee stain on his burgundy tie. "I look like shit."

"Doesn't matter, you don't clean up that well either," Doyle shot back. "And you don't say no to a drink with the President. Come on."

Coulter stood and unfolded to his full six foot three like a clumsy puppet rising from its box. He pulled on his suit jacket, shut down his laptop, and locked it in the small file cabinet jammed under the carrel desk. He followed as Doyle, a short man growing stouter every month from rich meals taken in the Navy Mess, puffed heavily up the narrow stairs leading from the warren of basement offices to the West Wing's first floor press room. They walked through the Palm Room into the Residence, nodding to the silent uniformed secret service agents on night duty seated along the walls of the long narrow Center Hall. Their footsteps on the stone floor echoed through the vaulted corridor.

The elevator bumped to a gentle stop in the family quarters in the center section of the White House. Doyle led Coulter through the Yellow Oval room. Lightning flashed in the night sky outside the French doors opening onto the Truman Balcony. The storm was somewhere to the southwest, over the Blue Ridge Mountains, and left a distant scent of ozone on the night air.

Doyle knocked, opened the doors to the Treaty Room, and found it empty.

"President must still be changing, he got a call from the Russian president he had to take," Doyle said. "Shouldn't be long unless they've invaded somebody. Wait here."

Under President Charles McConnell the Treaty Room had been returned to the configuration George H.W. Bush had preferred and again served as the President's personal library and evening home office. The *Resolute* desk, crafted from the oak timbers of a 19th Century British arctic exploration ship and gifted by Queen Victoria to Rutherford Hayes, was aligned to the west wall facing the marble fireplace across the room. An enormous gilt framed mirror hung above the carved mantel between tall flanking mahogany bookcases. Two heavy leather armchairs were placed along the room's south wall, a cocktail table poised between them, a brass reading lamp stationed beside the chair the President favored at night. Chartran's *The Signing of the Peace Protocol between Spain and the United States* hung on the wall behind the *Resolute* desk. A formal, seated portrait of a sour-faced Ulysses S. Grant, painted late in Grant's disastrous second term, faced the President's reading chair from across the room.

Coulter wandered briefly around the room, then stepped closer to the President's reading chair. A 2005 *Time* Magazine cover and accompanying news story had been framed for display on the wall above. The cover photograph showed a U.S. Army Humvee in tawny camouflage paint exploding into an intense orange-red fireball in a narrow Baghdad street as a tall man dressed in desert fatigues pulled another man out of the Humvee's front passenger seat and away from the flames. Both men's clothes were on fire. Coulter glanced at the photo caption he knew by heart: "As Baghdad explodes into violence, Chicago *Tribune* war correspondent Paul Coulter rescues Senator Charles McConnell, R-North Dakota, from his burning HMV in Sadr City."

"Paul," President Charlie McConnell said briskly, striding into the room. McConnell was less than six feet tall but had a bullish neck and heavy shoulders, the product of childhood labor on a wheat farm in his native North Dakota. He was freshly showered and casually but carefully dressed in a pressed blue oxford shirt, knife-creased khaki slacks, and the kind of expensive dark tobacco Italian loafers that no sane politician ever wears in public. At sixty, McConnell retained a thatch of thick white hair and pale blue eyes, but the burn scars on the left side of his squared off, even-featured face gave him an aspect of age and pain. When McConnell's Presidential portrait was painted the scars would be softened and given a faintly heroic glow, as in Shoumatoff's unfinished portrait of the dying, war-ravaged Franklin Roosevelt, painted at Warm Springs, Georgia on the morning of Roosevelt's death. Here, without television makeup, the scars were an angry reminder of the thousand degree sheet of flame that had torn through McConnell's Humvee years before. Coulter unconsciously touched his left arm, where the worst of his own burn scars remained, hidden beneath the fabric of his suit.

McConnell paused and extended a hand to Paul Coulter while appraising Coulter's rumpled suit and stained shirt with eyes full of skeptical good humor. "You look like a hobo, Paul. We need a dress code for the Press Room."

Coulter shook the President's outstretched hand and said, "It's good to see you, sir. A dress code would be a wonderful idea. But," Coulter added sarcastically, "your poll numbers would drop another seven points by the time we got even with you."

"Yeah, there's that," McConnell replied, chuckling. "Would you like a drink? Walter," he added, gesturing to his elderly valet, hovering in the doorway, "I'd like three fingers of Booker's on some cracked ice, please. Paul?"

"I'll have the same, Mr. President. Thank you. How are your daughters?"

"They're good, good, thanks for asking," McConnell replied, waiting for his drink. "Diane's busy with her kids. Barb just tried her first jury case for the Hennepin County District Attorney in Minneapolis. She sent me a disk from the courtroom video. She was nervous, but pretty darn good, if you'll forgive a father's pride. The jury was out a day but came back and convicted." McConnell smiled. "I told Barb when I get out of this gilded jail we'll go hang up our shingle together in Grand Forks. McConnell & McConnell, the Peoples' Lawyers."

Coulter laughed out loud. "You'd finally make some money, Mr. President," he replied.

"Damn right," McConnell replied. "I'm going to need a few bucks to retire." It was a joke on all sides: McConnell, once a modestly successful Grand Forks lawyer, had purchased a small bankrupt commodity trading firm thirty years before and built it into Agricorp, the world's third largest grain trader, before leaving business for politics and winning election to the Senate from North Dakota.

He was easily worth a hundred million dollars, perhaps more, and cared nothing for it.

McConnell let the grin fall from his face as he took a heavy crystal tumbler of bourbon and dropped wearily into his favorite leather reading chair. McConnell paused and sipped his drink while Coulter was served. "Take a seat, Paul." McConnell gestured toward the second deep leather chair and raised his glass. "Cheers."

"Cheers," Coulter replied automatically, then added, "If you're in a generous mood tonight, Mr. President, I'd love to know who you are going to nominate for Vice-President."

McConnell snorted. "Here's a scoop. It will not be our esteemed current Vice-President, the honorable James Babineux Robinson of Louisiana. And, nice try, Paul, but I'm not going to give you a head's up on the nomination. To be honest, I haven't made up my own mind yet. I'm going to stick to the schedule I've laid out and announce as planned on August 15, three weeks before the convention."

"What becomes of Robinson in the meantime? Coulter asked. "We've never had a sitting Vice-President challenge an incumbent President in the primaries, much less one who ran attack ads against his own administration the way Robinson did against you. Or had a Vice-President barred from entering the White House before his term's expired."

"Son of a bitch won't quit, you know." McConnell sighed, exasperated. "The situation is untenable and I put out a public call for his resignation. No dice. So I send a military aide and a briefer from the National Security Council out to the Vice-President's House at the Naval Observatory to brief him once a day, just in case somebody takes a shot at me."

"Do you think Robinson will bolt the party, start a third-party campaign after the convention?"

McConnell swallowed the last of the bourbon in his glass and rattled the ice cubes as if trying to ward off evil spirits. "He might. He's probably too late to get on some state ballots, particularly New York and Texas. We've heard he's been doing some polling."

"And?"

"And it doesn't make any fucking difference, Paul. I made one hell of a mistake coming back to the Republican Party after Brett was killed. I knew that I couldn't get the Democratic nomination away from Miranda Cardwell, but I should have run as an independent. Instead I tried to buy off the religious right by putting Robinson on the ticket. I've done some stupid things in my life, but that was stupid for the ages." McConnell leaned forward intently. "I am *not*, by God, going to let that bastard Jimmy Robinson become President of the United States. If he starts a third party and throws the election to Ben Giles that would be much better for the country. Ben and I have our differences on policy but we are both adults, we both love this country, and we both have some notion of *why* we want to be President—and it's not just because we want people snapping salutes when we get on the cool plane or because our daddies had the job once and we're trying to work out our Oedipal issues. If Ben's the one with his hand on the Bible come next January, I'll wish him well and ask that the country get behind him."

McConnell got up and walked to the drinks cart that his valet had left, pitched three more ice chunks into his glass, and poured more bourbon. He paced for a moment and then planted his rump against the *Resolute* desk, a pensive look on his face. "Every President is, in some sense, an accident, Paul. Especially me." McConnell gestured toward the framed *Time* cover on the wall behind Coulter. "If you hadn't pulled me out of that Humvee in Baghdad I'd have been killed for sure," McConnell continued. "But if that IED hadn't gone off I would have remained just another back bench senator, a guy who'd gotten lucky in business, made a bunch of money and decided on politics as a hobby. It was almost losing my life that jolted me hard enough start to think seriously about what a mess of things we were making in this country and how to try to fix them. When Brett asked me to defy my own party and join him on a unity ticket, I was ready. I sure as hell never thought I would have to take his place. But it happened."

McConnell fell silent, staring into some invisible middle distance, as if counting his losses. Coulter knew that Brett Campbell had been McConnell's closest friend in the Senate and that McConnell was godfather to Campbell's youngest daughter, Rachel, born in the White House a year before Campbell's assassination. In the five years since becoming President McConnell had lost both his best friend and his wife, Helen, dead from breast cancer at 50, just three years before.

"A hell of a night that was," McConnell continued. "Helen and I were up at our fishing camp in Devil's Lake, just getting ready to turn on the All Star game when Marine Two came roaring in overheard."

Coulter remembered: it had been his first week as a White House correspondent, assigned by the *Tribune* to the deadly dull task of pool reporter covering then Vice-President McConnell as he vacationed in godforsaken North Dakota. Coulter had been shoved by a frantic Secret Service agent into the helicopter for a lurching, gut empty-ing flight through a fierce Dakota thunderstorm to Grand Forks Air Force Base, where McConnell had hurriedly taken the Presidential oath from an elderly, visibly frightened federal judge aboard an un-gainly Air Force C-17 cargo jet, christened for that flight only with the majestic call sign *Air Force One*. McConnell had ordered the plane, over the vehement objections of his Secret Service detail, to fly him to Chicago to take personal charge of the disaster. McConnell's ashen, weeping aides and the press pool had huddled together on the plane's cargo floor and watched the news feeds from New Comiskey on phones and tablets as a desperate McConnell and his chief of staff sat in the cockpit's observer chairs, working the military communica-tions network for information. At midnight that awful night, when at least some details of the tragedy had become known, McConnell had made his first Presidential address from the lighted courtyard of Daley Center, tears running down his face and fire in his eyes as he promised continuity and justice to a grieving—and angry—nation.

"I'm sorry, Paul," McConnell said, breaking their mutual silence. "I called you in because I know you've got troubles of your own to-night," he added softly.

Coulter turned to the President. "She left me," he said quietly, be-fore he could stop himself. "Three days ago. I don't even know why."

"I know, Paul, I know," McConnell replied. He hesitated, and then turned his clear blue merciless eyes to confront Coulter. "It's not your fault, you know. I told her to."

Chapter Two

"*Where is she?*" Coulter demanded.

McConnell glanced away. "Out of the country. When she's here she's staying in a safe house, and working from the secure Homeland Intelligence facility in Liberty Crossing."

Coulter stared, his face a mask of confusion. "I don't understand."

"I do. People have tried to kill her. Paul, do you know what Elizabeth's job is?" McConnell asked.

"Not really. She is a major in the United States Army on detached duty, a staff deputy at the National Security Council, one you like as a briefer, I guess. I had to find that out by googling her. Beyond that she would not tell me a thing."

"Good for her. I will. Paul, Elizabeth Gray is my personal assistant for counter-terrorism. She also works in the field, both here and abroad. The NSC staff position is simply a cover."

"Homeland Intelligence," Coulter said, keeping his voice neutral. "Our domestic spy service."

"Call it that if you want. Fifteen days ago I assigned Elizabeth to lead a small group of people investigating what I regard as potentially the worst domestic security threat since World War Two. In Panama she had a very close call in a drive-by shooting. We killed the shooters but can't identify them. We don't know why she was attacked. Until we get some answers she will be exposed to a fair amount of personal risk. I did not feel that she could do her job, maintain security, and keep herself and you safe while leading a normal life with you. An impetuous break up was an effective cover. So blame me, not her."

Coulter shook his head, tried to keep the dismay out of his voice. "Sir, you can't do this to her. Elizabeth did two tours in the Second Iraq War, works a hundred hours a week in the White House. She lives every day with the fear that she will make a mistake, miss something, and that there will be another 9-11, another Comiskey Park, and people will die. The stress is killing her. She doesn't eat, she doesn't sleep. We've talked this through. She was going to train her replacement, go back to regular duty, finish her PhD, teach if the Army will let her." Coulter hesitated, and then added, "And I want to marry her."

McConnell spread his hands in a placating gesture. "Paul, I know that. Elizabeth did try to resign. I told her I couldn't afford to lose her, not yet. I don't like having to push people to the point where they are risking their health or their sanity. But Elizabeth *is* a soldier, without doubt a better soldier than you and I ever were or could have been. She is one of the smartest people working in this White House, with a unique ability to integrate complex data and shake solutions out of it. No one else can assess a threat situation like she can." McConnell set his glass on the cocktail table to his left and leaned toward Coulter. "You know how this government works. The people in senior staff positions in critical functions—state, defense, treasury, homeland intelligence—are the ones that keep us going. They are the only reason that *I* can ever sleep at night. And by way of thanks I burn them out and nearly kill them."

"How long?" Coulter demanded.

McConnell pursed his lips, a gesture Coulter knew meant frustration. "Don't know. Three months. Possibly four."

Coulter shook his head, dismayed.

"What's happened, Mr. President? What is this threat that you are so concerned about?"

"You know I can't answer that, Paul. Not even off the record. You're going to have to take it on faith—

"No sir."

McConnell's face creased with anger. "Are you saying my word—

"I honestly don't know what your word is worth on this subject, Mr. President." Coulter stood, unable to keep his emotions under control while seated, and paced the room as he spoke.

He turned back to confront McConnell. "You've become obsessed, Mr. President. You've created a national security state far beyond anything done by Truman, Nixon, or even Bush and Cheney. You rammed the Third Patriot Act through the Congress, using the public's grief over Brett Campbell's assassination to enact the most repressive laws since Wilson's administration in 1917. We have security cameras on every street and in every shopping mall. We have real-time satellite photo surveillance spanning the entire country that can pick up images as small as a golf ball. Every commercial and financial transaction is required by law to flow through a federal computer. Every piece of cargo is scanned, every cargo ship boarded for inspection ten miles offshore, every passenger in a plane or train or bus given a retinal scan and an RFID tag they must wear at risk of being yanked out of their seat and jailed. You've created a Homeland Intelligence office that's ten times the size of Britain's MI-5. You repealed the *Posse Comitatus* laws. There are five heavy brigades—20,000 combat troops—on active security duty on American soil, four under NORTHCOM at Fort Carson, Colorado with their own transport planes standing by at Peterson Field, and a full Brigade Combat Team at Fort Belvoir that trains to put down civil disorders right here in Washington. Now you tell me there is a new and secret threat worse than anything we've gone through before. Who are we fighting, Mr. President? Where's the goddamn war?"

McConnell sat motionless, rigid with anger.

"The war," he said tightly, "is with the same people it has been for years now, Paul. The names change. Al Qaida. Islamic State. Boko Haram. Caliphate. The threat doesn't change and it doesn't go away. These are the people who attacked on 9/11. The people who burned down Iraq and nearly killed both of us. The people who, in the name of a merciful God, murdered two thousand Americans and the President of the United States at a fucking *baseball* game to show their displeasure with liberal western customs and norms. Jesus *Christ*, Paul, how can you even *ask* a question like that?"

"How do we fight a war with a sixth of humanity, Mr. President? Is it a war? Or are we policing against deluded criminal factions? Which is it? There are days I agree with you, that all of this—that the gigantic national security apparatus you've created—is necessary. But we are choking to death. The recession is endless. We can't afford to put people to work on our crumbling infrastructure because every dime you can wring out of this economy is swallowed up by the national security state."

To Paul's surprise McConnell did not explode. "What else can I do, Paul?" he asked quietly. "For the love of God, what else can I do? I cannot 'preserve, protect, and defend' the Constitution if my fellow citizens are being slaughtered in the streets, subways, shopping malls and churches. The Bush-Cheney methods—kidnapping, torture, indefinite detention in military bases or secret prisons—didn't work. A thousand drone strikes didn't stop Al Qaeda from recruiting European converts to Islam and training them in the mountains of Pakistan and the back streets of Lahore and London to attack New Comiskey and murder Brett. That means I have to use defensive measures. I have to protect every port and airport and rail yard. I have to make sure that we review every communication that could be suspect. I have to have verifiable, fraud proof national I.D. cards that can be used to control movements and access to critical facilities. I have to have the ability to track and control financial transactions."

"Charlie, listen to yourself," Coulter replied softly. "Listen to how much power you've concentrated into one pair of hands—yours."

McConnell's face reddened as his anger deepened. "We—I— have not abused these security systems, Paul. I specifically set up Homeland Intelligence to separate the domestic intelligence function from the FBI and the CIA. I *prevented* those agencies from abusing their powers to spy on American citizens as they have in the past. Homeland Intelligence submits every data mining and analysis request involving U.S. citizens to the Federal Intelligence Court. If the Court doesn't issue the warrant, the data stays sealed and no human examiner gets to look at it. The video feeds from satellite and the monitors on streets and highways and in public buildings are analyzed and then erased if there is no criminal activity. Whenever we capture a terror suspect, anywhere in the world, American or not, they're flown to Washington D.C. and provided with a lawyer and a hearing within seventy-two hours. Each domestic security agency has an independent inspector general whose sole job is to enforce the privacy and civil liberties protections built into the laws. Those inspectors report every year to Congress. In the four and half years since Homeland Intelligence was set up we haven't had a single major breach of privacy or civil rights."

"That's ever been made public," Coulter shot back. "If HI wanted to hack their way into the raw data, they could—and no one would ever know the difference."

"Any system can be abused, Paul. That's why the character and ability of the people assigned to Homeland Intelligence and the White House are so critical—they enable me to keep the systems from being abused. That's one of the reasons I had to ask Elizabeth to stay." McConnell reached for the long-ignored drink on the table beside him, then thought the better of it and put his glass down again. "I'm sorry, Paul. My position doesn't leave me the luxury of making people happy. Even for a man who saved my life."

Coulter faced McConnell again, anger plain on his face. The men remained silent, each staring down the other. Coulter walked to the cocktail cart and placed his drink carefully on the surface.

"Thank you, Mr. President, for taking the time to tell me yourself. I will say nothing to anyone. I can only hope that the woman I love will come back some day." He turned toward the doors to the Yellow Oval, and then paused to look back, his hand on the door.

"Goddamn you, Charlie," he added.

McConnell rose. Dark fatigue suddenly surfaced on his face. "Good night, Paul. I'm bushed. Agent Ross will see you out."

Chapter Three

The Seattle Times
Sunday, July 17
Internet Edition, 4:04 A.M. PDT

NATION STUNNED BY PRESIDENT'S DEATH

By Paul Coulter, Pacific News Consortium
Special to the Seattle Times

Washington, D.C.

A stunned Capitol and Nation awoke this morning to learn that President Charles David McConnell has died. He was 60 years old.

The White House issued the following statement:

"President Charles D. McConnell died this morning. The President was stricken by what appears to have been a stroke at approximately 3:45 A.M. E.D.T. The White House Medical Unit, which had been treating the President for sleep apnea, responded immediately when monitors showed that the President had stopped breathing. The President's personal physician, Rear Admiral

Mike Warren, was in the White House at the time and attempted to revive the President. The President was flown to Bethesda Naval Hospital for continued treatment but did not regain consciousness and was pronounced dead at 5:37 A.M.

Secretary of State Donna Ribikoff, after being notified of the President's condition, met with Vice-President Robinson at the Vice-President's Residence at the United States Naval Observatory at 4:45 A.M. Upon learning of the President's death, the Secretary and the Vice-President returned to the White House. Vice-President Robinson will take the oath of office as President at 12:00 noon EDT today. Chief Justice Marilyn Lichtenberg will administer the oath of office.

President McConnell was preceded in death by his wife, Helen Schultheis McConnell. The President's daughters, Diane McConnell Johnson and Barbara Schultheis McConnell, have been notified of his passing and are en route to Washington aboard a United States Air Force transport. President Robinson, the Cabinet, and the leaders of the House and Senate will meet this afternoon to plan funeral services, as the President left no instructions."

Coulter's story continued, in his own words:

"There were no reports that President McConnell was seriously ill prior to his being stricken. The President's last physical examination revealed that he had elevated but controlled blood pressure and mild sleep apnea, but was otherwise considered in good health.

"Charles D. McConnell succeeded to the Presidency following the assassination of President Brett Campbell. Although elected Vice-President as an independent on the Democratic ticket, McConnell subsequently sought and won the Republican Party's Presidential nomination. He was elected President in his own right over his Democratic opponent, Speaker Miranda Cardwell of California, by the vote of 26 states in the U.S. House of Representatives following the second tie vote in the history of the United States Electoral College. President McConnell's five years in office were marked by his insistence on strong national and homeland security measures to prevent future acts of terrorism. The McConnell Global Anti-Terrorism Initiative included the passage of a toughened Third USA Patriot Act, the development of advanced surveillance technologies, a world-wide anti-terror treaty that sixty-seven nations have joined, and the deployment of American, Franco-German, Japanese, British, Polish, Korean and Australian special anti-terror combat units throughout the world. President McConnell created the first official domestic intelligence service, the Office of Homeland Intelligence, and authorized America's Northern Command to field the first standing military forces intended to fight within the borders of the United States since the Civil War. President McConnell's national and domestic security policies drew sharp criticism from both political parties. Many regarded those policies as a threat to traditional civil liberties, and blamed McConnell for failing to direct enough attention and resources to repair of the nation's long-stagnant economy.

The President's passing unleashes a political earthquake in Washington. President McConnell was estranged from Vice-President James B. Robinson, who challenged him in this year's bitterly disputed Republican primaries. Mr. Robinson, who suspended but never withdrew his own campaign for the White House, will take office confronted by a White House staff known for its loyalty to his predecessor and a deeply split Republican Party holding its nominating convention in just six weeks."

Chapter Four

Homeland Intelligence Applications Office
National Security Agency Complex Four
Fort George Gordon Meade, Maryland
Friday, August 26
11:35 p.m. EDT

Francis Benson sipped nervously at a cup of cold black coffee, intensely awake despite the late hour. He surveyed the open work area below his glassed in office on the mezzanine level of the Homeland Intelligence Applications Office. Homeland's data center filled most of the newly added fourth NSA complex building below him. Real time reports flashed across wall sized video displays. The wall screens were flanked by two seals: The NSA's eagle clutching a key, and Homeland Intelligence's heraldic shield with symbols that represented the American land, water and sky it surveilled. Fifty software engineers were spread out in two curved rows of workstations on the situation room floor below, the leadership cadre of the seven thousand software engineers and programmers who had designed TRIPLEX, a new data integration system for domestic security, the most thoroughly intrusive form of national surveillance ever created in the United States.

Benson slid a new piece of nicotine gum into his mouth. He'd started smoking during his initial tour in the Navy, a lonely 18-year old computer geek and gamer who'd joined up to get the hell out of Nebraska. Twenty-six years later Francis Benson held one of the first doctorate degrees in software engineering ever awarded by the U.S. Naval Postgraduate School and was the Chief Software Engineer for the Department of Homeland Security but still couldn't quite shake his dependence on nicotine.

Benson studied the screens in the room below, and then glanced down at his own work station, hands pressed against his desktop, bone-thin frame rocking forward and back with tension. He picked up the handset by his computer. "What's our status down there, Mike?" he asked softly.

The burly lead engineer from Dark/Star, Michael Burton, raised a fist, thumb extended up, into the air as he spoke into his headset mike. "I think we're good, Frank. Vandenberg confirms that we have all three satellite systems—the Lacrosse radar imaging birds, BASIC IMINT, and INTRUDER signals intelligence—on station and their data streams are coming in to us."

"Okay," Benson said, "Let's start up the system."

"We are initializing TRIPLEX," Burton confirmed. He began the software upload into the NSA's Roadrunner 9 Supercomputer, capable of sustained speeds of more than 12 quadrillion operations per second. Even at those speeds, minutes passed before the TRIPLEX software was fully uploaded and the system initialized to carry and cross-analyze thousands of data streams.

"Ready," Burton said.

"Let's run," Francis Benson replied.

"We are running."

"Start the test query series."

"Ok, Frank."

Burton's engineers fed hypothetical problems designed to test TRIPLEX's ability to combine and mine real time data from the vast data streams of email, cell phone and telephone transmissions, satellite images, internet postings, news feeds, and cable traffic. The system was also designed to enable simultaneous translations from more than 460 languages and dialects and to keyword search in all translations from any of those languages across the entire intelligence database as well as the internet.

Error messages began to appear on screens across the room.

"What's going on, Michael?" Benson demanded.

"Kernel panic, I think. System is shutting down."

Benson looked down at the screens on his workstation. "I'm getting it. Kernel memory message being dumped."

"Right. Can we reboot manually?"

"Go ahead."

Burton huddled briefly with his engineers on the operations floor, then nodded up at Benson. "Rebooting now."

The engineers' screens briefly turned black, then flared into life with the Homeland Intelligence logo before returning to black. Burton stared incredulously at his silent, empty screen.

"Frank?"

"I see it. What is it?"

"If this were an old PC I'd say we fried the hard drive, Frank. But that's not possible. Some kind of general systems failure, though. We're going to have to take the code and the system apart."

"How long?" Francis Benson asked.

"Absolutely no idea. Best case, three to ten days, if we put everybody at IBM, BAE and Dark/Star on it. Worst case? Months."

"You'll have the people. Can you return the data streams to the original analysis systems?"

Burton tapped at his keyboard, pointed to one of his engineers, waited. "Uh, problem, Frank. We're going to have to get inside TRI-PLEX. It's not letting us in to disengage."

Benson dreaded the call he would have to make. He reached reluctantly for the archaic, but secure, land-line phone at his workstation. He did not need to dial a number, because the phone was answered instantly.

"White House," a nasal voiced operator said.

"Major Gray, please."

"I will connect you."

Elizabeth Gray stirred uneasily. The air conditioning in the small, anonymous studio apartment above an M Street office building that doubled as a federal safe house had failed and the air was thick with Washington's summer humidity. Her hair was damp and her skin slick with sweat, the product of heat and bad dreams. The insistent ringing of the secure phone on her bedside table snapped her into consciousness. She grabbed for the phone, simultaneously propped herself up against the headboard.

"This is Gray," she said, her voice slurring from the Ambien tablet she'd finally taken to force herself to sleep.

"This is the White House Communications Office, Major. I have a call for you from the Homeland Intelligence Applications office at Fort Meade."

"Put them through."

Elizabeth waited through a silent pause, then a loud click as the lines were joined. "Major Gray?"

"Yes, who is this, please."

"Frank Benson. Chief software engineer for Homeland AO."

Elizabeth cleared her throat, tried to concentrate. "Yes, I remember you, Frank. What's up?"

"We were initializing TRIPLEX tonight."

"And?"

"We had a systems failure. The system booted fine, but when we began the test sequence there was a kernel fault, then a full systems breakdown."

"How quickly can you repair the fault?"

"Not sure at this point. That's not the worst of it."

"Yes?"

"We're having some difficulty restoring the old systems. It's as though the data streams are now embedded in the TRIPLEX software and we can't get them out without damaging the entire system."

"I'm not sure what that means."

"It may be 72 hours or more before I can restore the backup systems."

"So what's going to be missing? Signals, geospatial imagery, data mining, networking, internet surveillance, what?"

"All of it, Major. All of it."

Elizabeth tried to keep her voice level. She was fully awake now, bolt upright in bed, adrenalin coursing through her veins. "I thought this was an upgrade, Frank. Why in *hell* weren't we told that if there was an installation failure the entire system could be compromised?"

"Major, this is not just an upgrade." Benson was aware that his voice was tight and rising but kept talking. "We've written more than 400 million new lines of source code. That's like building everything Microsoft ever developed from scratch."

"Get the fucking backup systems restored, Frank. Now."

"That—"

"Get them restored. Pull your teams off of TRIPLEX if you have to, but give me my eyes and ears back, Frank."

"I'll need—"

"If you need Admiral Thrace to come down there and break heads, Frank, I can arrange that. I want a report by 0700 on the status of restoration."

Elizabeth Gray broke the connection and pressed an auto dial button on the secure phone.

"White House." The voice was male, soft, and southern.

"Locate Admiral Thrace and connect me, please. This is Major Gray."

"Immediately, ma'am."

Francis Benson dropped the phone handset into its cradle. He rummaged in his desk, came up with a half-empty box of Camel filters and some matches. He walked down the stairs from the catwalk outside his office to the operations center below.

"Anything, Michael?" he asked.

Michael Burton shook his head grimly. "Not yet."

"Focus on de-linking the old systems and restoring them to function."

"Frank?"

"Orders. Get the old systems up, even if you have to forego work on TRIPLEX. I'm going to want a repair estimate for restoring access to the original systems in…shit. About five hours."

"Right," Burton responded grimly. "Out for a smoke?"

"It's been a long fucking day, Michael. Twenty minutes."

Francis Benson took the elevator to the ground floor of the building, the fourth and newest of the glass cube structures that made up the heart of the NSA Fort Meade complex. He turned right, toward the sea of parking lots that accommodated the 19,000 NSA and Homeland Intelligence workers who commuted every day. Benson stopped at an open pavilion that served as one of NSA's few remaining smoking areas. He paused to light up a Camel and blew the smoke out of his lungs in a thin blue stream.

A younger Air Force staff sergeant in his late twenties wandered into the smoking area and nodded to Benson.

"Could use a light," he said, gesturing with an unlit cigarette between his fingers.

"Sure thing," Benson replied, passing the sergeant a cardboard pack of matches. The sergeant lit his smoke and waited. He looked quizzically at Benson.

Benson drew a deep breath. "It's down," he said. "For at least seventy-two hours. Go."

Chapter Five

**Tularosa Depot National Superfund Cleanup Site
45 Miles Southwest of Las Cruces, New Mexico
Friday, August 26
4:50 A.M. MDT**

A pair of battered M35 Army cargo trucks rolled east on the narrow unmarked road through the desert nineteen miles south of Deming, New Mexico, flanking the Florida Mountains. The night was clear but there was little moon and the scrub wasteland around them was a patchwork of grays and browns and blacks in the starlight.

Thirty minutes later the trucks stopped at a fortified gate post shielded by steel plate and sand bags. A twelve foot electrified fence stretched to the dark horizons from both sides of the gate. Two enlisted men emerged from the gate post, weapons drawn. The driver of the lead truck, a grizzled chief warrant officer well past fifty, opened the truck cab door and stepped cautiously onto the running board, then to the ground, his hands raised. He produced his identification, saluted, and passed them a sealed envelope.

"Special orders for the Lieutenant's review," the driver said.

The senior guard nodded, went to the gate post, and returned with his Lieutenant. The officer was about twenty five years old, under six feet tall but with the thick build of a weight lifter. He was well dressed for gate post duty in the middle of the night: pressed digitized camouflage uniform, infantry patch with three Iraq campaign ribbons on the sleeve, black polished jump boots, and black beret worn with a crisp fold on his shaved head. The name "Keeler" was stitched on a Velcro patch above the left breast pocket.

The driver saluted again and waited as the young officer glanced at the orders, reading with the aid of a pocket flashlight. Keeler finally folded the orders and stuffed them back into the envelope. He tapped the edge of the envelope nervously against the palm of his hand. "Corporal, I'll be proceeding into the control area with these men. I want a communications blackout until the trucks exit at the South portal gate at 0630 hours. Understood?"

The gate guard looked dubious. "Sir, standard procedure is to notify the security unit at Fort Bliss of any entry or egress from the control area."

"I know that. These are special orders that supersede standing procedure. If there's any shit about it I will square it with your CO. Carry out my orders, Corporal."

The Lieutenant snapped off a salute and scrambled up into the cab of the M35. The warrant officer followed, settled behind the wheel, and struck a kitchen match on the truck's steel dashboard. He looked the young Lieutenant over in the brief flare of light as he lit a cigarette.

"How far to the control perimeter, Lieutenant?" he asked, shifting the heavy truck into gear and beginning a slow grind forward through the gates and across the desert.

"Half a mile, Chief."

"Big place." The driver blew smoke from his nose and the corners of his mouth, cigarette still in place, both hands on the truck's big steering wheel as the track grew rougher over broken, ancient pavement.

"Tularosa was built as an ammunition depot during the Korean War," Keeler told the driver. "There was nothing out here then."

"Pretty much nothing now. At least nothing that anyone is going to admit to."

The young officer laughed nervously. "True fact, Chief. Can I bum a smoke?" He paused, accepted the cigarette, and held it unlit. "Your men ready?"

"They're suited up. You're going to need to stay about twenty-five yards back until they have tested the area. Are the monitors down?"

Keeler nodded. "I have a security tech working with me on this. He killed the remote access back at Fort Bliss, then disabled the systems inside the units when he came out for repairs. Bliss is getting a signal—a dozen different alternating thirty seconds of nothing, looped in a random program."

"And the door codes?" The old warrant officer persisted.

"The ones you have are good until 2300 tomorrow."

"Sounds like we're on our way then, sir."

They passed through a second gate in an inner fence marked with warning signs reading "Contaminated Munitions Area." Eight low concrete structures loomed out of the desert ahead. They looked like oversized Quonset huts half buried in the dry rocky ground. The trucks stopped.

"Second unit on the left," Keeler said, pointing ahead. The driver nodded. "Best you get off here, Lieutenant, while we make sure there's been no leakage."

"What about you, Chief?"

The driver coughed heavily, then stubbed his cigarette out against the dash and dropped the butt on the floor of the truck cab. "Hell, my cigarettes have probably killed me already. I volunteered for this, knew I'd have to take my chances." He shrugged. "I'll pick you up here when we've loaded. The load will be in rad-proof containers."

"Right." Keeler nodded and dropped from the truck's running board to the ground. The two trucks moved forward, gears clashing. He looked at his watch, a black titanium-cased Special Operations model that had cost him half a month's pay. They had a little less than two hours to get to the south portal gate before the guard changed shifts at 0700. Keeler settled himself against the half-crumbled concrete wall of an abandoned building, the chill of high altitude night biting through his fatigues. He fiddled nervously with the unlit cigarette, waiting.

The trucks turned toward the concrete bunkers and paused outside the unit Keeler had identified long enough for four men to emerge from their rear cargo areas. The men wore black rubberized Demron radiation suits with full face shields and carbon-graphite gas masks capable of screening out most radioactive particles. The man leading the group stopped on the loading dock at the blunt end of the munitions bunker to take a radiation reading, and then waved the others forward. They quickly picked open the heavy padlocks that secured the iron chains around the handles of the rusted iron doors, then pulled the doors open, grunting with the effort.

Inside the 1950s vintage iron doors twelve inch thick reinforced blast doors had been installed, similar to those used in MX missile silos. The leader entered the access codes through a numeric keypad located on the arched frame between the doors. The codes had to be entered twice, in the exact same sequence, within a thirty second time period. He sweated inside the hot radiation suit but did not falter or hesitate. The detached calm he had acquired defusing perhaps a thousand IEDs and booby traps in Iraq served him well. The blast doors swung open on massive, silent hinges.

The old munitions bunker had been secretly rebuilt. Squat yellow rows of lead lined radiation storage casks, oversized coffins five feet tall and eight feet long, filled the bunker, carefully spaced with twenty foot gaps in all directions to prevent any spontaneous chain reaction. The leader quickly moved to a cask in the center of the building. He verified a number on the cask's identification plate and then motioned to his men. They unbolted the cask's top hatch using thirty inch long hardened steel torque wrenches, the kind used on oil rigs to break open recalcitrant inch thick bolts. Four steel cylinders stood in separate, lead-lined compartments inside the opened casks, each cylinder about three feet long and one foot in diameter.

The men removed four cylinders, three from one cask and a fourth from another with the aid of a block and tackle mounted on a cart purchased from a Sears automotive shop in Albuquerque. Each cylinder was rolled to the loading dock. The men then pulled four identical-looking storage cylinders filled with depleted uranium from the trucks, rolled them into the storage bay, placed them into the casks, and re-bolted the hatches. Throughout the operation the leader kept his eyes on a radiation monitor and a dosimeter worn on his radiation suit. There were no leaks; the radiation was well within tolerable limits, scarcely above natural background.

When the cylinders had been loaded and the bunker doors closed the leader pulled back his faceplate and hood, unhooked his face mask, and approached the driver of the lead truck. "How's the time, Chief?" he asked.

"Good. We've got about forty minutes until we're supposed to check in at the south gate. We'll be out of here in less than ten minutes."

"That works. Where's our soldier boy?"

"The Lieutenant has been very busy counting up his money and keeping a safe distance. He's over by the old administrative building."

The leader nodded. "I should tell him we're all clear. Pick me up there, okay?"

The grizzled driver nodded, his expression blank. The M35's diesel engine growled into life.

The leader walked over to the ruin of the administration building where Lieutenant Keeler waited. The young officer finally lit the cigarette he had been holding for an hour and smoked nervously.

"Relax, Lieutenant," the leader said, smiling, his voice casual. His helmet was thrown back behind his head, the Demron suit unzipped to his chest, revealing a desert-tanned face with dark eyes and a Marine regulation sidewall haircut. "I won't offer you my hand until I've been through a scrub down, but I did want to thank you for all your help tonight."

"And the money?" Keeler demanded.

"Deposited as agreed. Check your phone."

Keeler slid a thumb across the surface of his Samsung, pulling up his email. It confirmed a deposit received into a numbered account at Bank Royal in Panama City.

Keeler relaxed, a triumphant grin spreading across his face. He dropped the cigarette he was holding and ground it out with his heel. "Let's go, then," he said, as the trucks approached.

The leader gestured to Keeler to pass first. When Keeler's back was turned he slid a Ka-Bar Short Black Tanto knife from a sheath strapped to his chest and severed the Lieutenant's spinal cord with a single thrust above the C-4 vertebrae. When the truck pulled up he watched as his men lifted Keeler's body into the back of the truck. He picked up Keeler's cigarette butt and raked the area where they had been standing with a plastic garden rake produced from the back of the truck, dispersing the small pool of blood into the dark sand. He was a man who believed in preparation and attention to detail. Those qualities had kept him alive for five long years in Iraq.

Chapter Six

Homeland Intelligence Special Working Group
National Counter Terrorism Information Center
Liberty Crossing, Virginia
Saturday, August 27
8:00 A.M. EDT

Elizabeth Gray took her position at the head of the conference table beside a large flat screen monitor and prepared to present the Power Point summary she had been working on since 5:00 A.M. that morning. *This is an unofficial and probably illegal group that's meeting today,* she mused to herself, *but this is Washington, and if it's not on Power Point it doesn't exist.*

It had been her third consecutive night with less than four hours sleep. Her eyes burned and a dull headache throbbed in the back of her head, but that was not what troubled her. She had functioned for years on minimum sleep, at West Point, in training units, in flying Blackhawk helicopters in Iraq, always able to bounce back physically and emotionally with even twenty-four off-duty hours. That gift had failed her in the week since she had returned from her third trip in four weeks to Panama. She now felt something new, a dark sense of foreboding that startled her awake every hour or two throughout the night, unsure of the line between nightmare and reality.

She caught a glimpse of herself reflected in the darkened mirror of the glass flat screen monitor and was not pleased with what she saw. At thirty-six, after three years in the White House, she was still tall and strong but beginning to feel and see the first signs of softness, a blurring at the edges of the body she had long prided herself on maintaining in tight condition. Never enough sleep or exercise, endless hours at the White House, the Pentagon, and Liberty, and meals taken on the run or not at all were going to ruin her.

"Suck it up, Gray," she told herself and straightened her blue pinstriped suit jacket. When she had gone on detached White House duty under cover of a staff position with the NSC, custom required that she not wear her military uniform to the office. Gray had developed little interest in clothes beyond jeans, riding breeches, ski wear, and Italian lingerie, having been in the Army since her 18-year-old plebe summer at West Point. When assigned to the White House she had simply gone to Brooks Brothers and purchased a dozen suits with skirts and pants in blue, gray, and khaki with two dozen white and cream silk blouses that she rotated through Washington's seasons with more regard to temperature than to fashion.

Gray waited until Derek Martin arranged his tablet PC, stylus, and oversized Starbucks cup on the table in front of him. Martin, a twenty-year officer in the CIA's National Clandestine Service, grinned sheepishly at being caught out as the last person to arrive. He was African American, nearing fifty, thick in the chest and waist, a quiet, genial man who once killed three Hamas operatives barehanded in an alley in Damascus. He nodded to Elizabeth, then to the three others already seated around a twenty-foot long mahogany conference table in the soundproofed, windowless secure room with smoke gray walls: Anthony Thrace, the Director of Homeland Intelligence; General Karol Horvath, the Joint Chiefs Staff Director for Intelligence, known in the Pentagon's own peculiar language as the J2, and Cable Hollings, the Deputy Director of the FBI. They were, out of the thousand senior appointed officials who run the federal government to the extent that it can be run, the five who had been most trusted by Charlie McConnell.

Anthony Thrace was a Navy Rear Admiral who had commanded an *Ohio* class nuclear missile submarine and taught foreign policy at the United States Naval Academy. At fifty-nine, he was small, balding but trim, who wore round black rimmed reading glasses and off the rack department store suits. His mild appearance belied a ferocious appetite for information and a cutting intelligence. "Tell us about TriPlex," he said, addressing Gray.

"The news keeps getting worse," she replied. "An hour ago I was told that the optimistic estimate for completing a diagnostic and repair would be seven to ten days. Worst case, several months."

"How blind are we?"

"Almost total. Pentagon intelligence services are on alert, manually reviewing satellite imaging on military locations around the world. CIA has called all its analysts in to manually collate reports from their stations. NSA is doing its thing with international data traffic, basically intact. HI is in the worst shape, since we were totally dependent on the TriPlex predecessor systems. We have no North America satellite data since the system crashed last night. Internet and telephone data surveillance are knocked out. The biometric cams are operating but no data is being analyzed. Basically, we're reading the newspapers, chatting with the FBI, and looking at incident reports from police departments. You should go to the Secretary and raise the threatcon to level three."

"Agreed," Thrace replied, jotting a note. "Everybody else report up and take equivalent steps. We're going to need to brief the President and NSC regarding TriPlex. But I also need to make a decision about whether, and how, to report on Charlie McConnell's project."

"It might help if I knew what that was, Tony," Derek Martin responded. Thrace nodded toward Elizabeth Gray, who tapped her laptop key board to put her first slide on the screen.

"President McConnell was contacted in early June by a retired senior Army NCO who had been approached by members of an organization composed of present and former members of the armed forces. They told him that their group consists of several thousand clandestine members who had served in Afghanistan and Iraq or had worked for private military contractors there. The vaguely stated purpose of the group was to 'rebuild American authority', 'unify America under God,' and 'and restore America to its place as a Christian nation.' That source—we designated him Confidential Source 1, we're not very imaginative—was noncommittal but played along. He was eventually told that the group had members currently serving in all five uniformed services and within Homeland Security, Defense, DEA, NSA and Justice. He learned that he was being recruited specifically because he had substantial experience in urban warfare, peacekeeping and security. When he would not commit to membership, his contacts withdrew. Three days later he came to Washington and talked his way into a meeting with the President, who sent him on to us for debriefing.

"After interviewing Source 1 we still had nowhere near enough information for Homeland Intelligence to seek surveillance warrants from the Federal Intelligence Court on the people who solicited him," Elizabeth Gray replied. "Nor did we want to risk these people going to ground. President McConnell directed us to investigate; we researched all available public and security records on Source 1 and those who contacted him. Director Hollings lent us staff to construct a social network analysis."

Gray displayed the next slide, a graphic data analysis. "Social network analysis isn't new—sociologists developed the basic concepts a century ago. It was first conceived of as an anti-terror tool fifteen years ago. DARPA developed the first usable analytical software in 2002, but it has since gotten much more sophisticated. A lot of the detailed software code that was developed for Facebook and other social networking sites has since been incorporated. Patriot Act Three permits Homeland Intelligence to access and trace email and twitter connections, email addresses and telephone numbers without a warrant," Gray added. She aimed a laser pointer to the social network diagram. "Using that data we were ultimately able to identify about four thousand individuals who had at least some connection to Source 1 and the people who contacted him, using their telephone and cell phone contacts, email distributions, church membership rosters, property tax records and apartment rent rolls. The network diagram on the screen expanded until there were thousands of points connected by a seemingly random maze of lines. "Each person is a *node*, each connection is a *tie*. One of the most powerful analyses we can do is to establish the clustering coefficient, which measures the likelihood that two or more associates of a node are associates themselves. The higher the coefficient, the greater the cohesion in the group."

"By expanding the search to identify persons who in turn had ties to the four thousand nodes, we increased the data set for the analysis to more than a hundred thousand people—useless information, in and of itself. But watch what happens when we cross reference." Gray slid dissolved to the next slide. "This is the result of the cluster coefficient analysis carried out to identify the group that had three or more ties to other nodes. Anyone who took Political Science 301 may recognize it."

Derek Martin broke in quickly. "That's a cell structure?" he asked, his voice rising with surprise.

"Correct," Gray answered. "It is a clandestine, fault tolerant cell structure, with side links that enable this organization, whatever it is, to repair broken links and maintain communications. It is large, it is here, and we don't know what its real purpose or intent may be."

A tense silence filled the room, finally broken by Derek Martin. "Well, there's a bright side here," he drawled. "This time it *isn't* the CIA's fault."

Chapter Seven

"Whoever these people are," Elizabeth Gray continued, "they are organized into the classic revolutionary cell structure: three members who each know only each other as members of the cell, but who also know at least one other member in parallel cells, and one member above. Each in turn each recruits three new cell members in a cell below them."

"How many are there?" Karol Horvath demanded.

"We don't know," Gray admitted. "We can only see the structure. Best estimate? Between three and five thousand people."

"What's this group's purpose?"

"We don't know that either," Elizabeth replied. "We *can't* know until we are able to tap their phones, intercept their cell calls and text messages, read their emails, look at their bank and credit card statements."

"The major's being a bit modest here," Cable Hollings interjected. Hollings, the FBI's lanky associate director for national security, tapped a long finger on the table top, one the few impatient gestures he was ever known to make. Hollings was descended from an old South Carolina political family with political skills both inherited and acquired. He had survived the FBI's internal headquarters politics for more than a decade and outlasted four directors and five Attorneys General. "I had our analysts take Source 1's statements about the people trying to recruit him and ran it through our conceptual databases. The output wasn't much better than we would've gotten through Google, but I can tell you this much. This group, whatever it is, shapes up along lines of being classically anti-government, with strong feelings of economic and political betrayal. Yet they also seem to be culturally conservative, religious, and with a strong connection to the military or past service in the military."

"Interviews?" Horvath persisted.

"We arranged about fifteen interviews," Hollings replied. "We selected a small group with a high relationship coefficient, and that seemed about equally connected to the men who approached Source 1. I had them interviewed through a variety of local police agencies using different pretexts—everything from a DUI to a local tax issue. They were disciplined. We got nothing."

"Why not have them interviewed by FBI professionals?"

"Because at this early stage, Karol," Hollings drawled, "Charlie McConnell thought it was counterproductive to for me to send FBI agents around to say, "Hey there, Sport, are you part of a conspiracy of current and ex-soldiers to commit sedition? Seemed like it might give the game away and send them to ground before we knew enough to be useful."

Thrace shook his head, unimpressed. "Conservative ex-military with a religious orientation? Meaningless. We might as well be talking about the American Legion."

"That's not the best analogy, Tony," Cable Hollings said quietly. "Remember your history. In the 1920s the American Legion was pretty damned close to being a private army called out to break labor strikes. And some of their leaders flirted with Mussolini."

Thrace dismissed the historical reference. "I'm still not seeing a national security threat."

Elizabeth Gray broke in. "I disagree, Admiral."

"Tell me why, Major."

"It's the money. We don't understand the money flows." Gray threw a new diagram on the screen. "We have been tracking unusual inflows of cash from Islamic sources in the Middle East, Indonesia, and the Philippines, routed through China and the Caribbean. These are not the typical transfers that we have monitored for years, money being sent from Islamic charities in failed efforts to establish sleeper cells in Arab neighborhoods in Detroit, Chicago, or Newark. This is different; the money is going to very strange places. Small construction businesses. Gun shops. Liquor stores. Christian churches. And it is ending up with people who appear to be in, or connected to, the cell structure we identified."

"Where?"

"Virginia and the Carolinas. West Texas and Southern New Mexico. Georgia. Pueblo and Colorado Springs."

"And the funds have been traced to Islamic sources?"

"Yes. Here's one example from the Abu Dhabi/Panama channel." Gray put a flow chart onto the main screen. "This is the anatomy of a one hundred thousand dollar transfer we were able to trace back to its point of origin. The chain ends with the Tabernacle Freedom Church in El Paso, but it starts…Here. The funds originated with the Al Zahar Foundation in Abu Dhabi. Al Zahar has supported Wahabi madrassas worldwide for years—but to find them funding an evangelical Christian church is bizarre, to say the least. Once the money left Abu Dhabi, the transfer was routed through six cut-outs—an air freight forwarder in Cairo, a wine wholesaler in Johannesburg, a shipping company in Dakar, Bank Royal in Panama City, a restaurant in Dallas, and a small meat packer in Amarillo, then transferred to the Tabernacle Church under more than thirty different names."

"Do we have this through Swift?" Thrace named the Brussels-based banking consortium that still processed the bulk of the world's financial wire transfer traffic.

"No, sir. The transfer we examined was run through Shanghai, Grand Cayman and Panama City. It had to be hand researched from cable intercepts, mostly from the *Carter*." The fact that the USS *Jimmy Carter*, a *Seawolf* class nuclear submarine specially fitted for intelligence work, had been tasked to sample the world's subterranean financial transactions traffic by tapping the global network of undersea fiber optic cables was an open secret.

"We have north of sixteen million dollars in payments going to these unusual destinations, within the last four months," Gray continued. "These people are being exceptionally cautious—as if they know the sources and methods we are using to track the money. Somebody is trying to keep this very tight."

"So what's your conclusion, Major?"

Elizabeth took a long breath. "This is a severe enough threat that it should be reported to the Presidential/NSC level. Terrorism is asymmetric warfare. Ten million dollars invested in attacks could buy a billion dollars' damage. I'm worried about ghosts, sir. Islamic agents of American, European or Mexican descent who can slide through a checkpoint with simple, decently faked I.D. The money is being broken up and moved in very small amounts. That takes a lot of people. One limit on Islamic terrorism has always been racial—they could not recruit enough radicalized American Muslims of European, African or Latino descent, which meant that attacks had to be planned, supported and carried out by Arabs. What if they are reaching out, forming alliances, looking for their own Timothy McVeigh? American militia movements in the south and west have made a comeback in the past several years because of the economic depression. Homegrown terrorists would be extremely difficult to detect or stop until after they reach their targets. With two hundred people, properly placed and armed, they could do twenty Mumbai-style swarm attacks across the country."

Thrace frowned. "Cable, can you set up a joint investigation with Treasury and FINCEN—to document, hopefully prosecute this thing from the money side? Seems like tax evasion and money laundering is taking place, regardless of the security implications."

"Already working it," Hollings drawled. "Treasury has an existing operation in Panama City that's been looking at these transfers—Elizabeth knows the details. By Monday I will have four active money laundering investigations—Columbus, Georgia, El Paso, Texas, Colorado Springs, and Fayetteville, North Carolina."

"Why those cities?" Horvath demanded.

"It's where the money is going."

Horvath tapped a key on the open laptop in front of him and a map of the United States' military installations across the country filled a wall-sized screen across the room. "Columbus, Georgia—Fort Benning. El Paso—Fort Bliss. Colorado Springs—Fort Carson,

Peterson Field, NORAD, NORTHCOM. Fayetteville, North Carolina—Fort Bragg." He turned to Gray. "This could be terrorism and these bases could be targets," he acknowledged. "Or, this could be sedition."

"We know we're looking at a clandestine organization with off-shore funding," Gray replied. "We've got an idea of its potential size, maybe its name, something of its politics, and—god forbid—that it might be a threat to the security of the government. What we don't know is if it has been able infiltrate the upper reaches of the government, or the military."

"I want to send a message through the counter-terrorism complex that we know something is up.," Thrace said. "I'll circulate it as part of the priority issue list for coping with the TriPlex failure that's going out at noon. I want to know if someone is listening and may act."

Elizabeth Gray looked carefully at Thrace. "How much will you tell the President, Admiral?"

Thrace looked doubtful. "I'm not sure. I guess I'll get that figured out on the way to New Orleans. Elizabeth, I'll want you with me. There's an Air Force C-37 headed to New Orleans at 5:45 P.M. with White House staff; I'll get seats. I'll ask for time with the President and the Acting NSA tonight, but we may not get it until tomorrow." Thrace turned to Horvath. "Will you brief the Chairman, Karol?"

Horvath smiled grimly. "Jack knows. But he'll want the details."

"Fine," Thrace replied. He turned to Hollings. "I think you should bring the Director in on this now, Cable."

"Not," Hollings said carefully, "unless you want to be reading about it in the Washington *Post* tomorrow morning. We have a strict rule against giving our fearless Director any information that might involve an ongoing investigation.

Thrace frowned. "All right, I leave it in your hands. But at some point we'll have to get a Presidential finding so we have authority to act and Robinson's the only president we've got. I guess we're going to find out what he's made of," Thrace concluded.

"Mush," Cable Hollings replied, his voice cold. "Mush and venom and bile."

New Orleans

Chapter Eight

PBS Studio
Morial Convention Center
New Orleans, Louisiana
Saturday, August 27
6:00 P.M. CDT

Paul Coulter looked uneasily around the hastily erected television set in a windowless second floor room in the Morial Convention Center. He noted the cheap blue fabric on the backdrop behind the faux wood commentator's desk and the hotel folding table covered with dark red cloth.

"I thought we were getting PBS," Coulter complained in a low voice.

"This is what PBS can afford with a budget that's about half what they had in 1999," Graham Taylor replied, nodding his head to whisper in Coulter's ear. Taylor was freakishly tall for an Englishman—nearly six foot six—and painfully thin, dressed in a slightly worn and very rumpled tan tropical-weight wool suit. He retained a gray fringe of close-cropped hair above a high forehead, a long nose that appeared to have been broken long ago, and brown eyes that watered constantly from an unknown allergen growing somewhere around New Orleans. Taylor turned away, took a puff from an asthma inhaler, and continued. "The good news is that this webcast gets about a quarter million hits a night and our personal sites will be linked to the main PBS website for at least the next couple of weeks. That and $2000 apiece towards our respective bar tabs for two hours work. Be grateful."

"Right." Coulter turned to greet the show's host, a dark-haired, portly and ambitious former New York *Times* editorial writer in his early thirties named Gerald Morrow. "Gerald! Good to see you. Thanks for having me on." Morrow was a Washington native who had grown up in the incestuous D.C. world of law, politics, government and press, the son of a powerful Washington litigator who was in turn married to a former assistant director of the Central Intelligence Agency.

"My pleasure," Morrow replied, a make-up bib still tied around his neck. "You're looking good, Paul," Morrow lied cheerfully, "but you *do* need to get into makeup." He assessed Coulter's pasty indoors complexion. "Didn't you get away from the White House at all this summer? I'd be *crushed* if we didn't sail the Chesapeake on the weekends. Don't worry about the sets, my engineer will adjust and fill in the backgrounds on the visuals before we stream the video to the web. We'll have as good a production value as any network news broadcast. This'll be a good show for you; we're up and coming, and if we continue to trend up on the web we'll be carried live on the nightly *Ifill-Dixon* news cast throughout the campaign. And we'll remember the friends who helped us get there when we book."

Morrow turned away from Coulter held out his hand in greeting. "You've got to be Graham Taylor," he said excitedly. "I went to military school as a kid and one of my instructors assigned us your book about your Special Air Services unit in the First Iraq War. Amazing stuff, incredibly heady reading for a mousy thirteen year old boy."

"Well that properly ages me," Taylor replied dryly, shaking hands, but Morrow had already begun to turn away to huddle with his producer before settling into the host's chair. Coulter returned from makeup to find Taylor receiving just a light coat of powder; the older man's habit of five mile morning walks through Washington in all weather kept his face tan. A producer adjusted the angle of one of the three small cameras as Coulter, Taylor and the other guest settled into their chairs.

"Welcome to this PBS web cast of *The First Draft of History*, your source for thoughtful political news and commentary, brought to you from New Orleans' Ernest Morial Convention Center on the eve of the Republican National Convention. I'm Gerald Morrow, and with me tonight is a distinguished panel covering this year's turbulent Republican Convention from three perspectives—working reporter, public opinion analyst, and professional historian. On my left, Paul Coulter, White House Correspondent for the Pacific News Consortium and proprietor of *Coulter's Politics,* a blog hosted by many daily newspaper and television websites. Next, Dr. Graham Taylor, retired British Army officer and well known military and political historian, essayist and commentator. Colonel Taylor is an affiliate professor of Military History at American University and the author of several best-selling books, including *Whiskey Tango Foxtrot,* his memoir of service behind Iraqi lines with Britain's elite Special Air Services during Operation Desert Storm. Finally, we bring you A. Michelle Dugan, pollster and public opinion analyst, and a columnist for *Internet Newsweek.* Paul, let's begin with you. Has there even been a more divided national convention in living memory than this year's Republican convention?"

"There's been nothing like this since at least the Republican Convention of 1940, or the deadlocked Democratic Convention of 1924," Coulter replied. "President James Robinson took office in July after Charlie McConnell's death from a stroke, just two months after the conclusion of the bitterly fought primary campaign in which Robinson broke with McConnell and sought the Presidency for himself. McConnell had won enough delegates for renomination, but those delegates have now divided between Governor Roger Blessing of Nevada and Michigan Senator Harry Purcell. No candidate has a first ballot lock, and as a result we expect two more state governors, Tyrone Brackett of South Carolina and Keith Anderson of Minnesota, may announce favorite-son candidacies tomorrow morning. With no candidate's support gelling, this convention could go on for many ballots before it chooses a nominee."

"Michelle, what effect has the loss of President McConnell had on Republican chances of retaining the Presidency?"

"Devastating," Dugan replied. A former economic statistician who'd once worked for Bank of America, after becoming a political pollster Dugan had been remade for the media: hair blonded, glasses replaced by contacts, slimmed to the point of emaciation by a drastic diet. "President McConnell was the only Republican candidate who polled within seven points of any potential Democratic candidate during the past year. Senator Ben Giles, the Democratic nominee, wrapped up his primary campaign in April, came roaring out of the Democratic Convention in Los Angeles, and has been campaigning nonstop ever since. Senator Giles now stands twenty-one points ahead of *all* potential Republican nominees, including President Robinson."

"No sympathy swing for President Robinson? New Presidents usually get an upsurge in support after taking office," Morrow continued.

"None," Dugan said firmly. "President Robinson has not polled well outside of the South or the religious right wing of the Republican party. McConnell's mainstream conservatives never warmed to him, even before Robinson challenged the President in the Republican primaries. Independent voters, who in the past have always gone strongly for McConnell, show no sign that they will support Robinson in the general election."

"Are any of the other Republican candidates—declared or otherwise—igniting voters?"

"Not so far, Gerald. Former Florida Governor Jeb Bush polls surprisingly well, given his brother's excruciatingly low public approval, but that could reflect simple name recognition. Senator Harry Purcell has the highest favorables of any potential nominee and could likely pull his home state of Michigan into his column, but fares poorly in the Deep South. It appears that the Republican nomination is a poison chalice in the hands of anyone other than President McConnell."

Morrow seemed to wince at Dugan's metaphor—a cup of poison in the hands of a man dead for less than two months—and ducked toward what he hoped was a safer historical analysis. "Professor Taylor? What's the historical perspective we should be considering?"

Graham Taylor smiled lazily. "That occasionally, very occasionally, Gerald, the voters in a democracy will administer a good swift well deserved ass-kicking," he said, and happily launched himself into the all purpose history lecture that kept him on the minor league chatter circuit and helped sell his books.

"American history has been well analyzed for its periodic swings between conservative and liberal eras," Taylor continued. "In the past twenty years, we've twice seen how elections that turned on fears of terrorism shifted normal political alignments. The conservative movement used its Supreme Court-blessed *coup d'etat* after the 2000 election to install the most regressive social and economic policies America had seen since before the Great Depression. The Bush Administration successfully waved the bloody shirt of 9/11 to barely retain power in 2004, but self-destructed soon after. Brett Campbell broke the conservative hold on the White House by building a coalition of the left and center, and pledging to turn public policy toward repairing the damage of the Great Recession. But the terror issue still has a hold on American voters. The Comiskey Park suicide bombings, the assassination of President Campbell, and the emergence of New York Mayor Andy Stern as an independent third-party candidate gave Charles McConnell the opening to force his election through the House of Representatives, even though he collected just 38% of the popular vote. Now the stars have turned the other way again. There has been no major terrorist incident on home soil since Comiskey Park. Given that we are now suffering through the third major recession in the past eight years, this election may finally bring the realignment that Brett Campbell sought: a majority center-left coalition firmly anchored in the Democratic Party, drawing independents and the few remaining moderate Republicans into the tent."

Morrow turned back to Coulter. "Paul? You're considered a thoughtful moderate—even conservative—commentator. Is Graham right? Is this just one of those times—like FDR's victory in 1936, or Goldwater's defeat in 1964, when the political tide is so sweeping that the losing party's politicians are going to have to hunker down, hold the Congressional and statehouse seats they can, and regroup to fight another day?"

Coulter tried to look thoughtful in the face of the banal question. "Gerald, that's an acute insight," he began, ignoring Graham Taylor's off camera expression of amused disdain. "But I do think the problem for most Republican politicians is going to be, how do they regroup when the party is so split between business-oriented conservatives, libertarians and the religious right? The last Republican attempt at a bridge ticket, McConnell-Robinson, blew apart so completely that the Republican Party as we have known it may no longer exist. I would not be surprised if one side or the other leaves this convention before a ticket can be nominated."

"Michelle?" Morrow asked, turning to the pollster. "Would there be support for a third party movement in the Republican center, or on the religious right?"

"Absolutely. Both could break away," Dugan replied firmly, brushing away her blonded hair as though it were an annoyance. "Senator Purcell could lead a breakaway movement for the moderates and libertarians, and either President Robinson or Governor Brackett could lead a new party for the Christian conservatives. But Purcell can't win in the South, and Robinson, based on his losses to McConnell in the primaries, has little following in the industrial North and no support on the West Coast. The Reagan coalition has shattered, and there is nothing on the horizon to replace it."

Morrow turned towards Graham Taylor. "Colonel Taylor? Any final thoughts about how this will look from the perspective of history?"

Taylor turned suddenly serious, mulling his answer. "This will be the fourth election in the last five that will be decided along almost purely sectional, racial and religious lines," he finally replied. "Historically, that's never been good for America. There's something in the air here, Gerald, with these delegates, especially the Robinson and Brackett groups—a hardening of the heart, a deepening anger as they sense that the rest of the country is drawing away from them." Taylor paused, looked soberly into the camera. "American culture is dividing again into separate nations. Both nations seem to be looking for the opportunity to have it out."

"For a minute there I thought you were going to tell us that Ty Brackett was planning to open fire on Fort Sumter," Paul Coulter said sarcastically as they left the Morial Center.

"Well, Brackett *is* the Governor of South Carolina, and we *do* have the historical precedent," Taylor replied smugly as they emerged from the Morial Center into the hot muggy twilight air, dodged a group of republican delegates huddled around a map, and crossed Convention Center Boulevard. "Of course, things didn't turn out so well for South Carolina last time." Taylor laughed, took a red box of Dunhill cigarettes from his pocket, drew one and lit it, ignoring Paul's disapproval.

"Damn it, Graham, you said you'd quit. With your asthma—"

"Sorry." Taylor drew in smoke and released it gratefully. "Republicans make my ass itch, as you well know, and New Orleans is the last city in America with a civilized view towards vice. Let's go on walkabout and get a drink. Or four drinks. I've got a sovereign duty to keep your mind off Elizabeth."

It was just before eight o'clock, the sky darkened by a band of thunderstorms that hung in the distance over the Gulf, emitting brief flashes of lightening. Streetlights switched on as they walked through the lower downtown area and into the arts district. New Orleans had painted on its best face and put on its party clothes for the Republican convention, but the bright streamers over the dark streets and fresh-painted murals on the old brick buildings could not hide the empty storefronts and cracked pavements. The city had never been fully rebuilt after Katrina; its economy had dwindled with the end of federal disaster aid, and was now sorely dependent on diminishing oil and gas revenues and a fading trade in sex, gambling and tourism.

"I don't think I can handle Bourbon Street," Coulter said. "Too many young Republicans will be puking their guts up on the sidewalks. Suggestions?"

Taylor nodded firmly. "The Windsor Court. It's Saturday night and we just got paid, as that song goes, and I want to take my alcohol with the ruling classes tonight."

Coulter grinned. "Fair enough." He followed as Taylor turned the corner onto Poydras Street and they strolled south past a line of delegates and political staffers that had formed on the sidewalk outside of Mother's Restaurant. The Windsor Court was on Gravier, which dead ended at Peters Street and formed a short, almost enclosed courtyard in front of the hotel. They paused on the corner of Tchoupitoulas and Gravier as a black Cadillac Escalade roared past them, headed for the hotel. The windows were darkened but a light came on briefly inside the car and both men could see the famous hawk-beaked profile and white bristle hair of the back-seat passenger. The light went off as the Escalade whipped past the Windsor Court's parking valet and disappeared into the parking garage.

"Well, that's interesting," Taylor said, taking a last meditative draw on his cigarette before crushing it out and dropping it into a trash barrel.

"I didn't even know Royce Reed was in New Orleans," Coulter replied.

"Of course he is. No doubt he hopes to engage in the favorite sport of preachers throughout history."

"Which is?" Paul demanded.

"Anointing Kings," Taylor replied dryly. "Do you think he uses the traditional olive oil, or something more modern? Canola, perhaps? Come along, Paul. I really could use that drink. Especially now."

Chapter Nine

"Major, I am so sorry. We just heard about Admiral Thrace here a couple hours ago." Gary Berthoud, the new White House Chief of Staff, held both of Elizabeth Gray's hands in his own, a sympathetic gesture he had practically trademarked as a mortician-turned-Congressman from Broken Arrow, Oklahoma.

"Thank you, sir." Elizabeth Gray was dry-eyed and composed, masking the wrenching pain she had felt since the White House communications office had patched the news about the death of Anthony Thrace through to the Air Force C-37 flight she had just boarded at Andrews Air Force Base. Thrace had been killed along with his driver in a head on collision on I-295 approaching Andrews. Elizabeth had done her weeping huddled in the cramped Gulfstream bathroom, but for now she was determined to keep to her duty first and attend to her grief later.

"I know what your real job is, Major. I'm going to want you to step up and take Admiral Thrace's place as acting Director of Home-land Intelligence for the time being," Berthoud began. "God knows we need to keep somebody working there who knows where the hell the files are, won't call up the goddamn New York *Times* every ten minutes, and can keep the fucking Arabs from trying to kill us." Berthoud was a bulky man with a round face, receding chin and hairline, and shrewd colorless eyes obscured behind rimless glasses. He had an unhealthy pallor beneath his reddened face, the stress of his new position plainly taking a toll, Gray thought. Berthoud had been James Robinson's Vice-Presidential chief of staff, but after Robinson's break with McConnell Berthoud had been exiled from the White House along with his boss, cut off from daily access to the flow of information that cascaded through the West Wing. Now Berthoud was working twenty hours a day trying to manage the flow of policy and decision paper, as well as recruit and select new White House staff to replace departed McConnell loyalists. His few off-duty hours were spent worrying about how to keep James Robinson from failing as President before he had served two months in office.

Elizabeth pondered how to take Berthoud's remark, and hesitated before answering. She did not equate being the acting Director of Homeland Intelligence with a file clerk's position, but she could understand Berthoud's burgeoning paranoia over the loyalty of the people who worked around him. Most of Charlie McConnell's White House staff and cabinet level officials—including, not that he would ever have admitted it, Tony Thrace—deeply loathed James Robinson. Over half had tendered their resignations within a week of Robinson's swearing in. The holdovers were a fertile source of embarrassing and exquisitely well-timed leaks to the media. Only the reluctant decisions of the Secretary of State, acting National Security Adviser, and Secretary of Defense to remain at their posts until their resignations were accepted gave the government any appearance of stability.

"I'm an army officer," Elizabeth finally replied, her voice neutral. "I will serve in whatever capacity the President directs."

"Thank you, thank you, that's a great relief," Berthoud responded. "I'm very glad you are here. I want you to attend the senior staff meeting tomorrow morning at ten, meet the new group," he added.

"But sir," Gray protested. "I came here to brief the President. With Admiral Thrace. There's a developing homeland security issue—"

"Yes, yes, Thrace requested the time," Berthoud replied testily, "but events have moved forward. The President's got a critical meeting tonight, and I just can't get you in. I want you to put your briefing in writing and run it through the National Security Advisor's staff before we go any further with this."

"Sir," Elizabeth insisted, "Admiral Thrace and I were coming here to brief President Robinson on a threat that, while not yet clearly outlined, we think has perhaps the most potential for damage since the Comiskey Park suicide attacks."

Berthoud looked up at Elizabeth Gray with narrowed, suspicious eyes. "All Thrace said was that he needed thirty minutes with the President, the Acting NSA, the Homeland Security Secretary, and the senior staff. If this was that important, why wasn't it briefed through channels?"

"Congressman, what we have is difficult to interpret but very significant information. A wave of funds has been flowing from the Middle East to non-traditional groups in the southern and western United States. There may be an effort to fund a radical terrorist movement here in the United States."

Berthoud closed his eyes as if in prayer and shook his head. "Look, Major, if there is some kind of domestic law enforcement issue here, why haven't I heard this from the Director of the FBI? Or the Attorney General?"

"You will. Treasury and FINCEN have been tracking the flow of funds for three months. But they haven't been able to get anyone inside the groups, or close to the individuals receiving the money."

"If you've got nothing definite on this situation, then why are you here, Major?" Berthoud demanded.

"It's because of the TriPlex situation…" Gray began.

"What TriPlex situation?" Berthoud demanded.

"You didn't read our briefing?" Gray was incredulous.

"I have a lot of daily briefing, Major, including multiple briefings from Homeland Intelligence—which, by the way, I want made shorter and *much* more succinct in the future. The President is not a big reader. I'm also trying to completely restructure the White House staff during a national political convention where, it just so happens, our President is a candidate." Berthoud's jaw set in anger. "Now, what briefing are you talking about?"

Gray paused. "Sir, thirty-six hours ago the new TriPlex national intelligence analysis system crashed. We have lost our ability to access and interpret our satellite and security monitor image data, telephone, cable, and internet intercepts and signals pattern recognition for at least 72 hours. After that—if we're lucky—we will be limping along on the original, inadequate systems for at least ten days, possibly much longer. We have a threat we do not understand. Our director was just killed in a suspicious auto accident. And we are blind."

Berthoud sighed dismissively. "Look, if you just want to raise the level to Threatcon 3, we could probably do that," he said. He paused and did a quick political calculation. "The President certainly wants to *appear* vigilant to the public. But, damn it, I've *got* to have better information than what you've given me so far. The media will be all over us, claiming we're playing politics with national security during the Convention."

"Sir, Threatcon 3 is basically a public awareness campaign, some fine talk, but no active measures. We need to go to Threatcon 2."

"Gray...that's just not realistic," Berthoud replied.

"Sir, it's what is called for by the policies set out in President McConnell's Homeland Security Directive, NSPD 2012-9, issued the year after the New Comiskey attacks. When we have credible evidence of a potential threat on a national scale, we take preventive measures, *even if the threat is not well defined and no specific target has been identified.*"

Berthoud pressed his lips together, still controlling his temper before he spoke. "Let's talk about those 'preventive measures', Major. I'm sure it will come as a surprise to you, but I've actually read all of those Homeland Security Directives. The Directive you're quoting calls for *reasonable* measures to be imposed, *up to and including* enhanced airport, passenger rail and mass transit screenings, military or national guardsmen to be stationed at rail yards, ports, power plants, electric transmission towers, and key pipeline junctions, and institution of national identification card systems. Which of those are you talking about?"

"All of them."

Berthoud stared in disbelief. "You're talking about cutting the number of airline flights in this country in half, shutting down heavy truck traffic, hand inspection of every freight container in every port from Boston to Long Beach. We'd have massive lines at national border crossing points to Mexico and Canada. Jesus Christ, Major, you can't shut down half the country—

"In an election year," Gray cut in.

Berthoud's face flushed dark with anger. "When this country is barely recovering from the worst depression since the 1930s. Goddamnit, Major, don't you fucking *dare* accuse me of putting politics ahead of national safety. I'm not. But I am not going to have the President humiliated if we disrupt the country and kill the economic recovery, and all this threat talk turns out to be nothing but talk. You brief this threat and bring it up through channels. There's an NSC deputies meeting when we get back to Washington. A week from Tuesday. If you get consensus by then that we should go to Threatcon 3, and can articulate plausible reasons that we can give to the public, I'll give you your time with the President to make your case."

"Sir, I—"

Berthoud turned away. "That's my decision, Major. I'd suggest you get back out to Fort Meade and get your damn computers fixed. No need to attend the senior staff in the morning. You aren't going to be in my White House very long."

Ten minutes later Berthoud picked up his secured phone, listened briefly, then said, "No, that's not necessary. I've got her buried for at least a week. No, she won't leak it. She's Army, and they'd crucify her. Stay with the program."

Chapter Ten

The Windsor Court Hotel
Gravier Street
New Orleans, Louisiana
Saturday, August 27
8:55 P.M. CDT

H*e does not carry himself like a President*, Royce Reed thought as the doors to the Windsor Court's Penthouse suite opened. Reed had known five Presidents since rising to political prominence with the founding of his church, The Christian Nation. Clinton could fill a room with the sheer hurricane force of his personality, even if you hated him. The younger Bush demanded attention, if only for his arrogance and ill-concealed contempt for anyone who disagreed with him. Campbell charmed his visitors with baseball stories while he played them like a chess grandmaster, always working the sixth move ahead. McConnell outworked and outlasted his opponents by stubborn, single-minded dedication. But James Babineux Robinson merely paused for a half-moment before entering the living room of the suite, as though bracing himself for a confrontation he did not want and feared he could not win. He squared his heavy shoulders, drew in his slumping belly, and forced a grin onto his broad flushed face as he sauntered into the room.

"Royce," James Robinson said warmly, his Cajun accent thicker than usual, reaching out for Reed's hand. Reed drew himself slowly to his feet, smiled thinly, and shook the outstretched hand.

"Mr. President," Reed replied. He nodded to the two men who had followed Robinson silently into the room: David Harrell, Robinson's new White House Counsel, and Mack Woods, Robinson's campaign manager. Both men were in their mid-forties, polished, barbered and well fed. Both wore the standard Washington political uniform: blue suit, starched white shirt, and conservative foulard ties—one pale blue, the other deep red—despite Robinson's own casual dress: chinos and a blue golf shirt with the presidential seal embroidered over the heart.

"I've been concerned about you, Mr. President," Reed continued, then fell silent. His voice in conversation was low and even, nothing like the sharp, high-pitched buzz saw of his preaching voice. In either voice he spoke with the flat rootless absence of accent that marked those raised in blue collar Southern California. The calming voice contrasted with Reed's harsh-featured, deeply tanned and lined face, his thick, almost Mohawk-cut white hair, and intense black-eyed stare. Reed, now in his late fifties, had ridden with the Mongols motorcycle gang in his native Southern California during the early 1980s and did four years in the California State Prison at Pelican Bay for dealing methamphetamine. In prison he had studied philosophy and religion as a means to the hearts of his parole board. He ultimately adopted the Christian Determinist doctrines that had their origins in the preaching of John Calvin of Geneva, made their way to America during the Great Awakening of the 1730s, and found current form and acceptance among the leaders of the 20th Century religious right, from Pat Robertson to Nixon's henchman, Charles Colson. Reed's prison commitment to Christ helped secure his early release, and in 1988 he founded an evangelical church in Sacramento that grew to more than four thousand members in three years. Reed's church services were fiery combinations of profanity and brimstone, sex and pop culture and Calvinism. Men were told that faith required them to fight, women to sexually submit to their men. Jesus was not some weakling who wanted to be a personal savior; he was a warrior God with a bad temper and scores to settle. By the early 1990s Reed's church had begun to morph into the Christian Nation, the Word spread by web sites and music videos that combined metal rock with Reed's black leather jacketed, foot stomping sermons. Reed founded dozens of social networking sites that spread his influence across the Internet. By 2010 he had absorbed a half-dozen older evangelical ministries into Christian Nation, taking over their cable television shows, websites and marketing. He built up their businesses—book publishing, video production, home schooling, internet advertising, insurance sales, banking, and investments—until they produced well over seven billion dollars in revenue per year.

Robinson smiled nervously as the silence in the room lengthened. "I appreciate your concern, Royce," he finally replied. "Yes, of course I do. But I'm holding up under the burden the Lord has seen fit to task me with."

"I hope you are, Mr. President. As you know, the thirty-six million people of Christian Nation have been praying for you ever since you took office."

"And I appreciate that, Royce, I do feel uplifted."

Reed smiled again, without warmth. "I'm glad." He gestured at Harrell and Woods, both flanking the President, a respectful two steps behind. "I was hoping that we could speak privately, Mr. President."

"What? Oh, of course. I guess Mack and David have been with me so much these past two months that sometimes I forget they're even in the room. Give us a few minutes, will you, gentlemen?"

Mack Woods began to speak, clearly concerned. "Mr. President—

"Thank you, Mr. President," Harrell cut in swiftly, placing a firm hand on the small of Mack Woods' back and ushering him out of the room.

"Please sit down, Royce," James Robinson said when they were gone. "When we're by ourselves it's just family." Robinson crossed to a bar that had been set up on a credenza against the far wall of the living room and splashed a double shot of Jack Daniel's into a cut crystal tumbler filled with cracked ice. "Get you something?"

"No, thank you." Reed's voice, still soft, took on an edge. "You're becoming a drunk, Jimmy. Among other things. You've gained forty pounds since the primaries ended and you got locked in that big house up at the Naval Observatory, nothing to look forward to except your daily briefing and a fifth of Virginia Gentleman every afternoon. You're fifty-nine years old. Six more months like this and you'll eat and drink yourself to death."

Robinson froze, momentarily astonished, and then defiantly raised his glass in a mock toast. "Here's to you, Royce. Now what the hell is this all about?" He swallowed bourbon and sat down heavily in a white damask covered arm chair

Reed leaned forward intently. "You are a failure, Jimmy," he said bluntly. "In the eyes of God, in the eyes of Christian Americans, and in the eyes of the foreign leaders who hold you in such contempt."

Robinson's eyes narrowed. "You forget your place, Royce. And who you are talking to."

"Do I? Twenty-five years ago you were a washed up country singer running a backwater TV station in Baton Rouge that couldn't pay its bills."

"Thirty-five years ago you were a convicted meth cooker locked up in Pelican Bay Penitentiary," Robinson shot back.

Reed nodded and suddenly smiled, but there was still no warmth in it. "That's right, Jimmy. We both were what we both were. But remember how you got here. I bought out your failed TV station and gave you a job, wrote the editorials you gave over the air every night, raised you up in the eyes of the Christian Nation. I raised the seven million dollars we had to spend to get you elected Governor of Louisiana. Four years ago *my* delegates blocked Charlie McConnell from gaining the Republican nomination and forced him to accept you as Vice-President. I provided the Christian Nation foot soldiers in the primaries this year that knocked on every door in Iowa and New Hampshire and South Carolina for you. You were running with the breath of God at your back against a wounded President with forty per cent approval ratings in his own party, and he *crushed* you."

Robinson's heavy face flushed, but he kept his wits. "Taking on McConnell," he began, "was—

"No excuses, Jimmy," Reed said, cutting him off. "No excuses. None for me either. We've both failed. The Supreme Court has reaffirmed *Roe v. Wade* and the two justices McConnell appointed joined that opinion, so the murder of infants remains the law of the land. Thirty-nine states now recognize homosexual marriage. We have lost two wars, withdrawn from the Middle East, and failed to protect ourselves or Israel from Islamic terrorists. The followers of Mohammed now possess nuclear weapons in Iran, Egypt, Pakistan, and Saudi Arabia. Europe will cease to be a Christian continent within our lifetimes. No, we have all failed."

Robinson said nothing, thinking hard. He had long since grown immune to Reed's preaching—and his rants. The Christian Nation had been his employer and then his political ally, but nothing more. Robinson had endured two baptisms by full immersion, one at 16 at the behest of his crazy stepmother, the other for the benefit of the TV cameras during his Louisiana gubernatorial campaign. He had come away from each convinced that bourbon whiskey and women both had spiritual qualities, but the subject of God Almighty left him uninspired. Robinson had formulated his own version of Pascal's wager: there was no harm in being Christian because if there was a god your ass was covered and if there wasn't, well, in the meantime, the yokels paid your bills, and preachers were always negotiable at a price.

"What are you asking me for, Royce?" Robinson finally said.

"I'm not asking, Jimmy. I'm giving."

"Giving me what?"

"A Vice-President, Jimmy. His name's Kyle Jackson."

The argument grew heated. The President of the United States poured himself a third drink.

"It's really heaven calling you, isn't it, Royce?" he asked sarcastically. "Calling down the wrath of God on me. Fine, God blesses you and not me. Is that why all those wonderful tax free donations from the faithful have been diverted from the church and invested every year in your personally owned cable channels, your banks, your insurance companies, and, especially, your offshore accounts?"

"What are you talking about?" Reed hissed angrily.

"Charlie McConnell hated your fucking guts, Royce," Robinson continued. "Charlie didn't mean to leave me any gifts, but he did. He's had a hundred FBI and IRS special agents taking apart your empire for the last three years. Hard to keep the rumors away from a Vice-President even when he's on the shit list. The very *first* thing I did when that self-righteous sonofabitch's brain blew out was order every fucking Justice Department confidential investigation put on my desk. The pricks didn't want to do it, but they didn't have a choice. Your file is seventeen feet thick, Royce. I read it all. Good stuff. Wiretaps. Emails, FINCEN money transfer reports, Suspicious Activity Reports, FBARs—I didn't even know what a Foreign Bank Account Report *was*. The draft indictment is a hundred pages long. And I must say the lawyers did one hell of a number on you, Royce. That indictment, it's a thing of beauty. Would love to show you a copy but, of course, that'd be against the law and all that."

Reed stared, shocked for the first time in years. "You bastard."

"You betcha, Royce. I got a brand new acting Attorney General, Ramon Acosta, promoted him just last week. He's a Cuban lawyer from Florida. Wants me to make sure his family gets back all their plantations in Cuba—and we extend the sugar subsidy—now that the Castro brothers are both dead and we have a light Marine division handling public order down there until the elections. Ramon has been in charge of building the case against you. He has what they tell me is called prosecutorial *discretion*. Meaning he will handle your case the way I want him to. And I'm thinking that possibly the best way to show my independence, assuming that I'm nominated—and especially if I'm *not* nominated—might just be to have your ass indicted."

Reed thought hard. He remembered, too late, that James Robinson had governed Louisiana with an unexpected cunning and ruthlessness that had surprised even him. "A good play, Jimmy," he said at last, breaking into a genuine grin. "Very good. Just not good enough." Reed paused. "Renee Barber, Jimmy."

"Who?"

"Please. The mother of your three-months-along unborn child. Who works for me."

Robinson exploded. "But she never told me—"

"Of course she didn't. I'm pleased that you can still get it up, Jimmy, given age, weight and the booze. You didn't think I'd let you go catting around without waiving properly vetted Christian pussy under your nose, did you? The DNA will be just as telling in your case as in Bill Clinton's. Your problem is that everyone understood that Clinton was a rascal. They forgave him. You're not in the same position." Reed paused, went to the bar at the far side of the room, selected one of the four Cabernets open on the bar, an Opus One, poured himself a small glass, and returned to the sofa, resting the wine glass on his knee.

"It does seem like mutual destruction, doesn't it?" Reed asked, suddenly expansive, almost friendly. "Let me explain how my end of it will play out. On Monday, *Christian Family Morning* will broadcast on satellite, cable and the web to more than thirty million Americans. We will disclose your multiple instances of sexual misconduct, not just Renee Barber but the score of women in the last two years. We will announce, more in sorrow than in anger, that Christian Nation cannot possibly support so immoral a candidate. And then our surprise guest will appear: Governor Ty Brackett, the Christian Nation's new candidate for President of the United States. After that, of course, you can indict me."

The deal was cut swiftly. By eleven o'clock Royce Reed had settled into the back seat of the black Escalade, closing his eyes for a moment and indulging a deep breath of satisfaction. He was joined by Daniel Eilat, the chief of marketing and statistical analysis for both the Christian Nation and Reed's personal business empire. Eilat, Israeli by birth, had once served as an intelligence agent for Mossad in the United States, a specialist in the care and feeding of the American evangelical right and its use as a political tool of Israel.

"I still don't get it," Eilat said, pouring a glass of mineral water from the small refrigerator tucked behind the Escalade's front seats. "Even if you could salvage Robinson's image after his disastrous primary campaign against McConnell, Jackson doesn't add anything to the ticket. He's got no name recognition outside of North Carolina. His connections with Dark/Star are going to be spread all over the press. An ex-military officer always appeals to a certain segment of the population, but Ben Giles has a hell of a military record himself. The economy's been on its back for nearly eight years now, a recession that turned into a depression that will not go away. Voters are going to be more concerned about having a job than gay marriage or any of our social issues. Our internal polling shows that a Robinson/ Jackson ticket will start out twenty-four points behind the Giles/ Kraft ticket—losing by four hundred electoral votes. We won't even hold Georgia and the Carolinas. And if Robinson performs as badly in the debates as he did against McConnell in the primaries, the only state Robinson *might* win outside of the South is Utah."

Royce Reed smiled. "Daniel, you don't understand. It's not about winning this time. It's about Dominion."

Chapter Eleven

Hyatt Regency New Orleans
Sunday, August 28
12:35 A.M. CDT

Coulter was dreaming.

He felt Elizabeth's breasts sliding along his back, her hand stroking his side. He began sweating; the dream was too real—

He came awake with a start.

"Shush baby, shush baby, it's alright, it's me," she said softly into his ear.

"But—

"Shush." She ran a hand through his curly brown hair, already tousled by sleep.

Coulter turned his head and looked up at her, smiling above him in the hotel room's dim half-light. "The locks—"

"I'm good with locks, remember?" Elizabeth's smile turned sly. Coulter stared at her: long intelligent face, high cheekbones, brown eyes courtesy of a grandmother from one of the old *Norteno* families of Santa Fe, blonde hair let down for once so that it could fall to her bare shoulders—and his heart broke, as it had every time since they had met, two and a half years before, at a White House Christmas party and had run away with each other just before midnight.

"*Where have you been?*" Coulter demanded. His voice was still thick from sleep.

"The answer to that question is too long, and way too classified," Elizabeth replied, her tone suddenly sober. "But I'm here, for seven more hours, anyway."

"What time is it?" Paul Coulter asked, finally coming awake.

"A little after midnight. I got in at seven. I was supposed to the see Robinson with the Admiral. Berthoud canceled. With Tony dead it was just too much…so I slipped my security guy and went looking for you and finally found you here." With that she broke down for the first time since locking herself in the bathroom on the Air Force flight from Andrews. "You know about Tony?" she asked in a whisper, tears streaming down her face.

Coulter nodded. "I am so sorry, Beth. I heard about it on CNN when I got back here tonight. Graham and I were out taping a webcast panel program for PBS. I wanted to call you…but didn't know how. You're cell phone doesn't work, your emails have been closed down." He shifted and got Elizabeth's head pillowed on his shoulder. She wrapped herself around him, arm across his chest, long muscled leg thrown over his hip. "Do they know what happened?" Coulter asked.

"It was a head on collision at high speed. The driver of the other car did not survive. The FBI is investigating." She shuddered in his arms. "I feel like I'm coming apart at the seams, Paul. First having to leave you, then the President dying, and now Tony—"

She broke down again and he simply held her for a long, allowing her to let the grief escape without question. When she was silent again he placed his hand along the side of her face and looked into her eyes. "I love you, Elizabeth," Coulter said firmly. "I won't quit you. I'm forty-four years old and know that you are the love of my life and always will be. But you have to tell me what is going on."

She stared back at him, eyes somber, tears again beginning to flow. "I can only say this much. I was assigned to conduct an investigation that had to be done quickly and with total secrecy. I didn't want to leave you. I'm living alone, Paul, out of a suitcase in a studio apartment inside a federal safe house in the D.C. security zone. There is no one else."

"Charlie told me that much, three nights before he died. But it was still hard to understand."

"What else did he tell you?"

"That you were working on something that was…deadly serious. That you had nearly been gunned down in Panama. I wasn't sure that I believed him. I was convinced that Charlie had driven himself out of his mind with his obsession about security …or was getting close to it."

"He wasn't, Paul. This is real."

"You've got to tell me what this is about," Paul repeated.

"I can't."

"Horizontal Rules."

She grinned suddenly, even with tears still in her eyes, a radiant smile he could both see and feel. "We invented the Rules. After making out like mad in the taxi from the White House Christmas party to your place in Capitol Hill, and shedding most of our clothes just inside the front door."

"I've always honored those rules, Elizabeth," Paul said, his voice serious and formal. "I've never printed, or followed up on anything you said when we were alone. I scarcely know what you do in the White House, and I've covered it for five years. I haven't asked, I haven't even tried to ask. But when you are at risk I have to know. Not knowing is going to break me."

The grin faded away, replaced by a fixed, flat expression—what Paul knew as Elizabeth's duty face. "Paul, this is like nothing else I've ever dealt with," Elizabeth said soberly. "It involves…potentially, the security of the government itself."

"But how long can you keep living like this?"

"I don't know," she said quietly. "Gary Berthoud, Robinson's chief of staff, told me to fill in for Admiral Thrace, at least to keep the intelligence flow intact, until a new Homeland Intelligence director is named. God knows I don't want to work for that man, but it's a dangerous time, Paul. There's a kind of….slack in the national security structure right now. No, that's not the right word. What I mean is…the new President doesn't know how to handle national security issues yet. He doesn't yet know how to credit good intelligence or to how disregard some fantasy that a staffer is trying to stovepipe. The people presently in position are not his people. Robinson's people don't know how the systems work. And with this…investigation going on, I don't know who I can trust. I have to know that I can trust you to stay for me, wait for me, no matter how long it takes or bad it gets."

"Of course you can." Coulter's voice was husky but he met her gaze with his own and knew as well as he had ever known anything that, regardless of church or state, they were married at that moment and nothing for him would change that. He was still trying to think of more and better words for her when Elizabeth rolled him onto his back and pressed herself against him, as though trying to absorb all of his skin through her own. "For now," she whispered, kissing him, "we still have six more hours."

Elizabeth spent the next morning, a Sunday, laboring in an empty cubicle in the White House staff's temporary office warren on the third floor of Morial Center. She pushed away her thoughts of Paul and of Tony Thrace and struggled to focus on the work of producing the daily Homeland Intelligence brief. It would be far less complete than usual because of the TriPlex breakdown. She was nearing the 2 P.M. EDT deadline when her government issued cell phone vibrated against her hip.

"Major? Cable Hollings. I'd like you to call me back on a secured land line."

Elizabeth shook off her annoyance and asked, "When?"

"Now. I've got to back in with the Director in ten minutes. It's important."

She quickly finished the brief, emailed it over the secured data network, and searched for an office with a secure land line to make the call. Eighty feet down the long corridor running through the middle of Morial Center's third floor she found an Army E-5 with the crossed flags-and-torch badge of the Signal Corps on his shoulder, scanning a checklist on a hand-held computer pad.

Elizabeth spoke quickly. "Sergeant, I need you to direct me to a secure land line as fast as you can."

He glanced at her civilian suit and started to brush her off but Elizabeth held up her Army identification and the soldier snapped to and saluted. "Sorry, Major. I'm Sergeant Aragon. We're still trying to get the bugs out of the temporary secure voice installation here. Some of the President's staff has been a little pushy with us."

Elizabeth gave him a rueful grin. "I know how it works with the staff, Aragon. Can you help me out?"

"Yes, Ma'am." He pointed toward the open door of an empty office with a newly installed land line telephone, a metal desk, and a worn secretarial chair. "This one's lit up."

"It'll do, Aragon. Thanks. Anybody need this room for twenty minutes or so?"

"Not that I know of, Ma'am. There's a couple more White House staffers coming in tonight, the rooms are for them. I can send my tech over to guard the door if you want."

"No need, I think. Hang in there, Sergeant, and don't let the politicians bug you. Carry on."

"Thank you, Major."

Elizabeth entered the office, closed the door, picked up the phone, and hesitated, wondering if the line would be recorded. Not if it is being installed for the political staff, she decided, and a call placed from a White House line to the FBI could be explained in a thousand ways. She punched numbers.

"Hollings," Cable responded, in his usual grumbling drawl.

"Elizabeth Gray. What's up, Cable?"

"I've had a team going over Tony Thrace's 'accident' on Saturday afternoon," Hollings said, putting just enough emphasis on the word 'accident' so that Elizabeth understood immediately that Hollings did not believe it was an accident at all. "For once the Director backs me up. He's become sensitive to the subject of senior federal executives meeting untimely deaths ever since he left the Fifth Circuit Court of Appeals and became a senior federal executive himself."

"And?"

"Maryland State Patrol hasn't issued any statement yet. But my folks are not buying this 'accident' at all."

"Why?"

"A lot of things. Tony's car was in its lane and within the speed limit. The other car, an old 2012 Chevrolet dually pickup, came over the median at better than seventy miles an hour. No skid marks, no evidence of any brakes applied. Damn thing weighed over two tons curb weight, had a pallet of bricks in the back, so you're talking three tons of mass. Tony was in one of the government-issue hybrid utility sedans. They're pretty light. It was like hitting a pop can with a sledge hammer."

Elizabeth's grip tightened on the phone. "What do we know about the driver?"

"Not much more than *Post* reported. Harland M. Boyd. Thirty-two year army man. Medically discharged with terminal lung cancer late last year. Boyd might have been pretty close to the end—there was an exploded oxygen tank in the cab of the truck. The tox screen on his blood showed Oxycontin, Xanax, alcohol—I'm guessing Jim Beam. Not enough of any one of them to black him out, but he was probably not feeling any pain. No wife. Not every suicide bomber needs a bomb, Elizabeth. As we know too damn well, a plane—or a truck—can function the same way."

"I have a sense that this is going to get even worse."

"It does. Boyd's passport file says he was in Panama when you were. And he showed up on the social network analysis." Hollings voice grew harsh. "If this was an assassination I want to smash these people, *now*. I've got fifteen agents working on this. I want Boyd's full DOD records."

"You can request—

Hollings cut her off with a laugh. "DOD's been holding out on the FBI for years. So get them to me quickly. In the meantime, here's a number." Hollings rattled off a toll-free 888 number with no meaning for her. "Call that number when you're on the ground back in D.C. tonight," he added. "I'm having you moved. We've already got your stuff, and my people will pick you up at the airport. I have an unused FBI safe house in Anacostia and you are going there."

"But—"

"No arguments. Tony put the bait out there Saturday morning and somebody took it right quick. You're more exposed than ever. Now we've got to figure out where the hell we go from here."

The C-37 she flew back to Washington was mostly empty. It had dropped off twelve additional White House staff to augment Robinson's campaign for the nomination in New Orleans, but Elizabeth was one of only three people deadheading back to Washington. Robinson's new chief domestic advisor was on board, and since he carried political tonnage and lived inside the District in Adams-Morgan, the C-37 would land at Reagan National, not Andrews AFB. As the plane banked low over the Potomac on final approach, Elizabeth could clearly see the brightly lighted monuments— the temples erected for Lincoln, Jefferson, the veterans of World War II, and the greatest of all: Washington's Monument, the white stone obelisk shining against the dark sky. For the first time in her life she began to fear for the Republic she had sworn to serve.

Chapter Twelve

Republican National Convention Press Center
Morial Convention Center
New Orleans, Louisiana
Monday, August 29
3:04 P.M. CDT

A kinetic storm of strobe lights flashed from a hundred photographers and filled the Republican National Convention press room as White House Press Secretary Mitchell Garson took the stage behind the traveling Presidential podium. The room was jammed with sweating, cranky reporters suffering from the stuffy air. Garson seemed to brace himself for a moment, as though summoning the face of a soldier preparing for battle. It was not a successful look for Garson, a small balding man in his forties with carefully combed-over hair who had never been closer to armed combat than reporting from the sidelines of an LSU-Texas football game with the Southwestern Conference title riding on the outcome.

"Is Robinson going to quit?" Paul Coulter yelled from the edge of the press gallery. Four other reporters followed with the same shouted question. Garson raised his arms to quiet the surging crowd of reporters and get them back into their chairs.

"Sit down!" Garson shouted repeatedly, his face reddening under his television makeup. He looked sourly over the press corps as they returned to their seats, assigned, even in this temporary press room, by their seniority on the White House beat.

"Is Robinson going to quit?" Coulter demanded again, popping up again from his chair. Garson waived him down. "Shut up, Paul. Listen. The President will be here for a very important announcement at 3:15 P.M., ten minutes from now. We have asked for and obtained live coverage from the networks, the cable news channels, and the major web-cast sites. That's all I have."

Andy Dworkin, an ancient gnome-like print reporter, balding, bearded, and nearly blind at an age somewhere in his eighties but still writing for the Internet-only Boston *Globe* jumped to his feet from the chair beside Coulter, choked with rage. "Text!" Dworkin shouted, pointing at Garson. "If it's an announcement, where's the fucking text?"

"No text until after the announcement," Garson replied. "If you'd ever learned to type with all ten fingers, Andy, you wouldn't have so many problems." Satisfied that he'd gotten in at least one insult, Garson hastily left the platform.

"Christ," Dworkin said, reclaiming his seat and mopping his bald head with a soiled red bandanna. "Lousy President, lousy air conditioning, no text. The fucking internet. Things have been going downhill ever since Clinton cut back the hot food on the press plane in '93."

Coulter laughed. "Come on, Andy," he replied. "This is great. Did you ever think that you would get to cover an open convention? So what do you hear out there? Is Robinson going to drop out?"

Dworkin shook his head and pushed his thick glasses up onto his forehead, old eyes gleaming with excitement. "No fuckin' way. Do the math, Paul," he said shrewdly. "Robinson won ten primaries and six caucuses, all in the south except for Idaho—McConnell didn't win enough delegates to be renominated until June. Almost all of the states Robinson carried have laws or party rules that bind their delegates to vote for the candidate that won their primary or caucus on at least the first ballot, sometimes the first two. Robinson suspended his campaign in June after the Montana Primary but never *released* his delegates. McConnell's death released *his* delegates, and the National Committee delegates are never bound to a particular candidate under the Republican rules. So Robinson goes into the first ballot with the biggest bloc of bound delegates—about 550, if I remember right—and most of those delegates are required to vote for him on the second ballot as well. That might be enough to keep somebody like Ty Brackett from gaining any momentum on Robinson's right. So that leaves the more centrist guys like Purcell or Blessing trying to pick up all the McConnell delegates. But remember, these are *Republican* delegates—in their hearts they are far more right wing than Charlie McConnell ever was. A lot of them are evangelicals, too, even if they don't always broadcast it. Blessing's a Mormon. Some of McConnell's evangelical delegates are going to have to be pushed to support a guy like Blessing that they think follows a false cult religion."

"So Robinson's still in it?"

"Very much. I think what we're hearing right now in the background—and what's gonna get announced in five more minutes—is the sound of a deal being cut. Robinson's going to try and pick off one of McConnell's guys and take him as Veep. It worked before, in reverse, when McConnell had to suck it up and take Robinson."

"Purcell?"

"Nah, Harry's too weird. Won't be Roger Blessing, either. Could be some other Governor—McFadden down in Arizona might have a lot of appeal to the McConnell people. But Robinson had better be sure about getting the right guy. I figure he'd better go over the top by the second ballot, third at the latest, unless they can kill off Purcell—he's their worst nightmare. If Robinson doesn't have the votes by then, he's cooked. Purcell's got the same problem. He better go over by the third ballot, maybe fourth. Otherwise all hell's gonna break loose. And then all bets are off—it could be some guy who isn't even a candidate right now, at least not somebody we *know* is a candidate."

"You got a name?"

"Nah. A feeling. I could be dead wrong. But remember that I was born in Philadelphia in July 1940. We Want Willkie."

Coulter grinned. "You had me going there for a minute, Andy. But Willkie was a liberal."

Dworkin returned the grin. "Doesn't seem like we'd get a liberal here, does it, Paul? Unless they decide to throw in the towel and nominate Ben Giles themselves." The sound in the room pitched up ten decibels. Coulter looked at the stage; there was movement behind the curtain.

Mitchell Garson emerged, a wide smile stitched across his face for the benefit of the cameras. "Ladies and Gentlemen, the President of the United States."

James Robinson, his bulk draped over the podium, spoke slowly and carefully.

"My fellow citizens, I have come before you today to announce my choice, not only for a candidate for Vice-President, but for a man who can and will immediately join my team, the better to protect America from the threat of foreign terrorism." He paused, looked somberly at the cameras. "It is no secret in my political party, or in America, that I did not agree with President Charles McConnell on many issues. Our disagreements grew so large, especially on domestic and moral issues, that I felt compelled to challenge President McConnell in the Republican primaries this year. But despite our disagreements, we always remained united on the protection of America's security at home and abroad, keeping America safe from the terrorists who despise and would threaten our very way of life. That is why, in considering and choosing a running mate to share the mission to make America safe from terrorism, I have looked for a man that not only understands the threat of islamofascist terrorism, but has direct experience in bringing that threat to its knees."

Robinson paused, sipped from a water glass, and mopped his brow. "I have found that man and made that choice. Many people will say this is not smartest political choice I could have made. Whether I win or lose this election to Ben Giles, an honorable man with whom I profoundly disagree on almost all issues is beside the point. I have chosen the man who can best help me keep Americans safe while I hold this office. A man who served his country in the United States Army Special Forces with honor and valor, and has built a business that serves this country and keeps it secure. A man who keeps Jesus Christ close to his own heart. *That man, and the next Vice-President of the United States, is Kyle! Hunter! Jackson!*"

Robinson turned and began applauding. Music rose from off-stage speakers and James Robinson's primary campaign theme song, a sanitized version of the forty-year old Doobie Brothers anthem *Takin' It to the Streets* swelled from the speakers mounted behind the stage. The curtains parted, the lights rose, and a very fit older man, modest in height, with gray brush cut hair and a tentative smile stepped out onto the stage, his younger blonde wife and four energetic children ranging from six to nineteen arrayed around him. The oldest child, a son, wore the dress grays of a cadet at the U.S. Military Academy at West Point. Kyle Hunter Jackson paused and shook the outstretched hand of the President of the United States before moving to the podium to speak.

"Mr. President," Jackson began. "I cannot begin to thank you for the honor you do me today by asking me to join your team as Vice-President. I accept this honor in the name of the men and women I served with, living and dead, wounded and whole, and all those in the United States Armed Forces and their civilian contract allies who have protected the American people during Operation Desert Storm, the second fight for Iraqi Freedom, and against the Taliban and Al Qaeda in Afghanistan. And I will—

"So who the *fuck* is he?" Andy Dworkin asked Coulter, his voice suddenly shaken, unsure, and old. "And why in *hell* would Robinson or any other sane politician fucking *want* him?"

"Beats me, Andy," Paul Coulter replied, equally stunned. "Beats me."

Four hours later Paul Coulter had more facts but fewer answers. He sat in his bland room at the Hyatt, his laptop charging on the desk while he paced the room talking into his cordless Bluetooth headset, trying his damnedest to do his job, work the story, and not to worry even harder about Elizabeth Gray.

"Listen, Mark," Coulter said, running his notes by his editor at Pacific News Consortium. "Here's what I've got and most of it is from secondary published sources. Jackson's sixty-four. West Point. Retired from the Army in December 1998 as a full Colonel, a funny time and way to retire since he was apparently just days away from being promoted to Brigadier General. A professional hard-ass, Special Forces for most of his career. Had a pair of academic stops, the War College and a master's in foreign policy from George Washington University. One year in J2, the joint staff intelligence operation, at the Pentagon. Among other things, Jackson led Special Forces groups that went into Iraq on Scud hunts during Desert Storm, went into Serbia to acquire bombing targets and take out war criminals in 1994 and 1995. God knows what else he did in between. He's won a Silver Star with three oak leaf clusters and a bunch of other commendations."

Coulter listened to the question from his editor, replied. "Jackson comes from an old North Carolina family. The family had some money from farming, textiles and newspapers but not much more than comfortable. Jackson bought into his company, Dark/Star— yeah, the big defense contractor—in early 1999. Dark/Star started pretty small—protection contracts for State and IAD and UN and NGOs in Bosnia and Rwanda and Jordan. Unsafe places where bureaucrats want a bunch of hard boys with Oakley sunglasses and automatic weapons to go with them every time they take a piss. Dark/ Star went big with Second Iraq. Jackson tried to get his commission back when the war started but no dice—don't know why. Dark/Star made a fortune—had a billion dollars in government security contracts alone by 2004, expanded into software, communications, and a bunch of other stuff. Jackson sold the company to run for Congress, and he's represented the North Carolina district around Fort Bragg for six years. Now Dark/Star's part of Cornwall Group, a *very* private offshore holding company headquartered in Grand Cayman. You might try putting somebody on Jackson's Congressional financial disclosure filings to get an idea of the size of his money."

Coulter listened to a barrage of questions. "Slow down, Mark. I've pulled Jackson's Congressional Quarterly voting record and issue ratings and emailed them to you. He's the most down the line Neo-con since Cheney. The CQ tables are in Excel. Have somebody in graphics create some bar charts contrasting his ADA and Conservative Political Action ratings. I bet he's 95% or higher every year on the CPA scores."

Coulter listened to his editor complain for another thirty seconds, and then checked his watch. "File? Fuck no, Mark. Run tonight with the generic story based on the bio, the backgrounder, the text of the announcement, and Jackson's congressional ratings. Amy can rewrite what I've sent if you'll give her some help. The real story is why Jackson's on the ticket in the first place. Politically, he's an unknown evangelical. From a potential swing state, okay, but he doesn't capture any moderate voters in North Carolina. He's an arms dealer and ran the biggest mercenary shop in Iraq. It's like designing a plane with two right wings. We should try to have some kind of a take on why Robinson put him on the ticket by morning. It's only nine here. I'm going to stir around and buy people a lot of alcohol and see what shakes loose."

Chapter Thirteen

The French 75 Bar
Arnaud's Restaurant
813 Rue Bienville, French Quarter
New Orleans, Louisiana
Monday, August 29
10:30 P.M. CDT

"Do you know why they call them French 75s, Paul?" Vince Magruder asked. He held up his glass. It shimmered in the light reflected by the bar's mirrors and polished wood paneling.

"No. I've always been more of a Jack Daniels from the pint kind of guy," Paul Coulter replied.

Magruder, the now former Deputy White House counsel, a holdover from the McConnell Administration whose resignation was just six hours old, shook his head sadly. "You should get out more, Paul." Magruder was a heavy bodied man in his mid-forties, a larger, somewhat softer version of the small college offensive tackle he once was at St. John's College in Minnesota. He had clear green eyes and an infectious smile that had seduced juries and clients and the press through his twenty years as an Assistant United States Attorney in Manhattan and Washington, D.C., the Securities and Exchange Commission, and as a partner in the D.C. office of the enormous Madden Broyles law firm. Magruder's rumpled suits and jovial patter concealed a highly accomplished, necessarily ruthless litigator adept in the kill people and break things school of American jurisprudence.

"The French 75 was originally invented by Raoul Lufbery, a French-American World War I flying ace in the Escadrille Lafayette squadron," Magruder continued. "Lufbery liked champagne, but wanted something with more of a kick to it, so he mixed it with cognac, a dash of lemon juice, and a tiny amount of sugar. Don't believe the morons who make them with gin—Lufbery specified cognac, and Arnaud's follows the true religion. Lufberry said that drinking them felt like being shelled with the French 75mm howitzer."

"He was probably referring to the way he felt the next morning."

"Perhaps, one always has to be careful around alcohol and sugar in combination. Unless it's your last day on the job and you are fucking well rid of it."

Coulter gestured with his own drink, a French 75 he had ordered at Magruder's insistence. "There's that," he said, then toasted: "To new horizons. So are these cocktails the reason that you have a twenty-nine year old wife clerking at the Supreme Court who looks like she just walked out of *Vogue*—or possibly *Maxim*—even though you personally could pass for a small water buffalo?"

"Absolutely. Oddball cocktails are part of my charm," Magruder answered. "Actually, the toast should be to unemployment." He downed his cocktail and raised a meaty hand in the crowded bar to signal for another round. "But I'll catch on somewhere. Maybe Giles is looking."

"You that pissed?"

"Well…yeah. We under the rose here?"

"You are officially half drunk and off the record."

"Great. That leaves me free to go to full drunk, and still be off the record."

"Be my guest. Still, I have to hand it to you. You held your nose and did your job for Robinson. You kept total secrecy on the Veep selection—I'm impressed. We knew Robinson was vetting Purcell, Brackett, Carmichael, Jeb Bush, even what's his name—the Governor of Minnesota, Anderson. But we never heard any kind of whisper that Robinson was looking at Kyle Jackson, much less going to nominate him."

Magruder did not reply, merely leaned forward on his elbows and hunched his heavy shoulders as though trying to ease a pulled muscle in his upper back. His fourth drink came and he tasted it carefully. "Not enough cognac. The proportions are off."

"You're dancing on me, Vince. I said you're off the record, I meant it."

"I'm not even background, Paul. Think of this discussion as an interesting fable of modern politics that you did not hear from me. Or anyone connected with the Counsel's office."

"All right."

"So. My boss, the real President, Charles David McConnell, died exactly 45 days ago today. Robinson didn't wait until Charlie was in the ground up in Grand Forks before announcing that he would again run for President. With Charlie's delegates released and splitting two or three ways no one is coming away from New Orleans with a first ballot win. So Robinson now has the biggest fucking poker chip in politics, the Vice-Presidency, free to trade and take out one of his main rivals, possibly lock up the nomination on the first ballot, almost surely by the second. Gary Berthoud, Robinson's chief of staff, is not a fool despite the guy he works for. Berthoud and my ex-boss, David Harrell, had Robinson's domestic political operation, the FBI, and the Counsel's office doing background on every potential vice presidential nominee you could think of before they'd stopped doing CPR on Charlie Mac. Except one."

"Kyle Jackson."

"Exactly."

"Why?"

"I don't know. I mean, what does Jackson bring to the ticket? Robinson won the Republican primary in North Carolina, so the delegates are already pledged to him for two ballots. Jackson's not well known, doesn't pull any of McConnell's old delegates from any other candidate. He might make it harder for Ty Brackett to get support, but Robinson's already got ninety percent of the South and religious right delegates locked up, unless some of the rumors on the bimbo watch turn out to be true. Of which I have no knowledge. Bimbo protectors get indicted."

"When did you get told to start vetting Jackson?" Coulter asked.

"You know I can't tell you that, Paul. That'd be a direct violation of attorney client privilege. But I can tell you that I, six other lawyers on my staff, and fourteen FBI agents developed severe cases of sleeplessness around 11:30 last…" Magruder glanced at his wristwatch and shook his head. "Sorry. Saturday night."

"What's the normal time allowed to vet a candidate?"

"For something serious, like the Cabinet, Court of Appeals, or the Supreme Court? At least eight weeks. We can do a lower official in three or four if there's a narrow political window for getting a nomination to the Senate before the session ends. But nobody in their right mind vets a potential Vice-President in two days."

"So why did it happen this time?"

"Fuck if I know." Magruder pursed his lips, looked at his glass, then shoved it away. "I shouldn't be talking to you about any of this, even off the record, Paul. But you knew Charlie, you were his friend, you saved his life in Iraq. And I hate this. I hate every, last, single stinking thing about this."

"I'm not following you."

"How much information did you get when you tried to find out about Kyle Jackson to file your story tonight, Paul? How much? I'll bet you a hundred bucks that you filed a pretty skinny story."

Coulter shrugged. "The first story is almost always written off the press release and the public statements anyway. What did I get? The bare outline of his military record, some business and financial press stories on Dark/Star. The sale of Dark/Star to a Caribbean private equity firm. The fact that he has a lovely blonde wife and four lovely Anglo-Saxon children and that, at least publicly, he loves his Lord Jesus and has said so in every congressional campaign and at every other public opportunity."

"Yeah." Magruder picked up his fifth French 75, considered its temperature, and downed it in a single massive swallow. "You gotta drink these fuckers cold. If they get warm and the champagne goes flat it's no good." Magruder turned away from the table and flagged the waiter. "Henry! Time to get serious. Coffee with cream and a snifter of Calvados. The Boulard. A *large* snifter, Henry. He turned. "Paul?"

Coulter considered the number of French 75s he had consumed—four, to Vince Magruder's five, along with his need to write a major story in the morning if he could, and promptly chickened out. "Perrier, lemon, aspirin, hope of redemption," he said.

Magruder nodded and gestured again to the waiter. "Sound choice, if a chickenshit one. Redemption's one of the many, many things on sale in New Orleans, one of the reasons I love this town so much. So, we were talking about Kyle Jackson."

"You were telling me what you got in the vetting," Coulter replied. "Or didn't get."

"I got about as much as was in the press release, Paul. And that *really* started to make my ass itch. Remember that when I was a hale and younger man, I did three years at the Manhattan U.S. Attorney's office, another three with the USAO in D.C., and four years as a trial lawyer for the old SEC. When I joined Madden Broyles in '06 they were still doing a lot of deal work—the last burst of mergers and acquisitions, private equity deals, public offerings—before the economic collapse in '08. Part of my job was to go through the due diligence on the deals and the guys doing the deals, ask them the questions that none of our white shoe corporate lawyers or underwriters or investment bankers wanted to ask because they were afraid to offend the client. I always insisted on a private interview—and a locked door. Man, I learned a lot of shit. Unacknowledged bastard children. Offshore bank accounts. Blow-jobs in anonymous Miami park bathrooms. I was pretty good at asking questions."

"And?"

"That's what you do when you vet someone for high appointed office, or as a running mate. Every other vetting job I've ever done, both for McConnell and Robinson, involved walking the candidate through their SF-86 disclosures *and* a special background questionnaire that I personally designed as a perjury trap. I'd sit there with a stack of paper eight inches high, birth certificates to tax returns, and depose people for six, eight hours. It was one of my specialties.

I never got to ask any questions about Kyle Jackson. Nobody on the White House staff except Berthoud and Harrell has ever even met him."

Magruder's coffee and Calvados arrived and he paused to swirl the liquor before tasting it. "There are a few questions that I'd like to ask Congressman Jackson," he said, his voice low.

"Like?"

"I'd like to review his military records. In detail. He was hot shit, you know. Special Forces. Promoted to full Colonel at thirty-five— less than 13 years out of West Point. He was on track to be the youngest Brigadier General in more than sixty years. This guy was like Petraeus on steroids. But suddenly, in December1998, when he's served just under 20 years on active duty, he resigns his commission."

"There could have been personal reasons."

"None that I could find. Then there's his company."

"Dark/Star. Peculiar name."

"Yeah. I tried to figure out what it meant. The only thing I came up with was a song by the Grateful Dead. 'Dark Star crashes, pouring its light into ashes.' Seems unlikely that Colonel Jackson is a Deadhead. It is a very peculiar company."

"It's a military contractor, Vince. The website says it has three business units. Executive Protection, Intelligence, and Software development and services. Eighty percent of its sales are to the U.S. Government."

"That's the surface picture, all right. Let's break it down. Executive Protection?"

"That's where they started, in Iraq Two, right?" Coulter decided to play dumb and let Magruder take the conversation as far as he chose.

"No, actually, Dark/Star was started by an ex-MP named Romey. They got their first contracts to protect U.S. State Department and UN personnel in Bosnia after the Dayton Peace accords were signed. They branched out, got business from NGO charities in Africa, and protected UN diplomats in Kosovo, Serbia and some of the crazier Middle Eastern states like Yemen. Jackson bought into the company in '99, controlled it a year later. He was smart, got investors to back him for a relatively small slice of the equity, did some very cute things with shell companies that left Dark/Star looking like a U.S. company but in fact moved control and ownership offshore. The big expansion came with Iraq II, the sequel from Hell. The private security contractors flooded in after the insurgents blew up the UN offices in Baghdad in 2004. Within two years Dark/Star had over 4,000 armed men, their own fleet of helicopters and armored vehicles, over a billion dollars a year in contracts with the U.S. Government and even more with the big infrastructure contractors: Halliburton, Exxon, Chevron, and Bechtel— all the firms supposed to be rebuilding the country. On top of that, Dark/Star got paid for running security in about half of Afghanistan after Little Bush pulled our troops away and sent them to the Great Iraq Oedipal Snipe Hunt. Jackson took the revenue from the mercenary business, used it to buy National Security Solutions, which became Dark/Star's intelligence information systems division, and Logical Integrations, which became Dark/Star Software."

"But Jackson sold Dark/Star before he was elected to Congress. To…uh…Cornwall LLC Group." Paul stayed dumb.

"Did he now? *Sold,* that's always an interesting concept for us lawyers, Paul. It's an act subject to some considerable interpretation."

"You're becoming cryptic as well as drunk now, Vince. What are you talking about?"

"You think that ownership or control of a private business actually gets disclosed on the website? Or in the publicly filed documents? Of which there are very, very few when offshore private equity's involved?" Jesus, Paul, you ought to audit the corporations and business organizations courses at a law school sometime, maybe learn something useful. At the time Jackson sold Dark/Star it was ostensibly 'owned' by fourteen different legal entities, spread out from the Cayman Islands to Dubai to Panama. Jackson still has interests in some of those companies, and in about thirty other companies spread across the globe, many of whom—drum roll, please—also have ownership interests in Cornwall LLC Group and its constituent brother-sister and subsidiary entities in Britain, Switzerland, Panama City, Grand Cayman, Singapore, and Hong Kong."

"But doesn't Jackson have to disclose those ownership interests? At least if he gets payments from them?"

"All tied up in four private blind trusts. The trustees are all eminently rentable senior partner types in major law firms in Charlotte and Raleigh, North Carolina. The reports show that Jackson's interests in the four trusts are valued at between $50 million and $500 million each, but they don't have to be more specific than that."

Coulter sat back, stunned. "You mean he's a billionaire."

"Yup. A billionaire with the brains not to show up on the Fortune list and, if I'm right in assuming that he still ultimately controls Dark/Star, a current mercenary force of several thousand exceedingly well armed, well-trained men taking orders from him. At least that's the way I'd spin it if I were doing the opposition analysis for Ben Giles. And if there was financial or contractor misconduct or padding or bid-rigging by Dark/Star—and there always is, you know, every defense contractor since the Revolutionary War has done it— Ben Giles will shove it up Robinson's ass. Which, frankly, wouldn't bother me all that much. This guy Jackson is the real scary deal, Paul. He makes Cheney look like a loud mouthed chicken-hawk draft dodger. Which, of course, he was."

"So why in hell did Robinson put Jackson on the ticket?"

"Dunno, Paul. The only thing I can think of is that Robinson thinks Jackson'll make the trains run on time."

"What does that mean?"

"They're working on a second announcement. It'll be made if Robinson wins the nomination. They're going to nominate Jackson as interim Vice-President, try to get him confirmed by the Congress."

"Why?"

"Well, for one thing, the Speaker of the House, Miranda Cardwell, is now second in line of succession. If something happened to Robinson, she'd be president."

"I can't see the Democrats voting to confirm Jackson as VP before the election, given his political record."

"Really? Think about it. Miranda Cardwell was the Democratic nominee last time. She ran again this year. I don't think Ben Giles' people would be too happy to see her in the White House before them, even for just a few months. You might be surprised how many Giles backers would vote 'present' in order to get Cardwell out of the line of succession."

Coulter shook his head. "I still don't see it. Even if some of Giles people might not oppose Jackson as interim Veep, getting him confirmed would take time and effort away from Robinson's campaign, burn up a lot of his limited political capital."

"There are a few other reasons it might be worth it."

"Like?"

"You remember how Charlie pushed through the Goldwater-Nichols Act amendments in 2013, as part of the Patriot Act III legislation?"

"Sure. That was after the Comiskey Park attacks. The amendments streamlined command structures and procurement in the military and put a stop to a lot of inter-service disputes. It was part of the reform package that took the counter-terrorism and intelligence functions out of Homeland Security, made Homeland Security what it should have been—an operating agency—and put the counter-terrorism stuff into Homeland Intelligence."

Magruder sipped at his Calvados, turning thoughtful for a moment.

"The Goldwater-Nichols Amendments did one other thing, too. They gave the President more flexibility and more power to maintain the continuity of government if we were attacked. Look at section 27 of the Amendments if you get a chance. I wrote it. Six weeks after Charlie was elected by the House over Cardwell he was already thinking of dumping Robinson and getting himself a real working Vice-President. He wanted maximum protection for the continuity of the government. Anyway, the amendment I wrote gives the President discretionary authority to designate not just the Secretary of Defense, but also the Vice-President as the Alternate National Command Authority, with direct power to issue orders to the military Combatant Commands. And thus to make the trains run on time."

Coulter was silent. "You're really just trying to see if you can scare me," he finally replied.

"Nah. I figure you got enough problems. The rumor going around the West Wing is that your girlfriend, the beautiful, mysterious and somewhat terrifying Major Gray, dumped you. No, don't bother to confirm or deny. I know you two were trying to keep your relationship secret. But I hope it works out." Magruder got up, wobbled slightly, and dropped a hundred dollar bill on the table. "My half," he said. "I'm unemployed." His crooked, infectious grin spread across his face. "Come on, Paul, fuck it, laugh," he said, slapping him on the shoulder. "I'm out of here, services no longer required, on my way home to the pretty wife back in Old Virginny. None of this is going to matter. If Robinson gets the nomination, he's going to lose by twenty points, no matter what they do with Jackson. No worries, man. No worries." Magruder lumbered out of the room, still chuckling to himself.

Paul Coulter pocketed the hundred, paid the check and eventually followed Magruder out into dimly lighted Rue Bienville. He stumbled on the broken pavement and cursed, realizing that he was drunker than he thought he was. He was going to have a hell of a time writing a story in the morning.

Chapter Fourteen

The first roll call ballot had been completed a little over four hours earlier that afternoon, and had given the country something it had not seen in over seventy years: a presidential nominating convention that had gone beyond the first ballot.

Graham Taylor could scarcely conceal his glee. "Christ, Paul, it's fabulous," he said, taking in the sight of the roaring convention floor below them, delegates and reporters scrambling between state delegations. The Convention Chair, the elderly Senator Harriett Collier of Nebraska, gaveled tirelessly in a futile effort to begin the second ballot as whip teams from each campaign worked the floor in a desperate effort to persuade delegates no longer legally bound to a candidate to switch their votes. With order only partially restored, the second ballot took over an hour to complete. Robinson and Blessing slipped; the Jeb Bush boomlet went nowhere, Ty Brackett withdrew but held back his delegates, and Henry Purcell began to build momentum among McConnell's delegates and took the lead with seven hundred sixty nine votes, still four hundred short of a majority.

Paul Coulter scarcely looked up from the stream of emails, tweets and text messages hitting his phone and his laptop, thumbing through messages with one hand while tapping out a blog spot update with the other. "Third ballot's going to start in twenty minutes," he told Taylor, then suddenly added, "Christ. *Fuck.* Graham, get your ass down to the Purcell campaign offices—they're two floors down below on the other side of the stadium."

"Paul, I'm a commentator, not a real reporter. And pushing sixty five—"

"Just shut up and get there, Graham. Take your phone and record it. Something's about to happen."

"With Purcell? I'd think he'd have the momentum now that Robinson's been shown to be so weak on the second ballot."

"Something's happening," Coulter insisted stubbornly. "I've got to go talk to someone. Go Now!" He grabbed his laptop, shoved his phone in his pocket, and ran down the stairs into the bowels of the Superdome. He followed the instructions he'd been texted: Section 27, the stairwell between the first and second levels. He dove through the fire doors and ran down two flights of stairs, grunting as his aging knees took the pounding from descending the stairs two at a time.

He found Diane DeLoren, Senator Henry Purcell's media director, on the stairwell landing just above the first level of Superdome seating. Coulter had known Diane since the second Iraq War. In those early, heady days, after the 2003 invasion but before things had turned to shit, DeLoren had been a triumphant Bushie, a brassy honey-blonde PR consultant with a truly dirty minded smile who had been recruited by The White House to go to Iraq with two impossible tasks: make the inept American Proconsul look good while he auctioned Iraqi oil to BP, Exxon and Conoco, and teach the Administration's pet Iraqis how to talk to the American media without having them come across as the opportunistic gangsters they were. The younger Coulter had been in serious lust with her, a mutual itch scratched on several three day weekends at the Egyptian Red Sea beaches at Sharm El Sheikh, where it amused Diane to have morning sex in the Fairmont Hotel just as the Muezzin's call to the *fajr* prayer drifted across the dawn sky. Thirteen years later her bright beauty had been worn down by two failed marriages and years spent in the political wilderness until Henry Purcell had pulled her into his last-ditch presidential campaign to take the Republican Party back to the political center.

There was no amusement in Diane DeLoren's face now. She was leaning against the bare concrete wall of the stairwell, dressed in a wrinkled beige suit that looked like it had been slept in and smoking a cigarette, her face bleak and her graying blonde hair a tangle. Her washed out pale blue eyes were reddened by tears. "You've heard?" she asked simply.

"No." The smoke hung in the dank hot air of the stairwell and stung Coulter's throat. "What is it, Diane?"

"Harry's going to withdraw."

"What? Why, for chrissake? Purcell is going to pick up thirty, maybe fifty votes from the uncommitted delegates on the next ballot. If Roger Blessing has half a brain he'll quit and throw his people—"

"It's about Jack."

"Harry's son? Jack's in the army, doing what every ambitious politician needs their 19-year-old kid to do: put on a uniform and get their picture taken with the old man. How can Jack hurt him?

"Jack's been arrested in Fayetteville, North Carolina. At Fort Bragg. For rape."

Coulter closed his eyes for a moment and flashed to a remembered image: a gap-toothed gangly twelve year old boy, the only child of Henry Purcell's late second marriage, who had made even Charlie McConnell laugh with his antics during his father's swearing in as a U.S. Senator seven years before. "How bad?"

"It's bad. Pictures all over Fox and CNN. I know that sounds crass. The girl was eighteen, just out of basic training, a medical orderly at the base hospital. A pretty girl, African American, sings in one of the chapel choirs. Good kid. She—well, she's been beaten pretty badly. But she identified Jack."

"Do they have DNA?"

"The Army Criminal Investigative Division isn't saying. But they're holding Jack in the Fort Bragg Stockade."

"What does Jack say?"

"He swears he's innocent, but he doesn't have much of an alibi. He says he'd gotten a call from a friend in trouble, borrowed a car and drove out of town into the hills up west of the Fort. He's refusing to say who called him—might have been something like a drug deal gone bad, with Jack trying to play rescue. They do that kind of stupid shit at nineteen, you know. They think they're bulletproof, and they love their friends more than anyone else." Diane dropped her cigarette, stamped it out, and immediately lit another. "I believe Jack's innocent. Harry does too. But he's completely destroyed by this. He loves that kid, and he can't function now. So he's going to pull out."

"When?"

"The story's going to break on Fox in about ten minutes."

"Is Harry going to face the cameras here?"

"No. We set up a link from the campaign plane. Harry's already on his way to the airport, heading to North Carolina. Nobody could stop him."

"Shit," Coulter said lamely. "I'm sorry, Diane." He reached out and put a hand on her shoulder for a moment, then pulled it away as he felt her tense up.

She looked up at him and blew smoke from the side of her mouth. "We're a funny tribe, aren't we Paul?" she asked. "All of us, political and media consultants, pollsters, reporters, bloggers, campaign workers. We wander around the country looking for work and every four years we latch on to someone, a candidate, for the money or for the jazz and even, sometimes, because we hope against hope that our candidate will actually make a good President. We're young, we've got time. And then suddenly we're forty-five or fifty or even pushing sixty and we end up with a small condo in Adams-Morgan and hope we can catch on as a visiting professor of politics for a semester or two each year at a small college. And we don't even have a cat. Fuck." She shook herself. "Sorry. I told myself I wasn't going to bleed on your carpet."

"It's okay, Diane. What can I do for you now?"

As he spoke the muted buzz of the convention hall grew to a huge throated roar that penetrated the dank stairwell where they were standing.

"That's the Robinson people. They've just gotten the news." Diane DeLoren's eyes flashed with anger. "This was a set up, Paul. A hit job. Five weeks from now Jack Purcell will be exonerated and then Army CID will issue an ever so polite apology to that fine upstanding young paratrooper of the 82nd Airborne Division. But by then somebody other than Henry C. Purcell will be the Republican nominee for President of the United States. This campaign was getting momentum and we were going to win this fight. Somebody just shot us in the head. That's why I reached out to you, Paul. Find out who fucking did this to us."

The drumbeat shouts of Vote! Vote! Vote! exploded from the Convention floor and the spectator rows above them in the stadium, as the Robinson supporters demanded a third ballot. The White House had, Coulter grimly conceded, done a decent job of seizing control of the convention machinery and installing their supporters on key committees after Charles McConnell had died. Now they controlled the floor as well.

"There was nothing at Purcell's HQ," Graham Taylor told Paul as Coulter returned to the press zone on the third tier of the Superdome. "They weren't talking and Purcell was already on the way to the airport. But I went 'round the Blessing camp and it is not good news there. They are have realized that Blessing had no business in this race and that Purcell was their only hope of stopping Robinson—and they know now that it is too late. Third ballot's about to begin, and everyone but Robinson's been maimed or killed."

At eleven forty-eight that night, after the seventh ballot, a flushed, sweating and triumphant James Robinson appeared at the convention podium flanked by his wife and three children, with Kyle Jackson and his family arrayed beside them.

"We have, by grace of the Lord Jesus' help, prevailed here tonight," Robinson intoned, his radio baritone echoing throughout the domed stadium. "I thank you, and I ask God's blessing on all who made this night possible. But even as we are victorious tonight, the enemies of America stalk this country. I cannot protect this country without the help of a strong team and a strong people. And that is why I ask—no, I *demand*—that the Congress of the United States come into special session within two weeks of this day and confirm Congressman Kyle Jackson as the Vice-President of the United States. The protection of this country doesn't take a village"—Robinson paused while the old Hillary Clinton jibe took hold and had the convention floor laughing—"but it does take strong, righteous people, like my friend and running mate, Kyle Jackson!"

"This is all wrong," Graham Taylor said, shaking his head. "Presidents don't talk about how much they need their Vice-Presidents—especially ones that weren't on the short list twenty four hours before being selected. Even The Yellow Rose of Texas maintained the fiction that he, not Cheney, was in charge of his own presidency. We've work to do, Paul. Something is very wrong here." Graham Taylor gestured to the convention floor below them. "Look at the Purcell people walking out. This party is going to split into pieces, and no one on the podium even seems to care."

Taylor paused as the Reverend Royce Reed mounted the podium. Reed raised his arms to the sky to invoke God's blessing, then placed his hands on the bowed heads of James Robinson and Kyle Hunter Jackson.

"Lord God, Protector of the American People and all that is just and good," Reed began, intoning the prayer. "We ask your blessing on these special servants, James Robinson and Kyle Jackson, the President and Vice-President of the United States, that they may follow your will and defend the American people against the false god of Islam and the terrorist threat..."

Coulter watched with grim dismay as the prayers at the convention podium droned on but said nothing.

Taylor suddenly grinned at him. "C'mon, brighten up, Paul. Really does seem like a case of divine fucking intervention, doesn't it?"

Chapter Fifteen

**New Harmony Farm
Lawrence, Kansas
Friday, September 2
9:15 A.M. CDT**

Ben Giles stared out through the open double doors of his office and across the flower-specked Kansas meadow. The morning was bright but cool, the thick heat of summer washed away by a week of thunderstorms. At the far side of the meadow an ancient hedgerow of Osage Orange blocked the dust of the soybean fields and provided good cover for the birds Giles hunted with his brothers each fall. He smiled as a stout old ring-neck pheasant was flushed from its hiding place by one of the New Harmony farm cats and exploded into flight.

Ben Giles was a compact man with a soldier's posture. At sixty he had graying, curly black hair, coffee skin, and deep green eyes that marked his mixed race legacy. He retained a younger man's springing, ready energy, eager to attack any problem before him or issue at hand. He had retired from the United States Army at fifty-two as one of its youngest Lieutenant Generals, having held both combat and staff positions, concluding his career as Commander of the Army's TRADOC, the training and doctrine command at Fort Monroe, Virginia. Giles had returned home to the Midwest to become

Superintendent of the Kansas City Public Schools. In three years he transformed a barren urban school district plagued by crime and high dropout rates into a model system that blended high academic achievement with community outreach and parent involvement. The Governor of Kansas then appointed him to a vacant U.S. Senate seat, which he won in his own right with 60% of the vote in the heavily Republican state two years later.

Giles took one last look at his cherished meadow, sighed, and reluctantly turned his attention back to the discussion around his conference table: the position that he should take on the pending Congressional vote to confirm Kyle Jackson as Vice-President of the United States.

"The count in the House of Representatives is the one I'm most worried about, Senator," Jeff Reardon said. Reardon, a top aide to Democratic House Speaker Miranda Cardwell, had the cadaverous look of a man constantly running on the ragged edge of exhaustion, but he possessed one of the best political minds in the Democratic Party. Reardon had understood Ben Giles' surging upset victories in the Illinois and California primaries as the writing on the wall for Cardwell's second campaign for the Presidency. He brokered an early withdrawal that gave Cardwell the opportunity to depart the Presidential race with her self-respect intact, and won Giles' endorsement for her to remain Speaker of the House. "The House is close. We hold a six-seat margin. The 25th Amendment requires only a majority vote of both Houses to confirm Jackson's nomination. There are twenty-two reps in our caucus from Southern swing districts who will be under tremendous pressure to approve Jackson on the basis of regional pride alone. Jackson's also reasonably well-liked by our members from the Carolinas that he's worked with on state and local issues. It's going to be tough to enforce party discipline. The Speaker might be able to do it, but it would be an ugly win."

"What do you think the White House's game is here, Jeff, trying to shove Jackson's confirmation down our throats only two months before the election?" Giles asked.

Reardon shrugged. "Robinson's probably trying to appeal to the base," he replied. "The Republican right responded pretty well to

Jackson's nomination, even though he was all but unknown before their convention. And when you read their blogs—they've driven themselves crazy at the thought of the Speaker being next in the line of succession until January 20. Robinson's strategists also probably hope that having Jackson as an incumbent, even if for just a couple of months, will help voters forget that this ticket is even farther to the right than Bush/Cheney was."

Giles shook his head. "Doesn't sound like Jimmy Robinson to me. He's a survivor—a nasty, shrewd one—but not a six moves down the chessboard kind of thinker." Giles stood and stretched to get the kinks out of his back, then paced around the room. When Giles had retired from the U.S. Army and returned to Kansas he had restored his family's ancestral home, an 1882 farmhouse, and rebuilt its adjacent dairy shed into a high-ceilinged open work space, with exposed white-washed heavy timbers, rough plaster walls, and a brown brick floor. A cast iron woodstove warmed the space in winter; twin ceiling fans and large clerestory windows cooled it in summer. The walls were covered with family photographs from the generations of Giles family life in Kansas since Amos Giles, a free African-American from Massachusetts, had come west in 1858 and joined other New England Jayhawkers in the abolitionist militias fighting to keep Kansas free territory. Amos Giles fought as a guerilla for three years, facing the risk that he would be sold back into slavery or tortured to death if captured by pro-slavery forces. When the wars in Bleeding Kansas finally ended Giles stayed on, homesteading the first 160 acres of what ultimately became New Harmony, a three thousand acre dairy, corn and soybean farm on flat rich tableland in a crook of the Kansas River. A faded sepia-toned photograph dated 1883 showed Amos Giles as a man in his early sixties, his bearing still straight and strong, with four handsome sons and their families standing in front of the proud white farmhouse where his great-grandson was poised to become President of the United States.

"George?" Ben Giles said. "What's your take?"

George Kraft, the Governor of Wisconsin and Giles' nominee for Vice President, spoke through a video screen from the Governor's mansion in Madison. "I don't think we should formally oppose it,

Ben," he replied with the calm voice of the Rhinelander family physician he had once been. Kraft was a man who had seen births and deaths and learned to view the world with a reserved Lutheran faith that the arc of human history was toward the better. "There's a real sense of fear about Presidential continuity. First Brett Campbell was murdered, then the mess we had last time, with the election taking six weeks to decide in the House of Representatives. And now we've lost Charlie McConnell so suddenly. I suspect the public wants the vice-presidency filled. What does Nate's polling show?"

Nathan Keller, the chief pollster for the Giles/Kraft campaign, defied the usual cliché of pollster as math geek. He had played tight end at Princeton, modeled clothes in *Esquire*, and wore hand tailored suits even to a meeting in the middle of the Kansas prairie. "This was a tough issue to poll, because how you frame the question determines the outcome," he said. "We tried six different variants with a reasonably large sample size for each and blended the results. My read is that Governor Kraft is correct: a fight in Congress to deny confirmation will be seen as obstructive and adding insecurity at a time when people are already unsettled by the long depression and fears of terrorism. It's one of the few things that could hurt us right now. Robinson got no convention bump. Even with Jackson appealing strongly to the right wing base they are only polling 39% nationwide against us, and that will drop if Purcell endorses us. We are leading above margin of error in states with 376 electoral votes, within the margin but ahead in another four states with 23 additional votes. We are winning over 270 electoral votes in 98.9% of the simulations. In short, we should sit this one out. We'll be winning the Presidency and picking up 36 seats plus or minus 3 in the House, and 6 seats plus or minus one in the Senate, in just under two months. Opposing Jackson's confirmation is not a risk worth taking."

Ben Giles frowned. "I hear it, guys, I really do," he said. "But there's something about this whole nomination that doesn't make political sense. And Jackson just gives me the creeps."

"Why, Ben?" George Kraft asked.

"Nothing I can put my finger on, other than an old army officer's distaste for a mercenary." He frowned. "George, I was in Iraq and

Afghanistan and saw the mercenaries, the contractors, swaggering around like little tin gods and shooting up civilians whenever they damn well pleased. Jackson's company, Dark/Star, was better trained and led than most, but it still guzzled billions of dollars from the public trough. It left a stench in my nostrils that I can't quite forget."

"Senator, it's not worth risking your campaign over it," Keller insisted.

"Isn't it?" Giles replied. "Think about what this means for the country for a second, instead of the campaign. We're talking about that old cliché, putting a guy a heartbeat away from the Presidency. And what do we know about him, Kyle Jackson? That he was one of the hard boys, Special Forces, and that he was pushed out of the Army for some reason so dark that I never got the straight story, even though I was already a Colonel when it happened. That he made a billion dollars, and maybe more, buying and building up a military contractor, sold it to some dodgy offshore investors, and bought himself a seat in the House. If you look at his voting record, he's got very little use for people in this country who don't share his religion, his race, his sexual orientation or his income bracket. This is a guy we want to put into the National Command Authority?"

"He won't be there very long, Ben," George Kraft said. "The country's not with them. I don't think Jackson can do much harm in four and half months."

"There's one advantage here that we shouldn't overlook," Jeff Reardon said. "There will be confirmation hearings, even though they will be very short, and we can have some of our attack dogs—Andy Ricardo on the Senate Judiciary Committee, Paul Rubin on Foreign Affairs in the House—appointed to the Joint Confirmation Committee. Their staffs would like nothing better than to get their bosses some media attention by ripping Jackson a new asshole. We could turn the whole media line into an examination of Jackson and the Republican hard right—and it wouldn't be over until just six weeks before Election Day."

"Gut him—and then call it a vote of conscience," George Kraft suggested. "Put it up to every member's own decision, so it isn't a partisan issue—but inflict the maximum damage."

"Four months until January, Ben," Kraft replied patiently. "Just four months."

"Okay, okay. When's the vote, Jeff?"

"The Speaker's willing to agree to September 20, but she wanted to make sure that works for you."

"Absolutely." Giles slapped the table in front of him. "I'll be there with bells on, and I'll vote against the sonofabitch myself."

Chapter Sixteen

XVIII Airborne Corps
82nd Airborne Division
49th Public Affairs Detachment
Fort Bragg, North Carolina
Saturday, September 3
10:30 A.M. E.D.T.

It did not take five weeks, as Diane DeLoren had predicted. It took less than four days.

Paul Coulter's head buzzed with exhaustion. He had returned from New Orleans to Washington late Friday night to file his last stories on the Republican Convention and the sudden elevation of Kyle Jackson, and then read and moderate the reader posts on his blog. He'd stopped at his Capitol Hill condominium long enough to shower, shake out his dirty clothes, heat and eat a frozen dinner, and fail to connect with any of Elizabeth's phone numbers before catching a cab at four thirty in the morning to Reagan National for the flight to Raleigh. He landed at dawn and transferred to the Delta Express turboprop to Fayetteville Regional Airport, sweaty and un-focused and cursing himself for what he was sure was a fool's errand.

The press briefing on the rape case against Corporal Jack Purcell was delayed twice and then moved from the regular press briefing room to the auditorium of the Fort Bragg Community Center to accommodate the overflow crowd of reporters and camera crews. A blue curtain wall with Army and the 82nd Airborne Division banners had been hastily hung across the back of the room to provide a visual backdrop. After the long wait, a bulky Army Criminal Investigative Division agent finally took the podium, wearing sharply pressed standard Army camouflage fatigues, the ACU. He had a Captain's bars on his rank tab, but wore a black CID brassard on his arm.

"I am Special Agent Jason Berger," he said, with the look of a man who would have preferred taking strychnine to facing the press this day. His close shaved skull bore a bright sheen of sweat. "I am the chief investigating officer in the matter of the sexual assault and rape charges brought against Corporal Jack Purcell of the 1st Battalion, 505th Parachute Infantry Regiment, 82nd Airborne Division. Today I am announcing today that all charges against Corporal Purcell have been withdrawn. Our investigation will continue until we have identified the person or persons who attacked Specialist Alicia Greene."

The room erupted with fifty shouted questions from the reporters. A public affairs officer from the 82nd's media operation, a Major Judson, dressed in regular army greens, took the microphone.

"Hold up, hold up," Judson pleaded. "One at a time. You, there. Front row." He pointed at Coulter.

"Paul Coulter, Pacific News. What was the basis for withdrawing the charges against Corporal Purcell?"

Agent Berger stepped forward. "There was insufficient physical evidence to link Corporal Purcell to the attack on Specialist Greene," he said. "We were also able to verify at least part of Corporal Purcell's statements about his whereabouts last Sunday night, which made it unlikely—although not physically impossible—for him to have been involved."

"Does that mean the DNA didn't match?" Coulter persisted.

"I am not able to discuss the status of DNA testing since this is an ongoing investigation," Berger replied.

Major Judson pointed to Sheila Dickson of *MSNBC*. "What about the eyewitness identification?" she asked. "Has Specialist Greene recanted her identification of Corporal Purcell as her attacker?"

"I believe that she has, in fact, withdrawn her initial positive identification," Judson replied. He pointed again, to Kurt Swenson of the Washington *Post*.

"Major," Swenson began, "The charges brought against Corporal Purcell may have influenced the political process in this country at the highest level. When did the CID form a conclusion that Corporal Purcell was *not*, in fact, involved in the attack on Specialist Greene?"

Judson looked at Berger and warned him off with a barely perceptible shake of his head. "We are not at liberty to discuss the details of an ongoing investigation," Berger replied.

Berger would utter the same statement twenty six more times in the course of the next hour, until the press conference was closed.

As the press conference broke up Diane DeLoren cut through the crowd and took Paul Coulter's arm. "Thanks for covering this, Paul," she said quietly. She'd looked as though she'd gotten some sleep since the Purcell campaign's disastrous end. Her eyes were dry and clear and some life had come back into her face, but her anger was still intense, undiminished.

"I did it for you, Diane," he responded, sounding a little harsher than he intended. "But I'm not going to get anywhere with this. I'm not a crime beat reporter or legal analyst and don't have any sources down here; no one's going to talk to me."

"That's not quite right," she responded. "I've got somebody for you to talk to who will make it worth your while." She led him out of the auditorium and into a small meeting room that someone had apparently arranged for the use of Senator Purcell and his staff during the press conference. "Harry's gone over to the stockade to meet Jack when they've finished processing him out. We've got a press conference scheduled in an hour, and I've got to help get Jack ready. But I wanted you to meet Jack's lawyer." As she finished speaking a tall confident man in his late forties with dark curling hair, a strong hawk's beak nose, and dark eyes strode into the room, hand extended. He was wearing about four thousand dollars of hand-tailored Brioni in pale gray.

"Ben Simon," he said.

"Paul Coulter," Paul responded, shaking hands. "I've heard of you," he added, "but I hope this isn't an office call because I can't afford you."

Simon laughed. He was a former United States Attorney from Philadelphia, now DC's premier criminal defense attorney, with all the intellect of a David Boies and some of the theatrics of an Edward Bennett Williams.

"What did you think of the press conference?" Simon asked.

Coulter paused. "I've never been a crime reporter," he responded. "But it sounded to me as if whatever case they had was thin at best, maybe non-existent."

"Not non-existent," Simon replied. "Any cop or a prosecutor who sees a good looking, terribly hurt victim who has made a positive perp identification knows that they've got probable cause dicked. But this case turned sour pretty quickly."

"What do you mean?"

"The attack on this girl happened at 9:30 Sunday night, in a dark wooded area north of the First Brigade's enlisted barracks. By 11:00 P.M. she was in the base hospital, CID had been notified, samples had been taken with a rape kit. Specialist Greene gave CID a fairly detailed description of her attacker, and I agree that description fits Jack Purcell quite nicely. CID pulled Purcell in on Monday morning for a line up with ten other soldiers, and Greene identified him. They took hair, fiber and blood samples from Purcell, and had his DNA worked up within four hours."

Simon smiled nastily. "Now, here's where it gets a little strange, Paul. They had everything they needed to charge Purcell by noon Monday. They didn't. Sounds good, sounds like they're being cautious. That was, in fact, the right way to play it. Because by four o'clock on Monday they know the following: there was no semen. There wasn't a single hair or fiber sample taken from Greene that matched to Purcell or the car he borrowed Sunday night. They'd found and impounded the clothes Jack wore on Sunday night, still in his laundry basket. And, surprise, there isn't a single hair or fiber on Jack's clothes that can be traced to Greene. Nor is there any trace of material that matches the soil and plants in the wooded area north of the barracks. Instead, the mud on his shoes matches the place up in the hills where Jack told them he was called to meet a friend in trouble who never showed up. They've got Jack's phone, which recorded the call he said he received, but the number recorded was not a working number."

"A burn phone, used just before it was deactivated," Coulter mused.

"Most likely. All that was known on Monday. So on Tuesday, knowing for over twelve hours that every piece of evidence they have is either contradicted or tainted, they charge Purcell and release the charges complete with video of a busted up eighteen year old girl. It goes viral on the web just before Henry Purcell's campaign for the Presidency reaches the third ballot at the Republican convention. None of that was an accident."

"These," Paul Coulter said soberly, "are big charges."

"They are," Ben Simon agreed. "But I don't believe in coincidence, fate, or the fairy godmother, Paul. When looking at a conspiracy case, a prosecutor ultimately thinks about who benefited, and who was in a position to create the conspiracy. We know who benefited— James Robinson has the nomination. And we know who was in a position to do this: Kyle Jackson. Hell, his company, Dark/Star, is the second largest employer in this part of North Carolina after Fort Bragg itself, Paul."

"So where are you going with this?" Coulter asked. "No news organization in the country—other than Drudge or the *Enquirer*— could run this story with the information you have so far. Nothing other than a 'questions are being raised' piece—and we'd better have people to quote for that."

"Oh, you will," Simon said confidently. "The lead on your piece will be, 'questions raised about Purcell investigation.' And you can follow up with a nice piece on the lawsuit that will be filed next week."

"So you're not announcing the lawsuit today?"

"No. I'm waiting for one more thing."

"What's that?"

"I'm waiting to see what Alicia Greene says. She had to know."

Coulter missed his connecting flight and got stuck in Raleigh, waiting for the last flight of the night out of North Carolina back to DC. Despite his exhaustion he chewed his way through a rubbery chicken sandwich in the terminal and roughed out a story along the lines that Simon had indicated, hoping to decide by morning whether it met his own smell test. If it panned out it would be big: it is no small thing to tamper with a criminal investigation, and if the Purcell rape allegations had been fixed to play Presidential politics there would be a firestorm.

Paul broke away from his writing to Google the video of the press conference. His search pulled up a new video: a statement from Alicia Greene. The video began without any preamble and showed a delicate young woman, her flawless sepia skin marred by bruises, a split lower lip, and a gash over her left eye that looked had taken a dozen stitches to close.

"My name is Alicia Greene," she began in a soft contralto voice with a thick Georgia accent. "I am speaking tonight because I want to…apologize…to my fellow soldier, Jack Purcell. I was raped last Sunday night, and the man who attacked me resembled Corporal Purcell. I identified Mr. Purcell in a line up, and I believed that I spoke the truth. I have since learned that I—that I must have been wrong. And I am sorry." Her voice broke down and tears streamed from her blackened eyes. "I am *so* sorry," she whispered. "Please forgive me." Alicia Greene's eyes dropped away from the camera and she wept, her shoulders shuddering with each sob, her hands covering her face.

Coulter watched the video twice, his expression grim. There would be no lawsuit and no investigation. Not even Ben Simon's legal skill could overcome the image of a beautiful, battered woman with the courage to apologize for a mistake, watched by sixty million people across the country by morning.

Grand Cayman

Chapter Seventeen

The Martial Club
Dr. Roy's Drive
George Town
Grand Cayman
British West Indies
Monday, September 5
1:45 P.M. Eastern Standard Time

Graham Taylor had been in a foul mood when he arrived in Grand Cayman just after midnight on Sunday. His plane from Washington to Miami was crowded and late and he had missed his connection, barely scraping into a back row seat on the night's last Cayman Air flight. When he landed the night air was dolorous and dense, hurricane season weather without a breeze. Taylor felt awash in his own sweat and bad temper. A cramped Chinese-made hybrid taxi finally deposited him at a small hotel on Seven Mile beach north of George Town. On arrival Taylor sent the drowsy night clerk scurrying for room keys, ice, lime and a fifth of local rum. The rum had turned out to be Tortuga Special Spiced, not at all bad. He finished a third of the bottle in just over an hour and dropped off to a troubled sleep.

When he woke early the next morning he found both himself and the world improved. The air had lost some of its humidity, the sun was bright, and on impulse Graham purchased sunscreen and borrowed fins, mask and snorkel from the hotel. He spent two hours in the water, exploring the local reef and remaking the acquaintance of the angel fish and nearly tame manta rays that his wife had loved so much when they had last been to the Caymans ten years before. When he saw that it was nearly nine-thirty by the stainless steel Rolex diving watch that was a relic of an earlier and better financed time in his life he reluctantly headed to shore for an English breakfast, eggs and bacon and grilled tomatoes. He felt himself by the time he had finished updating his notes, closed his computer, put on a twenty year old white linen suit, and caught a taxi to George Town for a late lunch.

The Martial Club in George Town was a sister club—barely—to Mossman's, the last club that Graham still belonged to in London. He had joined Mossman's more than thirty years before, chivvied into it by his supervisor during one of the several years when he had been detached to MI-6. He soon grew to appreciate Mossman's because in an emergency you could bunk in the rooms upstairs and drink decent scotch at something very near to cost. The food, sometimes dreary, was at least warm and available late into the night. He had kept up the two hundred pound annual membership fee, even when it seemed a waste, to have some remaining place in London that he could consider a sort of home.

The Martial had seen better days. It was on the ground floor of a 1960s-vintage office building not far from the Bank of Bermuda, a darkish cave with a patched carpet, the smell of old smoke, and what looked like a steam table and buffet where there would be the inevitable three hots, limp salad, and Normandy cheese, butter and biscuits that had been wrapped in individual plastic packets. Graham was nonetheless content. The Martial reminded him of when he had been young, just out of Sandhurst. Britain in the late 1970s had been poor, riven by strikes and the troubles in Northern Ireland, but remained proud and very, very, tough. Taylor had disliked his native country by the turn of the last century, with its estate-agent easy money prosperity and the kind of smiley false cheer that he had always associated with Tony Blair. *Well, we've learned that fucking lesson, haven't we?* He knew he was fortunate at sixty-four to still be working and somewhat relevant, not dying slowly drinking cheap gin in a fucking caravan park in Spain like so many others in his generation.

He ordered a dark rum and tonic and lit a cigarette, the room nearly empty around him. A few older men like himself—*Christ, I really do look like that, don't I?*—held positions at the bar, claimed by right of long occupation. Three or four middle-aged English expat couples sat in the dining room, chewing soundlessly and studiously avoiding conversation.

The booming voice at his elbow bumped Taylor out of his reverie. "Jesus *Christ*, Graham, I thought I'd never lay eyes on you again," said Barnes Powell—Barney—a Lieutenant who had served in SAS under Taylor's command in the First Iraq War. Once short, quick and lean, in his early fifties Powell had become sleek and padded, hair slicked back, face full and shaved smooth, the whole effect rather like an otter that had taken to wearing tropical weight Italian suits. He sat down heavily at the table. "I'd heard that you'd become some kind of lefty professor in the States, but lost track of you after that. Is Anna well? Are you still together, or have you succumbed to divorce like the rest of us?"

"She died," Taylor said quietly. "Six years ago."

"Ah, fuck, I'm sorry," Powell said sheepishly. His face turned sad. "I've been a fucking banker so long now, it's a habit, ask about the wife, make a joke..." he sighed, bleakly. "Have you a drink on order? And may I bum a cigarette? And may I tell you how absolutely sorry I am that your wonderful wife is no longer with us?"

"All of that, Barney." Taylor raised a hand for the waiter, who finally arrived with Taylor's rum and looked at Powell expectantly.

"Gordon's gin, ice, two lime slices. A double," Powell said. He slid a Dunhill from Graham's box, lit it, and sighed with pleasure. "Forbidden me, you know. New wife. Mychelle. With a 'y'. Does yoga."

"And banking is still good, Barney? Seems like a tough business since 2008," Taylor said.

"We're private bankers at Blagg and Bennett, Graham," Powell replied. "It's a service business. Quiet and boring. We didn't buy our clients any mortgages on over-priced suburban estates in Sussex or vacation villas in Spain, expecting the fucking things would go up forever. And we didn't buy any of the American RMBS or CMBS or SIVs or CDO squared or any of that crap; we let the hedge funders who bet long ruin themselves. A lot—not enough—of the little fuckers are broke now. God, after all, is just."

Powell's drink finally arrived and he finished it in two swallows, called back the waiter, and ordered another. "The curry's passable, or the dorado," Powell added. His small eyes narrowed a bit. "I'm delighted to see my old Boss, but I'm puzzled, Graham. You're a books, politics, history guy now. What on earth brings you to the Caymans?"

"New book," Taylor replied promptly. He made a casual show of filling out the meal ticket. "The curry? Right." He signed the ticket and handed it to the waiter. "It's a military biography. Of the fellow who's been nominated for the American Vice-Presidency, Kyle Jackson."

Powell accepted his second Gordon's from the waiter. "Yes, right. Jackson seems like a good soldier, admirable in many ways. Little too ostentatiously Christian for my taste, having always preferred our Church of England, which bothers us only for births, deaths, marriages, and the occasional installation of one's gay cousin Philbin as Vicar in some dusty parish."

"It's Jackson's financial interests that attract me, Barney," Taylor said.

Powell looked upset. "Christ, Boss, private banking is *private*, that's where we get the name, you know? But even if I was to break every rule in the book, I couldn't tell you much about Jackson or Dark/Star. He's not a client, neither is the firm. I only know what I read in the Financial *Times* or the *Economist*: he bought it, built it up on government contracts, bought shrewd in the defense contractor market, adding data analysis and policy services, munitions and computer software, and sold it to Cornwall."

"Really, Barney? That's not what I've heard. Or read. I've spent three days in the SEC's archives in Washington. It seems Jackson raised the initial money to buy Dark/Star in a private partnership offering in late 2001. It wasn't a huge deal, just thirty million or so, easily funded right out of Merrill Lynch's Miami office. You were the head of Merrill's Miami investment banking team at the time."

Barnes Powell raised his eyebrows, sipped his gin, and then smiled. "Absolutely guilty, Boss. Poor old Mother Merrill sold into slavery to a goddamn commercial bank. I still miss her. The Masters of the Universe, we were. In 2002 if you'd looked up the term *motherfucker* in the Oxford *Unabridged Dictionary* you'd have seen the picture of our CEO and his board, all smiles and bespoke suits." Powell laughed. "And any damn fool, even me, could make a million dollars a year. But to be perfectly honest, Boss, I don't even remember the deal. Thirty million wouldn't have built a medium-sized condo tower in Miami in those days."

"True enough. But the Dark/Star deal more or less sold itself, didn't it? The whole thing was bought up by a couple of Cayman-based investment trusts? One called The Corinthian Trust, the other The Dominion Trust?" Taylor sipped at his long ignored rum and tonic. "Do you know how I could find them? I've looked, but there don't seem to be any records."

Powell looked blandly evasive, swirled his gin. "They probably no longer exist, Graham. Cayman Trusts are usually special purpose entities—one shot, throwaway places to park assets, cash or notes or stock, until the next stage of a transaction occurs. They live tragically brief lives in lawyers' filing cases until they are paid off or new stock gets issued or whatever. Then they convey their assets to another entity or two and are closed down. It's a nice way to do business because there are no corporate taxes in Cayman, so you can complete a transaction without the taxman in Washington or London taking their cut."

Powell fell momentarily silent. His lamb curry arrived and he tucked into it with enthusiasm, forking chunks of lamb and rice into his mouth. A third double Gordon's appeared along side, while Taylor satisfied himself with grilled Dorado and a glass of Argentine torrentes.

"I'm impressed though, Graham," Powell said, pausing to finish his gin and gesture for a fourth. "Have you been attending business school on the sly?"

"I have some bright students," Taylor admitted, "who have helped explain the modern world to me." He paused to taste his fish. "Well, if these trusts are dead, what did Jackson do when he sold the company to Cornwall?" Taylor continued. "And who really *is* the Cornwall Group, Barney? Because I know for a fact that they *are* your client."

"In the smallest of ways," Powell conceded. "Look, Graham, Cornwall is exactly what you would expect it to be—something that would frighten the over-educated lefties in your faculty meetings. It is private equity, very deep pockets, third, fourth, fifth generation money—Swiss pharmaceutical heirs, German grocers and manufacturers, Hong Kong traders, Norwegian oil and shipping, a few not-stupid Americans, including a couple of former Presidents, and the ubiquitous Arabs."

"Why would Cornwall want Dark/Star?" Taylor asked, knowing he was pushing his luck.

"I'll answer that," Barnes Powell growled, "Only because you could get the same answer from any reasonably awake financial guy. Cornwall likes businesses with pricing power, a franchise, a history of delivering value, and steady customers. Since our governments still need hard men, military arms, software, and strategic planning to keep bureaucratic heads out of bureaucratic asses, Dark/Star is a wonderful investment for the long-term thinker."

"Cornwall is mostly off-shore, then?" Taylor asked.

"No one in their fucking mind is *on shore*, Graham," he answered, halting the metronome of his fork to ease into his fourth gin. "Only if you have to be—if you sell pharmaceuticals, or food, or heavy materials—anything where you have to have licenses and franchisees and local employees. Ever since the Campbell administration busted the Swiss' balls on tax evasion and bank secrecy, no country with a big financial exposure to the United States or the European Union can afford to preserve their bank secrecy laws—they have to adhere to OECD transparency standards regarding money laundering and reporting tax evasion. That leaves us. Cayman, Guernsey, Antigua, Aruba, Guyana, Panama. The Caribbean states, having gone broke in the Great Recession being good boys, reinstated their secrecy laws and took their money movement business from London and Brussels to Shanghai and Nairobi, where they don't have such tender sensibilities. We're not quite the Spanish Main anymore, but when it comes to banking us islanders are as close to pirates as you can get."

"But how can you close deals if you can't convert to dollars or euros?"

"Not a problem. Take Cornwall, for example. Every deal they do is done through Panama Bank Royal. Why? Near perfect secrecy, a local economy that uses the dollar as its own currency, or can set up direct swaps through Shanghai into nice hard emerging market currencies that you can always convert back to dollars later."

"So Cornwall bought Dark/Star through Bank Royal? Is that where Jackson's private trusts are set up?" Graham asked sharply.

Powell dropped his fork onto his half-eaten plate of curry, shoved it away, picked up his glass, and looked at Taylor with aspersion. "I've said too much," he said, "though it wouldn't have taken you long to find out. What the fuck are you after here, Graham?" He took another cigarette from Graham's box of Dunhill's and lit it with an air of exasperation.

"It's a part of Jackson's story, Barney. Nothing more than that."

"It's a part you might think about fairly carefully, Graham," Powell replied. His voice began to slur, only slightly, for he was an experienced drinker. "There's this notion about in the world that Brett Campbell crushed the old Wall Street after the Panic of '08. True, western governments put all the credit default swaps and derivatives onto exchanges and standardized their contracts, so everybody could see and understand what they were up to and the regulators could keep the leverage ratios under control. And it has worked, to a certain extent. For that I'm grateful—one should never bet Western civilization on what some twenty-something quant with a laptop and hundred to one leverage thinks is a great idea. But the deep money, the old money, and the *very* smart money—and for them that isn't an oxymoron, Graham—has gone very deep indeed. They like their privacy. And they like private offshore companies like Dark/Star." Powell stopped, tried to recover. "I meant Cornwall."

Taylor was silent for a long moment, and then raised his glass of wine in a toast, smiling. "Here's to you, Barney. You bastards do indeed still run the world."

"Horseshit," Barnes Powell replied. "Small private bankers like me are cleaner fish, Graham, just picking morsels off the great sharks' hides. But at least I'm living in a villa on Seven Mile Beach with a pool and a 32-year-old second wife with the most amazing tits in the history of the world instead of manning a desk in MI5 or even MI6 and training home each night to think about slitting my wrists in my moldy semi-detached in Kent."

"King and Country." Graham Taylor smiled again and signed the check. "Thank you, Barney. I'd ask you to call if you think of anything else—but I know you won't. So be well. And enjoy those amazing tits."

"Graham," Barnes Powell said, as though suddenly seized with a fit of conscience, "stay away from this. Write a nice lefty book based on Jackson's speeches and public utterances and call him a fascist or something. But stay away from the money."

When Graham Taylor returned to his hotel he placed a call to Paul Coulter, failed to get an answer, and decided to swim off his small indulgence in fish and wine. When he returned to his room an hour later his cell phone was ringing.

"Paul? I'm well, if a bit overfed. Listen. My lunch guest fucked up and let slip a couple of things. Jackson's purchase of Dark/Star was indeed funded by a pair of offshore trusts. Don't know who or what lies underneath them, but knowing the Caymans, it could be anything—hot money of any sort, from drugs to tax evasion to a government agency with a history of creating corporations to do its bidding—there's a certain outfit in Langley, Virginia that keeps coming to mind. At any rate, when Jackson supposedly sold Dark/Star to Cornwall the deal was closed through Bank Royal in Panama City. You know what they are famous for."

"Absolutely," Coulter replied. "They finance a third of the arms dealing on the planet. And every Mexican drug lord gets a free toaster with each deposit."

"Hush. You just drew the attention of one of Homeland Intelligence's satellites."

"Fuck them."

"The satellites don't like profanity either. I'm going to stir around a bit more here. You know, George Town is like a New Orleans cemetery, all marble mausoleums, but with bank's names instead of old dead racists on the brass plaques. I'm paid up through tomorrow night, I might as well see if there's anything else I can learn."

"All right. Be careful."

"Any bites on the piece?"

"*Atlantic* is willing to offer ten thousand based on the five hundred word summary if we can get it in before Jackson's confirmation vote on the 20th. It will double to twenty thousand if I can get an interview with Jackson. I've contacted them."

"The *Atlantic* isn't bankrupt yet? Praise god. Get the money up front. I'll email you a summary from Miami. I don't trust the encryption here. How're you doing?"

"Not great. Not something I want to talk about on the phone."

"Fair enough. I'll call in tomorrow night."

Barnes Powell checked his watch. It was nearly four. In another ten minutes the bank's car would take him home to Seven Mile beach. He would spend an hour in the pool, swimming the gin out of his system. What *had* possessed him to talk to Graham Taylor, anyway? The lure of the old Boss, he decided, the legendary Colonel Taylor who'd once had a god's powers over his life and career. Well, no longer. He was at risk if he made the call he was contemplating, but in the long run possibly very dead if he did not.

He picked up the phone, an old-fashioned land line that offered at least local security, and dialed a number that, after being switched several times, rang in a small but exquisitely restored stone farmhouse in a secluded forty acre vineyard in the Provence.

"Eric? Barney here. Listen, I think I may have been indiscreet today. Let me explain, alright?"

In the morning Graham Taylor took advantage of the fair weather to treat himself to another snorkel before settling in for breakfast on the hotel's terrace overlooking the beach. He ate with good appetite, somehow feeling stronger and more rested than in years…the years since Anna had died.

A younger man, strongly built and dressed in Brooks Bros. tan summer poplin, white linen shirt and a subdued blue tie approached Graham's breakfast table.

"Professor Taylor? I'm Derek Martin." He flashed a badge inside a leather case. Graham briefly caught the words *Special Agent* and *United States Treasury*. "May I join you?" Martin added politely.

Graham Taylor smiled. "Please. I've never been so happy to be under CIA surveillance. I was just remembering how MI-6 always provided us with taxman credentials when we were in other people's countries gathering intelligence." Graham poured coffee for his guest and added, "May I order breakfast for you? The food is really quite good, and I hope we have lots to talk about."

"That would be great," Martin said seating himself and adding cream to his coffee. He smiled, face serene. "In fact, there's a former student of yours who is very curious as to what you are up to. She's in Panama City. Are you free to join her for dinner?"

Chapter Eighteen

Eric Friedheim Library & News Information Center
National Press Club
529 14th Street NW, Washington D.C.
Tuesday, September 6
9:40 A.M. EDT

Paul Coulter leaned back in his chair and rubbed the fatigue out of his eyes. In the past four days he had spent every spare hour away from his routine daily coverage of the White House in the Smithsonian Library and the National Archives. The Friedheim was the only institution open to him on Labor Day, a day that Washington's chattering classes kept holy despite their lack of familiarity with manual labor. It was the last weekend at their Eastern Shore and Virginia Beach cottages before the courts got busy and Congress returned.

Paul had tracked the military and public career of Kyle Hunter Jackson through every conceivable database and source, from Congresspedia to Legistorm to the Library's Electronic Briefing Books of declassified national security materials, the LOUIS project archives, and the Library of Unified Information Sources, the database that contained and cross-referenced every federal executive and congressional branch document generated in the past fifty years.

The problem was not a lack of information. No man who had served nearly twenty years in the United States Army, built one of the largest private military companies in the world, and later won a seat in Congress could avoid leaving a data trail through the web and the proprietary databases that now held the vast majority of data on the planet. But the picture of Jackson that had emerged was maddeningly vague, shaded, somehow forced, more an extended press release than a history.

Jackson was born in Raleigh, North Carolina on December 12, 1957, the third son of a modestly wealthy banking, textile, and real estate family. He'd graduated from Oak Ridge Military Academy just northwest of Greensboro, North Carolina in 1976, then from West Point in 1980. He'd been in the top third of both classes, played lacrosse and captained the debate teams at both schools, worn a powder blue tuxedo to his girlfriend's high school junior prom but a more mature, military cut white dinner jacket to the senior formal. It was a genteel upbringing, far removed from the tumult of the 1970s.

But even though Coulter downloaded, read, viewed and chronologically sorted every word and image that had ever been published or recorded about Kyle Jackson, the man's public façade remained cast in stone: former military officer of considerable bravery, his career shrouded by the secrecy that surrounded the Special Forces. A committed Christian who married in 1997 and seemed to revel in the gift of his four children. A successful, if controversial businessman. Dark/Star had, like every other military contractor in the Second Iraq War, become despised for its enormous profits and the collateral damage it caused: employees killed, wounded and crippled, and Iraqi civilians shot at checkpoints and in protection zones when they didn't obey quickly enough. But those issues were, Paul knew, lost in the collective national amnesia about the war.

In short, with sixty hours' work Coulter had come up with no more meaningful information about Kyle Jackson's life than he had already obtained by strolling into Press Secretary Mitchell Garson's office and requesting a copy of the White House's standard bio. Jackson's Congressional financial disclosure forms were no more help. His wealth had been divided into four approved blind trusts, valued on the official disclosure forms as 'Block B, Category K'—in plain English, each trust was worth more than $50 million dollars, but less than $500 million dollars; no further information about the underlying assets was required to be disclosed, and none was.

Jackson's political press revealed little. When he entered politics he chose North Carolina's seventh district, which included Fort Bragg, Fayetteville, and the surrounding, military dependent and highly conservative communities. Jackson had overwhelmed his opponent, a young prosecutor recruited to the race with the promise of name recognition and future support for state-wide office if he would take the present role of mouse against the cat. Paul studied the video of the two debates held in Jackson's first race. Both candidates had been cautious, Jackson particularly so, his gestures restrained and wooden, his voice soft throughout even when the local television blonde talking head who moderated the debates tried to provoke him. Only once did Paul see real passion in answer to a question about whether his wealth made him callous to the poor:

> "Let me answer that straight on. I don't think that my
> military or my business experience limits me at all in my
> compassion for others. Service to this country, whether
> it is in the armed forces or in the Congress, is about four
> things: character, discipline, judgment and faith in God.
> I never checked my humanity at the door. I have held
> dying men and women, apologized to their grieving
> wives and husbands and families, counseled my soldiers
> about everything from faith to their troubled marriages. I
> will be the representative of all the people of this district,
> rich or poor, black or white, soldier or civilian. You need
> *never* ask that question again."

Paul played the sequence twice. It was good stuff, probably Jackson's best in any campaign. 'Character, discipline, judgment and faith in God' was still the signature line on Jackson's website years later.

Coulter knew he needed a loose thread, an anomaly, a small crack in the rock face of Jackson's public image that he could drive a piton into—anything that might give his research traction. He tried again, focusing on Jackson's resignation from the Army. It was not a RFGOS—resigned for the good of the service—that would have indicated misconduct or the potential for court martial. Only the timing stood out: by resigning on December 27, 1998, just before completing twenty years of service and on the eve of promotion to Brigadier General, Jackson had foregone substantial pay and benefits, but those amounts were nothing compared to the billion dollars he had made from Dark/Star.

"Why resign between Christmas and New Year's?" Paul asked himself aloud. He let the thought tumble around for a few minutes while finding himself another cup of coffee, then settled back into his chair to run random data searches around the date of Jackson's resignation. He finally found a small story in the now defunct Washington *Times* dated Saturday, January 16, 1999. The *Times,* then funded by the right wing Korean evangelical Sun Myung Moon, had featured pages of breathless Clinton impeachment cheerleading as the House Prosecutors' made their presentation in the Senate trial. Paul waded through it and found a short story buried near the bottom of page 19:

"Military Losing Senior Officers at Accelerated Rate?"
James Park, Special to the Washington Times

"The personnel records of the United States Armed Forces showed an unusual number of senior officer resignations during the month of December 1998. In all, nineteen active duty Air Force officers holding the rank of Lieutenant Colonel or above, including two Brigadier Generals, twelve naval officers holding the rank of Captain or above, six Marine officers, and a surprising fifty four senior Army officers submitted letters of resignation in a single month. Curiously, none of the resignations were denominated "Resignations for Good of the Service", which would have indicated that the resigning officer had breached military standards, or had resigned in lieu of a court martial. Captain Catherine Yang, spokeswoman for the Fort Belvoir's Headquarters

Command Personnel Service Center, refused comment on the unusual number of resignations."

Paul tried to narrow his search, and then broadened it again, looking for data from any source about military retirements in late 1998 and early 1999, but nothing else turned up. The only formal way to seek further information would be to submit a Freedom of Information Act request for each officer's resignation letter, but such a request would take weeks to process. Military personnel files were generally FOIA exempt, and the secrecy protections for all types of military information had been expanded since the enactment of Patriot Act III. Paul downloaded the short *Times* piece and headed out the door into the hot late summer afternoon, walking briskly to the Metro stop at McPherson Square to catch the Orange line train to Foggy Bottom.

The offices of the Center for American Military Information were in a rundown 1960s vintage building owned by George Washington University on 24th Street on the far side of Washington Circle, near Rock Creek Park. When Paul entered his office, Arne Kaplan, the Center's founder, had his feet up on his desk, nearly buried by the mountains of reports and books that surrounded him. Kaplan was a short, barrel-chested sixty-six year old retired Army Major General. He'd spent most of his thirty-four year military career in intelligence and planning functions, but had tasted dirt as an infantry scout late in the Viet Nam War, and had commanded a battalion in First Iraq. Kaplan's work on war gaming within the Pentagon's planning office had won him his second general's star—one of the few Jews in senior command rank—but he had grown fearful that the military's constant push toward secrecy and insularity was diminishing its effectiveness in the field and increasing its estrangement from civilian leadership. He resigned in 2008, accepted a faculty position at George Washington, and founded the Center for American Military Information with the avowed purpose of making the military establishment more transparent and honest for both civilian policy makers and concerned citizens. In short, Arne Kaplan knew where more bodies were buried in the Pentagon than any other civilian in Washington.

Kaplan looked up as Coulter entered his office. "You're my sixth fucking reporter today, Paul, and it's a goddamn holiday," he growled by way of greeting.

"Only sixth? I'm surprised you haven't had thirty."

"And you all want to know about Jackson," Kaplan added.

"That's true, Arne."

Kaplan sighed. "I can only tell you what I've told everyone else. I didn't know the man well. He was Special Forces. I attended some debriefings after his classified missions, read a number of after-action reports if they were relevant to what I was working on. He was an incredibly able soldier—effectiveness ratings off the chart. His men would—did—literally go through walls for him." Kaplan's wide, thick featured face scowled. "Dark/Star, the whole use of contractors in Afghanistan and Second Iraq, his politics…I can't say I like any of those things about him. But I'm not going to say any of that on the record, Paul."

"Not what I'm after. But I would like you to take a look at something, Arne."

"What's this for?"

"Graham Taylor and I are working on a biographical piece about Jackson together."

"Where the hell is Graham, anyway?" Kaplan asked. "I've got an idea for a seminar with him this winter, if he can make the time."

"He's researching something out of town."

"I hope he's staying sober. He always goes to pieces in the early fall. That's when Anna died."

"I know. I'm trying to keep him busy. We've got a pretty short deadline on this Jackson piece for the *Atlantic*. If we can write it at all."

"Why can't you?"

"I've spent four full days on this now, Arne. I've tried to pull Jackson's life apart and look at it from every angle I can think of. I've been through his official military record, as released by the White House.

His financial disclosures. All of his press, back to military school in North Carolina. His voting record. Jackson has the most private, tightly controlled public image I've ever seen in a Congressman."

"Some sense of propriety and personal discipline is not necessarily a bad thing in a politician, Paul," Kaplan replied, scolding.

"That's not the point." Coulter weaved through the piled stacks of books, journals and papers that surrounded Kaplan until he was standing at his shoulder. Paul handed him the short article he had printed out from the Washington *Times*. "Jackson resigned his commission on December 27, 1998—just shy of twenty years service credit *and* when he was on the short list to be promoted to General. It looks like a substantial number of other Army officers decided to resign that month—almost four times the normal rate of voluntary resignations, and all in the week between Christmas and New Year's. So what really happened, Arne?"

Kaplan narrowed his eyes as he read the story, and then read it a second time. "I had almost forgotten about this," he said.

"What's 'this'?" Coulter demanded.

"Let me think," Kaplan hesitated. "I don't think it's in any way classified," he finally continued, "but I'm going to talk to you off the record, Paul."

"Why?"

"Because I like you and this might be important for you, but it also might damage my ability to function. And because I don't have first-hand knowledge."

"So—"

"Off the record."

"Retired military source?"

"No. Not now. If you absolutely need to use a background attribution, come back and see me again and we'll talk."

"Damn it, Arne—"

"Hush. The key to this is the date. Christmas 1998. Remember?"

"No."

"Clinton had just been impeached over the Lewinsky sex scandal. The House voted to bring the charges on December 18th, if I remember correctly. Clinton had a long and troubled history with the military. Most of the officer corps hated his guts even before they knew about the Lewinsky thing. But for a number of conservative, religious officers it was the last straw. A group was formed. The plan was to get one thousand officers to sign a public demand for Clinton's resignation."

"Did you see it? The demand, I mean."

"Yeah, I saw it. It was an open letter for publication, cold and to the point. It accused Clinton of destroying the military's morale and effectiveness. Reminded Clinton and the world that the officers signing the document could be court-martialed for having an affair with a subordinate *or* for lying about it—although we both know that there's a long tradition of looking the other way when officers are deployed outside the country. The letter demanded that Clinton resign immediately to avoid threats to national security during an impeachment trial."

"Did you keep a copy?"

"Are you kidding? I know radioactive material when I see it, Paul."

"So what happened?" Paul demanded.

"It didn't get too far. Maybe sixty or seventy officers had signed on when senior command got wind of it."

"And?"

"It was not pretty for anyone who signed. Bit of a double standard—I don't remember Colin Powell resigning his commission when he told Clinton to go fuck himself over gays in the military in '93."

"So the signers were forced to resign?"

Kaplan nodded. "Word got up to General Nakasone, the Army Chief of Staff. He went ballistic. Had the signers—most were in Washington or the Pentagon, the letter hadn't gotten into the field yet—escorted to his office by MPs. Within 72 hours he had their nuts on his desk. Jackson contributed a pair, as I recall."

At seven P.M. that night Paul was opening a paper box of cashew chicken in his kitchen when his cell phone rang. His hopes momentarily rose at the thought that Elizabeth might have been able to break free from her security confinement, or that Graham might be reporting in from the airport saying he was back, but the voice on the phone was one he did not know.

"Hello," the caller said. "Paul, my name is Roy Conover. I'm chief of staff for Congressman Jackson. Can you be ready for the interview you asked for next Monday morning at eleven? 2448 Rayburn House Office Building."

Panama

Chapter Nineteen

Paseo Las Bovedas
Casco Viejo District
Panama City, Panama
Wednesday, September 7
7:40 P.M. CDT

They dined early at the Ramblas bar on Calle Primera, then walked off the pleasant effect of a liter of iced sangria in the warm night air on the Paseo Las Bovedas, the Promenade of the Vaults, named for the dungeons that the Spanish conquistadores had built into the old seawall that surrounded the Plaza Francia at the southern tip of Casco Viejo. They passed under the bougainvillea adorned trestle near the Union Club and on to the open promenade, noting the obelisk that honored the failed French effort to build a canal in 19th Century Panama before the arrival of the Americans in 1903. From the Paseo they could look out at the ships queued up to wait their turn for passage through the Canal, and at the sun-lighted glass towers in the financial district of modern Panama City across the bay.

Graham's dinner partner that evening was his former student, a now sober-minded woman in her mid-thirties named Karen Jenkins. She had much better than average research and writing talent, but like so many of Graham's other students Jenkins had considered the dismal job market for historians and opted for law school. Graham had not seen her for six years, since the memorial service the University had held for Anna Taylor one week after her death from cancer. Graham barely remembered Jenkins' presence; it had not been his finest hour. Only Paul Coulter's steady determination to keep Graham away from Scotch, valium, guns and razor blades before the service had ensured his attendance and left him with even a few memories, however unpleasant, of the day.

They had chatted lightly over dinner; Jenkins had read his books and enjoyed the truculent political essays he contributed to small magazines and websites. She tersely disclosed an unhappy childless marriage now a year in the past. Graham shifted to the more comfortable topic of work and quickly saw that Karen Jenkins was truly married to her job. She joined the Treasury Department out of law school as a staff attorney in the Tax division, and then trained as a field agent. She was now the Senior Special Agent in charge of the Internal Revenue Service's money laundering/tax evasion task force in Panama City, with over one hundred IRS special and revenue agents, FBI field investigators, FINCEN money laundering analysts, and security staff reporting to her. Her group worked in an anonymous suite of offices in a dingy black glass and concrete building a block off the traffic-choked Via Espana in the financial district. Graham's stay at those offices earlier that day had been mercifully brief, just long enough for Derek Martin's CIA field team to verify his identity, passport use, and previous whereabouts before Karen Jenkins arrived for dinner.

Graham stared out from the Promenade into the bay at the entrance to the Canal. "There must be twenty cruise liners alone waiting out there," he said, amazed. "If I were a terrorist wanting to make a purist Islamic point about decadent western civilization I would want a fleet of zodiac boats with about four hundred' pounds of C-4 or Semtex in each."

Karen Jenkins smiled and shook her head. "The Panamanian's aren't stupid," she replied. "The Canal's patrolled by a joint Panamanian National Police-U.S. helicopter squadron, with a not-very-secret wing of Marine Corps F35 Lightening II jump jets on standby, tucked into a remote hanger at the Panama Air Cargo field, which just happens to be our former Howard Air Force Base. We also have a pair of destroyers on station twelve miles off each end of the Canal, just outside Panama's territorial waters." Jenkins paused, and then gestured toward a bench on the Paseo. "Shall we sit and enjoy the air?"

"And talk?"

"And talk. This is a safe place. I had Derek's field team sweep you and your luggage in the office. They found that your other suit, the one in your overnight bag, had been chipped."

"Pardon?"

"Someone placed an RFID tag on it before or during your trip so that you could be tracked. Did anyone touch your clothing or baggage?"

Graham started to say no, but then remembered: he'd been pulled out of the screening line at Miami International and his bag hand searched. "At the airport. I must have been on a TSA list."

"It's been taken care of. The RFID tag was inserted into the lining, and we had to cut it open. Don't worry, the suit's been repaired, cleaned and pressed. It will be at your hotel tonight. Clean in all ways, I assure you."

Graham looked quizzically at Karen Jenkins' small, symmetrical, determined face, one that he would have described as neat or tidy rather than conventionally beautiful. He tried harder to ignore her fit, assuredly female body. His wife had those same qualities, and Graham found to his astonishment that he was not quite dead yet. "So let's get to the point, can we?" he said abruptly, trying to hide his sudden awkwardness. "You had your agents in Cayman pick me up because I was talking to Barnes Powell."

Karen nodded. "Yes. We've had Barnes and his bank under surveillance for months now. When you came into the picture—literally, Powell eats lunch at the Martial Club nearly every day, and we video him—I nearly fell out of my chair with curiosity at what my old Prof was doing with a lizard like Powell."

"One of the few contacts I could impose on. He was a junior officer in SAS under my command during First Iraq."

"Contact for what, Graham? Powell's running a money laundry." She leaned back and pushed her sunglasses up onto her light brown hair, her dark eyes appraising him. "So you've come into money all of a sudden?"

"I wish." Taylor thought furiously but could see no reason not to level with Jenkins about what he was doing. "I'm working on a biographical and political piece with Paul Coulter—he's a White House political reporter, an old friend from both Iraq Wars. The story is about Kyle Jackson, the newly nominated Vice-Presidential candidate. Paul's taking on Jackson's military and political career. I'm taking the money end because I had the contact with Powell, who raised the money for Jackson to buy out Dark/Star while an investment banker in Merrill Lynch's Miami office in 2002. Powell was also involved in Jackson's sale of Dark/Star to the Cornwall Group, but won't say what he did. Barney describes himself as a feeder fish. Is he being modest?"

"A bit," she replied. "Powell has turned Blagg & Bennett from being a small legitimate investment bank into a specialty firm repatriating laundered funds from offshore investments back into legitimate jurisdictions without being taxed. He uses all the tricks: false fee and invoice schemes, unsecured corporate loans that never have to be repaid, debit and credit cards direct-issued by SinoCard, the Chinese version of Visa that will not respond to American subpoenas. We have quite a history with Barney. I could have him indicted in the U.S. District Court in Miami next Tuesday if we wanted to. But since we've tapped into all his systems he's more useful to us as a source of information."

Graham turned away for a moment and watched the orange-red sundown light play on the glass of Panama City's office towers. He remembered Barnes Powell as an eager and intelligent young officer, and was saddened by what Powell had become.

"None of this makes any sense to me, Karen," he admitted. "Are there current connections between Powell and Jackson? There must be. Barney all but threatened me if I didn't stay away from Jackson and the Cornwall Group. And where do you fit into this? Surely you didn't have me brought here simply because you were curious about your doddering old Prof wandering around Grand Cayman."

Karen Jenkins stood up and began walking up the Paseo. Taylor was unsure whether he should follow her or not but eventually decided to follow and caught up with her, placing a tentative hand on her arm.

"That's good," Jenkins said, her voice low. "We look like a couple that just had an argument and now need to talk very intently to patch things up. So walk with me, Graham. Should I consider you a journalist? Can I go off the record?"

"I can be a journalist, I'm accredited, and we can use those rules. Or not."

"Let's say off the record then. Because it's quite a long story, and I'm pretty sure I'm going to be violating federal law at several points along the way."

They walked further along the Paseo as the sky darkened and found a place where the ancient wall rose above the path itself, blocking any view from the Plaza Francia—and, Graham noted, any long distance audio and video surveillance aimed at them from the Casco Viejo. The high rise financial district was too far away across the water to successfully intercept their conversation.

"This all started two and a half years ago as a major revenue push," Jenkins began. "Treasury estimated that it was losing as much half a trillion per year from high end tax evasion through offshore vehicles. They thought they had solved the problem with the 2010 Swiss tax treaty, but in the Caribbean it's just gotten worse. There are no international sanctions you can use anymore on a Cayman or an Antigua. The British Commonwealth tried to crack down—quaint, can you picture Charles III playing tough guy?—and the rogue islands just withdrew from the Commonwealth. The offshore banks *control* these governments. Banking is the dominant industry—it's well over half the GDP now on Cayman. The bankers bought themselves half-a-dozen Southern senators to block Treasury from mounting a frontal assault on them through new legislation. But we still needed the revenue to keep the deficit from bleeding us to death. So we adapted and initiated a campaign to target the biggest evaders on a case by case basis."

"Why are you in Panama, rather than in George Town or Antigua?"

"Panama," she continued, "is a very different situation. Although all of the military bases we had here are gone now, the Panamanians remember quite vividly how Bush the Elder came in and blew up the place in 1989 because Noriega had called him a pansy or something. The CIA and the Army's School of the Americas trained damn near every senior cop and public official in this country. So the Panamanians agreed to play ball as long as we didn't flat out crush their banking business."

"And?" Taylor asked.

"And we follow the money. Money that goes in and out of the tax haven islands usually travels through Panama on its way to the Middle East, Africa, China, and South Asia. If the money is reinvested offshore, many of the deals that start elsewhere get done here. Panama has a very sophisticated banking and legal infrastructure in place. And they've got bank secrecy laws—or so they tell everyone."

Graham smiled. "Except those secrecy laws don't apply to you. So for the past two years you have been—

"Investigating, developing and bringing *very* targeted, very *large* tax evasion and money laundering prosecutions against the thousand worst offenders we could find. We sink our teeth into them and don't let them go with plea bargains or soft sentences. We bring cases that have hundreds of separate criminal counts and score so high on the sentencing guidelines that the people we convict will spend the rest of their lives in prison, while we seize every asset they own down to their children's socks."

"How do you know who to prosecute? Tax evasion is a quite popular sport in America."

"We focus on three groups," she answered. "First, the people who transfer assets out of the United States and liquidate them offshore to avoid tax. Second, the people who ship cash out to invest it and evade taxes—the Mitt Romney IRA program. Third, the people who already have offshore assets that try to bring cash home without tax."

"Explain. I've never had enough money to ever worry about any of this."

Karen Jenkins smiled. "What are the biggest cash businesses in the United States, Graham?"

Taylor thought briefly. "Drugs. Gambling. Congress."

Jenkins smiled. "Congress is actually pretty small beer compared to, say, New Jersey's highway contractors and their state legislators," Jenkins replied. "But you are on the right track. Drugs, illegal gaming, legal gaming—what do you think the so-called legal casinos do with the skim? Prostitution, skin clubs, and pornography. Restaurants and bars. Even fast food. A good-sized chain of teriyaki stands in Los Angeles can generate four or five million dollars a year in cash under the table. But you'd be missing one of the biggest sources you can imagine."

"Which is?" Taylor demanded.

"The collection plate, Graham. That's where Congressman Jackson got the money to buy Dark/Star."

Two hours later they were still talking, sitting in the near-deserted cocktail bar of the Hotel Central, drinking twenty-four year old Flor de Cana Nicaraguan rum and the excellent shade grown coffee that never tastes quite as good outside of Central America.

"Why are you telling me all this, Karen? Graham asked, troubled. "The best you can hope for when this story comes out is that you will lose your job; if you're not careful you'll be looking at the business end of a federal indictment."

"Don't worry about that. I've got pretty advanced survival skills and know how to play the whistleblower statute. I want this story told, Graham. We were ready to nail Royce Reed's ass to the wall for embezzling half a billion dollars from his church members over the past ten years. The indictment was drafted; the prosecution had cleared both Treasury and Justice. And the day that Robinson and Jackson were nominated the White House shut us down."

"What happens now?" Graham asked.

"We're under orders to close out this site within ten days. We're going to lose four hundred person-years of work building contacts, recruiting moles within the Panamanian and offshore banks, as well as all the work we've done figuring out the systems that guys like Barnes Powell have developed to get around U.S. money laundering and anti-terror rules. Oh, yeah, there's a serious anti-terror issue here. Six months ago we started seeing black money being moved out of the Middle East via the Shanghai system into the U.S. via Panama and the Caribbean. We couldn't figure out where it was ending up, so we called in Homeland Intelligence. They sent people down here to work with us and started to make the connections, tracing the cash as it flowed through here to the States. That sure got somebody's attention, because when the Homeland Intelligence task force director came down here two months ago somebody made a real live honest to god move on her—a trap and shoot. The only reason she got out alive was that our FBI guys had picked up a local rumor and had a security car rolling a block behind her when the hit went down. They took out the shooters inside of a minute, but we were never able to trace the bad guys back to the source. No names, no Interpol records, no fingerprints or DNA that we could trace through the data banks of any country that cooperates with us. Our best guess was that they were maybe former Bolivian or Venezuelan security police."

She handed him a data key. "This is a summary. I'm going to try to find a way to use the shut down process to start taking electronic copies of our evidence files—might work, might not. But no matter what happens I want somebody in the real world to know what we know."

Paul Coulter's telephone rang at a little after 3:30 in the morning on Thursday, September 8. Paul was startled out of sleep and suffered momentary panic until he heard Graham's voice.

"Paul? I'm sorry about the hour."

"Graham?" Paul responded sleepily. It's three thirty in the morning. I've got to cover a press conference at the White House in six hours." Coulter's voice sharpened. "Oh, and by the way, where the fuck have you been?"

"I know, I know, I'm sorry. Listen, I'm in Panama City. Much to talk about. I'm not sure when I'm going to finish down here. I'm going to ship a contribution to the company assets, okay? So if I'm late you'll have to work it out with the company lawyers. If I'm late they will be in touch."

"Graham, what the fuck are you talking about? What have you been up to? You were supposed to be back here last night."

"Right, I was," Taylor responded. Paul could hear him chuckling, something Taylor had seldom done since his wife had died. "Just check on the company if I'm *really* late getting back, Paul, okay? Not too much to ask. I must run." The phone went suddenly dead and Coulter sat straight up in bed, suddenly gripping the handset hard, not knowing what the hell Graham had been talking about, or what to think next.

Washington

Chapter Twenty

The Arlington National Cemetery
Arlington, Virginia
Friday, September 9
11:00 A.M. EDT

The flag-draped coffin of Admiral Anthony Thrace had been placed on the catafalque above an opened grave in Section 51 of Arlington National Cemetery, not far from Custis Walk. A draining September heat and bright sun had caused several dozen umbrellas to be opened by the assembled mourners seated on an array of folding chairs in front of the grave site. Elizabeth Gray, along with eleven other military officers who had been detached to serve under Thrace in Homeland Intelligence, stood in dress uniform at parade rest on either side of his coffin. Thrace had not been a religious man, but his wife was a practicing Catholic, and a Navy RC chaplain had been called on to conduct the service. The Chaplain had the sense to keep both the homily and final prayer short and pointed:

> "O Lord, recall thy servant Anthony Thrace with love
> and respect, for having been trusted with great power, he
> held that trust sacred, and kept the people safe. We pray
> to the Lord."

Elizabeth, who had been baptized and confirmed under the watchful gaze of La Conquistadora, Our Lady of the Rosary, in the Cathedral of St. Francis in her native Santa Fe, bowed her head and muttered the requisite "Lord, hear our prayer." She then nodded to the Sergeant of the Third Infantry Old Guard, whose seven man detail fired the three volleys of the 21 gun salute. With that, Tony Thrace joined the long line of ordinary soldiers and able seamen, many now nameless and forgotten, who had died for their country.

Cable Hollings, anguished and reed thin in a threadbare black suit that had seen too many funerals, nodded to Elizabeth and gestured to a nearby grove of leafy post oaks and maples at the edge of Section 51. He strolled toward it and she joined him a moment later, both grateful for the shade and the slight breeze. Karol Horvath silently joined them less than a minute later.

"You holding up okay, Major?" Hollings asked, taking a handkerchief from his back pocket to mop the sweat along his receding hairline.

She nodded. "I'm fine. Just waiting to be court-martialed once Robinson appoints a new director of Homeland Intelligence."

"I saw Crane Dunham in the crowd. Think it will be him?"

"I'm not politically connected enough to guess," Elizabeth replied truthfully. "But Dunham's tight with Congressman Jackson, and I suspect that will be his best credential."

"Right enough," Hollings sighed. "This is what we have so far on Harland Boyd," he added, passing Elizabeth an inch long thumb drive. "Bank records, medical records, contents of his home, interviews with his neighbors out in Manassas, interviews with family. The most interesting thing we've got is Boyd's travel records. He's taken seven different airplane flights in the last two months alone. Pretty heavy schedule for a man with terminal cancer."

"Where did he go?" Gray asked.

"In addition to Panama City, he went to Albuquerque, El Paso, and Las Vegas, twice to each."

Elizabeth frowned. "Las Vegas I can understand, but as a native New Mexican I don't think Albuquerque and El Paso would be that high up on a dying man's bucket list. What do you want me to do with this, Cable?"

"Read it. Read Boyd's service records. Try to figure out whether, and why, somebody like Boyd would want to kill Tony Thrace." Hollings glanced back toward the gravesite, saw that the crowd of mourners was beginning to bleed away a little faster than a Washington crowd normally would from an A-list Arlington funeral. "We don't have much time," he added. "We're still pursuing this clandestine group from my end, but I haven't gone to the Intelligence Court for any warrants—didn't want to attract the attention from the White House."

"Can you keep the domestic investigation active, but less visible, by splitting it into different units, Cable?" Karol Horvath asked.

Hollings nodded. "I've buried my teams under every mission I could think of—firearms trafficking, counter-terrorism, fraud—hell, I even plugged the El Paso group into the bank robbery section. But Acosta isn't stupid; he will see through it eventually. "What's going on with your team, Karol?"

"We're still intact. We have begun identifying active duty personnel who have tries to this cabal, and they will be brought in for questioning once we think we have identified most of the membership on active duty. I have Jack's support, and nothing short of a public Presidential order will shut us down," Horvath replied. "Major?"

"The investigators from IRS and FINCEN in Panama City have been ordered to pull out within a week," Gray told him. "DEA's already been pulled back, and Derek Martin's people in NCTS have been given the word to pack up—which is more than a little unusual since there were only four of them and they were on the roster of the CIA station in Panama City. I don't think Gary Berthoud really knows what we were up to."

"Don't assume that," Hollings cautioned. "Whoever killed Tony was trying to make sure he didn't have a chance to brief the President directly about this. That does not mean people around Robinson don't know what's going on."

"What about the Homeland Applications Office? Do we have any eyes or ears yet?" Karol Horvath asked.

"We're getting NSA signals data from the satellites and the taps on the fiber optic cables, but with TriPlex not operational I don't know what's getting read and translated versus what we've missed. HAO's analysts are drowning the in the data. The FINCEN analysts in Panama report that money is continuing to move into the country—if anything, it's getting bigger. But without TriPlex I can't assess the threat situation."

"Is it time to make another run at briefing Robinson?" Horvath asked.

"No," Elizabeth replied. "If I go back to Berthoud now, with no new information, and tell him in detail what we are doing, he will shut us down. Or indict us."

Horvath nodded. "Let's keep our heads, everyone. If we've still got them at the end of next week, we might just get through this in one piece."

At 8:45 that night Elizabeth leaned back in her chair in her small office in the Old Executive Office Building and removed the reading glasses she wore only in the privacy of her office, and then only with the door closed. She picked up her coffee and finished the cold dregs. The White House served such excellent coffee, particularly compared to the Army, that she had developed a serious caffeine habit.

"I am missing something," she said aloud in the silence of her office.

Harland Boyd seemed to her a plain man: born and raised in Bowling Green, Kentucky; married early at eighteen and enlisted late, age twenty-two, after struggling to support a wife and two children on a mechanic's pay while studying engineering part-time at Western Kentucky University. With his engineering background he had quickly risen to warrant officer, supervising maintenance and upgrading the armor of the Army's ground vehicles. He'd received several negative ratings after a rough divorce in 1989, but served with distinction in Desert Storm and survived three duty tours in Second Iraq, keeping the Army's Second Brigade Combat Team in their tanks and strykers despite sand, heat and increasingly powerful roadside bombs. His roughest patch had come in Afghanistan in 2005. He'd been wounded twice, by shrapnel and then by sniper fire, while supervising the construction of a road in Kunar Province.

Twenty months' ago Boyd had been diagnosed with lung cancer, then medically discharged. He'd since lived quietly in Manassas, Virginia.

Elizabeth turned to the FBI field reports. Hollings had questioned Boyd's neighbors at his Manassas apartment, interviewed his superiors at Fort Belvoir, and sifted through Boyd's bank accounts, investments, and army insurance. The picture that emerged was of a cautious man who saved his money and lived simply, his only extravagances the enormous Chevy truck he drove and tithes to the evangelical church he attended.

She was still puzzling over the seeming contradiction of a modest Christian man who quite probably had turned his pickup truck into a murder weapon when her laptop chimed softly to announce a new encrypted email. She opened the email and ran the decryption program to access it.

It was from Cable Hollings. "Is there any military connection to the airplane flights Boyd took before he died? Here's the list again."

Elizabeth scrolled down and reviewed the flights, all to cities near major military installations. She thought for a moment, then rose, opened her office safe, and took out a loose leaf notebook that contained a listing of every United States military installation in the world, both acknowledged and clandestine. She paged for several minutes through the listings of domestic installations, and then reached for her secure line.

"Lieutenant Commander Sykes," please, she said, when the duty operator at the Joint Staff in the Pentagon answered. Sykes, a Navy intelligence analyst working in J2, had been tasked by Karol Horvath to be Elizabeth's primary contact for any needed DOD data, but not to be informed of the object of the investigation. Horvath kept his cards close, even with his junior officers.

Elizabeth waited while Sykes, who was off-duty, was tracked down on his pager. When he finally came on the line he sounded winded.

"Bad time, Jerry?" she asked.

"No, just playing basketball with the kids," he responded, still puffing. "What do you need?"

"I need situation reports and any unusual activity information for every installation we have, classified or not, in Nevada, New Mexico, and Texas," she said. "Starting from..." Elizabeth thought hard. Tri-Plex had been disabled on 31 August but Boyd had been in all three states during August. "Call it August 1, and run through today. How soon?"

"What kind of unusual activity?" Sykes asked.

"Anything. Everything. Daily staff, command, operations reports. Equipment breakdowns. Motor pool problems. Thefts. Disciplinary problems—assaults, criminal offenses, AWOLS, thefts. *Everything.*"

Sykes sighed. "There's going to be pushback on this from classified installations like Groom Lake."

"Everything and every installation," Elizabeth said firmly. "I'll get Horvath to cut you orders for whatever records and staff help you need."

"How soon?"

"Now. The kids are going to have to miss you at hoops for the next couple days."

She hung up. Her laptop chimed.

It was a second email from Hollings. "Almost forgot. We found Boyd's bank safety deposit box about two hours ago," Cable wrote. "It contained one hundred thousand dollars in cash. There's a second key and power of attorney on file in favor of a woman named Carlotta Johnson. What can you tell us about Johnson? She's apparently retired military and lives just a few blocks away from Boyd's place in Manassas."

Gray opened up the restricted Pentagon personnel data system and read the service records of Carlotta Johnson. 10th Mountain.

Medic. Afghanistan, Iraq, Afghanistan again. Seemed to be a solid soldier, clean sheet, awarded the MSM on her second Afghan tour, Purple Heart after being wounded on a recon mission. Recon? Weird. Stateside duty, then retired with 25 years' service. The last item in Carlotta Johnson's service record was a photo from her discharge ceremony taken two years before. Johnson had worn the then-new formal day dress uniform for women, a navy blue tunic with pale gray slacks. Elizabeth was about to speed forward when she noticed something unusual: a ceramic pin worn above the standard three rows of badges mounted on the left breast of the tunic. She zoomed in on the photos, then cursed and took out her reading glasses and looked again. The pin depicted a red square on a white backdrop. The square had eight points, the corners and four triangular points on the middle of each side. She had seen the peculiar symbol before: doodled in the margin of the notes Charlie McConnell had taken the day his confidential source had finally made his way through the White House bureaucracy to tell the President his story.

Chapter Twenty-One

"Major, have you taken *complete* leave of your senses?" Gary Berthoud snarled. He threw the Justice Department internal investigation memorandum he had received less than an hour before across the desk at her, his broad fleshy chinless face flushed with rage.

Elizabeth Gray snagged the bound memorandum out of the air and calmly placed it in an 'eyes only' security folder before returning it to Berthoud's desk.

"That is something others will have to judge, Sir," she replied. "My team undertook the tasks we were assigned by President McConnell in good faith, and under the direct operational control of the Director of Homeland Intelligence. If I may ask, Sir, why are you shutting down an investigation into a material threat to domestic security?"

Berthoud did not listen to or answer her. "*This* is what you came to brief the President about in New Orleans?' he asked, incredulous. "This…paranoid fantasy about a right wing terrorist group infiltrating the military and veteran's organizations? In case it has escaped your attention, Major, this is the Robinson/Jackson administration. We actually *are* conservatives, we *do* support our military and our veterans, and we don't give a flaming *asswipe* what the liberal coastal media thinks about it."

"Sir, this is not about politics. This is about a clandestine group, organized in cells, that is receiving funds from what appear to be Islamic sources—"

"Shut up, Major." Berthoud sat down heavily in the massive leather desk chair that visibly sagged under his near eighth of a ton. "Did you and Thrace have a Presidential Finding to support this alleged investigation?"

"Only a verbal one, Sir." Elizabeth felt a strand of fear growing in her spine. Domestic surveillance and investigation was still a touchy subject, no matter what the Third Patriot Act had authorized. Charlie McConnell had issued no written findings or orders; he wanted no paper trail linking him to an investigation that he feared might implicate people in his own political party. Gray and Thrace had gone along, knowing that the President needed political cover, but Elizabeth found that the prospect of spending the next three years going a million dollars into debt to pay for criminal defense counsel did not appeal to her.

"The President did, however, speak personally with the other deputies who supplied resources to this investigation," she added. "They will confirm what I have told you, that this project was authorized."

"Really?" Berthoud smiled maliciously. "How many do you think will back you after they've had a chance to lawyer up? Let me give you some *reasoned* advice, Major. We're appointing a new director of Homeland Intelligence tomorrow. His name is Crane Dunham. He's a former congressman from Florida. It is a recess appointment and takes effect immediately but he needs help getting up to speed. You will be his enthusiastic supporter and for the next thirty days you will school him carefully and thoroughly on every ongoing Homeland Intelligence issue and procedure…excluding this pile of pig swill you were involved in. With your help, he will be the smartest student in school and will eventually get confirmed in the Senate without difficulty. And *if* all that happens, I will *allow* you to be reassigned to your service and won't have a goddamn special prosecutor appointed to explore the possibility of your spending, say, four years in the Leavenworth stockade for conspiracy to violate the civil rights of your fellow citizens who have more patriotism and guts than you do. Am I *clear*, Major?

Elizabeth bit her lip, and then forced herself to smile. "Perfectly, Congressman. Like you, I love a good funeral. Whether it's mine… or yours."

She arrived at five o'clock that afternoon at the third floor Capitol Hill condominium she had previously shared with Paul Coulter, with most of the clothes and a few books from the FBI Alexandria safe house packed into two regulation Army duffels that she'd lugged up the stairs from the street, not bothering to wait for the building's poky, thirty year old elevator. On arrival she had kissed a surprised but very happy Paul Coulter for a good forty-five seconds. She'd then taken her bags into the bedroom and immediately began hanging her clothes in the closet and folding her lingerie into her side of their shared chest of drawers. Elizabeth would never admit it but she was secretly pleased that her spaces were empty and that no trace of another woman's clothes or scent could be found. When she was finished she changed her clothes, returned to the kitchen, rummaged in a cabinet under the counter, and emerged with a bottle of Johnny Walker Black, a glass, and a bowl of ice. Then she talked.

Coulter had enough limited intelligence about women to let Elizabeth tell her story without asking too many questions. "If I'd had my sidearm I'd have killed the fat little sonovabitch," she raged, stomping around the living room with a tumbler of Scotch on ice in hand, her Brooks Brothers suit replaced by an Army Lacrosse T-shirt and a pair of Coulter's sweatpants cinched in around her waist.

"That's why they don't let you carry in the White House," Paul replied. He busied himself taking a steak out of the refrigerator to warm to room temperature and uncorking a bottle of Alexander Valley cabernet to breathe. Elizabeth continued to vent.

When she finally paused for breath Paul asked, "So is this over? Are you out of this investigation?"

"There isn't any investigation," she replied. "The White House went around me and recalled everyone that had been assigned to the task force to their home agencies. By the time I knew what they were doing it was over." She splashed more Johnny Walker Black into her glass and pried another ice cube from the now half-melted bowl of ice on the kitchen counter. "Somebody at the Justice Department wrote up a report that summarized some of what we had done…and Berthoud threw it in my face. Literally. I've got thirty days to prepare Tony's replacement as Director, some dim bulb Florida Congressman named Dunham, and get him up to speed so he won't pee his pants when he's asked questions at his confirmation hearings. After that, if I'm a very good girl and don't further piss off the administration, they'll let me go back to the Army. I'll probably get assigned as a Battalion XO in, say, Kyrgyzstan."

"What did Cable Hollings say when you told him you weren't going to stay in the safe house?"

"He was pretty worried. I told him I wasn't—that if you can stop an investigation with a phone call instead of having people killed, it's really a hell of a lot easier to just make the phone call." She smiled. "But would you mind if I borrowed your Beretta tonight? My M9's in my locker out at the range."

On Saturday, September 10 an exhausted Graham Taylor flew out of Panama City, with a list of people to interview in Antigua, Cayman, and Nassau. As his flight idled on the runway he took out a throwaway cell phone he had purchased at a rundown electronics shop near the Mercado Nacional de Artesanias. The phone had been preloaded with three hours of international voice time; Taylor would need less than three minutes.

"Paul," he said, when Coulter's cell phone voice mail picked up the call, "Graham here. I've got useful stuff—more great new assets for the company. I'll be sending more to the office from along the road, but it's going to be at least four or five days until I'll be home.

If you get the face time you wanted with our friend, ask a lot of questions about how he started and funded the business. A lot of questions, Paul. Be well, and don't forget the company assets." Graham closed the phone, then removed the battery and the sim card. He would reassemble the bits and turn the phone back on when he changed planes in Guatemala City. If the phone was traced they would find it tucked behind dusty bottles of men's cologne at the duty free shop.

Paul's phone rang around eleven, an hour after both he and Elizabeth had fallen into the kind of sweet dreamless sleep that making love sometimes gives as its parting gift. He rose painfully from bed, remembered he had left his phone charging on the kitchen counter, and stumbled out of the bedroom to find the phone had gone silent. The caller used an I.D. block but left a voice mail. It was Graham. Paul listened to the message twice, confused again by Graham's odd phrasing—"company", "assets"? Graham had no investments; he'd poured everything he'd ever earned or saved into the bottomless pit of medical treatment, trying to save his wife's life. His University salary was small and his British Army pension would not have kept a roof over his head in D.C. Paul finally gave up, still puzzled, and saved the voice mail to his laptop. He would to listen to it in the morning with a clear head.

When Paul returned to bed he found Elizabeth stirring. "Something wrong, baby?" she asked.

"I don't know. It was a voice mail from Graham. He said something about staying in the Caribbean for four or five more days. That would make him a full week overdue."

"Maybe he's actually having a good time?"

"He wouldn't just chuck this project to take some vacation. He knows I'll need him to help me write up the *Atlantic* piece after I interview Jackson on Monday. The magazine wants to publish it, at least in the web edition, before the confirmation vote."

"What is Graham doing down there, Paul?"

"He went down to Cayman to interview an investment banker who worked on some of the financing deals that Jackson used to buy Dark/Star. It seems the banker had been one of Graham's junior officers during First Iraq. Graham talked to the banker, and the next day a CIA guy posing as an IRS agent picked him up and took him to Panama City. Some kind of tax evasion and money laundering investigation is going on down there. Is that investigation connected to what you were doing?"

Elizabeth came fully awake and sat up in bed, frowning. "Graham's too old for this shit," she said, by way of avoiding an answer. "I think I'd better go to the office tomorrow and see if I can find him."

Chapter Twenty-Two

The Rayburn House Office Building
United States Capitol Complex
Monday, September 12
11:37 A.M. EDT

The collar on Paul Coulter's dress shirt chafed uncomfortably, a reminder that his neck had thickened and he needed to get his ass back to the gym and out on the running path of the National Mall to knock off the seven pounds of red beans, rice, fried shrimp Po'Boys, and Jax beer he'd larded on during the Republican Convention.

Coulter remained seated as a small mob of aides and supplicants surged and receded through Kyle Jackson's reception room. Jackson was running thirty minutes past the agreed time for the interview, but by Washington standards that was not a snub or a message, not from a Vice-Presidential nominee in the post-Labor Day heart of a campaign. He slid his interview outline back into his Filson canvas shoulder bag and had just picked up the New York *Times* when Jackson's Chief of Staff, Roy Conover, appeared to greet him.

Coulter stood and the two men shook hands and appraised each other. Coulter saw that Conover was an inch taller than his own six foot three, African-American, somewhere in his middle to late thirties, lean and nearly model handsome, with a long forehead and intelligent, somewhat wary eyes. Conover dressed well in a dark gray-striped suit with a pin on each lapel—on the right, the obligatory American flag, on the left, a white enameled pin that contained a smaller red square, with red arrows or darts on the outer perimeter of the inner square.

"Thanks for being willing to take this on with just a couple of days notice," Conover began politely. He touched Coulter's arm and pointed him across the long reception room toward Jackson's private office.

"I'm delighted," Coulter replied, walking with him. "Your guy is a tough get, especially for a print reporter. Why'd you pick me instead of Rachel Maddow? Scared of her?"

Conover laughed. "We think you're an honest guy, Paul," he began. "All we're asking for here is a chance to be heard, to let Vi— *Congressman* Jackson explain what he's about." Conover paused and then added, "The Congressman and I both respect your service to the country. You were in the Marine Corps during First Iraq, an embedded correspondent during second Iraq—and you rescued President McConnell under fire in Baghdad. That's a pretty hot record. It sets you apart from most Washington reporters."

"There were a lot of reporters," Coulter responded quietly, "who died in those wars and had a hell of a lot more guts than I do. Even if they were never in the military themselves. But thanks for the kind words. Mind a question?"

"Not at all."

"The pin on your left lapel. It feels like I've seen it somewhere before. What's it mean?"

Conover reached his hand to his lapel and rubbed the enameled pin with his thumb, as if it were a talisman, then smiled. "I doubt it you've seen it, Paul. It's a personal thing from Afghanistan. I was in the 10th Mountain Division, with an intelligence company. I was a green LT less than a year out of the Point, getting through my missions only because my master sergeant was holding my hand and telling me what to do, and my platoon—you'll never find better soldiers. We were doing a recon mission in Nuristan Province overlooking the Pakistan border. The Taliban came down on top of

us from over the ridge to the west and pinned us down. We had
the Kunar River canyon behind us so we couldn't retreat, and the
weather was so bad we couldn't get airlifted. We had to fight our
way out, but we all made it. So when we rotated back to Fort Drum
we had these made up, a reminder of how much we meant to each
other."

A door opened in front of them. Kyle Jackson emerged in white
shirtsleeves and dark blue tie, hand offered in greeting. "Mr. Coulter,
it's a pleasure," he said, his deep hoarse voice softened by his North
Carolina accent. Jackson moved gracefully and gave off an air of
easy—and expected—authority. Coulter had a sudden flash to a television documentary about the Mercury astronauts, and was struck
by how much Jackson resembled Alan Shepard, the first American
in space.

Coulter took the outstretched hand. "Congressman, thank you
for the time," he responded. "I imagine your world has been turned
upside down in these last ten days."

"That's putting it mildly," Jackson said, grinning. "Let's go into
my office. Roy, have you got the voice transcription system working?"

"I do," Conover replied. "Good thing I took electrical engineering at the Point. Paul, you'll have transcript in hand when you walk
out of here."

"Thanks," Coulter replied. "But you won't mind if I take a few
notes? I can't think unless I'm scribbling something at the same
time." He followed the two men into Jackson's private office. It was
not what Coulter expected. The furnishings, like most congressional
offices, ran to dark leather and traditional mahogany. But Jackson eschewed the usual trappings of power, the high trophy walls
of self-aggrandizing photographs taken with Presidents and CEOs
and Kings. Instead, Jackson's walls were thoughtfully decorated with
tribal and indigenous art: Dan masks from East Africa, Masai spears,
Tlingit baskets, water color sketches by Sioux warriors taken prisoner
in America's Prairie wars. Jackson also collected primitive paintings
from Latin America and Africa with Christian heroes and themes: a
Ghanaian Christ, a Mexican San Sebastian shot with arrows, an odd
Peruvian portrait of Joan of Arc painted in muted colors on wood,

the Maid depicted with *mestizo* Indian features but in full armor and with blood, presumably English, on her sword. One large framed glass case behind Jackson's desk stood out: it held a dozen modern military mission patches sewn to a black velvet background.

Jackson settled into a leather armchair in front of his office's decorative fireplace. "I understand you were Marine Recon, Paul," he began.

Coulter laughed ruefully. "I was nineteen years old, very scared, not very bright, and praying every night that I would not, pardon my language, fuck up or wash out."

Jackson laughed with him. "Some screw up. Bronze Star with a V from the Battle of Khafji. The one battle in First Iraq actually fought on Saudi soil. Fourteen marines held off most of an Iraqi battalion for twenty-four hours by calling in air strikes less than fifty yards from their own positions. You guys did good work."

Coulter shook his head. "I don't remember much of that day or night. I'm partly deaf from the bombs," he added, brushing back the graying brown hair over his left ear to reveal his hearing aid. "I'm pretty sure I killed eleven people, plus or minus two, given that I hit an Iraqi armored car, a piece of Soviet era junk, with an RPG round that took a one in a million bounce, skipped into an open port and blew the car apart."

"Does that bother you?" Jackson asked quietly.

"No. I've never had PTSD. But I still think about the pieces of war that I fought."

"So do I, Paul. And I appreciate your honesty. Shall we get started?"

"Sure. But I thought we were waiting for someone from the campaign media staff to sit in."

Jackson shook his head, no. "I eat my own cooking. Fire away."

"Congressman," Paul began, "you've served most of your life in the armed forces. You started military school at age 12, graduated from West Point, and had what appears to have been a very distinguished Army career until your resignation in 1998. Yet your official service record has major gaps. Can you explain those gaps?"

"I can, to a certain extent," Jackson replied evenly. "My records do show the units I was assigned to, and they fully disclose all of my staff and headquarters assignments. However, almost all of my active duty career assignments were with the Special Forces. I can talk about some of those missions—for example, in First Iraq I commanded a team that fought behind Iraq lines prior to our ground assault to take out Saddam's command and communications systems. Other missions...remain classified, as do most Special Forces missions. Nothing out of the ordinary, that's just S.O.P."

Coulter gestured toward the framed collection of mission badges behind Jackson. "I noticed the mission badges you've had framed, sir. Can you tell us anything about them?"

"The ones in the top row are from First Iraq, Mr. Coulter. The next three are from missions in Somalia, Bosnia, and Kosovo—and that's all I can tell you about them. I can't talk about the others—and that's part of the reason we create these badges. Special Forces in all branches design mission badges to commemorate accomplishments that we cannot talk about. It's part of a long military tradition of heraldry that goes back centuries."

Coulter's eye was drawn to a badge in the last row, presumably close to the end of Jackson's career. It depicted an eagle flying hard to clear a mountain range with a golden casket clutched in its claws. "Can you tell us anything about that mission badge, sir?" Coulter said, gesturing. Jackson turned, glanced, and shook his head. "Sorry, Mr. Coulter. That one is still classified."

"Was that mission near the end of your career?"

"Yes." *He seems more wary now,* Paul thought. *Is it his resignation?*

"Congressman, when you resigned from the Army in December 1998 you'd already won the Silver Star with oak leaf cluster for 'conspicuous acts of gallantry in the service of the United States,' from a mission that still remains classified. You were on track to become the Army's youngest Brigadier General in over sixty years. Why did you resign?"

Jackson's expression closed a bit but he did not hesitate. "Several reasons. I had recently married and started a family. Becoming a general involves accepting more staff and headquarters positions. I wasn't sure, based on the tours I had done at the War College and at the Pentagon, that staff work was my cup of tea. Not to denigrate staff officers—staff officers are critical to the function of any modern armed force—but I was not a staff officer by temperament."

"There were an unusual number of relatively senior Army officers—Majors and above—who resigned in December 1998," Paul continued. "Was your decision to resign your commission related in any way to similar decisions by other officers?"

Jackson hesitated. "Only in this sense," he began carefully. "December 1998 was a difficult month in the history of the country. The President had just been impeached for immoral conduct in office, with a Senate trial to come. So I suppose a third factor in my decision was my sense—and I did hear similar sentiments from other officers—of embarrassment at being unable to whole heartedly support a Commander in Chief whose actions offended Christian values I hold."

"Did officers who felt similarly...embarrassed...undertake any formal action to make their views known?"

"Formal? I don't understand."

"A public statement, an open letter, a demand that President Clinton resign?"

Jackson shrugged. "My personal belief, of course, was that a man who disgraced the office of President as he had *should* resign out of common decency and respect for the Nation. But I did not publicize those views."

"So there was no pressure from your Commanders to resign?"

"My discharge was honorable and never designated 'for the good of the service', Mr. Coulter." *Nice,* Paul thought. *Technically true and completely evasive.*

Paul shifted subjects. "Can we talk about Dark/Star?"

"Certainly. I know that's a piece of my background that the public may not fully understand."

"First," Coulter said, smiling, "Can you explain the name? What is a 'Dark/Star'? You've got me completely baffled."

Jackson laughed. "No, I can't really. As you probably know, I bought into the company after it was formed by three other guys. One of them, Roy Romey—a good man who died last year—was a former Marine who grew up wild in San Francisco and an over the top Grateful Dead fan. I didn't even know who the Grateful Dead were, or about the song that has the phrase 'Dark/Star.' Just not the kind of music I ever listened to. But I have to say that I thought the name was kind of cool. So when I bought control of the company, I kept it."

"What kind of business was Dark/Star doing when you bought into it?"

"At the time, the Company's focus was on executive protection for

diplomats, doctors, United Nations personnel and NGOs in rough places like Bosnia, Kosovo, Somalia and Rwanda."

"How did you fund your purchase?"

"Initially? With savings. A second mortgage. My father and my brothers and sisters also kicked in seed money."

"And later, when you took over the Company and bought out the founders?"

"Is this pertinent?"

"I don't know, sir, but your television ads are touting you as a self-made entrepreneur in the finest American tradition. So if you can claim it I think I can ask about it."

Jackson nodded. "Hoist on my own advertising. Fair enough. But I'm going to have to get you more detail from the Company if you are going very far into this, because I wasn't that deeply involved in the process. My lawyers worked with Merrill Lynch—the firm's nearly forgotten now, but in 2002 they were top investment bankers. They put together a couple of partnerships, pitched them to venture capital funds, and made it work. I never met the investors, never took part in the sales pitch. I was in Sudan, trying to keep the *Janjawid* away from the French docs who had set up field clinics in Darfur. It was pretty surreal, talking deal points on a satellite phone in the middle of a dusty village in Africa where the standard of living didn't come close to what the ancient Hebrews had."

"You're saying you don't know who the investors were?" Paul persisted.

Jackson stiffened. "I knew that the investors were vetted by my lawyers and Merrill's lawyers, that everything was on the straight, and that all funds that were invested were legitimate. I do not know every entity, partnership, or investor in the funding group. That was, to a certain extent, not my issue. I insisted on clear control and a free hand to grow the company enough to justify their investments."

"And then Second Iraq happened. And growth was not a problem for Dark/Star."

"That's true," Jackson said evenly. "General Shinseki was absolutely right; we invaded Iraq with too small a force to govern it once we had destroyed Saddam's military. We couldn't keep public order; we couldn't protect our own officials, much less the Iraqi infrastructure and the U.N. The Bush Administration panicked and the missing hundred thousand boots on the ground were filled by security contractors.

"But that does *not* make me or my company mercenaries, Mr. Coulter. We were hired by the American government and we served its purposes, followed its orders. We protected American officials, American supply lines, and American civilians doing their best to reconstruct Iraq and support the democracy that America wanted to take root there. Dark/Star hired only professionals—most of them soldiers that I knew, had worked with, fought with, prayed with. We had the lowest rate of casualties and injuries, both for ourselves and for Iraqi civilians, of any contractor. In every case where an Iraqi civilian was killed, we voluntarily sought out their families and paid them compensation out of our own pocket, even if we suspected that their lost relative was an outright member of Al Qaeda. There were contractors in Iraq that took advantage of the panic—guys who three months before the war couldn't make a pickup truck payment, and suddenly had a thirty million dollar contract with the Commerce Department or one of the big reconstruction contractors like Bechtel or Halliburton. Those guys were idiots who hired anyone who could sober up long enough to hold a carbine. We were never like that."

"As the Second Iraq and Afghanistan wars continued, Dark/Star made an enormous amount of money on its government protection contracts, correct?"

Jackson nodded. "We did very well. We eventually had over 4,000 contractors working for us, and we made enough money to recruit and train and pay the best. We had an attrition rate of less than four percent. And none of my men were ever charged with a crime in Iraq."

"That doesn't mean much. As security contractors you were immune from prosecution."

"No. Not true. We waived that right as a company, and all of our employees individually waived their rights. We didn't want to hide behind that order."

"But you hide behind secrecy, even now," Coulter said, challenging him.

Jackson bristled. "For example?"

"You provided services in Afghanistan."

"Not a secret, Mr. Coulter."

"But some of it was. And still is. Did Dark/Star participate in renditions from Afghanistan and Pakistan?"

"You know I can't talk about the specifics of Dark/Star's contractual obligations, Mr. Coulter. You're taking a cheap shot."

"I don't think so, Congressman. Aren't people entitled to know what we did there? Or is the answer so dark that the United States Government cannot acknowledge the actions of its forces and agents, even now?"

"All governments do unpleasant things in war. And all of them decline to discuss the details. You might as well ask Al Quada, or Saddam's Iraq."

"Did Dark/Star provide services to the United States government regarding interrogations?"

"The same answer, Mr. Coulter, regardless of what you think about it."

"I just ask questions, Congressman. My thoughts are not relevant. Did Dark/Star provide services to the United States government to assist any program of assassination or executions between 2001 and 2009?"

Jackson looked away, mildly disgusted. "Move on," he snapped.

Chapter Twenty-Three

The room grew close and heated as they talked through the lunch hour. Jackson limited himself to two meals a day—a luxury compared to his Special Forces regimen. Paul, far more indulgent, never ate while he was working. Each man probed the other, searching for any weakness. The tension in the air was thick.

"Do you still own Dark/Star, Congressman Jackson?"

"No. It's owned by the Cornwall Group, a private equity firm. I paid some pretty amazing tax bills when I sold it."

"Do you have any interests in Cornwall?"

"None that I know of. All of my family's assets are now held in blind trusts administered by the best lawyers in North Carolina. I report their size and their income on my Congressional disclosure forms, but that's all I know about the trusts."

"Do you have any form of control, direct or indirect, over Dark/Star at this time?"

"I'm a member of the House Appropriations Committee and the Defense subcommittee. I vote on bills that probably authorize programs that Dark/Star is involved in. Other than that—no."

"Let's talk for a moment about Dark/Star itself now," Coulter said. "You leveraged the cash flow from the security business to build your company into a major defense contractor. It advises the federal government on intelligence and homeland security policy and is one of the three largest information technology contractors to Homeland

Intelligence. Dark/Star develops cyber war software for the Defense Advanced Research Projects Agency. It builds and operates its own armed intelligence drones. Dark/Star also does a huge business in emergency management, providing continuity of government plans and emergency facilities for federal, state and local governments, not to mention half the companies in the Fortune 500. Aren't these functions that are normally carried out by the U.S. government and the States? Isn't it dangerous to turn so many government operations over to a private company?"

"Mr. Coulter, private companies have been taking over business functions from the U.S. government, particularly in defense, for over sixty years. The reality is that our systems have grown so complex that government managers simply cannot cope with them."

"But haven't you done what Eisenhower warned us against? Created a self-perpetuating military industrial complex that feeds on public resources, and then uses those resources to lobby for even more?"

"I agree there is always that risk. But we are an empire now, and we do what we must do to defend it."

Coulter sat back in his chair and thought, *keep him talking.*

"What kind of an empire are we, Congressman?"

Jackson shrugged. "A unique one. We do not seek to conquer, we only seek to liberate. We are the bulwark of the western world, a world more challenged now than at any time since the seventeenth century, when the Ottoman forces stood at the gates of Vienna."

"By 'Western' I take it you mean 'Christian' world. What role does being committed Christian play in your political beliefs, Congressman?"

"My Christian beliefs are…the basis of my political beliefs, and certainly define my political beliefs. I have never felt the need to apologize for Judeo-Christian civilization, nor to deny that America was founded as, and is, a Christian Nation."

"So you do not believe in the separation of Church and State?"

"Not in the sense that you probably do, Mr. Coulter. I view our Constitutional guarantees of freedom of religion as protecting the right of each of us to seek the face of God in his or her own way.

That does *not* mean that the Constitution requires, or allows, the government to drive people of faith, or religion itself, from public life. The way I think of it, government is like the town square that you will still find at the heart of a lot of our small cities in North Carolina. There are four sides to that square. On one side you'll find the courthouse; on the next you'll find the mercantile row of shops and restaurants; on the third side you might find the town high school, and on the fourth side of that public square, you'll find the local Methodist or Baptist or Episcopalian Church. Government, education, commerce and religion all share that public space."

"And where do the Buddhists go? Or the Muslims? Or the Jews?" Coulter pressed.

"I think we could certainly arrange for them to rent some meeting space," Jackson replied, smiling. "But it might not front directly on the Square. The primacy of place on the American public square has been decided by our nation's Christian history and heritage."

"Demographically, in twenty years or so, people of white ancestry will no longer be a numeric majority in this country. What happens to your public square then?"

"Why, nothing," Jackson replied. "African-Americans are predominantly Christian, Latinos Catholic or evangelical. We will remain a Christian Nation."

"Speaking of the Christian Nation, what is your relationship with Royce Reed?"

"I would say we are friends. I admire his work, his faith, and his personal redemption. I've been on his television and web cast programs to give personal testimony, and to talk about political issues, foreign policy issues. I would always listen to his advice, and I would certainly hope for the support of his prayers."

"Did Royce Reed have anything to do with your being named the Republican nominee for Vice-President?"

"You'd have to ask the President and Royce that. I don't think President Robinson would have selected me if Royce had advised him against it. They are very close."

"I was in the press conference in New Orleans the day your selection as President Robinson's running mate was announced. And I have to tell you, in all honesty, that the reporters and political professionals in that room were puzzled by your selection."

Jackson nodded. "Let me guess. 'Nobody knows who he is. A right winger from the South who won't bring any new voters to the ticket.' Is that close to accurate?"

"Pretty much."

"That's conventional wisdom. But you know, Mr. Coulter, the conventional wisdom just doesn't work anymore. Trying to mate Charlie McConnell and Jim Robinson on the same ticket was a disaster. People saw that it was a cynical alliance born in desperation. McConnell/Robinson got just 38% of the vote in 2012. If Mayor Stern hadn't run as a third party candidate, split the vote, and thrown the election into the House, Miranda Cardwell would be President today. Jim Robinson and I have a slightly different idea: that committed people attract other committed people. And because most Americans have lost faith, lost hope, and lost trust in both government and business, the decisive factor will be whether they have retained their faith in God. If they have, they'll vote for us, give us a chance to build on their Christian faith to restore other faiths. If they haven't kept faith with God, their disillusion with all of our failed institutions will keep them home, and our voters will carry the day."

"So you'll be appealing to the Republican base?"

"Yes. But the Christian Nation embraces a great many people outside the Republican Party. I consider those people part of our political base."

Coulter swallowed a half dozen potential follow up questions; his time was growing short.

"What do you bring to the Republican ticket that complements James Robinson?" *A puffball question, but sometimes politicians say more when not attacked.*

Jackson thought. "I have experience in areas that complement the President's own—in national defense, the disposition of the military, emergency management and control. I believe that I can appeal to the voters on national and homeland security issues."

And thus to make the trains run on time, Paul remembered Vince Magruder saying, the night that Jackson's selection was announced.

"So you anticipate having a larger role, perhaps, than has been usual for Vice-presidents, in military, homeland defense and anti-terrorism issues?"

"I hope so—but of course my role will always be up to the President. On a personal level, I'd also like to work on military family issues. We have not done well by our Iraq and Afghanistan veterans, or those still on active duty. Their health care needs haven't been met and they are not getting the education and training benefits they deserve. Pay has been stagnant. No group has suffered more from sub-prime mortgages, shoddy mutual funds, the housing market collapse, and this endless recession than veterans. I talk to career soldiers every week who are still trying to dig out from unjust debts—but they're too proud to default or declare bankruptcy."

"So you're saying the career military has been hit harder by the long recession than the rest of America?"

"Yes. Look at all the foreclosures and empty houses around any major military base."

"I have," Coulter replied, "And I agree with you. But I was also struck by the sense that the active military community has separated itself in many ways from the core of American society."

"The core?" Jackson asked, genuinely incredulous. "We—the career military—*are* the core of American life, the protector of its values. If anything, it is the rest of society that has separated from *us*. When the Second Iraq War began, how many Congressman and Senators had children serving in the armed forces? As I remember, it was six out of five hundred thirty-five. The career military has been tasked over and over again to defend America's interests over the past two decades—and has been underpaid, under respected, and over-burdened." Jackson's hands closed into fists, as though he was subconsciously containing an old anger.

"How do you see the role of the military in American political life?" Coulter asked.

"We are the servants and protectors of the American nation," Jackson responded. "Every soldier swears an oath to preserve and protect the Constitution."

"So you believe in civilian control of the military?"

"Yes. But the military has its own constitutional role."

"Constitutional role?"

"Have you read the Constitution recently, Mr. Coulter?" Jackson's voice shaded toward sarcasm. "Look at the repeated references to the military. One of the most basic purposes the Constitution sets forth for government, right in the Preamble, is to provide for the common defense. Congress has the power to raise armies and navies, and to call out the militia. The President is commander in chief of the army, navy, and militias. Article III, Section 4, guarantees to each state a republican form of government and the protection of the United States against invasion or domestic violence. You cannot read the Constitution without seeing that the Framers crafted a role for the military to protect the Constitution, the national government, and the states themselves."

"And if there is a dispute as to the whether the civilian authority is protecting the Constitution?"

"Every means of preserving civil authority should be undertaken, but if necessary, the Constitutional imperative and intent should be followed. We have procedures for ensuring the continuity of government. Some of them require declarations of martial law and temporary military control."

"Who decides to implement martial law?"

"The President would, or his designee in the National Command Authority. Under extreme circumstances, a decapitating nationwide attack, the commander of NORTHCOM could make that decision."

"As Vice President you would be in the National Command Authority?

"Yes. Subject to the President. And to anticipate your next question, if I am confirmed and then elected I would have the authority to order military measures to preserve the nation."

Paul was slightly shaken by Jackson's calm assertion of the military's right to take control as long as it was cloaked as continuity of government. "And if there is this special role in the Constitution for the military, should members of the military vote? Or be politically active? There used to be a tradition in this country by officers who may have interpreted the Constitution as you do—General Marshall, for example—to refrain from voting in national elections."

"I think that's a confusion of the two roles. Service members can and should vote their conscience, knowing that their duty to the Constitution may require them to place their political preferences aside and obey orders while they are on duty."

"America presently has the smallest number of troops in the Middle East since 1991," Coulter said, launching into his last subject. "Does this mean that our involvement in the region is finally going to end sometime in the foreseeable future?"

Jackson shook his head. "I don't believe so. We have made progress in weaning ourselves from Middle Eastern oil, and President McConnell's insistence on strong anti-terror defenses has kept our Homeland safe these past few years. But, I regret to say, I think that President McConnell's views were short-sighted and isolationist. The goal of radical Islam is world domination—nothing less. Israel, the Palestinians, OPEC pressure on world governments keep oil taxes low, Iran's demand for a seat at the U.N. Security Council—those are simply side issues. Islam seeks dominion. We seek dominion. There may be another collision."

"*We* seek dominion?" Paul asked. "What do you mean by 'dominion'?"

Jackson sighed. "Mr. Coulter, this country was intended to be a dominion of Christ, and for its citizens to be primarily Christian. That's a truth that has been long ignored, suppressed, and scorned by the liberal elites, the media, and the entertainment industry, throughout most of the 20th Century and into the 21st. *We* have been laughed at, called yokels, bigots, crackers, and fascists. Just watch any comedy program on cable or the Web. Who's the butt of the joke? The dumb white Southerner, the crazy born-again, the dopey private soldier, the dim-witted straight guy who can't keep up with his cool gay friends. Who are the bad guys in the conspiracy shows? They used to be Al Qaeda or ISIS—for once Hollywood got something right. Now it's the Christian preacher with sins to hide, the businessman or corporate executive who's always corrupt. But despite the laughter we've had leaders that understood American dominion—Ronald Reagan, George W. Bush. They understood that we had a common purpose, a common identity, as Christian Americans. They understood that the road would be difficult, and that we would have to harden and purify ourselves through sacrifice—including the sacrifices we made in Iraq and Afghanistan to hold Islam at bay. We will probably be called upon again—and the sacrifices might well be much greater next time. We have a common identity and purpose as Americans. And we *will* have a common faith."

Jackson looked at his watch. "Sorry. I'd like to continue this. It's always good to talk to a brother soldier. But I'm due in Atlanta in three hours." Jackson stood, pulled on his suit jacket, and ushered Paul to the door.

Chapter Twenty-Four

The Old Executive Office Building
Washington, D.C.
Monday, September 12
4:45 pm. EDT

Elizabeth Gray closed the door to her office and tossed the short blue jacket from her Army uniform onto the chair beside her desk, glad that the day was nearly done. She blamed the breach of White House protocol on her dry cleaner; in fact, she had worn her uniform for the purpose of playing a small head game with Crane Dunham, the ex-Florida Congressman who had morphed from 1968 draft dodger to right-wing car dealer and politician. During twenty undistinguished years in Congress he had cheerfully voted to send other people's children—never his own—to war not less than four times. Dunham was oblivious to Elizabeth's intended slight. He believed himself, with the touching child-like faith of Congressmen in their own greatness, the perfect man to run Homeland Intelligence despite having no competence or prior interest in domestic security issues.

Despite the aggravation of having to begin Dunham's preparation for the job and his ultimate confirmation hearings at the kindergarten level, Elizabeth was relieved that the world had stayed quiet for once on a Monday—at least so far as anyone knew. The work to restore TriPlex dragged on; the human anti-terror analysts at Liberty Crossing were days behind in satellite intelligence review and weeks behind in translation, and god only knew what was sliding unnoticed through the internet. But nothing had blown up on her watch, and she began to understand Tony Thrace's relief and joy at the passing of every calm day.

At five o'clock, having skipped lunch, Elizabeth had notions of slipping out early to M Street for a drink when she returned from Dunham's EOB office and saw the bulky package waiting on her credenza. Sykes had done his duty, she decided, and she'd better do hers. She ripped open the three inch thick envelope and groaned; having asked for anything and everything that happened at any military installation in Nevada, Texas and New Mexico during the preceding month, she had gotten it. She picked up the phone, asked for one of the Navy stewards to bring her more coffee and a ham and Swiss on rye from the mess, and settled in to read.

An hour and forty minutes later, two-thirds of the way through the stack of reports, she thought she had something.

It was a routine disciplinary report out of Fort Bliss. A base security officer, an army lieutenant named Adam Keeler, had been reported missing on 31 August and was believed AWOL. Keeler had drawn a three day pass on Friday the 26th. A civilian base employee said that he had seen Keeler leave late that night, in uniform fatigues but driving his own car. Reluctant statements taken from Keeler's fellow junior officers had yielded an unconvincing tale involving a romantic triangle with a woman in San Antonio. Most stories like this, Elizabeth knew from experience, ended with the young officer involved returning to base a day or two past orders with head throbbing and tail between legs, to be resolved administratively with reprimands from their company or battalion XO. But there had been no sign of Keeler for nineteen days; his car had not been reported stolen, nor found. The Fort Bliss personnel office had finally called in the C.I.D., inexcusably late, Elizabeth thought, for an Army that had in the wake of withdrawals from Iraq and Afghanistan suffered from elevated rates of depression, PTSD, suicide, and domestic violence.

She accessed Keeler's personnel file from the Army's database and read it on screen, with growing unease. Keeler had three tours in Iraq as a security and intelligence officer with lousy performance ratings: altercations with two enlisted men, fault unclear, and several run-ins with superior officers. In the manpower-short post-war Army he'd been competent enough to keep a job, although the odds against his ever being promoted to Captain were pretty damned long. He'd turned in his most able performance in a recent assignment as a security advisor on a Columbian army base. Elizabeth guessed that weekends in Cartagena or Panama City were probably the best thing that ever happened to Keeler, sexually and otherwise, and had motivated him to get his ass in gear.

She picked up the phone and called Jerry Sykes.

"I got the package," she told him.

"Sorry," Sykes replied, "but you did say you wanted everything."

"No, you got me exactly what I wanted. Have you ever been assigned to Fort Bliss, Jerry? I noticed that we had a junior officer go AWOL from there."

"Once. Six week desert survival course, just what every Navy officer really wants. Why?"

"I've never been assigned there, thank god, even though I grew up only three hundred miles away. What can you tell me about it?"

"Huge. HQ is in the City of El Paso, but the base has facilities and training grounds all over southeastern New Mexico. A lot of it goes back to World War II and Korea."

"This missing lieutenant was a security officer. Do they provide security out of Bliss for any other installations?"

"Three or four active sites, I think. Possibly some inactive or dark stuff. Want me to check?"

"No," she said thoughtfully, "I can do that much myself. I'll be sure to send an email to General Horvath detailing your fast good work, Commander."

"Words from the White House," he responded, "never look bad in the promotion jacket. Thanks, Major."

She turned quickly to the list of off-base installations associated with Fort Bliss, then cross-checked the list against the stack of incident reports Sykes had provided. She found one report dated July 26, the same day Keeler had gone AWOL. The report had been filed by a guard team at the Tularosa Weapons Depot, noting that at the request of the security officer at the Depot a two-truck incursion had been permitted, but that the officer had not returned to the guard post to sign out the trucks upon departure. She squinted to read the blurred print of the report. The security officer who had authorized the trucks' entry was the same missing Lt. Keeler.

Elizabeth finally left her office just before 8 P.M. She grabbed a cab on Constitution Avenue to return to Paul's and, she suddenly realized, her own home again. She ran up the steps and let herself in quietly, knowing that Paul might be writing; his interview with Jackson today was a potential career coup and he would be feeling the stress. She found the door to his writing room closed with a note pinned to the dark varnished wood:

"I will emerge at 9 P.M. looking for food, booze, and your fair naked body."

She smiled to herself. Two of three she could provide; food was impossible. She ordered a pizza and salads from a reasonably good brick oven joint not far away, poured a scotch, peeled out of her sweaty uniform, and dove through the shower. By the time the pizza arrived she smelled much better, had finished a second scotch, and had a mild buzz. Careful, she told herself, alcohol is the Army's functional equivalent of black lung disease. She passed on a third scotch, plated a piece of the pizza and a large chunk of the salad, and poured herself a big glass of mineral water and a half glass of Paul's favorite jug red.

He emerged at nine as promised. She looked at him carefully, as though suddenly afraid she might lose him and have only his memory left to her. Paul's curling brown hair looked grayer at the temples than ever before. She thought again about Paul's standing offer to marry her anytime, anywhere, and began to wonder, with seventeen years in service, whether commanding a battalion was what she really wanted if it meant leaving him again, possibly for good.

"What?" he asked, searching her sober expression. She slipped inside his arms and stuffed a small piece of pizza into his mouth.

"The food part," she responded. Paul simultaneously chewed and laughed, maneuvered around her into the kitchen, got himself a shot of vodka from a bottle in the freezer, and downed it one swallow.

"How was it?" she asked.

"Way complicated," he answered. "Jackson's good—thoughtful, intense and disciplined. He's skilled at using partial truths to evade questions. The interview transcript reads like it was written by a speechwriter—clipped, organized, mostly complete sentences, good grammar. But he's got ideas about the role of the military and religion in government that make me seriously nervous—you'll see that part when I give you the draft."

She nodded, knowing that Paul hated to talk out a story while he was trying to write it. "Have you heard from Graham?" she asked.

"Not a word since Saturday night. Were you able to find out anything?"

"No. Nobody's seen him since he left Panama City."

"Damn."

Elizabeth, standing at the kitchen counter, started to pick at a Caesar salad. Paul filled a plate to take back to his work room but suddenly stopped. "Hey, I've got a question for you. Have you ever seen anything like this?"

He pulled a red felt tip drawing pen from an oversized ceramic coffee cup that held a hundred pens at the end of the kitchen counter, and drew a square symbol on a piece of 3x5 card stock salvaged from their junk drawer.

"Red square on white square field," he continued. "Arrows—darts?—in the midpoint of each line. Makes me think of something like an old log fort from the Indian wars. Something military."

She stared silently at the drawing he had made. "Where did you see this?" she asked slowly.

"That's the weird part. On a lapel pin."

"Who was wearing it?"

"Jackson's chief of staff, named Roy Conover. West Point graduate, mid-thirties, Afghan vet, so GQ he must get looks in the steam room."

"Did he say anything about his pin?" Elizabeth asked.

"I asked him to explain it. He said he was a newbie lieutenant in the 10th Mountain in Afghanistan, and his squad got pinned with their backs against the Kunar River, had to fight their way out. This was their talisman, or something. But after drawing it a couple of times and thinking about it, I have a feeling I've seen this symbol someplace before. Have you?"

"I really don't know what it is." She changed the subject. "Are you done for the night, or is this a guest appearance?"

"Guest. I've got three more hours at least."

"Then I'm going to bed in the next hour, I'm beat."

"Dunham arrive today?"

She nodded.

"Bad?"

"Only if I throw him off the roof of the Eisenhower Building. Which I'm considering."

"Probably not a good career move." Paul reached around her for his plate of pizza, poured himself a water glass of red wine. "I'm going back to it. Forgive me?"

"Make millions and get a job on MSNBC."

"Okay." He kissed her. "I'll try not to wake you when I come in." He smiled. "I am so...you're here and that's all that matters."

She kissed him back. "Go. Be brilliant."

Elizabeth sat upright in bed, her laptop plugged into the hardwired and encrypted broadband internet connection that Paul had installed when he bought the apartment.

She logged in to the Army's secure military history website. Within four minutes she had found a reference to Conover's story in the Army's still classified day by day chronology of the Afghan War, keyed to a detailed after-action report. In November 2007 a

10th Mountain Division intelligence squad monitoring the Pakistan border had been pinned down on a high escarpment in the Hindu Kush by a Taliban force with five times their number. The mountain storms had been so fierce that neither Blackhawks nor the twin rotor Chinooks could fly in to evacuate the troops. Combat air support was committed elsewhere. The squad was saved only when a specially modified Dark/Star Apache intercepted their distress calls and drove the Taliban back over the ridge, enabling the unit to hold out until morning.

Elizabeth scrolled through the names of the soldiers involved in the action. The squad's medic had been replaced by Staff Sergeant Carlotta Johnson, who had been wounded by sniper fire in the opening skirmish with the Taliban that night. Elizabeth verified Johnson's social security number (soldiers' personnel files and dog tags had carried the SSN rather than a separate military ID since the mid-1960s) and matched her name and the number to the power of attorney that Harland Boyd had signed at his bank in suburban Virginia. Finally, she looked up Boyd's service record: he too had been assigned to the 10th Mountain's Firebase Oneida, its primary outpost in Nuristan, as its chief operating engineer.

Elizabeth dug deeper, into the individual statements about the engagement attached to the formal after-action report. The gunner of the Dark/Star chopper explained the decision to separately evacuate Carlotta Johnson and praised the poise and courage of the young Lieutenant Conover and his squad as they held their piece of frozen mountain dirt until morning. His statement was given great weight when he turned out to be the legendary Kyle Hunter Jackson.

Elizabeth thought back to her own memories of the cold barren mountains of Afghanistan and understood. "So that's how it started," she whispered, speaking only to herself in the dark.

She had one last thing to check. She returned to the DOD secure database and went through a long tiresome clearance protocol and was finally logged on. She searched for "Tularosa Weapons Depot—assigned mission". Her eyes widened as the screen slammed shut on her request, the query page replaced by the word 'DENIED' in 24 point font. She would have a call tomorrow morning from Pentagon security by 0600. Why? The only aspect of the entire military establishment that she did not have clearance for was nuclear.

In the morning, Elizabeth Grey canceled her appointments and slipped out of the apartment early, walking four blocks east to pick up a Zipcar from a parking lot behind Eastern Market. She selected an anonymous Chevy hybrid and forced her way through inner Washington's dense traffic to Interstate 66, heading southwest. Traffic thinned after she crossed the Beltway and finally passed the last cut-off roads to Dulles Airport. She found the right street in Manassas less than an hour and half after leaving the District.

The townhouse in the 8700 block of Bretton Woods Drive in Manassas was about forty years old. The cosmetic brick facade on the lower level and the clapboard on the exterior walls of the second floor both indicated that it had been built during a neo-colonial revival in the 1980s. The area seemed tired but the homeowners, largely retired military, worked hard at it: paint was new, roofs were clean, yards were trimmed, and the neighborhood, not far from Bull Run Regional Park, was holding its own.

Elizabeth parked in front and approached the front door. The door was locked and there was no answer to repeated knocks, but the view in the living room window showed that the owner had not been gone long: a laptop was open on a desk placed behind the living room sofa, a coffee carafe beside it.

Elizabeth was startled by the sound of a woman calling out, "Hey there!" She turned to find an African-American woman in her sixties standing on the porch of the house next door, a watering hose in her hand. "Can I help you?" the woman asked, her voice polite but suspicious.

"I'm looking for Carlotta Johnson," she said. "Is this her house?"

"Sure is. But I don't think she'll be back for a while."

"Why's that?"

"Well, she left this morning, about an hour ago. Two men helped her with her bags, and they drove off."

"In Carlotta's car?"

The neighbor woman looked momentarily troubled. "No. Not her car."

"Did she talk to you as she left?"

"No, I was inside, just happened to look out the window."

"Do you know the men she left with? Have you ever seen them before?"

"Can't say. Possible they were friends of Harland. He'd been Carlotta's man for some years, but he passed a couple weeks ago. Terrible car crash, but in a way it was a blessing for them both, he was so sick with the cancer, but he worked right to the very end."

Elizabeth nodded sympathetically. "Yes, I heard about Sergeant Boyd, and wanted to offer Carlotta my condolences. I'm Major Elizabeth Gray, by the way." She crossed through the yard to offer the woman her hand.

"Marian Langston," the older woman replied, smiling. In this neighborhood Gray's uniform was her friend. "I'll tell Carlotta you called for her."

"Please do," Elizabeth said, smiling while she calculated the value of attempting a small lie. "We're going to miss him," she added. "Last time I saw him was in New Mexico."

"Harland liked it out there. New Mexico and Nevada. Said the dry air was good for his lungs. He worked three or four long jobs. Worried Carlotta some, his being gone, but he always came back a little stronger."

Gray smiled. "A good soldier. Thanks for your time," she added, heading for her car.

She would have the FBI at the Marian Langston's door within the hour. But before calling Cable Hollings she paused behind the steering wheel and opened a bulky looking portable phone, one that was routed through a Pentagon satellite, not the local cell network. She punched in numbers, waited for the encryption protocol to negotiate entry into the system.

"Duty station," a gruff voice answered.

"General Horvath, please. Major Elizabeth Gray."

Elizabeth waited again while her identification and the security status of her phone were verified.

"Horvath."

"General? Major Gray. I think there's a problem in New Mexico."

Chapter Twenty-Five

The Center for American Military Information
1106 24th St. NW
Washington, D.C.
Wednesday, September 14
9:00 A.M. EDT

"Paul, I just can't do it." Arne Kaplan sat hunched forward, elbows on his cluttered desk, his third monstrously large paper cup of black coffee of the morning clutched in one hand. The morning was cloudy and Kaplan's close-cropped hair was iron gray in the dim light. "I won't go on record, even on background, when everything I know is based on hearsay."

"Arne," Paul said, trying to keep the tinge of desperation out of his voice, "I'm on deadline. "I've got to get this piece in by the 16th, Graham is still missing. Jackson's confirmation vote is on the 20th. Don't you think the country has a right to know that the man the Congress is voting to confirm as Vice-President has a history of challenging civilian control of the military?"

"That wasn't what those officers were doing during the Clinton impeachment, Paul. They weren't challenging civilian control; they were issuing a political challenge, based on their version of personal morality, to a sitting President."

"It amounts to the same thing," Paul shot back. "Let's say the whole officer corps had made the demand, and Clinton told them to piss up a rope. What was next? Having the Third Infantry take down the Secret Service on the White House lawn?"

Kaplan leaned back in his chair, spread his arms and opened his hands. "I repeat myself," he said, exasperated. "I called thirteen people I knew in senior rank in 1998. Nobody would admit or confirm anything. I even called General Nakasone, the Army chief who cracked down on those officers. He would not say a word. Nor has turning eighty improved the legendary General Jack's sense of humor, I might add."

"So where does that leave me?"

"You or the country? Make up your mind."

"The country, then."

"The country's fine. It leaves you with no story. But options you still have."

"You're being cryptic. Yoda did the talking backwards thing better, without the Bronx accent."

Kaplan grinned. "The goyim I put up with," he responded. "You know what it means. Go talk to Ben Giles' people. Get their opposition research. Ben must have heard about this."

Paul met Jeff Riordan for lunch on the garden patio of the Tabard Inn. The brick-floored walled garden was still summery, and the waiter seated them at a table beneath a patio umbrella to shield them from the autumn sun that had broken through the clouds the hour before.

"Thanks for meeting me, Jeff," Coulter grumbled. "But why the Tabard? We could have taken out an announcement on WaPo or Politico that told everyone we were tying the knot and invited all comers to the wedding."

"Nonsense," Reardon said. His gaunt visage and papery skin made him look older than his fifty years. He was a Washington mandarin of the first order, a Yale-educated K Street lawyer of independent means and a long time senior adviser to House Speaker Miranda Cardwell. Cardwell had given Reardon leave to join the Giles/Kraft campaign. Whatever blood Ben Giles had drawn from her during the Democratic primary campaign had been forgiven and forgotten; the Speaker now wanted to get even with James Robinson and Royce Reed. Robinson and Reed had turned the votes of three born-again Blue-Dog Democrats in the House of Representatives away from Cardwell, swinging two states and electing McConnell in the last election. Reardon, the Speaker's sword arm, had personally arranged Cardwell's revenge on the apostate Blue Dogs. Each had faced well funded primary opponents in the following mid-terms. The two that survived their primaries drew independent candidates in the fall that split the fragile moderate vote in their districts; they lost by double digit margins. The shock that greeted the three defeated Congressmen when they tried to get jobs in D.C. was much worse; they would have no place in the Washington Club. The Speaker had declared all three radioactive: Democratic congressmen would not see them; staffers would hang up the phone on any government agency or lobbying firm that employed them; the caucus would vote as one against any bill they were associated with. Reardon had personally delivered the news to each man that life as each knew it was over: they should sell insurance, or cars, or stocks and bonds, but never, ever think about politics again. One, from Nashville, sought election to the City Council there and found that seven primary opponents and a well funded personal morals investigation had been arranged to welcome him home. He was selling second-hand Fords three months later. The McConnell White House never admitted to conceding the Speaker her revenge but was deaf to the Blue Dogs' pleas that they had delivered McConnell the Presidency and then been sold out.

"The whole town knows you got the only detailed print interview Jackson has given prior to the confirmation vote," Reardon said, looking around for a waiter. "So I'm not surprised to see you following up and asking what we've got."

"I'm asking, but I'm not selling the transcript to you," Coulter replied.

"We already have it," Reardon replied serenely. "Nor did we have to burgle for it, Paul. The White House can't keep anything secret because too many people with access there believe Charlie McConnell never died. Tell the *Atlantic* to publish quick before we post it on the Web."

Reardon picked up his menu, gestured impatiently to a passing waiter, and ordered a half-dozen Maine oysters and the salmon with an Oregon Pinot Noir. Paul grimly stuck to his diet and ordered salad with grilled chicken. He wondered how a man could eat as well as Reardon did without having any perceptible body fat at all.

The wine arrived. Reardon looked at Paul inquisitively. "And so, Paul? What do you really want?"

Coulter hesitated. "First, a question: What do you know about Jackson's military career and the reasons behind his resignation?"

"Not enough," Reardon admitted. "What are you suggesting?"

"There was a group of military officers during Bill Clinton's impeachment trial that prepared and circulated an open letter demanding Clinton's resignation. They might have taken some further steps towards building an organization to confront Clinton politically. But the Army Chief of Staff at the time, General Nakasone, got wind of it. He sacked the officers. All of them"

"Jackson was among this group?"

"A leader, I suspect. Jackson admits to having agreed with the demand that Clinton resign in my interview with him."

"And this goes where? Reardon asked, tasting the pinot noir and nodding to the waiter. "There were very many people in politics who thought Clinton should have resigned, including many of us on the left who thought that a President Al Gore would then have won the 2000 election with fair ease."

"That's not the point," Coulter replied. "To have a military officer, or group of officers, especially those of relatively senior rank intervening in politics is something that has never been accepted in this country. George Washington set the precedent at Newburgh, New York, in 1783, when he faced down a potential insurrection from his own officers against the Continental Congress."

Reardon ate his oysters and pondered. "You want our opposition research."

"Right," Coulter responded. "You've always done first rate opposition research, Jeff. I'm one guy, and I need a second source on this. You have fifteen, maybe twenty people in the Giles/Kraft campaign doing a work up on Jackson. You have a lot of retired senior military who are supporting Ben Giles. The vote is coming down on September 20, but there hasn't been a leak, a squeak, from your guys about...let's call it a most unusual vice-presidential choice."

"Unusual?" Reardon asked, laughing. "You're missing a rich history. William Rufus Devane King, the largest slaveholder in America. Chester Alan Arthur, the most corrupt man in New York. Henry Wallace, a serious leftie who practiced spiritualism and searched for the lost kingdom of Shambhala. Imagine what Fox could have done with *that*."

Coulter dropped his fork and pushed his tasteless lunch aside. "*Unusual* is a polite term for dangerous. Jackson is a man who believes that the military has a permanent Constitutional and political role in running the government. I don't think he'd be afraid to exercise that role if he thought it was necessary to preserving his notion of a Christian America." Coulter's frustration boiled over. "Damn it, Jeff, we've known each other for nearly twenty years. You're deflecting me. What's really going on here?"

"Paul, why should I leak you our opposition research? You're not a member of the Club anymore; the web and cable have pretty much cast you aside. Your social media presence is non-existent. And you're a conservative at heart, Charlie McConnell's old friend. If I was going to do favors for anyone on this, I'd do them for a reporter that...had significant media heft and would be more reliably favorable."

Coulter glared, stung by what Riordan had said. "Fine, I'm not big enough for you. But you haven't given your research to anyone. What are you holding back? The vote's a week away. If Congress puts Jackson into the Vice-President's chair, it also puts him into the National Command Authority. Do you understand the implications of that?"

"I think we've got a pretty good handle on military issues, Paul, given that our nominee is a retired Lieutenant General."

"What are you holding back?" Coulter insisted

Reardon finished his fish. "The man has some...connections we can exploit. Disclosure will have much more impact in the general election campaign. Robinson and Jackson are no threat, Paul. They have less than four months in their term of office. The military seems pretty calm. And that's really all I'm going to say."

"You don't get it, Jeff," Coulter said. "When it comes to military issues you're like ninety-nine per cent of Congress, the bureaucracy, the political and media elite. You wouldn't know one end of an M4 carbine from the other, because you've never been there. You've just paid poor people to do the dirty work for you."

Coulter grabbed the lunch tab, shoved his chair back so hard that it scraped on the brick floor of the garden with an audible crack, and stalked away.

Arne Kaplan looked surprised when Coulter braced him late that afternoon as Kaplan stepped on to the 20th Street sidewalk behind the imposing four story brick building housing George Washington University Law School, where Kaplan taught a seminar in National Security law. Kaplan was an approachable and genial man, but no man or woman who had served as a general officer expected to have to say no twice, on any subject.

"Paul? We're done with this," he said, exasperated.

"I'm not asking again about 1998, Arne," Coulter replied. "This is something else, something I should have shown you before."

"All right," Kaplan said. "One more question."

Coulter produced his drawing of the symbol he had seen on Roy Conover's lapel, the square with points on each side. He handed it to Kaplan. "Do you recognize this? It's military, I think."

Kaplan squinted at the card in his hand. "Can't say it looks familiar. Where'd you see it?"

"On the lapel of Jackson's Chief of Staff, an Afghanistan vet."

"Did he explain it?"

"Said it was made up after his observation post was attacked and his unit had to fight off the Taliban until morning."

"Lots of small unit fights in Afghanistan. He tell you when this happened?"

"No. It's not the fight, it's the symbol. I can't help feeling I've seen it somewhere before, and it's got something to do with Jackson. Some kind of military group he was or is affiliated with."

Kaplan frowned, and then shrugged. "Ok. I'll check it out with some people who have a fetish about this kind of military symbolism. It's a long shot, though. See if you can find me something more to go on."

Paul locked himself into the Friedheim Library in the National Press Club building, getting special permission from the library director to remain past hours. He left a message for Elizabeth and brought with him a pair of sandwiches and a large coffee from the Potbelly Sandwich Works on 14th and New York, hoping it would not take all night to find what he was looking for, but prepared for the worst.

He found it around 1:30 A.M., in archival footage from WNCN, the NBC news affiliate in Raleigh, North Carolina. They had covered a Jackson reelection campaign appearance at the annual Fort Bragg Fair in Fayetteville. The sound portion of the story had been lost when it had been converted to an MPEG but the visuals were crisp. It was a fine sunny late spring day and Jackson, dressed in a tan suit, white shirt, and blue tie had been doing his best to work the supportive crowd, mostly soldiers and their families, the human side of politics not his strength. Paul caught it in the close-up, when Jackson had paused to be interviewed by a young woman from the WNCN outlet, her cameraman catching him close and square from the chest up. He had two pins in his lapels. One was the obligatory American flag. The other depicted a red square on a white field, with spear points on each side.

Chapter Twenty-Six

Stanton Square
Capitol Hill District
Washington D.C.
Thursday, September 15
3:35 A.M. EDT

The cop who picked up Paul Coulter at his apartment in the middle of the night drove him in silence six blocks to the edge of Stanton Square, the juncture of Massachusetts and Maryland Avenues five blocks northeast of the Capitol. Paul sat rigidly in the back seat of the squad car, his mind frozen with fear. Graham Taylor had had not yet called him. And Graham lived on the top floor of a three story townhouse near 7ᵗʰ Street NE, just a quarter mile away.

The young patrolman escorted Coulter through the dark humid night to a group of men and women huddled at the side of the square, away from the heroic equestrian statue of Nathanael Greene, a Rhode Island Quaker and one of the more gifted and least political generals in the American Revolution. Temporary work lights had been set up, mounted on eight foot stands, the light focused down on to an object hidden by the milling group of people. As Coulter approached a middle-aged African American woman with short cropped hair stepped away from the group. She was tall, about five eleven, and strongly built. She wore dark slacks and a white shirt, her jacket discarded on the hot night, her brassard and gun clipped to her belt.

"I'm Lieutenant Elder, D.C. Homicide," she said, unsmiling but extending her hand. "You're Paul Coulter?"

"Yes. Is this about Graham Taylor—"

"I'm sorry, yes it is. He's dead." Elder's voice was low, precise, and unemotional. "Mr. Taylor was shot twice in the back and then once in the head with a small caliber weapon, perhaps a .22, almost certainly silenced. We think the shooting took place shortly after midnight. No one in the nearby homes or apartments heard the gun. He was found at approximately two-thirty by a couple from the neighborhood whose air-conditioning had broken down and decided to take a walk."

Coulter closed his eyes and clenched his jaw and said nothing for a moment. "May I see him?" he asked.

"We should have the crime scene worked up within another ten minutes," Elder replied. "Let me ask you a few questions." She guided him away at a slow pace, toward the other side of the square.

"How did you find me so quickly?" Coulter asked. His eyes still burned from the long night at the Friedheim Library; when the police had knocked he had been asleep on the living room sofa to avoid waking Elizabeth.

"Your name was on the medical consent card in Mr. Taylor's wallet," she responded. "You related, involved, what?"

"Graham was my friend," Coulter said. "We met during the First Iraq War. He was a Major in the British Army, their Special Air Services unit—like our Special Forces. I was a 19 year old Marine. Dumb as a brick. There was a card game, and Graham took every last dime I had. Then he stood me to a drink from the illegal still that the Brits had set up in their base, and slipped my cash back to me. We've been friends ever since. I've never had a better friend."

"What kind of work did Taylor do?"

"He was a historian. He'd retired from the British Army, took a Master's in history at Cambridge, then a PhD at the University of Virginia. He taught history at American University. He was also a journalist, wrote books and essays, and covered political events."

"And what do you do?" Elder continued. Coulter was grateful for the numbing repetition of her questions, which gave him purchase on his grief and enabled him to keep it suppressed, if only for the moment.

"I'm White House Correspondent for Pacific News and the Coastal Press Consortium—what's left of the big newspapers on the West Coast—The Seattle *Times*, the Portland *Oregonian*, the San Francisco *Chronicle*, the Los Angeles *Times*." He fumbled for the White House press pass in his wallet, presented it for her inspection.

She took it, looked it over with the aid of her pocket flash, and returned it, unimpressed. "Why would Taylor be out in Stanton Square at midnight?" she asked.

Coulter hesitated, and then told her the truth. "He might've just flown back into D.C. tonight," he responded. "He'd been traveling. Ever since his wife died, Graham's had a terrible problem with sleep. Traveling, working extra long days—those kinds of things made it worse for him. When he couldn't sleep, he walked. Sometimes he walked all night, and then would walk another five miles after breakfast before going to his office."

"Do you know where he was returning from?" Elder asked.

Coulter paused again. "Could I have three minutes to think about that?" he responded. "We were working on a story together. I don't think I have any information from him about confidential sources, but I need a couple of minutes to think. My brain's not working well right now."

Elder turned slightly and saw that the Medical Examiner's field team was beginning to take down their lights. An ambulance backed slowly into the Square, to retrieve Graham Taylor's body. She tipped her head toward the scene. "Come on. It's a lousy way to say goodbye to a friend. But it's better than not saying good-bye at all."

They walked towards Graham's body. Elder nodded her head, and an M.E. technician raised the shroud. The final wound was on the right side of Graham' head, a coup de grace shot taken after he had been driven to the pavement by the first shots in his back. Tears flooded Coulter's eyes and he turned away as Graham's body was loaded into the waiting ambulance. The thought that flashed through his mind was the prayer that his platoon leader in First Iraq had muttered every time their company had suffered a casualty.

"Dear God," the Sergeant prayed. "Please help us find the motherfuckers that did this. So that we can use knives. Amen."

It was after four in the morning by the time Paul Coulter guided Lee Elder to Graham's townhouse at 635 Acker Place, a quiet tree-lined lane between E and F streets just east of 7th Street NE. It was a three-and-a half story red brick row house that Anna Taylor, blessed with a bit of family money, had purchased for them after marrying Graham at the University of Virginia in 1997. The Taylors had lived in the top floor flat and built an eight hundred square foot duplex upper story on the roof, with a walled garden deck on the south side of the structure. Since Anna's death Graham had lived in that rooftop studio, with a kitchenette, a single bathroom, and a small living room that was mostly office—the home of a man who seldom received visitors. Money had grown tight, and Graham had leased out the three main floors and the basement apartment to a small law firm that did tax, estate and probate work—the ideal tenants, as Graham pointed out, because they went home at six o'clock each night and almost all of their clients were dead.

"So there was a security system?" Elder asked.

"There was, but it was installed and maintained by the law firm," Coulter responded as he let them into the front door, which opened into an elevator vestibule. He showed her the law firm's lighted security panel, at the left side of the French door entrance to their office. "The elevator was keyed, and Graham and I had the only keys to the roof level." He inserted his key, switched on the elevator power, and pulled the door open, ushering Elder inside. They rose with a jolt, passed the entrance to the law firm's upper floor offices, and waited as the elevator settled into its place on the roof level. Coulter pulled the door open.

The inner door to Graham's apartment had been smashed, as if with a fire ax.

"Jesus," Coulter exclaimed. "Who hit this place?"

Elder put a finger to her lips, pulled her nine millimeter side arm, racked it, and slid inside to clear the apartment. When she returned she took two sealed packets containing powder free latex gloves from her pants pocket and handed one to Coulter. "Put them on. Now," she ordered.

Coulter complied. "What am I looking for?"

"For now, concentrate on what's missing. I'll have my back-up do a complete search and contents inventory when he comes on duty at seven."

Coulter followed her through the studio he knew so well. Graham's desk, in the rear of the studio overlooking the roof top garden deck, was covered in its usual messy swarm of books, journals, and print-outs from various blogs and web pages, but Graham's laptop was gone. He checked the luggage that Graham had dumped at the foot of his bed, but the laptop bag was empty, and the suitcase contained only Graham's used linen.

"His computer's gone, for starters," Coulter replied. "And the safe...Coulter opened a large storage closet in the bathroom that contained shelves for towels and linens, a small stacked washer and dryer, and, nearly invisible behind a jumble of vacuum, broom and cleaning utensils, a small home safe mounted between the studs of the wall. The safe had been found. It was gone, pried from the wall with a heavy steel bar.

"Did Taylor keep money or valuables in there?" Elder asked.

Coulter laughed briefly. "He had precious little of either. He spent a million dollars on his wife's medical care after their insurance ran out, went heavily into debt. He couldn't abide having Anna's jewelry in the house after she died, and gave it away to her nieces. He didn't own a car. The house was mortgaged. The only things of any value that he owned were a computer, a wedding ring, a Rolex diving watch, and—

Coulter rushed to Graham's bedside table and opened the top drawer. The weapons box was intact; by weight Coulter could tell that it still held Graham's Glock semi-automatic pistol and at least two clips of ammunition, a prize an ordinary thief would not have missed.

"Graham was out for a walk," Coulter finally said, straightening up and closing the drawer of the bedside table. "Whoever trashed this place was watching the house and knew he was out. They tossed it, then went looking for him on the streets."

Elder nodded. "Ok, he's home from a trip, too tired to sleep. So where was Taylor coming home from? And what was he doing?"

"He was in Grand Cayman, then in Panama."

"The boarding pass stub we found in his pants pocket was from a U.S. Airways flight from Nassau, Bahamas direct to Reagan National. That was the flight he came in on tonight. The plane landed at 9:30. Why didn't he call you?"

"I don't know. He might just have been waiting for morning."

"I'm assuming he didn't go to the Caribbean in the middle of hurricane season just to snorkel."

Coulter took a breath. "No. He was working for me."

"Doing what?"

"We were writing a biographical, political piece together. On the Republican nominee for Vice-President, Kyle Jackson."

"What does that have to do with the Caribbean?"

"Jackson purchased his military contracting company, Dark/Star, with money he raised offshore. As it turned out Graham knew one of the people involved, a former officer in the British Army. Graham flew to Grand Cayman to see that man ten days ago. He said he was intercepted in the Caymans by a CIA agent and flew to Panama City at the agent's direction. That's all I know. I've been half crazy worrying about him and half crazy trying to get the project done without him."

"Why would you worry about him?"

Paul looked away. "Graham drank. Especially in the fall—his wife died in September, six years ago. He barely ate. He had chronic bronchitis and asthma and still smoked."

"Did you think what he was investigating was dangerous?"

"Not at the time. We thought there might possibly be a financial scandal involving Jackson. But people don't get killed for those things."

"Well," Elder drawled, "you might be surprised on that one. I think that your friend was pretty clearly hit by somebody who knew what he was doing. And in this town that probably means it wasn't sex or money, it was power. So I have, Mr. Coulter, the proverbial case from hell that's going to fuck me up with interference from every kind of black suit, no-we're-not-really-here federal agency that you can imagine. I've been on duty for eleven hours. I know a 24 hour diner, not far away, where the hash browns are good and the grits are even better. While we are eating you will tell me everything you know about Graham Taylor and why someone might want to kill him. I'll flip you for the check."

Coulter did not reply. He took a final look around Graham's messy, lonely aerie. Then he put his face in hands and wept.

The *Atlantic* was good to him. They accepted the interview, his introduction, and his memorial comments about Graham Taylor, and published it all on their website on the 18th. They paid only half, but Coulter was in no position to argue. The piece would go to actual print in the November issue, with Graham's name first on their byline.

Coulter arranged for Graham Taylor to be cremated and his ashes joined with his wife in her family ground in rural Anne Arundel County, Maryland, with services to follow.

The Washington D.C. police reported that they had been unable to question Cayman Islands banker Barnes Powell, who had drowned in his pool on Seven Mile Beach two days before Graham had returned to Washington.

Elizabeth Gray stayed close to Paul Coulter, made sure she came home every night, held him, slept with him, made love with him, and tried very hard to say little as Coulter alternated, as he needed to do, between grief and anger.

On Monday, September 20, despite the heated objections of Senator Ben Giles, Kyle Jackson was confirmed as Vice-President of the United States, by close votes of 219-216 in the House, and 51-49 in the Senate.

Chapter Twenty-Seven

Fairchilds, LLP
555 13th St. N.W.
Washington, D.C.
Wednesday, September 28
10:30 A.M. EDT

"Mr. Coulter?" I'm Lonny Sanderson, managing partner of this office. I was terribly sorry to hear about Graham. I appreciate your coming down here."

Paul Coulter rose from a low couch in the sleekly modern, marble floored lobby of Fairchilds' Washington branch office. "Thank you," he responded politely, extending his hand, "but I don't know what this about, Mr. Sanderson."

Sanderson was about six feet tall, with graying, carefully styled sandy hair, a tanned jowly face, and linebacker shoulders that, combined with good tailoring, distracted attention from his comfortable belly. They shook hands and Paul experienced a subtle pull toward the double glass doors at the far side of the lobby that opened to a wing of offices set along a tall hallway walled with legal books. "Best we discuss this in my office."

Three minutes later they were seated at a small teak conference table in an office surprisingly free of clutter and paper. Sanderson's glass topped desk contained only four files, arrayed in the order of his appointments. One old fashioned red cardboard folio, the kind with a flap closure tied off by a string, lay in the center of the conference table.

"How long had you known Graham, Mr. Sanderson?" Coulter asked.

"Call me Lonny," the lawyer replied, his Georgia accent thickening. "Long time. As you know, Graham was detached to MI-6 during parts of his military career. And, well let's just say we met while I was a United States Government employee with offices in Langley."

Sanderson put on his reading glasses and opened the file. "Did Graham ever mention Annabelle, Limited, to you?"

"No," Coulter replied. "His late wife's name was Anna. She was from an old Maryland family. Graham used to tease her by calling her Annabelle."

"That would explain it. Annabelle, Ltd. is a Guernsey limited liability company. Our Guernsey office incorporated it five years ago. It has two shareholders. One was Graham, the other is you. I'm the secretary and general counsel. On behalf of the company, do you have dollar?"

"A dollar?"

"A formality."

Coulter fished a dollar coin out of his change and examined it. "Millard Fillmore. Not a very auspicious omen."

Sanderson chuckled as he accepted the coin. "Legal tender, no matter how bad a president is on the coin. I'll forward this dollar to Graham's executor—which is me, and I'll be sure to give myself a receipt. You are now the sole owner of Annabelle Ltd. and all its assets, Paul." Sanderson slid the cardboard folio to Coulter.

Coulter looked puzzled, untwisted the string, and opened the portfolio. It contained about three dozen old fashioned DVD-ROM disks and a half dozen flash drives in small envelopes. There were also two DHL Express Courier envelopes, unopened. They had been sent from Nassau, Bahamas on September 14.

"You're Graham's dead drop," Coulter said.

Sanderson nodded. "If you want to keep something private, there's few better ways than wrapping it in an offshore corporation with 'offices' inside a twelve hundred lawyer London-based law firm. Per Graham's instructions, our tech people made two copies of everything he ever sent in to me. One set is here for you. One set is in our Washington wills and trusts vault. The third set is in Guernsey. The new materials haven't been copied—we didn't receive them until after Graham was dead. It's my fault we didn't get you in here sooner—I was in Shanghai, and my staff missed it. Under the circumstances I thought you might want to see what's in there before we copied anything. I've had them set up a sanitized laptop, not connected to our network, in the conference room next door. Let me know what you want to do when you've finished viewing the contents." Sanderson stood up to show Coulter the way. "With any luck," he added, "this will help you get the fuckers."

Arne Kaplan sat behind his desk and stared at the screen of Paul's laptop, transfixed by Graham Taylor's haggard image, recorded by his laptop cam in a dreary room in the Towne Hotel just off Bay Street in downtown Nassau.

"Paul," Graham began, his face slightly distorted by the cam's fishbowl lens effect, "this is a summary of what I've found. The two other flash drives contain .pdf images of the documents I was allowed to copy, my handwritten notes summarizing what I couldn't copy, and my summaries of my interviews. I've tried to double source every statement I received on background, but it's been damned hard to get people to talk."

Graham took a swallow of rum from a glass resting on a rickety bamboo side table, and then continued. "The key to this goes back to Jackson's acquisition of all of Dark/Star in 2001. The buyout funds came from a private equity partnership structured by Barnes Powell, my former officer, then an investment banker at Merrill Lynch's Miami office. The entire ownership not remaining with Jackson and his family was transferred to two Cayman Island Trusts, the Corinthian Trust and the Dominion Trust. The beneficiaries of those trusts are four separate Panamanian corporations, referred to, none too imaginatively, as Omega One, Omega Two, Omega Three, and Omega Four. Each corporation paid for and held twelve percent of the beneficial ownership interest in Dark/Star via the Trusts. Those four corporations had no real existence outside of the offices of Morgan Suarez, a Panamanian law firm. But the source of funds they used to purchase their pieces of Dark/Star was quite interesting. Each issued convertible corporate notes in Panama that were privately sold to four different American corporate investors: Regency Medallion Insurance, Masterworks Media, Brookside Properties, and NetShare Telecomm. All four purchasing companies are subsidiaries of Royce Reed's various private holding companies. When the time came to sell Dark/Star to Cornwall Group, the American companies sold their notes to a new Panamanian company owned by the Corinthian and Dominion trusts, at par. It converted their notes to stock and took control of the Cayman Trusts, which received the buyout payments and equity interest in Cornwall. Later, very quietly, the Corinthian and Dominion Trusts conveyed their assets to a successor offshore trust, Revelation Trust, and were themselves dissolved. Royce Reed and his companies thus avoided paying capital gains taxes on about four hundred million dollars in profit. Apparently Reverend Reed's theology accepts manna from Heaven, but God forbids that it be taxed. "

Graham paused again, lit a Dunhill, and said waspishly, "I can hear you bitching about the cigarette, Paul, but the fact of the matter is that if you're watching this, then smoking didn't kill me after all." He took another sip of his drink. "I couldn't have found out anything beyond the initial funding of Dark/Star but for the fact that there was an enormous American financial intelligence operation being conducted in the Caribbean and in Panama. One of its targets was Royce Reed. According to the Treasury and intelligence officials in Panama City, Reed has been skimming from the collection plate since Christian Nation was founded in 1994. Collection plate dollars go to Reed's companies to pay for goods and services that aren't delivered, fees that aren't real, expenses that aren't incurred. Charlie McConnell's Justice Department went after him…and turned up the rest of the story of how Reed funded Dark/Star. The indictment was prepared and ready to go to a special Grand Jury sitting in Miami when the new acting Attorney General, Ramon Acosta, stopped it. According to the woman heading up the Panama operation, a lawyer and IRS Special Agent named Karen Jenkins, they were ordered to shut down the operation the day that Robinson and Jackson were nominated at the Republican Convention.

"I tried to find out more about the Cornwall Group. It is smaller than Carlyle or Blackstone or the other major private equity groups, and nastier, much more opaque. Dark/Star, ostensibly a North Carolina corporation but that is actually controlled though a second holding company, known as Triad LLC, comprises about forty-five per cent of Cornwall's holdings and revenues. Cornwall's arms manufacturers—Dnieper Design Group in Ukraine, PKI in Indonesia, Nordic Resources in Norway, PRL in Poland, Carter Arms Limited, in South Africa—all focus on small and medium arms, light artillery, ground to air missiles, short range ground to ground missiles—in short, the least regulated part of the military arms market. That's about another thirty per cent of their revenues. The remainder is banking, real estate, and oil and natural gas around the world. They finance their acquisitions through equity and their majority ownership of Bank Royal in Panama. The best guess of the financial experts in the task force here is that if Jackson's trusts, which own most of Triad, and Reed's Revelation Trust pool their interests, they effectively control Cornwall. The other investors are international—and are mostly politically connected, especially in Europe and the Mideast. Since Cornwall is totally offshore and entirely private, under 300 investors for American rules, there is no public reporting at all."

"So Cornwall, together with Bank Royal, acts like a kind of big revolver fund. Government dollars paid to Dark/Star and to their arms manufacturers are recycled into oil investments, and in turn petro-dollars from the Gulf States and South Asia flow back in to be invested. There have an enormous capability to move money, with Bank Royal acting as conduit. That's what has the American intelligence agencies scared shitless. They've been watching the money flows. Some of it they can see—but a lot of it they can't. It can take weeks for the FINCEN money laundering analysts to reconstruct a series of transactions that moves as little as $50,000."

Graham took a last drag and stubbed out his cigarette. "Final developments. Things got a little more alarming when I learned that Jenkins' tax people weren't the only ones down here. I knew that CIA would be here—it always helps to use your intelligence agencies offshore when you're chasing tax elephants to cover the budget. But it's not just CIA, it's also Homeland Intelligence. There was talk in Panama that money is flowing into some kind of *sub rosa* group inside the U.S. The dollar flow is increasing. Drastically. Six months ago there were perhaps a million black dollars a month flowing back into the U.S. and landing...somewhere. In the past thirty days it's apparently increased to a rate of twelve million dollars a month—and yet the Robinson administration is still shutting this task force down."

Graham looked drawn. "I'm sorry, Paul. The best that I could do— I know it's going to take too long to verify all this into a well documented story that can be published before the Jackson vote. My only thought is that we might try to take this directly to Senator Giles. It might square up with things they know—or at least they can use it to slow down the confirmation hearings, put it over until after the election."

Graham took a final sip of rum. "It's fascinating. Nobody really knows—or will admit—what the hell goes on down here once the money begins to move around. There are new pirates and new pirate nations. China, Indonesia, Nigeria, Brazil and Russia are all willing to do business with the rogue banks down here. It's going to be a dangerous world." He sighed. "I'm looking forward to coming home. Will Elizabeth be there when I get back? I'd like that, for both your sakes."

Taylor reached forward to shut off the web cam. The computer screen went black. Arne Kaplan looked at Paul, as if making a decision.

"There's a guy," Kaplan finally said. "He's in Minnesota. I think you need to talk to him. I think you should go as soon you can."

Cass Lake

Chapter Twenty-Eight

It had taken Coulter all of Thursday and most of Friday morning to write the backlog of stories and blog posts that had piled up in his paralysis after Graham's death. The White House itself was relatively quiet as the news operations shifted to the campaign. Mitchell Garson's daily briefing had been transferred to Air Force One, which the AP pool reporter would report for Pacific News. By one o'clock on Friday Coulter was able to catch a Delta flight to Minneapolis, where he rented a car and headed northwest on I-94 before turning due north on State Highway 71 at Sauk Centre. He chose the route for sentimental reasons: it would take him past the boyhood home of Sinclair Lewis, the 1920s novelist who had accurately, and sometimes cruelly, poured the essence of his Midwestern neighbors onto the pages of *Babbitt* and *Main Street* and won a Nobel Prize in the bargain. Coulter admired Lewis more for his later, political novels, the acid portrayals of religious hypocrisy in *Elmer Gantry* and of the 1930s proto-fascist movements of Huey Long and Father Coughlin in *It Can't Happen Here*.

Past Sauk Centre Coulter could feel the growing presence of forest and water as he followed the narrow two lane highway under the enormous prairie sky. The road climbed north from the sand plains, dotted with lakes and dairy farms, into Minnesota's North Country. Here white birches and aspen blazed gold and red as they ringed rock-shored lakes, tamarack bogs alternated with granite outcrops, and the second growth forest of White and Norway pine, spruce and fir extended to the far eastern horizon of the Chippewa National Forest, underlain by the hard stone of the Canadian Shield.

At eight-thirty Saturday morning Coulter was the only customer at the fishing camp's small café, consuming eggs scrambled with ham and peppers while looking over the copies of the Minneapolis *Tribune* and *Wall Street Journal* he had grabbed from the airport the day before. The morning was cool and snatches of low fog still clung to small bays and creek mouths that entered into the lake. The birches and pin oaks were in full color; within a few days the fishing camps and houseboat resorts would begin to close down for the ice-bound winter. Coulter liked the emptiness and what seemed like the first peaceful morning he had spent in the months since Charlie McConnell had died.

The man who entered the café promptly at 9:00 was of medium build, a young looking sixty with coarse black hair barely flecked with gray and deeply tanned, chiseled features. He wore khaki fishing pants with a black long sleeved t-shirt, sleeves rolled up, under a Filson fishing vest. His hands, wrists and arms were thick and powerful, with multiple scars.

"Mr. Coulter?"

Paul pushed his chair back and stood to offer his hand. "That's me. Mr. Troyer?"

"Dane Troyer." They shook hands and Paul decided that he would never want to cross the man; there was a difference between the kind of strength one could build during three gym visits a week and the kind of strength that came from a lifetime of hard training. Troyer definitely had the latter.

Paul gestured to the table. "Coffee? Breakfast?"

"I've broken fast, thanks, and I've a thermos of coffee in the boat. Nice morning out there. Join me?" Troyer's voice was mid-pitch and soft, with a pronounced Dakota accent.

"I'd like that." Coulter dropped a twenty dollar bill on the table to cover breakfast and followed Dane Troyer to the dock. They stepped down into Troyer's classic fifteen foot Boston Whaler. Troyer cast off the lines and they set out for Star Island, on the northwest side of the lake.

"There are nine lakes in the Cass Lake Chain," Troyer said, voice rising to be heard over the drone of the outboard motor. "We're part of the headwaters of the Mississippi River. In the summers we use boats for everything—even to shop in town, or visit friends. Everything revolves around the lakes." Troyer cut the engine speed and the boat loafed in the shallow bay. Troyer set a pair of fishing poles with Walleye lures into the trolling rack on either side of the boat. "There," he said, returning to his chair behind the boat's wheel. "We look proper now." He set a slow course at one-eighth speed parallel to the island.

"General Kaplan speaks pretty highly of you, Mr. Coulter," Troyer continued. "Said you'd been a Marine, yourself. That's why I agreed to see you. This isn't an easy thing for me. I spent thirty-four years in the Army. I don't like reporters. And I don't betray my comrades."

"I hope I'm not asking you to do that," Paul replied. "Are you willing to talk on the record? Be quoted by name?"

"Not yet," Troyer replied. "But Arne said that you might be able to use what I know to link things up, make sense of what's going on."

"I understand," Coulter replied. "Will you tell me something about yourself?" he began.

"I joined the army a week after finishing high school and stayed in until 2008. I had no interest in being an officer—I liked the field, plain and simple. I was a good Sergeant, good at breaking in young officers. Went to Ranger school. Served in a lot of different units. Got a college degree when I was stateside, during training assignments. I was in Panama, First Iraq, Bosnia, Second Iraq, and Afghanistan. My last combat posting was with the 10th Mountain Division. I got bumped up to Sergeant Major just before I retired."

"Did you ever get married?"

"I did. I was going to leave with my twenty years. But my wife died in a car accident so I stayed in."

Paul fished in the chest pocket of his flannel shirt. He pulled out the same drawing he had made for Arne Kaplan: the red square with spear points on a white field. "Have you ever seen this symbol, or design before?"

Troyer nodded. "I have. It's called a Phalanx. You know what that is?"

Coulter shook his head. "Dictionary would say an ancient Greek or Spartan military formation. A square of men in close formation with shields up, spears out."

"That's right. That's what this symbol represents."

"But what does it mean?"

Troyer looked back at Coulter with a mixture of sadness and self-loathing at what he was about to say. "The Phalanx began as a group of soldiers in Afghanistan, late in the Bush years—a bad time there. The Taliban were recruiting, resupplying from Pakistan, taking the war to us. We were fighting at high altitude, on the worst terrain I've ever experienced, and didn't have enough soldiers and material to do the job properly—too much had been diverted to Iraq. A lot of our missions involved putting squad or platoon-size units in forward posts to observe, and then calling in air strikes or assault teams to interdict the Taliban coming from their safe havens. Many soldiers began to feel that they were used as bait.

"The Phalanx started as a fellowship," Troyer continued. "Almost everyone who joined was a Christian, but it was the evangelicals who built it up and urged that the group be kept secret from senior command, although many junior and mid-level officers joined as well."

"Why?"

"They thought the Army might see it as political, as insubordination. People didn't want to lose their careers, and some of the officers who were in it had already taken shit for Christian proselytizing in uniform. And we knew the Army wouldn't want to admit to the existence of a Christian organization inside the military when we were fighting in a Muslim country. So it stayed underground."

"What was the organization doing while you were in Afghanistan?"

"At first, and for a long time, the Phalanx was just…well, nothing political. People would get together off base, have a prayer service, and gather in groups to talk. Some of it was classic military griping, some of it was Christian fellowship, some of it was group therapy for guys who'd been wounded, seen their buddies killed, gotten dumped by their wife or girlfriend at home. After a while a secure email network evolved—never with the name 'Phalanx' attached, but you knew who it was. The network reached out to veterans' groups and churches for support for soldiers who'd gotten into financial trouble with credit cards and mortgages, or needed a lawyer to help them keep contact with their kids after a divorce. It did a lot of good for a lot of people. But then it got political."

"When did it get political?" Coulter asked.

"When Brett Campbell became President. That really tore it."

"Why?"

"A lot of people couldn't handle the color of his skin. Or the fact that he was way smarter than they were. But it went deeper than that. The military draws conservative people who don't want the world to change, who think that once you have been called to battle, no matter how spurious the reason, you stay no matter what. Campbell knew…they knew…that he'd have to do triage, cut our losses in the Middle East. And that freaked a lot of people out. It got pretty raw. Brett Campbell, the secret Muslim. Brett Campbell, the Anti-Christ."

"How did the Phalanx change?"

"Even more secretive. Organized into cells. All emails ran through darknet websites; IMs and texts went through Tor. Evangelicals took over completely. I'll give you a list of some of the websites they had, you can pull them up through wayback.com or another one of the archive sites."

"Is that what drove you away?"

Troyer shrugged. "Not entirely. I always thought the politics was bullshit, but I liked that the group always found a way to get help to ordinary soldiers. But the religious side eventually got to me. My family's Lutheran, German and Danish—we're pretty reserved people. And none of the Hallelujahs or Praise Jesuses or Thank you Lords saved my wife during the three weeks she was dying." Troyer shrugged. "So I drifted away."

What is the Phalanx doing now?"

"Well, it spread out of Afghanistan, of course. Soldiers finished enlistments or duty tours and went home, and new cells were formed on military bases. A lot of people who left the Army and joined up with one of the military contractors were members too."

"Did you ever work for a military contractor?"

Troyer nodded. "After I retired I spent two years working with Dark/Star, protecting civilian reconstruction firms in Iraq. I made more money, managing a group of thirty contractors, than I'd made in my last ten years in the Army." He laughed grimly. "I never could understand the logic in that, paying contractors fifteen times what you'd pay a platoon for doing ordinary garrison duty. But I have to admit, the money was there and I took it."

The last of the morning low clouds and fog were gone and the autumn sun was high on the waters of the lake. Coulter took a pair of sunglasses from his shirt pocket and slipped them on to cut the glare. He looked at Troyer, who waited patiently—painfully—for the next question.

"Do you know Kyle Jackson?" Coulter asked.

"I do," Troyer replied, seeming unsurprised. "At least I met him. On the night he saved my life." And then he told Paul the story.

An hour later Troyer pulled in their troll lines—he had carefully failed to attach hooks to the lures, lest they actually have to deal with landing a Walleye—and drifted the boat into the shade close to shore.

"I love late September, early October," Troyer said. "You try this in June, you'll be eaten alive by mosquitoes before you can get the boat back out on to open water."

"So this is what you do now?" Coulter asked. "Guide in the summers, here and up in the Boundary Waters, and then winter down at the Gulf?"

"Yes. Or Mexico. 'Each day provides its own gifts.'"

"Marcus Aurelius," Coulter responded.

"My college senior thesis subject, at the age of 39," Troyer replied.

"Sounds like you'd lived that advice by then. What happened, Dane? Why did Arne Kaplan send me here?"

Troyer bit his lip, hesitated. "I told you I'd drifted away from the Phalanx."

"Yes."

"They came back to me. About five months ago."

"Came back?" Coulter was confused. "To rejoin, get religion, what?"

"No, this time the offer was professional. Fifteen thousand dollars a month to start. The smell of even more money in the air."

"For what?"

"Training. At a new Dark/Star facility in Nevada."

"Doing what?"

"Same thing I did in my last year in the Army, after Afghanistan. I was an instructor in counter insurgency at the Zussman Urban Combat Training Site, at Fort Knox. This contract… would be the same thing, but for Dark/Star. It didn't smell right. I've a decent pension, have money saved, and don't need much—so I turned it down."

"Then what happened?"

"I got asked again, in early summer. Roy Conover called me. Best new LT I ever broke in. He came out here himself to make the pitch even though he's a busy guy now, Kyle Jackson's chief of staff in Congress. He said they needed the best trainers they could get, and that their operational time window might be getting short."

Coulter was puzzled again. "Time? Time to do what?"

"Roy was a little vague there," Troyer replied. "He's learned to speak politician. Said they had to be 'prepared to protect the country.'"

"What did you do?"

"I told him I'd think about it. I was actually stalling for time, thought maybe I could find out a little more if I held out. They made one last run at me in late June. Not Conover this time, two management suits from Dark/Star. By then they were staffing up their new Nevada training facility, someplace outside of Elko; they needed an answer, now or never. I tried to get into specifics with them—who I'd be training, how many soldiers, who the contract agency was, where the money was coming from, where the people I was training would be deployed. I got the same vague crap about 'protecting the country.' And when I wouldn't sign the contract they left."

"Protecting the country?" Coulter asked. "From what? I still don't understand."

"I didn't either. But I added it up. The hard right politics. The use of Dominion and Empire and all the other religious code words. Every meeting I went to in the last two years seemed to be run by some preacher from Christian Nation. And Dark/Star, with unlimited amounts of money, suddenly setting up a second training camp in rural Nevada when they already had one of the biggest combat training bases outside of the U.S. Army in North Carolina, and a satellite technical center not too far from Las Vegas."

"Maybe they were asking you to train people for a new contract overseas?"

"If that was in the job description, they would have said so. It didn't sound like it. One of the few specifics I got was about the rules of engagement that I would be training to. They were very limited, very restrictive. I was told that in conducting training I would need to teach coordination with local police and armed forces that were presumed loyal."

"So?"

"Paul," Troyer said patiently, using Coulter's first name for the first time, "we *never* assumed the cooperation and loyalty of the local forces in urban warfare. Not in Iraq, Afghanistan, Kosovo or Bosnia. Not anywhere."

"Except, just possibly, you might assume that if you were doing counter-insurgency work inside the United States," Coulter said slowly.

Troyer turned his hard-planed face to Coulter, eyes hidden behind the dark bronze lenses of his shooting glasses. "That was what I figured out," he said.

"What did you do?"

"I decided I had to tell someone I could trust."

"Who did you tell?"

"My boyhood best friend, from Devil's Lake, North Dakota. Our mutual friend. Charlie McConnell, the President of the United States."

Chapter Twenty-Nine

The National Mall
15th & Constitution Avenue
Washington, D.C.
Sunday, October 2
1:30 P.M. EDT

It was a golden afternoon on the National Mall, pure high Indian summer: clear skies, bright warm sun, enough of a breeze to ruffle the surface of the Reflecting Pool in front of the Lincoln Memorial. Flags flew from every standard around the Washington Monument. Thousands of tourists from a hundred countries swarmed the Ellipse for the view of the White House and the South Lawn. Hundreds of Viet Nam veterans with their children and grandchildren, many of the once-boy soldiers now in wheelchairs or pushing walkers, moved slowly along the paths in Constitution Gardens leading to the black marble of their Memorial Wall.

Paul finally found Elizabeth near the Washington monument, playing touch football in one of the half-dozen games played most fair Sundays on the Mall's grassy pitch, an informal league of teams from the White House, Treasury, the Smithsonian, Congress, and the museums. Elizabeth wore a Corcoran Gallery Cormorants' loose blue sleeveless jersey over a gray-green Army t-shirt and running shorts, blonde hair tied back in a pony tail. She took a shovel pass from the slot back and ran for the sidelines, trying to turn the corner before the pursuit could reach her. She made a respectable gain, perhaps ten yards, before being forced over the chalked sideline marker. Paul said nothing, waiting on the far side of the field next to her blue nylon gym bag for the game to be over.

She jogged across the field after the final play and looked up and saw him standing there. "Paul?" she called out. "Are you home?"

He didn't answer. She stopped in front of him, sized up the set of his jaw, and waited.

"When in hell were you going to tell me?" Coulter demanded.

"Tell you what?" she asked, suddenly cautious.

"What you were doing. What was really going on. Say, in Panama. Or around a half dozen American military bases."

"Paul, you know I cannot talk about what I do. It would violate my oath. It would be a criminal offense."

Paul ignored her. "You've known what the Phalanx is for months, haven't you? I found your 'source number one.' Dane Troyer. In Cass Lake, Minnesota."

"Did he—

"Shut *up*. I don't know what in hell you're doing. You say don't ask. I don't ask. You disappear. You come back. I still don't ask. Instead I send Graham Taylor to use what slender connection he has with a banker in Grand Cayman to try and see if there was anything not kosher about the way Kyle Jackson built up his military contracting empire. Graham disappears. The next time I hear from him he is in Panama. He has stumbled across a secret financial intelligence task force that's been investigating tax evasion and money laundering in the pirate islands for two years. He also finds your Homeland Intelligence group, complete with its CIA liaison, Derek Martin, who everybody over the age of six in this town knows is the Number three guy in the National Clandestine Service. Seven days after that Graham returns to Washington, and is quite professionally shot dead at midnight in Stanton Square."

"Paul—

"I'm not done. What Graham has discovered is the political secret of the century: that newly installed Vice President Kyle Jackson's military contracting empire was acquired with money embezzled from the collection plates of the second largest church group in America by its own preacher, Royce Reed. That Jackson and Reed together control the Cornwall Group which in turn owns military contractors, weapons manufacturers, and a very dirty bank in Panama. When you add up their assets you probably have the seventh or eighth most potent conventional military force on the planet. The Cornwall Group is using its banking connections to move black money into the United States, making it appear that the source of the money is Islamic, maybe headed for sleeper cells, or maybe headed for a group of two, three, maybe four hundred of the kind of whacked-out people that blew up the Oklahoma City federal courthouse and regularly stockpile mortars and RPGs in the basement. That's what you thought you had on your hands. Am I right?"

Elizabeth said nothing but nodded slightly, almost involuntarily.

"But maybe, just maybe, the Phalanx is not a collection of mouth-breathers, militia, bigots, tax cheats, and gun nuts. Maybe, just maybe, it started out with good intentions and with good and frustrated people who were sent to take the weight of two wars, one botched, one unwinnable, and in that frustration developed a political cast, an ideology based on fears that America is no longer very Christian, no longer white enough, that is going to contain people who speak a dozen different languages, and that America cannot win a war with a sixth of humanity. They don't want to come to grips with any of those things. They know they're getting screwed by their own politicians, by the banks, by Wall Street, by the crony capitalism that gets fatter as the country gets poorer. They know they will be poorer than their parents, and that their children will likely be poorer still. And maybe, just maybe, this group came to be organized and dominated and led by some people with a very specific political and religious agenda that does not embrace the messy, unpopular life of a representative democracy. A fifth column, organized into sleeper cells. Waiting."

"Paul, I cannot say anything. You know that. This is juvenile." She began to shovel her gear into her gym bag. Paul grabbed her arm and pulled her up to confront him. Elizabeth started to react out of instinct, to put a palm shot underneath his chin, but stopped herself, willed herself to do nothing, angry and yet horrified at how close she had come to striking Paul.

"So who's leading this, Elizabeth?" Paul asked. "Your 'source number one' knows. Because the approach to him to rejoin the Phalanx came from the last young officer Sergeant Dane Troyer trained in Afghanistan: Roy Conover. Kyle Jackson's congressional chief of staff. You know what Dane Troyer's special skills are? Counterinsurgency. Urban warfare."

Paul released his grip on her arm, still barely able to contain his anger.

"Well, congratulations to Homeland Intelligence. Because while you guys were on a snipe hunt for homegrown Al Qaeda terror cells and the friends of Tim McVeigh, the world moved on. And because you were all silent, the man who runs the Phalanx was just installed in the National Command Authority. He made it by two votes. *Two votes.* If any piece of this had come out, if *anyone* had leaked any part of the truth, Kyle Jackson would not be Vice-President."

"Troyer didn't tell us about Conover," Elizabeth responded slowly, still angry but beginning to think. "Charlie McConnell talked to Troyer directly, and Charlie didn't link this group to Jackson. There's no proof that Jackson has anything to do with the Phalanx."

"There's another connection that come close to proof. The woman Graham knew, Karen Jenkins, his former student, the woman who headed the financial intelligence operation in Panama. You know her too—you worked with her. She's mad as hell that James Robinson killed the indictment against Reed, shut down her operation and wasted years of work. She made the same connection that Graham and I did: that Royce Reed stole the money that funded Jackson's purchase of Dark/Star and still controls it through Cornwall. And that Cornwall was moving the money so it looked like it was coming from the Middle East to parts of the Phalanx set up around the army bases in the south and southeast. According to the notes Graham left for me Jenkins is ready to tell big chunks of this story. But you know what? I can't find her. The operation in Panama's completely shut down. The IRS in Washington says she's on 'extended personal leave.' None of her friends or co-workers have heard from her. She's simply *gone*. I hope like hell she's found a good place to hide. But if I were you and Cable Hollings I'd be making damn sure she doesn't die like Tony Thrace and Graham Taylor. Because I don't know how much time is left. There's an election in thirty-six days. At least I hope there will be."

Paul shook his head with utter self-disgust. "If I had known any of this—any single piece of this—I would not have sent Graham to get himself killed." He turned on his heel and left, long strides taking him quickly across Constitution Avenue and into the crowds. Elizabeth watched him go, silent tears welling in the corner of her eyes. She brushed them angrily away and then reached into her gym bag and took out her satellite phone.

"Cable Hollings, please. Major Gray. This is an emergency."

Coulter took out his own telephone as he reached the far side of Constitution Avenue.

"Jeff Reardon," he demanded. He paused, listened to the excuses. "Fuck that," he replied angrily. "Tell him Coulter called and said that if the Jackson story doesn't go out he will lose this election just like the last two he fucked up."

The West Coast
Black Monday

Chapter Thirty

D Wing
Magnuson Health Sciences Center
The University of Washington
Seattle, Washington
Monday, October 3
6:57 A.M. PDT

Roxanne Dawson jogged down the dim D Wing corridor toward the microbiology labs. As she ran she juggled her coffee cup, yoghurt carton, bike helmet, and a stack of journal articles remotely printed and delivered to her campus mailbox from the Health Sciences library the night before. The morning had been so achingly beautiful—soft rose and peach sunrise, cloudless sky, a perfect autumn day—that she had chosen to bike from her Sand Point Way apartment down the Burke Gilman trail to the University of Washington's Magnuson Health Sciences Center. As a result she was running late for her 7:00 A.M. conference call with two genomics scientists at Johns Hopkins, her partners in their joint research project on cell signaling. As she reached the door to D Wing she paused to press her face against the eyepiece of the biometric security system so her retinas could be scanned. The security system had been installed the previous year when the D Wing had been remodeled and the Biohazard Level 3 and radiological 'hot' labs had been rebuilt.

Dawson, like most of the technicians, researchers and grad students working in D Wing, referred to the security system as "O'Brien," a derogatory salute to Winston Smith's interrogator in Orwell's *1984*.

When the explosion came it rocked the entire massive Magnuson structure—the ninth largest building in the world—and threw Dawson against the far corridor wall. The reinforced windows in the outer labs blew out and air rushed into the corridor. Dawson lay stunned, staring up at the ceiling as her vision came slowly back into focus. The sound of the blast wave had nearly deafened her. She turned her head from side to side to ease the ringing in her ears. As her hearing slowly returned another sound, a high pitched wail that filled the dust-choked corridor, took over her senses.

The radiation alarms were going off.

Chapter Thirty-One

Crane Dunham sat behind the partner-sized mahogany desk in the office reserved for the Director of Homeland Intelligence in the Old Executive Office Building and fitted the fingertips of his manicured hands together with irritated precision.

"I believe you are enjoying, this, Major," he said peevishly. "I presume that I am not going to be the *only* employee of Homeland Intelligence and will have *staff* to deal with at least *some* of these technical issues?"

Elizabeth Gray placed three additional binders containing procedural guidelines for the handling of citizen data obtained from Homeland Intelligence collection systems on the desk. "It's like learning a new language, sir," she responded. "Your staff will be able to carry out your instructions, and brief you on alternative courses of action, but you have to be able to speak the language. And when you are in front of Congress you will need to be able to translate the technical policy issues—and their language—into English for Congressional consumption."

Gray's diplomatic explanation had no good effect. Color rose in Dunham's heavy jowls and spread across his tanned face, under his perfect helmet of styled blue white hair. "I *know* how to talk to Congress, I was *in* Congress for twenty years, Major," he snapped.

Most of it whoring for the sugar lobby, Elizabeth thought, but said only "Of course, sir."

She was saved by the harsh tone of Dunham's secure telephone. He nodded brusquely for her to pick up the call.

"Gray," she said.

"This is the NCTC Watch Desk, Michael McMasters," the caller responded. "Better get the Director, Major. We have reports of a major explosion in Seattle."

"Industrial?"

"Doesn't look like it. It's at or near the University of Washington. We're getting some images." The watch director's voice was grim.

"Send the feed to the Situation Room. We'll be there in—call it four minutes." She broke the connection, ignored Dunham, and punched numbers.

"Situation Room. This is Commander Vuong."

"Major Gray, Homeland Intelligence. NCTC has a serious incident report they will patch to you. An explosion in Seattle."

"The President's en route to Seattle," Vuong replied.

"I know. Who's senior in the building?"

Vuong hesitated. "Nobody. Almost nobody. The Chief of Staff's with the President. The Acting National Security Advisor is out—he's having surgery this morning at Johns Hopkins. And the Vice-President's leaving for Dallas in twenty minutes."

"Flash Jackson's office and hold him. Set up a video conference with the Emergency Response Group, but don't activate it until I tell you to. Understand?"

"Yes, Major."

"We're on our way."

Elizabeth turned to Crane Dunham. He was sitting back in his chair, anger gone, face suddenly pale beneath his Florida tan.

"What now?" he asked.

"This appears to be an emergency and you will have to function, Congressman. Follow me."

Paul Coulter arrived at the White House Press Room at 9:45 A.M., two hours later than usual. Elizabeth, still furious with him, had chosen to stay the night in visiting officer's quarters in Crystal City, near the Pentagon. Paul had stayed late in his writing room, mind churning in frustration, roughing out the Dark/Star story while simultaneously trying, with increasing desperation, to reach Jeff Reardon. Reardon refused his calls, as did other contacts Paul had within the Giles campaign and in his Senate office; Reardon had apparently declared him toxic.

Coulter settled into his Press Room cubicle. He quickly scrolled through the morning press office feed, discarded it as crap, and turned back to his long jumbled draft of the Jackson-Dark/Star story. It remained more a cut-and-paste compilation of his and Graham's notes than a publishable article. In cold daylight Coulter knew that the sourcing was too thin: too many holes, too many what ifs, too many undocumented assertions. Without Karen Jenkins, without someone with access to the full story and the documentation, he couldn't publish. Even if he could persuade an editor to take the piece, any paper's media lawyers would go batshit crazy and kill it. If he posted what he had on his own blog, a fleet of lawyers from Cornwall and The Christian Nation would grind him into dust. He was out of his league on a story of this size. Pacific News was no help; it was understaffed and underfunded, a fig leaf of respectability for the dying Left Coast newspapers. Paul needed a newsroom with fifty reporters who could be mustered as a group to tackle the research and the interviews, to drag the story kicking and screaming from those who knew. But those newsrooms didn't exist anymore; the great roaring days of the big rich papers, the *Times* and the *Post* and the Miami *Herald,* were over. Their descendants were bankrupt ghosts surviving as nonprofits on table scraps from the foundations of the 1990s software and Internet billionaires, Gates and Allen, Brin and Bezos and

Zuckerberg. It did not seem to Paul a sufficient recompense for what the technology they had created had done to the news.

Bloomberg, Coulter thought to himself, drinking lukewarm coffee and absent-mindedly pulling a protein bar from the stash in his file drawer for breakfast. They still had the resources, and could get extra bodies on the ground. He would have to get permission from Pacific News, but they would grab at a deal for even a piece of the credit, and find someone else to cover Paul's daily beat so that he could pursue it.

He had started to email his editor when he heard someone scream "*Jesus Fucking Christ!*" from the opposite end of the press room, where an array of flat screen monitors displayed the 24-hour news feeds.

Elizabeth Gray bolted into the Situation Room with Dunham, her putative boss, puffing hard on her heels. "Cut in the main feed from Liberty Crossing," she snapped at Lt. Commander Julie Vuong. Vuong pointed to her tech sergeant who immediately jumped back to her station in the support area in the next room and tapped keys on her laptop. "I have NCTC coming through. The links to the Emergency Response Group of the National Security Council have been set up. Should I tell them to get the Principals into their chairs?"

Elizabeth said, "Not yet. Get me somebody in Seattle first."

She looked at Dunham, who seemed frozen by the speed of events. "What do I do?" Crane Dunham asked, voice shaking. Gray shook her head and pointed at the screen, now split between NCTC's day watch chief, Michael McMasters, and Roger Daniels, the Seattle Fire Chief, who appeared on screen from the back cabin of an SFD First Response command truck speeding through the University campus. A flickering black and white diorama of broken, burning buildings and blackened cars was projected on a screen behind Daniels.

Gray clipped a wireless Bluetooth earpiece into place. "What are we looking at on your screen, Chief?" she demanded.

"This is taken from a security camera at far end of the South Campus of the University of Washington, near the Lake Washington Ship Canal," Daniels responded. "We're looking at the aftermath of an explosion just south of our Health Sciences complex that took place about seven minutes ago. We've lost two smaller buildings that have collapsed. My guys think this was an ANFO or ANNM device, probably carried in here by a truck or van left in one of the loading docks near the Lake Washington Ship Canal on the south side of the campus. We can smell caustic ammonia in the air as well as smoke. The blast radius looks to be about six hundred feet through buildings, maybe two thousand five hundred feet in the open—bigger than the Oklahoma City courthouse bomb back in the '90s. That's not the worst of it. The bomb went off about three hundred feet south of the Magnuson Health Sciences Building—it's the largest medical and biological complex on the West Coast. The façade looks mostly intact, but a lot of the building windows were blown out, even some of the reinforced windows in the labs. We've got a BioHazard Level 3 containment lab in there. The interior sensors seem to show that the lab hasn't had any changes in air pressure so far, but—"

"You're afraid the bio-hazard containment will break down? What do they have in there? Gray asked.

"Some human pathogens, but not the nightmare stuff—there's no smallpox or Warburg's or Ebola. No, I'm more concerned about the hot labs. The radiation detectors throughout the complex are all going off. And the first team coming in from the hospital side, away from the blast zone, is picking up some radiation as they start to look for survivors."

Gray closed her eyes and took a deep breath. "Chief," she said a moment later, "I think you should get all of your first responders into their radiation suits. It may not be just the labs. This could be a dirty bomb. Do you have airborne radiation monitoring capability?"

"Washington Air National Guard does it for the City of Seattle. They're ten minutes away by air, down at Joint Base Lewis-McChord outside Tacoma."

"Get 'em up, Chief," Gray responded. She turned back to Commander Vuong. "Activate the video conference with the Emergency

Response Group. Get the Principals or their senior deputies into their chairs." Gray then ran the eighty feet to the Vice President's West Wing office. She flashed her security badge at Jackson's secret service agent, knocked hard, and opened the door to find Jackson working at his standing desk, handing edited speech pages to a deputy.

"Sir," she began. "You're needed in the Situation Room. Immediately."

Jackson looked up at her over his half-moon reading glasses. "It's Major Gray, isn't it?" he said, seeming puzzled. "I'm supposed to leave for Dallas in ten minutes."

"Sir, the Acting NSA, Dr. Arlen is in surgery this morning. His deputy, Colonel Hotchkiss, is traveling with the President, as are the Chief of Staff and his deputy. There has been an explosion in Seattle. The Seattle Fire Chief believes it may be ANFO. That's—"

"Ammonium nitrate fuel oil. Go on."

"The President's flight plan has him less than an hour from landing at Boeing Field. We have no idea whether there is a threat to the President. We have concerns that radiation may be leaking from nuclear medicine facilities in the University Hospital complex or even worse, that the bomb could be dirty. We are assembling the ERG conference and you are the senior official in the building. With Arlen unavailable and Director Dunham not up to speed I need you to chair the Emergency Response Group."

Jackson nodded. "Let's go, Major." They ran together down the hallway.

Lt. Commander Vuong rose to her feet from her station at the back of the Situation Room and saluted the Vice-President. "Sir. The ERG is assembled. I have State, Defense, NORAD, CIA, FBI, Energy, Transportation, Homeland Security, Treasury, and NCTC on video conference. Within five minutes we should have Director Edwards of the Secret Service, acting Attorney General Acosta, Brigadier General Roper, the director of the White House Military Office, and Lt. General Horvath, the director of the Joint Intelligence Staff of the JCS, present in the room. Homeland Intelligence Director Dunham is here and will return in just a moment. He stepped out feeling somewhat... indisposed." Vuong kept her face straight, her back rigid. "He will—

Jackson cut her off. "Thank you, Commander. I want Major Gray to sit in the NSA chair and run the board. Activate the videoconference."

One by one the department secretaries and agency directors' heads filled the teleconference screens.

Jackson spoke quickly, his voice confident. "This is the Vice-President and I am taking charge of this conference until we can sort out what's going on and contact the President. We are proceeding under crisis rules. Keep your microphones off unless responding. If you have something to say, flash the Sit Room and Major Gray will keep you sorted out. Communications. Get Air Force One on line and tell them to stand by to get the President. First, I want an update. NCTC, go."

Michael McMasters filled the largest screen at the far end of the Situation Room. "Mr. Vice-President, at 0657 PDT what we believe was an ANFO truck bomb exploded on the University of Washington South Campus, near the Health Sciences Complex and University Hospital. There are suspicions the bomb was dirty. We have now picked up two of the University's surviving security camera feeds as well as the visuals from two news helicopters. This is what they show."

The primary situation room screen cut away and split into four sections. The ground security cameras were barely functional now as the fires spread to their circuitry. The image of a half collapsed brick building was dimly visible on one camera through a thick curtain of fire and smoke. The aerial shots from the news helicopters were much more useful. They showed the blackened blast area, with two buildings collapsed and a third nearly so. The blast had fractured the exterior concrete wall of the Magnuson Health Sciences Center, but the wall had not yet collapsed. The lab areas seemed much more damaged than the adjacent University Hospital. A thick smoke plume rose from the still burning buildings.

Gray's monitor flashed and she cut Air Force One into the conference. "Sir, the President."

James Robinson's fleshy pale face filled one of the screens. "Kyle? Why aren't you headed to Dallas? We need to nail down Texas."

"Mr. President, there is a possible terrorist bombing in Seattle. We need to get Air Force One turned around and get you safe on the ground and we have to do it now. I need you to authorize your flight deck to turn the plane and head toward….the nearest air force base is McChord, outside Tacoma. Too close. Sir, I need you to patch in your pilot." Robinson nodded, eyes fearful, and gestured to an aide. Gray added an audio circuit to the pilot of Air Force One.

"Air Force One Flight Deck, go," Jackson said.

"This is Colonel Jacobs on the flight deck. Mr. President?" The pilot's voice sounded puzzled.

Robinson cut in. "Yes, Colonel. The Vice-President is in the White House and has instructions for you."

"Colonel, this is Vice President Jackson. Where are you and what's your fuel status?"

"We are about half way between Eugene and Salem in Oregon, and we have four plus hours fuel, sir."

"Fine. Mr. President, I think you should head for Mountain Home Air Force Base in Idaho. There is a secure facility there with good communications and you will be safe while we sort this out. NORAD, go. How fast can you get fighter escorts scrambled from Mountain Home?"

"Six minutes. The F-22s from Mountain Home should be able to rendezvous with Air Force One about twelve minutes after takeoff. Say over the Hanford Nuclear Reservation, we have good radar coverage there. We have also scrambled two Oregon Air National Guard F-15s. They will not make contact but will guard the flight corridor to Hanford until rendezvous."

"Air Force One, do you copy?"

"Yes sir, we will be turning to course two four one, that's two four one, and we will look to pick up the escorts in Hanford's air space en route to Mountain Home."

Gray signaled Jackson. "DOD needs CAP authorization," she said.

Jackson nodded. "Mr. President, you need to authorize CAP."

"What?"

"Combat Air Patrol, Sir. We need your authorization to shoot down any aircraft, including passenger aircraft, that threatens Air Force One, and to place air patrols over our twenty-five largest cities."

Robinson's wide face and shaky voice were filled with fear. "Is this an assassination attempt?"

"We don't know, Mr. President. Do you authorize CAP?"

"Yes, damn it, yes. Do what you have to do."

Chapter Thirty-Two

Jackson ran through the Emergency Procedures check list with a force and efficiency that Gray could only admire, calmly keeping his place and jotting notes in the classified manual she had handed him when he had entered the Sit Room. As Jackson gave orders, the federal zone encompassing the White House, the Capitol, the Pentagon, and the major federal department buildings was secured as soldiers from Fort Belvoir's Special Brigade Combat Team and the Third Infantry moved their armored Humvees and Strykers into position. Separate units were dispatched to secure Homeland Security's new headquarters in Anacostia, north of the Navy Yard, and the NCTC/Homeland Intelligence offices at Liberty Crossing in Virginia. The Secretary of Commerce, an otherwise obscure former Congressman from Wisconsin, was removed to the fortified bunker at Mt. Weather in the Blue Ridge Mountains to provide a constitutional successor if the Seattle attack proved to be a precursor to a broader assault on the government. The stock, bond, derivative, and commodities markets were closed so their books could be balanced and the Federal Reserve would know how much liquidity to provide the financial system the following morning. Banks were ordered to remain open late and disburse cash to panicky customers; emergency shipments of cash left the vaults of the regional Federal Reserve banks in armored cars and courier jets. Ports, power plants, oil and gas pipelines, electric transmission lines, airports, railroad switching stations, internet server farms, fiber optic communication nodes and satellite ground stations were placed on alert and their security teams put in place. U.S. airlines were directed to begin landing their planes and to keep them on the ground until given permission to resume flying. U.S. Embassies, consulates, and military bases across the planet raised their guard. Coast Guard vessels were ordered to power up and move into protective positions around major ports. Naval destroyers and frigates were dispatched to provide special protection to oil refineries and liquefied natural gas terminals at ports in Massachusetts, Texas, Louisiana, Maryland, Georgia, Washington State and Puerto Rico. AWACs command planes launched with their flanking F-22 interceptors and moved to their monitoring stations above the United States and the Atlantic and Pacific sea lanes. NSA and Homeland Intelligence satellites were repositioned to expand surveillance over the United States. STRATCOM and local air bases launched National Guard F-15s and F-16s and Air Force twin-tailed F-35 Lightning IIs on their Combat Air Patrol routes. NORAD monitored every aircraft in North America as well as the principal satellites and manned spacecraft in low Earth orbit. NORTHCOM put two of its airborne combat brigades on twenty minute alert at Peterson Field.

Elizabeth, who had spent three years helping write and game out many of these procedures, could only watch in something close to awe as the enormous weight of federal power was deployed by the small, tough man seated with rigid posture at the head of the table, his suit jacket still on and tie still knotted. *I hope to God Paul's wrong about Jackson,* Elizabeth thought. *He must have been one hell of an officer.*

Lt. Gen. Karol Horvath entered the Situation Room with a brief nod to the Vice-President and replaced a junior DOD undersecretary at the main table. The smaller man moved aside and took a briefer's seat at the back of the room.

"Karol," Jackson said, cordially if not warmly. "What's our defense status this morning?"

"It was quiet, Mr. Vice-President," Horvath replied, his face and voice without affect. It was obvious that the two men had known and not liked each other at some point in their past. "Even the Iranians were behaving today. I notified the Chiefs before coming in here that you might have military deployment considerations in addition to the CAP, port security procedures and the Fort Belvoir team that is securing Washington. We are bringing the combat commands on line, waiting for orders."

Jackson nodded. "State, DOD," he said crisply. "Emergency notification to all the nuclear powers, Russia, China, Israel, U.K., France, the Koreas, India, Pakistan, Iran, and Saudi Arabia, and to NATO Headquarters in Brussels. Tell them we have an internal incident and are going to DefCon 3 in North America and at our bases as a *precaution*. We are not, repeat *not*, alerting any of our strategic forces. Karol, make sure the Chief of Naval Operations keeps the submarine fleet, especially the missile boats, on normal patrol patterns. They should come to communications depth but not surface or take any other unusual action. The NATO Supreme Commander should get on the phone with his Russian counterpart and explain that no European forces are being alerted outside of base security. Have CENTCOM make the same call to the Israelis and the Saudis. But Karol—"

"Yes, sir?"

"Tell the Chief of Naval Operations to begin moving the surface fleet. Do we have carrier task forces in port?"

Horvath checked his pad. "Yes. Carriers are in port at Everett, Norfolk and San Diego."

"Tell them to fire up their reactors and move to sea. Get them three hundred nautical miles clear of their ports. No aircraft launches other than normal patrols." Horvath nodded and moved off to the adjacent communications room to comply.

Jackson turned back to Gray. "Get Seattle," he directed. "They should have their radiation detection gear over the site now."

Gray nodded and the image of Seattle's Fire Chief, Carl Daniels, returned to the primary screen. "We have the word," he said, his broad-featured face grim under his helmet. He was now out of his command truck standing at the south edge of the blast zone, fully suited in protective gear, with bottled oxygen on his back and a breathing mask dangling below his throat. The blackened and fractured concrete walls of the Magnuson Health Sciences Center loomed behind him. "We've got high levels of radiation in the zone. Where I'm standing, about three hundred yards from the center of the explosion, we've taken about twenty-five REMs. The bomb was dirty."

"Any idea what radioactives were used?" Jackson asked.

"We've got a rough spectrometer reading taken from the air. Uranium and plutonium. We're also picking up Cesium, Strontium and Americium." *Oh shit,* Gray said silently to herself.

Jackson noticed the grim expression pass over Elizabeth's face. "Summarize, Major," Jackson ordered. "What are the risks to responders and the civil population?"

"Uranium is primarily an alpha emitter. Alpha particles can be stopped by clothes, or even skin. Plutonium is a beta and gamma emitter; direct exposure presents more significant risks but is still survivable; ordinary protective gear is very effective. They may have juiced the bomb with radioactive Cesium and Strontium because those isotopes are gamma emitters, and create more direct radiation. The primary risk to the responders and population not directly injured from the blast is from inhalation or ingestion. The explosion turns the uranium and plutonium into a fine particulate aerosol. It spreads in the smoke plume from the explosion and then contaminates water and ground surfaces. If inhaled or ingested both can cause radiation sickness and death. In low dose concentrations uranium, and especially plutonium, are highly carcinogenic."

"Clear the news choppers out of the airspace," Jackson quickly commanded. "They could be flying through the plume, and if there's plutonium in the smoke—

"We've already ordered them out," Daniels said, cutting in. "I've got our police and fire first responders and our two Nuclear/Radiological/Biological teams searching for anyone in the immediate blast area who is injured and still alive. We have pretty limited decontamination ability at the Seattle/King County level but our National Guard's emergency teams are on their way. We are evacuating the hospital from the north side of the complex, away from the blast zone, but that's going to take at least four hours. They've got a lot of critical care patients, and at least thirty patients were in surgery when the bomb went off."

"Okay," Jackson responded. "What do you need?"

Daniels grimaced. "Everything."

"You'll have it. DOE, go. Where are the closest Nuclear Emergency Support Teams based?"

The Secretary of Energy, an unconfirmed Robinson political appointee who'd managed to lose his safe Idaho Senate seat after a sex scandal, had a background in advertising but not in energy or engineering. He looked blank. An assistant secretary literally shoved him aside to respond. "DOE has NEST teams at Nellis AFB in Nevada and at Hanford."

"Do they have their own flight support?"

"Yes, sir."

"Get two NEST teams to Seattle. I want NEST's Airborne Measurement Systems to make systematic over flights of the city. We need to know how big and intense the radioactive plume is, and what direction it is going to spread to. Transportation, go. I need FAA."

"Mr. Vice-President," the Secretary of Transportation responded, "FAA on line to you now.

""I want both Sea-Tac Airport and Boeing Field open for emergency support units. Divert inbound commercial flights. See if Canada will take some of them at Vancouver, otherwise Spokane and the Boeing field at Moses Lake. Move whatever planes are on the ground at Sea-Tac to clear at least fifteen gates close to the main terminal and at the air cargo terminal," Jackson directed. "Homeland Security, Coast Guard. Close the Port of Seattle and clear two heavy cargo piers for relief vessels. FEMA, go. I want you to set up an emergency command center at the nearest location to the site that is outside of the radiation plume."

"FEMA has a regional office about twenty miles north of Seattle," the long-time, apolitical FEMA director replied. "There's a former Naval Air Station at Sand Point, about two miles north of the University of Washington. It's now a Seattle city park but it still has the old hanger buildings in place. They have thousands of square feet under roof. We'll set up there."

"Very well," Jackson responded. "Major. I need the Governor of Washington."

"I'm on the conference," Mr. Vice-President," Governor Marion Sanchez Tyler responded. Tyler, a tough-minded former Sheriff of Yakima County, Washington, appeared on the room's center screen, a stocky Hispanic grandmother with a short helmet of steel gray hair.

"Governor, I think you need to declare martial law."

"I have, Mr. Vice-President. The Washington Army National Guard has been mobilized to cordon off the radiation risk zone and begin an evacuation. They are blocking streets and freeway on-ramps to keep cars out of the area and to keep possible escape routes clear. We have temporarily shut down the light rail system to the University campus, but we are checking the tracks. If there is no damage we will reopen it for evacuation within the hour. I need to have the best radioactive risk measurements and some notion of which way the plume is traveling so that we can give specific instructions to our people as soon as possible. We're going to have people killed trying to flee who are not at risk unless I can convince them to shelter in place."

Jackson nodded agreement. "Agreed. DOE, go. I want that deputy secretary for nuclear security who seemed to know what he was talking about tasked with being the Governor's liaison with the NEST teams and get her intel on the radiation plume. Governor, what else?"

"There's an Army combat engineering battalion, the 864th, at Fort Lewis with armored recovery vehicles and bulldozers," Tyler responded. "I think we're going to need them to get the roads cleared. My Transportation Department's sensors and video cams are showing every major freeway in the Puget Sound area has already gridlocked. We have hundreds of accidents."

Jackson nodded again. "DOD. I need Lewis-McChord—the Commander of I-Corps. What airlift capacity do we have at McChord? The Governor's got the right idea. I'd rather keep the Army's vehicles off the roads until we can deploy them, and then shift all the traffic on I-5 and I-90 to outbound so that all lanes can be used to evacuate the city."

Horvath returned to the Sit Room as Jackson waited for the commanding general at Lewis-McChord to be patched in. It took less than three minutes; DOD and the Washington Governor's office had already alerted her. "We are loading two companies of the 864th and their gear onto C-17s and should have them at Boeing Field inside of an hour, Mr. Vice-President," the I-Corps commanding officer, a Lt. General Sheila Wallace, responded. "But you're going to need to designate a task force commander."

Jackson hesitated, but only briefly, looking up over the rim of his reading glasses at Marion Tyler on the screen. "Governor, if I do that, I'm going to have to federalize your guard troops."

Tyler simply nodded. "Give me someone that I and my Guard commander can work with, that's all I ask. Can General Wallace do this? We've had a terrific relationship since she took command at Fort Lewis."

"General Wallace, take command with FEMA at Sand Point. Send an operations officer to Boeing Field to get the 'dozers moving as soon as they land. DOD, cut the orders."

Jackson paused, just long enough to jot a note in his Procedures notebook and then take off his reading glasses and rub the dryness out of his eyes. "Everybody takes a one minute breath," he said. Elizabeth checked her watch; they were just two hours into the crisis, but many days' worth of fatigue and sweat and fear had filled the Situation Room. Jackson stood up, stretched his lower back briefly, and squared his shoulders.

"Major Gray," he said, "I'm going to a need a timeline, in power point, detailing every action taken in the past two hours since this thing broke," he said.

Elizabeth nodded. "Two of Commander Vuong's techs have been recording and generating a summary of every decision you've made. I can have that for you in—

"Jesus God, *No!*" a woman's voice shouted from the linked hook-up of federal officials. Gray looked for the source and found it at the NCTC Watch Desk in Liberty Crossing. The deputy watch commander there, a woman named Gordon, seemed almost paralyzed as her image filled the screen.

"It's San Francisco," she finally said, unable to keep the fear and anger out of her shaking voice. "Oh, Christ, they did it to us again."

Chapter Thirty-Three

Walter E. Washington Convention Center
801 Mount Vernon Place Northwest
Washington, D.C.
Monday, October 3
12:09 P.M. EDT

The Google satellite feed patched through to CNN showed a black explosive plume rising above Van Ness Avenue near Fulton Street, just north of the ornate San Francisco City Hall. There was no sound yet but the resolution sharpened and again the shapes of blackened buildings and shattered cars filled the screen. The press corps, who had been evacuated from the White House along with other nonessential personnel a half hour after the Seattle blast, groaned aloud and shouted questions that no one from the Press Office came out to answer. The reporters and camera crews finally settled down, but they filled the room with an uneasy, angry buzz, mixing curses and speculation as the temporary press office was literally assembled around them in one of the basement meeting rooms inside the Washington Convention Center, a mile northeast of the White House. Most of the video screens in the room were still not working; techs from the White House and the convention center staff moved frantically to install servers and lay cable. The Convention Center's Wi-Fi and cell phone access crashed under the sudden demand. Wi-Fi from nearby buildings was sketchy and unreliable. Another half hour passed and still no one came to brief them. A hundred reporters were staring at the story of their lifetimes, yet were suddenly more isolated than they thought possible in the 21st Century.

Paul Coulter considered making a run for the Press Club or the Washington *Post's* offices, six blocks northwest along Massachusetts Avenue. He ultimately decided against it—he had no back up this day, and his job was to report the news from the White House, not try to take the lead on a story three thousand miles away. His phone, wifi, and 4g laptop connection were still blocked. Suddenly a deputy White House press secretary, a thin and nervous red-headed man in his very early thirties named Nolan mounted a small dais in front of a hastily rigged blue curtain with the White House seal. Television lights suddenly flared across the room.

"Where's the President?" shouted a half dozen reporters. "Is he in Seattle?"

"No," Nolan replied. "The President was on board Air Force One just prior to the attack on Seattle. His plane has been diverted to a se-cure facility at Mountain Home, Idaho, where he is actively involved in the response to what we now believe is a very serious terrorist at-tack on the Homeland."

"Who is in control in the White House?" Coulter shouted.

"The Vice-President is in the White House, leading our national response from the Situation Room under the President's guidance," Nolan replied. "We are emailing every reporter on the listserve a statement summarizing every action that the President and the Vice-President have directed in response to the emergency. We'll also have that in hard copy—

Nolan paused, listened to the blue tooth web piece in his ear, and suddenly fled the dais, disappearing behind the secret service cordon standing at the back of the room.

"What the fuck?" the AP reporter standing next to Coulter shouted. The NBC feed came alive, and audio suddenly blasted through from both CNN and NBC. Both networks' anchors were nearly shouting, their words tumbled over one another.

"San Francisco's Fire Department has stated that it will take radiation precautions on the assumption that the attack on the San Francisco City Hall may have been a dirty bomb, a Radioactive Dispersal Device," Lester Holt intoned for NBC. "There are reports that the Seattle bomb attack at the University of Washington involved a dirty bomb."

NBC then shifted to stock footage of wedding couples standing on the steps in front of San Francisco City Hall's elegant 19th Century rotunda, one of the most popular venues for gay marriage in the country. "When the San Francisco bomb exploded at nine A.M. today Pacific Time the City Hall area was crowded with government workers arriving for work, along with hundreds of couples applying for wedding licenses, a San Francisco gay tradition," Holt continued. "California state authorities estimate that one to two thousand people may have been killed by the blast."

"How bad?" the Vice-President said grimly.

"Bad, Mr. Vice-President," Ray Quinones, the Governor of California, replied. He was still in the Governor's office in Sacramento, his shoulders slumped, his face ashen. In the background Elizabeth could see his aides working the phones for news from the city and to coordinate the evacuation of Sacramento's government buildings. "We're reading the same type of radioactive materials, principally uranium and plutonium but also with some strontium and cesium, similar to what we've been told was found in the Seattle attack."

"I've scrambled Nuclear Emergency Support Teams from New Mexico and Texas to assist you," Jackson replied. "Have you activated the California Guard?"

"Yes. The Guard's 79th and 81st Combat Brigades are setting up a field hospital and decontamination facility at the Polo Field in Golden Gate Park," Quinones replied. "I'd like the FEMA and the NEST teams to set up there as well. We have other units shutting down traffic into San Francisco and redirecting BART and Cal Train to evacuate the City, but it is going to be a hell of a mess on the highways no matter what we do," he added. "The only good news is that our main hospitals are not within the blast zone and, so far at least, are outside of the radiation plume. I'm ordering the Guard to clear Union Square, the area around AT&T Park, Dolores Park and Jefferson Square for medical evacuation teams to chopper in."

Jackson nodded his approval. "I'm designating Major General

Volker of the Northern Command as the federal task force commander for San Francisco, Governor," Jackson said. "We're sending you a summary of his service record now. He should reach Sacramento in two hours to coordinate with you and assume command of your Guard units. NORTHCOM will muster one of its military police teams trained in peacekeeping. They can be in San Francisco in as little as three hours, but you should meet with Volker and agree on a deployment plan first. In the meantime, please post your guardsmen on the bridges, the waterfront, San Francisco International, your rail yards, and at BART stations. We don't know if they will try to hit the infrastructure next." Jackson paused to think. "Please stand by, Governor," he added to Quinones. Jackson turned towards Gray. "Communications," he said.

"Go ahead, sir," she replied, and pointed at Commander Vuong to carry out the order.

"Get the mayor of Los Angeles—I don't know the name. Get him or her on the conference while you still have the Governor, patch them together. I want Los Angeles to start an evacuation."

Paul Coulter continued to watch the NBC monitor in stunned silence as a long line of University of Washington students from the dormitories on the east and south sides of campus and east of University Avenue, were guided out and herded into a long column to make the two mile walk north to the FEMA decontamination facility being set up at Magnuson Park, the site of the former Sand Point Naval Air Station. Most wore dusk masks or bandannas over their nose and mouth to limit the risk of inhaling radioactive smoke. Coulter had seen mass evacuations as a soldier and war correspondent, from First Iraq through Bosnia, Kosovo, and Afghanistan, but only once before had he seen an evacuation on his own native soil, that terrible morning when New York had been brought to its knees on 9/11.

"FEMA," Jackson said, "Go. I want an atmospherics update for both Seattle and San Francisco."

The FEMA director turned away while an aide crouched behind his shoulder whispered in his ear. "Seattle looks better," he finally replied, turning back to face his camera. "Winds are light, blowing from the west south west at about seven knots. If it continues, the smoke plume, now about a thousand meters across, should spread and dissipate over Lake Washington. Radiation levels should drop below 5 REMs one mile out from the site. Particulates and possible ingestion of radioactive materials will still be a risk. We should consider having the eastern suburbs across the lake, Kirkland and Bellevue, evacuate and pull back say twenty miles for forty eight hours."

Jackson shook his head. "They'll have to self-evacuate. We don't have the resources on the ground yet to do anything but try to control the panic in the city areas."

The FEMA director nodded. "We'll work with the Governor's people and local media to start publicizing the emergency routes east," he said. "As for San Francisco—

"Yes?"

"Not good. There is a small system about a hundred miles off the coast that is causing a slight flow from the southwest, call it two knots." The FEMA director grimaced as he reviewed the data. "The plume's going to move very slowly over downtown San Francisco and the Financial District," he said. "A lot of the particulates will begin settling out. We need to clear out everybody there. Now."

At 1:45 that afternoon the deputy White House press secretary, Timothy Nolan, finally returned to the temporary stage that had been set up for him in the Convention Center.

"We are confirming that the Seattle and San Francisco terror attacks involved the use of Radiation Dispersal Devices," he began.

"How dirty were the bombs?" a new woman reporter for AP that Coulter didn't know shouted from the second row.

"No questions until I get through the statement," Nolan replied angrily as the reporters in the room erupted. "Now listen. The RDDs did have some radioactive material packed into them. There were no nuclear explosions. The total effect is much less than the fallout one would associate with a nuclear explosion. Therefore, we have directed people in both Seattle and San Francisco who are not in danger of exposure to take shelter in place. Anyone a mile or more from the blast sites and not in the direct path of the smoke plumes should take shelter in place. They will be much safer if they stay home, so please help get that word out—we are emailing evacuation directions to those of you who report for local media in the attack zones. People who were in areas near the bomb sites and exposed to radiation from the initial explosion are being directed to decontamination units by FEMA and by units of the Washington and California National Guards, as well as by local police."

As Nolan paused to take a breath, the room erupted again.

"What are the casualties?" a Reuters' reporter demanded.

"We're trying to estimate," Nolan replied. "Preliminary word— From the FBI and from the Red Cross, as well as local officials, puts the number around 400 dead in Seattle, perhaps as many as 2000 people dead in San Francisco. These are estimates only. It will be at least a week before the forensic examinations are completed. And we're not sure yet what the ultimate health effects from the radiation will be."

"Who's behind this?" Coulter shouted.

"We don't know," Nolan admitted. "Every effort will be made—

"Right," a skeptical reporter from the left wing *Nation* growled in a thick Australian accent. "So who the fuck are we going to invade *this* time?"

An hour later Los Angeles was hit.

"The L.A. evacuation was at least partially successful," California Governor Ray Quinones said later that night, shortly before 1:00 A.M. EDT. "We think we lost about two hundred people in the L.A. blast zone. We think most of them were tourists who were in the streets or in nearby shops on Hollywood Boulevard that didn't hear the warnings in time. But we got a lot of people out in the four hours prior to the bomb going off. Good call, Mr. Vice-President."

"What do we know about the plume?" Jackson asked, rubbing his face hard with the heels of his hands, one of the few gestures he had allowed himself to make that revealed his fatigue after eleven hours in command in the Situation Room.

"We think it might be dissipating essentially in place," the FEMA director said. "It was a hot day in Los Angeles. The bomb exploded at a loading dock behind the W Hotel at Hollywood Boulevard and Argyle. The Hollywood Hills to the north cuts off most of the local breezes. There's not much wind coming up tonight. So the Hollywood area is going to be the most heavily contaminated. Nobody will be touring Grauman's Chinese Theater this week. "

Jackson nodded. "Okay. Focus our decontamination resources there. What have we got?"

"We had to split our units," FEMA replied. "The terrain on the way to the open areas to the north of the Boulevard, in Griffith Park, is too hilly and too far for anyone injured to walk. So we've set up the smaller decon unit in the Park; it will treat people who are driven in by ambulance or National Guard trucks. The larger unit has been set up in the Hollywood Forever cemetery south of Santa Monica Boulevard. The terrain's flat, it's close, people can walk there. We've set up water distribution points and marked a path out for them, and arranged for transport from there to get them home, to hospitals, or to temporary shelter."

"Acceptable, FEMA," Jackson pivoted to another screen. "Governor, I've ordered NEST teams and units from NorthCom comparable to what we have provided in San Francisco to move into L.A. The task force commander will be…" Jackson paused, looked to Horvath.

"Brigadier General David Foster," Horvath replied promptly.

"He will go to L.A. or Sacramento by 0500 hours your time to meet with you—tell him where you'll be. We'll get you back in this loop tomorrow morning after you meet with him…say 0700 your time." Jackson nodded to Gray, who then dropped the California participants from the conference.

Jackson stood, seemed lost for a moment in thought as a sudden silence filled the room. "FBI, CIA, Homeland Intelligence," he finally said. "In order. Is there any indication of any additional attack of any sort, in the cities that have been hit, or anywhere else around the country?"

"FBI, no," Cable Hollings, who had taken over for the Director, said quietly.

"CIA, no," replied Derek Martin, sitting in for the DCI.

"Homeland Intelligence…" Crane Dunham said slowly, while gesturing impatiently for the latest analysis. Elizabeth pointed and a senior analyst she had summoned from NCTC handed a one page brief to Dunham who read it. "We're not sure," Dunham replied. "With TriPlex still down we can't rule out another attack." Dunham turned to glare briefly at Elizabeth Gray, who during an earlier sidebar conference call had demanded Homeland Intelligence take a neutral stance. Dunham crumpled the briefing paper into a ball and tossed it on the table.

Jackson looked up at the conference camera over the rims of his reading glasses. "OK. Four hours ago I asked everyone in this room to designate a deputy to keep watch overnight. Get those people in their chairs. The lead team needs to go get six hours sleep and reconvene at 0700. We will need your input before the President addresses the American people tomorrow. We need to explain what has happened. So I will see you in…sorry. A little over six hours."

Chapter Thirty-Four

Elizabeth briefed her replacement as the ERG Coordinator, a Navy Captain whom Jackson had just named as his principal national security aide. As they worked through the procedures sailors from the Navy Mess came through the Sit Room bringing fresh water, juices, coffee and sandwiches. The sailors had been ordered to evacuate in the first hour after the Seattle attacks; every man and woman on duty had refused the order and stayed.

When Gray was finished she stood, straightened the jacket on her Class A uniform, and prepared to leave the Sit Room, wondering how the hell she would get home.

"Major? A word," Jackson said.

Karol Horvath looked up, suddenly intensely alert.

Gray nodded. "Sir?"

Jackson frowned. "I am directing that you be relieved, Major," he said bluntly.

The words could not have had more impact on Gray than if Jackson had punched her in the gut. Stunned, fighting down a sudden wave of nausea, she said, "I do not understand, sir."

"This is the worst intelligence failure since 9/11. Your agency was set up to detect and *prevent* surprise terror attacks. Yet fifteen years later we are apparently still defenseless. There will be an inquiry…by Congress and by the Justice Department.

"I don't understand what the hell you and Thrace thought you were doing," Jackson continued, his voice rising in anger. "From what I'm told you were hell bent pursuing some groundless, even bizarre investigation into the loyalty of former American military personnel, yet you missed the first nuclear attack on American soil. Pending an investigation the Pentagon can reassign you to duties more suited to your abilities…however limited."

Horvath looked at Gray, expression neutral. "Major," he said, "you will report to me for reassignment to the Joint Staff tomorrow morning at 0800."

"Yes, sir," she said softly, still stunned.

Horvath walked with her in silence through the West Wing and out to the White House's north gate. His driver appeared with a black Pentagon sedan. As Horvath started to get into the back seat of the car he paused, looked out toward H Street, and saw no there were no cars and no chance of a taxi; all streets within six blocks of the White House had been closed to all but military traffic. "Come on, Major, get in. I can drop you on Capitol Hill on the way back to Fort Myers. The only other way you'd get a ride home tonight is by hijacking a Stryker."

When they were both seated in the back of the sedan Horvath leaned over and spoke directly into Elizabeth's ear, his voice lowered to a near whisper.

"Don't let that little bastard scare you," he said. "They're going to try to set up Tony Thrace for this, the same way the neocons tried to blame Bush's 9/11 negligence on Clinton. As for the Phalanx investigation, I've got a paper trail that shows that we were all following Charlie McConnell's orders. You'll be all right."

The lump of lead in Gray's stomach dissolved only a bit, balanced by the shock of Horvath's description of the Vice-President as "that little bastard". She wondered again what history had divided the two men. "What's my new job?" she asked.

Horvath smiled nastily, as though he was beginning to relish the idea of a public fight with Kyle Jackson. "Staff. For me. You're going to figure out who did this to us, and how they did it."

The Press Office, still in disarray, had put the lid on at eleven. News was embargoed until 7:00 A.M. Washington time to give local responders and FEMA personnel an opportunity to begin identifying the victims and give notice to their families. The last scenes Paul watched on the CNN, Google and NBC screens in the temporary press room showed the black tents that had been set up at the FEMA sites in Seattle, San Francisco, and Los Angeles as field morgues. Sickened and depressed, Paul decided to file his story from home rather than remain in the sterile confines of the Convention Center. He wondered if his editor would notice if he wrote the damn thing drunk.

DC Metro was shut down; there were no cabs. Paul walked east on K Street, at the north edge of the military security cordon that now surrounded the federal zone around the White House and the Capitol. The night was still balmy with Indian summer and under other circumstances he might have made a game of the walk, stopping in an all night store or maybe a bar or two to see what was shaking in his neighborhood. The stores and bars were all closed; soldiers from Fort Belvoir manned the security line in their armored Humvees and Strykers, weapons at ready, ignoring the few late pedestrians who, like Paul, walked carefully on the north side of K Street.

When Elizabeth arrived home after 2:30 A.M. Paul barely glanced up from the large flat screen video monitor in their living room.

"Paul?" she asked sharply, hurt and exasperated that he had not so much as acknowledged her presence. He continued to stare at the screen, his laptop open and a story started but no words below the headline. He had an unopened bottle of Johnny Walker Black and an empty glass on the cocktail table in front of him; Elizabeth smelled no alcohol on the air. There was, she saw, a grim fury in his eyes.

"What is it?" she asked again, insistent.

"You were video recorded," Paul said slowly, finally coming out of his trance. "In the Situation Room."

"That's standard," she responded. "All Sit Room meetings are recorded, everybody knows that." Elizabeth went to the kitchen, found a glass and ice, and returned to the living room, intending to crack open the scotch, 0800 report or not.

"Do you post them on the Internet?" Paul finally responded.

She nearly choked. "What? Hell, *no.* Those recordings are classified for five, ten, twenty years."

"This one wasn't," Paul responded. "It was leaked. Looks like it was edited, too. Damn thing plays like a documentary film."

"What? Where?" Elizabeth said, dropping onto the couch beside him.

"Everywhere. You Tube. Google Video. Bing Current. *Everywhere.* CNN's been picking up feeds, editing them together. There's been more than fifty million hits in the last hour. And more segments keep showing up."

Oh Christ, Elizabeth thought, *another ground for my court martial. Could Vuong and her tech crew have somehow stored the Sit Room video in a public or hackable database?*

"Wait a minute," she finally said, as she watched the next segment pop up on CNN. This does look like a movie. With a star."

"Right," Paul said bitterly. "America's new man on horseback. Kyle Jackson."

Chapter Thirty-Five

The Seattle Times/The Portland Oregonian
Tuesday, October 4
Special to the Internet Editions
8:35 A.M. E.D.T.

NATION REELS FROM NUCLEAR TERRORISM
PRESIDENT WILL VOW JUSTICE, REVENGE

By Paul Coulter, Pacific News Consortium

There has not been a dawn like this in America since September 12, 2001.

Three Pacific Coast cities—Seattle, San Francisco, and Los Angeles—have suffered devastating terror attacks. Landmarks in each of those cities—the Magnuson Health Sciences Center in Seattle, the San Francisco City Hall, and the historic heart of America's film industry, the street of dreams at Hollywood and Vine— suffered massive truck bomb attacks. Each of the truck bombs, deadly in their own right, was laced with radioactive spent fuel, spewing uranium and plutonium into the air. No group or nation has yet claimed responsibility for the attacks.

Almost three thousand people in the three cities are now believed dead, killed in the blasts. Perhaps ten thousand more may have been exposed to deadly inhaled plutonium in the smoke from the explosions. No one can presently estimate how many exposed will contract lung cancer or other radiation induced diseases in the coming months and years.

In the twenty-four hours since these attacks began the nation has been convulsed by fear and anger. All major West Coast cities, including Portland, San Diego, and Sacramento, have seen hundreds of automobile accidents as desperate city residents sought to flee actual or feared attacks. Airline flights throughout the country have been grounded, stranding a million people far from their homes. Washington and other major cities are patrolled this morning by combat troops from the Army's Northern Command and by National Guardsmen from thirty different states.

At the White House, Vice-President Kyle Jackson took control of the Homeland Emergency Response Group in place of the traveling President Robinson, logging more than thirteen hours in the White House Situation Room yesterday as he directed the nation's military and civilian first responders in their tasks. Portions of White House Situation Room video recordings were leaked to the Internet, drawing more than 200 million hits by seven A.M. this morning. The videos, which show Jackson responding to the crisis, appear to have generated a huge wave of public support and admiration for the new Vice-President.

The President and Vice-President Jackson will travel to Los Angeles later today to review the damage and speak to the nation. Their joint speech is scheduled for 6:00 P.M. Pacific Daylight Time. Early reports say the President's speech will emphasize that the United States intends to bring to justice all those involved in the attacks. One senior official, speaking on background, vowed "There will be an eye for an eye."

As with the 9/11 and New Comiskey terror attacks, fear and anger against Muslim communities ran high throughout the country last night, based on the belief that these attacks are further battles in the long twilight terror war with Islamic extremists. Mosques in Seattle, Los Angeles, Minneapolis, and Houston have been burned to the ground; as many as fourteen people are feared dead. Congressman

Edward Al Masra, a Democrat from Detroit, Michigan was assassinated at 2:30 this morning in Southeast Washington as he attempted to head off a confrontation between angry crowds of Christians and Muslims. The White House offered its condolences to Congressman Al Masra's family and vowed that "the full power and resources of the Federal Government" would be devoted to finding his killer.

At 6 P.M. James Robinson and Kyle Jackson stood before a surging, weeping crowd of twenty thousand people at the Staples Center in downtown Los Angeles. Although the threat of direct radiation exposure had long since passed, both still wore the red Demron protective suits that they had worn earlier in the Hollywood district as they assayed the damage. Robinson, if nothing else a shrewd judge of political theater, had insisted that he and Jackson remain inside their hot radiation suits throughout their speeches. He spoke with sweat pouring down his face.

"I stand before you today as the leader of a proud but wounded people," Robinson said slowly. "For the third time in fifteen years, we have been attacked on our home soil. Once again, thousands have died. Once again, this seemingly implacable war with Islam—for there is little doubt that this attack originated in the Middle East—comes to the heart of the American Nation. And once more, we will preserve and protect our people and take the fight to the enemy." Robinson's reddened, sweating face set in anger. "And I promise you this: *our American dead will be avenged.*" Cheers rocked the arena.

"So while we mourn those we have lost," he continued, "let us recognize that we have among us a new American hero. My friend, my Vice-President, Kyle Jackson! Many, if not most of you, saw how he guided our response to this tragedy. I could not have more confidence in this man. There is no better man for the safety of America, than Vice-President Jackson." The ten thousand people in Staples Center roared their approval. He finally raised his hands for quiet. "It is time for you to hear directly from him. I give you Kyle! Hunter! Jackson!

Jackson stepped to the podium in his radiation suit amid the cheers.

"Thank you," he said simply. "Let us pray."

Cable Hollings fell asleep for a moment on the soft leather armchair he used for reading in his office on the Hoover Building's 11th floor, on the E street side of the building. It seemed as though he had just closed his eyes after thirty-six working hours when one of his personal deputies, a young lawyer three years' out from the University of Virginia Law School shook him awake. The television was still on, the sound muted as thousands of people appeared to be singing hymns in Staples Center arena.

"Sir? It's after ten P.M. The next update meeting on the RDD attack investigation is in twenty minutes," she said.

"Hell, breakfast and everything else in between," Hollings said, waking suddenly. "I suppose the Director will be there. Is there coffee?"

"Yes, sir. And you have four new reports to review before the meeting."

"Son of a bitch." He rose from the sofa, all bones and aches. He stepped into the small private bath adjacent to his office to splash water on his face. Something nagged at him. He was getting old and his short term memory wasn't what it once was, but the cold water helped wake up his mind. "I need to talk to Bob Rupert," he said, emerging from the bathroom and wiping his face dry with a towel. "He's the SAC in the Las Vegas office."

"Yes sir. Agent Rupert sent you an encrypted email about ten minutes ago that contains his report."

"Send in coffee and shoo, Deborah, I've got to get myself put together and some of the stuff I've got to read is above your classification. But walk me over to the Director's conference room, okay?" She nodded and left, leaving Cable Hollings to wonder for the hundredth time how the Bureau was able to attract such good people at such crap wages in the junior grades. He opened his secure computer and glanced down the list of emails until he found Bob Rupert's, then opened and decrypted it.

The email read, "Raids Unsuccessful. Phalanx gone. Both sites abandoned."

At 11:30 P.M. that October night Elizabeth Gray remained in her temporary office in the Joint Staff area at the Pentagon, sifting through the voluminous reports, paper and electronic, now making their way to her through the federal bureaucracy. Karol Horvath appeared at the door of her office. His uniform, unlike hers, was still immaculate, but lines of strain had appeared around his eyes and his voice betrayed his concern.

"Did you see the broadcast from L.A.?" he asked.

"No sir," she said, rising and saluting.

Horvath waived it off. "At ease, Major."

"Sorry sir, I need to practice being a real military officer again. What happened in L.A.?"

"The President and the Vice-President had themselves a prayer rally at Staples Center. The President blamed the bombings on 'radical Islamists.'"

She looked startled. "But we don't know that," she replied.

"No, we don't. That does not seem to bother the Administration." He paused. "I've got to go into the tank with the Chairman in fifteen minutes and he's going to want to know what in hell happened and why his J2 didn't have any idea of what was coming. That's my problem, not yours. You were sending up alarms four months ago." Horvath, paused, face grim. "We have to know who did this. The world can't take the uncertainty right now. Every nuclear power in the Middle East, as well as India and Pakistan, has gone to launch on warning. Israel seems particularly anxious. Rosh Hashanah, the Day of Judgment, was yesterday, Major, and the Israelis don't like the symbolic connection one goddamn bit. Jehovah seals his judgments on Yom Kippur, which begins at sunset on 11 October. I think that may be all the time we are going to have to figure this out." He started to step away. Elizabeth stopped him.

"Sir, for what it's worth…it does not make sense for any Islamic group or government to have done this. They know our doctrine, that we will meet any use of a weapon of mass destruction with a retaliatory WMD strike…and one D-5 missile with eight MIRV warheads from the *Henry Jackson* would turn all the major cities in Iran to glass."

Gray gestured to the reports filling her desk. "The casualties are awful…but they could have been much worse. Think of some of the WMD scenarios we've run: a 10 kiloton nuke in any of our ports, a subway nerve gas attack on Manhattan or BART in San Francisco; a smallpox or mutated flu virus attack deliberately spread by suicidal terrorists coming in on a hundred airline flights at once, armed only with a virus in their blood. Under those scenarios we'd have experienced tens, maybe hundreds of thousands of casualties. Why raise the WMD issue by such relatively small attacks? A conventional car bomb, followed up by suicide squads, could have killed hundreds of people at Magnuson in Seattle; a similar strategy aimed at three or four targets in San Francisco would probably have killed more people. Dirty bombs effectively spread fear and panic, but to be mass killers they have to disperse short-lived strong gamma emitters like cesium or strontium across wide distances—and the physics of these bombs didn't work that way. We have a radiological air pollution problem that will cause cancers, and cleaning up the contamination will cost billions, but…at the societal level of a country this big and powerful, it's *manageable.* It's as if they wanted to stun us or distract us, not seriously hurt us. Yet our retaliation doctrine says we will blow them and any country that sheltered them into rubble."

Horvath looked thoughtful, then at his watch. "Six minutes. Keep going."

"Think about it as a strategic problem in a war game—you're the Red Commander. If you wanted to hurt the United States and diminish its power over the long term, turn the country towards isolation, but didn't want to risk nuclear retaliation, what would you do? I'd go after economic targets—we have thousands of soft ones.

The undersea cables and satellite uplink stations that carry international Internet traffic. The Google and Microsoft and AT&T server farms along the Columbia River and in Texas and Virginia. Hell, the Columbia River dams themselves, the Texas and Dakota wind farms, the Joshua Tree solar plants in California, the new regional smart electrical power grids, and the whole network of oil and gas pipelines. All of those installations are relatively fragile, none of them as well guarded as a nuclear power plant. But they are all hugely important to maintaining the American standard of living.

"And if you were really crazy enough to risk using a nuclear device, why in hell wouldn't you deploy an Electromagnetic Pulse attack, fire off a megaton or bigger nuke two hundred miles above Kansas, disable all civilian communications and power systems, scramble the financial world, and put us even further into an economic depression that could last twenty more years? *But that would also be suicidal.* Most of the scenarios we've run show a high probability that Israel would launch a preemptive strike on every Islamic nuclear power— Pakistan, Iran, the Saudis—and possibly the small players like Jordan and what's left of Syria and Iraq, within ten minutes of an Islamic nuclear or biological attack on the Unites States. An Islamic terrorist using any type of WMD against the United States has to assume that three quarters of the Muslim population of the world would be killed. Yet none of our intelligence sources has ever revealed the existence of a group that wants to bring the apocalypse to the *ummat al-mu'minin,* the community of believers.*"

"I thought there was a millennial streak within Shi'a Islam."

"There is, but it doesn't involve mass suicide. In fact it's very similar to fundamentalist Christian beliefs. The Twelfth Imam returns to bring justice to the world, the faithful battle the unbelievers; there is a Day of Judgment, and a physical resurrection."

"Two minutes," Horvath replied. "Bottom line, Major."

"This doesn't make sense as an external terrorist attack. It's much more like three Oklahoma City attacks, combined for impact, and with a radioactive component to frighten and paralyze. It will disrupt, maybe halt, the elections, and give the administration an excuse to keep itself in power. I can't believe Americans would do this to their country. I don't have a word for how sick that makes me feel. But we know a group that is capable, funded, and out there."

"Are you suggesting the Phalanx carried out these attacks? Do they have ties to radical Islamist groups, or to Iran?"

"I don't believe they have ties to Islamists or Iran, General. I think they'd be ideological enemies—which doesn't foreclose cooperation. But what if it is the election? Washington, Oregon and California have seventy-four solidly democratic electoral votes that have just been knocked out. And the targets represent everything the Christian Nation hates. Seattle is software, biotechnology, stem cell research, the whole modern secular world. San Francisco is the internet, gay rights and gay marriage. Hollywood mocks their religion and values and brings moral decay."

Horvath closed his eyes, thought, nodded. "You're suggesting that this is our Reichstag fire. I'd really like to think you've lost your mind under the pressure, Major. If you're wrong—especially about Jackson's being involved with the Phalanx—you'll be broken out of the service. No one will be able to help you. But I'll tell the Chairman what you think. You'll have a couple of days, no more, before you have to prove it."

Chapter Thirty-Six

Shepherd Field
Eastern West Virginia Regional Airport
Martinsburg, West Virginia
Sunday, October 9
12:45 A.M. EDT

The aging Gulfstream G4 was parked at the rear of the small airport's single hanger building. Paul Coulter's eyes burned from the harsh fluorescent lighting as he exited from the unmarked Ford van that had picked him up from Dulles Airport and driven him the final sixty miles to Martinsburg. As Coulter walked toward the plane a black-suited, well-muscled man that Coulter could only assume was Secret Service opened the cabin door and lowered the folding stairs, gesturing for Coulter to enter the plane.

Democratic Presidential nominee Ben Giles stepped forward in the aircraft cabin from a conference table that filled much of the center of the plane, his right hand stretched out in greeting, but his dark green eyes betraying both exhaustion and a certain amount of caution. "I'm Ben Giles," he said, as Paul took his hand. "I'm sorry if I'm not at my most polite, but my country is under attack and it's going to be bitch to hold things together between now and the election."

"If there is an election, Senator," Paul replied.

Giles blinked once but gave no other sign of surprise. "So? I've got 45 minutes for you, because some of my old friends in the military tell me that I should listen to you. But make it march."

Coulter glanced over at two other men in the plane: Jeff Reardon, who had been evading his calls for weeks, and a senior Giles campaign lawyer named David Rivera, a plaintiff's class action lawyer from California who was reputed to be Giles' first choice for White House counsel. "Do they stay?" Coulter asked.

"They're my shit detectors."

"Fair enough. You listening, Jeff?"

Reardon's smile was a thin wire spread across bone. "I'm listening, Paul. I'm in the woodshed for not listening before."

Coulter did not respond. He turned to Giles, took a deep breath.

"We did not experience an external terrorist attack on the United States in Seattle, San Francisco, and L.A," he said.

"What?" Giles demanded.

"It's a false flag operation, to justify a constitutional coup and suspend the elections."

Giles tilted his head, focused on Coulter, his green eyes intense. "Ok. That's a little hard to swallow. You need to start at the beginning."

Coulter nodded. He took the same plain 3 x 5 card from his pocket that he had drawn for Elizabeth and showed to Arne Kaplan on the street on a bright day that seemed years in the past. "Have you ever seen this symbol, Senator?" he asked.

"No. I can guess what it is. A representation of an archaic Spartan infantry formation. A phalanx."

"Correct. "The Phalanx" is also the name of a clandestine organization formed by active duty and retired military, many of whom now work for military contractors. It started in Afghanistan a decade ago. And it has—best guess—around four to five thousand members. It could be more."

"How do you know this?" Giles asked.

"The Phalanx was the subject of a secret investigation that Charlie McConnell launched shortly before his death. Charlie told me about it because he had assigned my almost wife, girlfriend, partner—whatever the hell *is* the right word nowadays?—to investigate the Phalanx and its sources of funding. She is named Elizabeth Gray. She's an Army major who was on detached duty in the White House. Her cover was low level NSA staffer. In reality she was Mc-Connell's personal assistant who dealt with the nastier kinds of Homeland Intelligence security issues.

"Elizabeth's task was to identify who these people were, what their objectives were, and how they were funded. The Phalanx began as a cross between a Christian fellowship and a *sub rosa* soldiers' union—enlisted men and a few junior officers, angered by the endless repeat deployments, stuck in a forever war drawing bad pay and losing their families. It soon fell under the sway of right wing Dominionist Christian theology. It got political."

Giles shook his head in disgust. "The Dominionists. The Rambo Jesus. Where's the money fit in? You said Gray was trying to figure out where this group was getting its funding."

"The Phalanx seemed to be getting money from a variety of Middle Eastern sources, routed via banks in Panama City. When Elizabeth looked into it, she found an existing IRS/FINCEN tax and money laundering investigation."

Giles leaned forward. "I don't see how the trails cross."

"Neither did she at first. The IRS and FINCEN people in Panama told her the money was coming through one of the biggest banks in Panama City, the Bank Royal. It is owned by the Cornwall Group, a private holding company headquartered in Grand Cayman. Cornwall has an American subsidiary that you probably know pretty well. Dark/Star."

Giles paused, looked skeptical. "Where do you fit into this, Coulter?"

"I covered the Republican Convention with Graham Taylor. He was a retired British SAS Colonel, a journalist and history professor at American University. We were stunned by Jackson's selection as the Vice-Presidential nominee. And the decapitation of Harry Purcell's candidacy was just a little too neat. So Graham and I decided to take on a Jackson project, to see what we could find out. I took the military side and found out that Jackson was cashiered on the verge of becoming a Brigadier General in 1998 because he was one of the organizers of an officers' revolt against Bill Clinton that got squashed by the Army Chief Staff, General Nakasone."

"So that was it," Giles said slowly. "I was in Kosovo, a long way away, and General Jack clamped an iron wall around all those resignations. But go back to the money thing, Paul. What's Jackson's connection to Cornwall and the money moving through the pirate islands and Panama? He's supposed to have sold Dark/Star years ago, and denies any connection to Cornwall."

"Graham had sources in the Caribbean. He found out that Jackson got the funding to buy Dark/Star through a pair of Cayman trusts owned by Royce Reed, the founder of Christian Nation. Reed stole the money to buy Dark/Star from the collection plates of his churches. When Dark/Star was sold to Cornwall, Reed and Jackson kept the profits hidden offshore to evade capital gains taxes. They control Cornwall now. But Reed was in trouble. McConnell's Justice Department had built a hundred count indictment against him for tax evasion and money laundering...which the Robinson White House killed as soon as Jackson was named Vice-President. I've got a copy of the indictment."

"Taylor was murdered in DC last month," Giles said.

"The DC cops think it was a professional hit. So do I."

"Where's this Panama task force now?" David Rivera asked.

"Shut down. I've been trying to contact or locate a woman named Karen Jenkins, the head of the task force, for two weeks. She's gone, utterly gone. No trace. I hope she's in hiding, but I'm afraid she's dead. Like Graham Taylor. Like Barnes Powell, Jackson's banker, who was found dead at his home on Grand Cayman the day before Graham was killed. Like Tony Thrace, murdered by a Phalanx member who turned his truck into a suicide bomb."

Giles leaned forward in his leather seat. "Does Jackson run the Phalanx?"

"Yes. Through Dark/Star. It has set up a new urban warfare training base in Nevada, and they are training troops."

"But why would Dark/Star need another training base?" Giles asked. "The Army had three facilities that handled that kind of civil disturbance training for soldiers and guardsmen headed for the Middle East during the Wars. I set them up when I was head of the Joint Training Command."

"Because Dark/Star isn't training the Army," Coulter replied. "It's training the Phalanx. For deployment *inside* the United States."

Giles paused in thought, his expression grim. "The President," he said slowly, his distaste at applying that title to James Robinson quite plain, "will call Congress back into special session for next Monday, 17 October. Kind of peculiar timing, isn't it? So close to Election Day."

"If there is an Election Day," Coulter replied. Why is a special session being called? There's been no press statement about that, not even a rumor."

Giles looked grim. "If you are right...Robinson is going to try to invoke the continuity of government measures. Martial law." He paused. "So what do you want from us, Paul?"

"Smart people. You've got probably a thousand volunteer lawyers, recruited in case there are election law issues in November. Give me fifty litigators with backgrounds in securities, white collar crime, tax, corporate transactions. Let me outline this, tell them what to look for, and they can raise hell, file lawsuits and FOIA demands, prove this up, at least the financial end—the embezzlement of the money that Reed and Jackson used to acquire Dark/Star, the hundreds of millions in tax evasion. If you go after Jackson on the money, you can still smash him—phony national hero or not."

"Paul, if you give us your information, and we give you resources, you're not a journalist anymore. You're working for me. Given what's at stake, you'll never work as a journalist again. You prepared for that?"

Coulter nodded. "I knew that when I walked in here."

Giles turned to his aides. "Coulter gets his fifty lawyers. He'll need media people too. Jeff, free up as much money as you can for this—go back to the Billionaire Boys Club and shake them down. David, you head up the working group. You've got five days to get me something I can use to stop this in the joint session. But for chrissakes keep it under wraps."

Rivera nodded. "We won't set up in one place. We'll assemble the team in small groups across the country and hook them up in a private encrypted network. Lonnie Sanderson can get four or five big law firms to give us space and secure facilities access, no questions asked. Most of the people we will bring in will be either ex-Justice Department or state prosecutors who can keep their mouths shut. But there's always some risk it will get out."

"There's not a lot of time," Coulter replied. He took three data sticks from the pocket of his jacket and handed them to Rivera. "Start with these," he said. "This is everything Graham was able to find out about Dark/Star and Cornwall. It includes a copy the Reed indictment. And tell me where to go tomorrow morning."

Giles cut in. "Paul, David can take the lead on Graham Taylor's information. But there's something else we need to know. We're hearing that Jackson is going to blame the West Coast bombings on Iran. I don't think the Mullahs are crazy enough to supply the spent fuel, and maybe have us nuke them, but I need evidence. If the Phalanx did these attacks, then where did they get the spent fuel used in the bombs? I need you and your Major Gray to find out, Paul. As fast as you can."

Chapter Thirty-Seven

Fairchilds, LLP
555 13th St. N.W.
Washington, D.C.
Sunday, October 9
2:05 P.M. EDT

Coulter finally got home at 6:00 A.M. He hoped he would find Elizabeth asleep in their bed, the water in the shower actually hot, and that he could have a quiet hour to sit down, have a shot of whiskey, and contemplate the end of his career as he knew it.

It was not going to work out that way. Elizabeth was wide awake, seated in the living room in a Japanese silk robe with the gas fire burning, a carafe of coffee with the sadly skinny Sunday newspapers arrayed on the low table in front of her.

"I'm not going to bother you with any clichés like where have you been," she said. "I now know a bit like what you felt when I disappeared without a word—and I'm forever sorry, Paul. But there are just too many goddamn secrets in this room."

"I know," Paul replied quietly. "I agree. But you're already a political and legal target. If you get involved in what I am doing…it will be worse for you. Besides," he added, aiming for a little gallows humor, "our legal budget isn't that big."

"Great," Elizabeth responded sarcastically. "We *should* get married. That's the only way we can avoid being subpoenaed to testify against each other. Oh, and we could put our law firms on the registry. Ask each guest to give one billable hour. Pricey, but more useful than another coffee maker. *Fuck*." She got up and paced, restless. "What do we do now?"

"Giles asked a good question," he responded. He stood and reached out a hand to her; she reluctantly stopped her pacing and took it. "Where could the Phalanx find nuclear fuel that could be passed off as Iranian in origin to use in the bombs?"

"I don't have nuclear clearances, Paul. But the chemical residues at all the bomb sites have been sampled in great detail. Nuclear materials are typed by chemical composition and match it against our existing databases. My father started work on that problem at Los Alamos nearly forty years ago. Cable Hollings probably has the FBI lab working on it."

Paul shook his head. "Jackson wouldn't use FBI labs he couldn't control to test the bomb residues. Can you find out?"

"Paul, I'm already too far over too many lines."

"So am I. One more thing. Has the FBI found the Phalanx training site that Dane Troyer told us about? They would need lots of empty space, not too visible to satellite. Troyer also told me about a second Nevada site. He said it was 'technical'. Could it have handled the spent fuel and built the ANFO bombs? Ask Cable to talk to me directly. I can get any information he can provide to Ben Giles."

"So much for retired pay and benefits," Elizabeth sighed.

"I'll make it worth your while, Beth."

"Fat chance. There's one other possible connec—

The telephone rang.

Coulter cursed, thought, and then picked it up.

It was Graham Taylor's attorney, Lonnie Sanderson. "Hey Paul," he said brightly. "Sorry about the early hour, but I missed you yesterday. Anyway, seems like your company has acquired a new asset we should talk about." He chuckled. "Nothing…miraculous, probably speculative, but could be profitable."

"Think you'll be in the office this afternoon, cleaning up paper-work?" Coulter asked.

"Yeah, I had to give my 'Skins tickets to a client. They aren't any good this year anyway."

"How's two o'clock?"

"Sure, I'll leave your name with the security guard. I'll put a cou-ple beers on ice to make the trip worthwhile."

When Coulter arrived at the Fairchilds LLP law offices he was met not by a security guard but by a blonde pony-tailed junior as-sociate, dressed in a blue blazer and jeans for Sunday duty, who dispassionately checked Coulter's I.D. and led him directly to Sand-erson's office.

Sanderson's cheery deflective humor was gone. "Did you tell anyone about this dead drop?" he demanded. "There are risks for both—

"No," Coulter responded, cutting him off. "Whoever used the drop must have gotten it from Graham, not me."

Sanderson handed him a thin DHL courier envelope. Paul checked the transit label. It had been sent from Cartagena, Colum-bia five days before. He slit it open.

It contained a single piece of cheap printer paper, with two sen-tences printed in the center of the page.

"Your Englishman liked to stay three drinks ahead of the world, especially at lunch on the Day of Atonement." Coulter passed it without comment to Sanderson.

"Coded?" Sanderson asked after he'd read it.

"No," Coulter responded. "I know where and when, and I have a pretty good idea about who sent it."

Chapter Thirty-Eight

The White House Situation Room
The National Security Council
Washington, D.C.
Monday, October 10
8:45 A.M. EDT

"As you may know, Mr. Vice-President, when Homeland Intelligence was established by the third Patriot Act, the responsibility for forensic analysis in national security incidents was shifted from the FBI to Homeland Intelligence. We have analyzed all three disaster zones. The results were remarkably consistent." Crane Dunham gestured with a laser pointer and a power point filled the far screen at the end of the room. "Each of the bombs was indeed ANNM, an ANFO bomb juiced by a significant quantity of nitromethane to increase explosive power and intensity." Dunham gestured to an aide, who clicked to the next slide. "The proposal to add chemical taggants to fuel oil and fertilizer did not survive Congressional scrutiny in the final Patriot III bill legislation; therefore we cannot precisely trace the explosive material." Dunham neglected to add that, at the behest of the National Rifle Association, he had voted *against* the addition of chemical tags to potential explosives.

"As we all know," Dunham continued, "Iran was developing its domestic uranium mines even before the Islamic Revolution in

1979, part of the Shah's long term plan to acquire nuclear weapons. Despite the 'burning' process involved in using uranium fuel in a reactor, we can identify, by spectrographic analysis of trace elements, where the original uranium was mined: in the North Khorassan region of Iran. It appears to have been enriched to the 5-7% U-235 necessary to achieve a chain reaction in a pressurized water reactor. It very likely was burned in their Besheur I power reactor. The small pellets loaded into the fuel rods were subsequently ground into a powder for maximum radioactive distribution from the RDDs.

"I believe this is conclusive," Dunham said triumphantly. "We have our perpetrator. Directly or indirectly, Iran must have been behind this attack."

Jackson nodded approvingly. "Thank you, Director," he said. "I want our intelligence resources focused on the Iran/Alawite/Hezbollah nexus. I want confirmation of their guilt in seven days or less. The President and I will not tolerate more delays. Retribution must be swift."

Karol Horvath and Cable Hollings left via the North Portico and retreated to a far corner beyond the White House gate in the light morning drizzle. Both were convinced that Homeland Intelligence was now intercepting sound and cell phone signals from the White House grounds.

"They're stove-piping the intelligence," Hollings said. "Dunham has replaced the top twenty people in Homeland Intelligence in the last four days. Most of them come from Dark/Star. I doubt he even knows their names. He sure as hell doesn't even know what that crap he was reading from the PowerPoint means. None of the information he presented came from the FBI."

"Who's doing the forensics work, then?" Horvath asked.

Hollings took a red classified folder from his briefcase, scanned the document inside. "This can't be right," he said slowly.

"What's wrong?" Horvath asked.

"Well, shit," Hollings drawled. "When nuclear forensics was pulled from us we were told that work would be done at the national labs that had nuclear chemistry experience—Los Alamos and Fermi. But this is from a contractor. They outsourced this."

"Who was the contractor?" Horvath asked.

"Detail Chemical Forensics,"

"Yeah, I know it," Horvath replied, voice tinged with disgust. "It's a subsidiary of Dark/Star."

Hollings said, "I've still got forensic teams, Karol. With a little military cover I could dress them in ACU's instead of JC Penney polyester suits and send them in with your guys into the blast zones to take samples."

"Talk to Gray. Have them sample all three cities," Horvath replied. "That machine shop outside of Las Vegas, too. I'll contact Los Alamos and get them ready. Fast, Cable. Fast."

At nine o'clock that night Elizabeth Gray dumped the mostly uneaten remains of her cheeseburger into the garbage disposal in the kitchen of their Capitol Hill condominium, poured herself a third shot of Johnny Walker Black, and looked stonily at her lover.

"This is nuts," she said to Coulter. "It's a piece of paper in a DHL envelope. Even if you could find her, there's no way of knowing whether the two of you could make it back here alive," she said.

"There are three cutouts covering my tracks on the flight down there," Coulter responded. "If I find Jenkins we can interview her there. If there's a problem all I have to do is fly home from Costa Rica. The network of private jet charters that the big law firms and banks use is way better than the CIA's Rendition Air. I won't even have to fly sober."

"Why does it have to be you?" she insisted. "And why do you still need Jenkins? I thought you had a hundred lawyers working on this now."

"Given enough time, six weeks, maybe six months, those guys will get almost all of it right. But every story, every court case, needs a witness. Jenkins can go in front of Congress and the cameras. She was there through the entire tax investigation. There's nothing Acosta can say that will crack her credibility when she testifies that he trashed the Reed indictment in a deal with Robinson."

"Great. Terrific. Will they let you write the story? You'll get a Pulitzer. If you live long enough." She banged her empty glass on the kitchen counter. "What time do you leave?"

Coulter looked at his watch. "Five minutes or so."

She came to him, braced him, and kissed him hard on the mouth. "Don't fucking die," she said.

Coulter couldn't think of any reply that didn't sound stupid, or maudlin. He kissed Elizabeth again and descended to the lobby to wait for Lonny Sanderson's town car that would take him to the Leesburg Executive Airport to catch his charter. Elizabeth stayed in the dark kitchen for two or three minutes after he left, then went into their bedroom and tried to sleep. In the morning, in her office, they would be talking about plans for war with Iran.

Costa Rica

Chapter Thirty-Nine

The Gilded Iguana Hotel
Playa Guiones
Nosara, Costa Rica
Tuesday, October 12
10:55 A.M. CDT

Paul Coulter pulled up to the small surf-and-fishing hotel set back in a shaded, flowering garden a hundred yards inland from the Guiones beachfront. The drive down from Liberia had taken him nearly four hours because the rented Jeep was ten years old and lacked GPS, and the paper maps didn't show all of the unmarked crossings on the gravel roads that laced through the Guanacaste hills. The morning was hot and dry but this western province of Costa Rica was still on the shoulder between the rainy green season and the parched 'summer' that would settle in by mid-December. As he got out of the car he looked back down the road to the beach and saw towering clouds build over the Pacific, a thunderous tropical storm that would hit by six that night.

Coulter entered the welcome shade of the hotel restaurant and took a stool at the small bar. Before sitting down he reached up and rubbed his hand across the ancient teak plank mounted above the bar, a talisman for those seeking good fishing and good luck. The plank had been cut from a Key West fishing boat that had been tossed inland and wrecked in the 1935 Labor Day hurricane; an unknown optimist in the wake of that storm had carved his personal motto into it: "The rest of the World is three drinks behind." The sign had hung in a Duval Street dive for more than fifty years before being salvaged and brought to Costa Rica.

Coulter cleaned the neck of the tall Bavaria beer bottle with a lime and inhaled half the bottle in four long swallows. His late breakfast of steak, fried eggs and *gallo pinto* was brought to him by a slim ageless blonde woman who was, he remembered from a fishing trip with Graham Taylor, the owner of the hotel.

"Susannah Dunn," the woman said. "You've stayed with us before."

"Paul Coulter."

"I remember. DC reporter, something like that. Your friend the Englishman with you?"

Coulter shook his head. "He died a month ago."

"I'm sorry. I liked him. Funny as hell but sad underneath. You meeting someone?"

"Not sure."

"Man or woman?"

"Woman."

She raised an eyebrow. "Good luck. I think."

At first he did not notice the red-haired woman who entered the restaurant by the path through the shaded garden. She was somewhere in her thirties, he guessed, not tall but very fit, her sinewy arms and taut curves exposed by the black sleeveless tank top she wore above a red and gold sarong. Her short red hair was gelled into spikes, her eyes hidden by oversized sunglasses. She slowly crossed the room, not indifferent to the male eyes that followed her. She paused at the bar and rubbed the teak sign in the same good luck gesture Coulter had made, then sat down at the next stool and ordered a beer. Susannah Dunn placed the beer on the bar and said, "Hey Devin, you picked a good spot. This is Paul Coulter, back again after two years. As a shrewd judge of beach bum character I'd say he's not likely to bite....unless you want him to."

Coulter said nothing as the woman lifted her sunglasses, her look one of frank appraisal. She raised her beer bottle in a toast.

"Absent friends," she said. "Our mutual friend was English."

An hour later they were driving in Paul's rented Jeep south on the coast road to Playa Samara.

"I wasn't sure that you would understand the message," Karen Jenkins said. "But Graham told me a lot about you, and mentioned you were Jewish on your mother's side. So am I."

"It was a smart message," Coulter replied. "My mother is Ladino—descended from Sephardic Jews expelled from Spain in the 1500s who took refuge in Cyprus. She was born there but came to the U.S. as a small child. She wasn't observant; I grew up with Christmas trees. But I know when Rosh Hashanah and Yom Kippur fall every year."

They turned up into the hills. Four kilometers above the beachfront they emerged from the tropical forest just below a ridge crowned with a white cement house with a red tile roof and a large swimming pool commanding a view of the beach and the sea below. Coulter stopped the Jeep about a hundred yards from the house, still out of sight.

"I would never have recognized you," Coulter said. "Not from your IRS file." The woman in the passenger seat resembled not at all the sad overweight woman with mousy brown hair and thick glasses portrayed on the IRS website as a top special agent.

"Not my best picture," Karen Jenkins, now carrying a passport that identified her as Devin Janklow, replied. "But I got in shape again after coming to Panama City. So when it was time to hide in plain sight as one of many footloose American women on the Central American beach trail I attracted no attention—except from Latin men, who are endearing, if not serious about their long-term intentions."

"That's not what I mean," Coulter said seriously. "There's little tracking and surveillance down here, especially if you look like a slumming gringo, stay away from government offices, and have a couple of extra passports and some ready cash. You could hide safely in Central America for a very long time. Are you sure you want to do this? There's a long list of people who've been killed in the past four months. You don't have any obligation to join them. And once you are on record, you'll be at risk until—or if—your testimony goes public."

Jenkins looked hard at him. "You are Elizabeth—Major Gray's—reporter, aren't you? The one she is so conflicted about."

"Yes," Coulter replied, voice thick. "That's right."

"What would you tell her to do?"

"Run like hell. With me."

"And what would she do?"

"Her duty, as she saw it."

Karen Jenkins' look was sufficient reply. Coulter put the Jeep back in gear and drove the rest of the way up the hill to the house.

The house had been leased by David Rivera, who greeted them at the open front terrace of the house wearing the pants from a Brooks Brothers tan cotton suit, a blue dress shirt, and a rep-striped tie draped around his neck.

"Had to bring a suit," Rivera explained. "Can't save the country in a Hawaiian shirt."

Karen Jenkins said, "I agree. Is there something in the house I can wear?"

"My wife's about your size, *mas o menos*," Rivera replied. "She sent down some business clothes you might need for the video. The videographer will only be shooting you from the shoulders up, so her stuff should work. Let me show you the way." He touched Jenkins' arm and guided her back into the recesses of the house. Coulter eventually found his way through a pair of solid, dark varnished *Pochote* wood doors into a shelf-lined library that had been hurriedly converted into a miniature American-style law office with satellite internet access and a video camera for taping witness testimony. Two younger lawyers from Rivera's office, one male, one female, were already seated at a conference table. They briefly nodded their greetings and then returned to the task of updating the outline that Rivera was about to use in questioning Jenkins.

"We can get started in about ten minutes," Rivera said, entering the conference room. "Karen's ready, but she wants her look to be a bit more IRS agent than what she came in with. Not that the prior look was bad." He looked at Coulter and shrugged. "Married but not blind. Anyway, not to be rude, but I need you to stay off camera."

"I know that," Coulter said. "I'd be toxic. What chair is out of camera range?"

"That one in the corner should be ok. My video guy doubles as the court reporter. He will always announce when he is starting or stopping the camera and whether we are on or off record. So just grab a bottle of water, relax, and give me the high sign if you need a break or you think I'm missing something." Rivera took a ringing cell phone from his pants pocket, listened. "Ok, bring them up," he replied.

"Who's that?" Paul asked.

"A deputy United States consul from the new consulate in Nicoya. He's a former L.A. car dealer, a friend of a friend, and he's got the legal credentials under statute to administer an oath valid in an American court. I've also asked a member of the Supreme Court of Justice of Costa Rica to swear Karen in under Costa Rican law. We aren't going to leave any doubts about whether this deposition is hearsay, any of that crap."

They finished the deposition at four A.M. the following morning. Jenkins appeared calm and alert. Rivera, shaken by what he had just heard, was knocking back coffee laced with Nicaraguan rum.

"I started out as an LA prosecutor, and now I do nothing but big class actions involving white collar crime," he said. "I thought I had seen and heard the worst—murders and rapists then, and now pharmaceutical manufacturers knowingly selling drugs that kill, bankers selling worthless paper, bribery, systematic fraud. But this is surreal. A conspiracy to obstruct justice, headed by the President of the United States. A Vice-President making war on his own people."

"It's our fault," Coulter replied somberly, pausing to add rum to his sixth cup of coffee. "We need to face up to that. The things we have countenanced—stolen elections, unjust wars, over burdened troops, blank checks for military contractors, hyper-concentration of wealth, tax evasion, endless recession, the surveillance state in the name of protection against terror —can you really say you are surprised, David?"

"We can stop this," David Rivera said firmly. "I'm heading to Washington to talk to Ben. I'll tell him we need to get this out *now*. I have a plane standing by at the Liberia airport. I've got room for both you and Karen, Paul, and we can be back in Washington by 6 P.M."

Coulter shook his head, no. "Thanks, but I'm going to head back to my hotel and catch three hours sleep. After that I can drop the Jeep at Avis in Alajuela, near the San Jose airport and fly home from there. I don't think we want to come back into the U.S. under our real names, in the same plane, on the same day. That will get noticed."

Karen Jenkins agreed. "David, Paul can drop me in Playa Pelada," she said. "There's a local bus that runs up the coast and stops at all the beach towns between here and San Juan del Sur in Nicaragua. I'll pick towns at random and spend a day or two in each as I work north. I won't come back to D.C. until this is public. When I'm ready to come back, or if I need help, I'll make contact through Paul. He's given me an encrypted email address that will go straight to his dead drop."

"I know you've both been through a lot...but this kind of paranoia is...well, okay, it's understandable." Rivera paused, suddenly almost shy for a lawyer who had made a hundred million dollars over the past ten years. "Hey, I scramble good eggs," he said, trying to break the pall of worry. "Eat something, let's all have a beer. It'll take the techs another hour to get everything ready."

They did. As dawn broke Coulter and Jenkins went to his Jeep to follow their separate paths north. By 11:30 David Rivera had taxied his HondaJet F3 into position at Daniel Oduber airport and took off to the east. He bantered with his two junior lawyers and enjoyed the power of the light jet as it bit into the mid-day breeze flowing down from the mountains surrounding the Costa Rican *Meseta Central*. They rose quickly past fifteen thousand feet, with only a light chop as they turned north.

And blew up.

Chapter Forty

Fairchilds, LLP
555 13th St. N.W.
Washington, D.C .
Thursday, October 14
9:15 a.m. EDT

Coulter's eyes burned and his throat ached from twelve hours of dry and dirty aircraft air. He had been back in Washington for less than nine hours, having squeezed onto a Delta flight out of Costa Rica at 3 P.M. on Wednesday that landed him in Houston at 8 to clear customs and immigration before taking the last flight of the night to D.C. He'd bought the late edition of the *Washington Post* at a newsbox in Reagan National at 1:30 A.M. and found the story about Rivera's plane crash. Too paranoid to risk going home, Coulter checked into an anonymous motel on the outskirts of Alexandria and passed the rest of the sleepless night filled with a survivor's mix of terror, guilt, fear, and relief .

Do we know what happened to David's plane?" Coulter asked. His voice was shaky with fatigue.

"No, we don't," Lonnie Sanderson replied. His face was gray and lined, eyes streaked with red. "I still can't believe this," he said. "I've known David for twenty-two years. He was a terrific pilot. And the weather conditions were perfect."

"What about the crash site? Did they recover the data recorder from the plane?" Coulter demanded.

"We sent a guy from our aviation department in Tampa down there to watch what the Costa Rican authorities did," Sanderson replied. "They recovered the data recorder late yesterday afternoon, before our guy got there. By then the Ticos had given it to Honda's technical team to examine."

"That means we'll never see it."

"Don't be too sure, Paul," Sanderson replied quietly, grim determination on his face. "I'm the managing partner of this firm and I have 1,300 lawyers working for me. Honda and the Costa Rican government will deal with us. Because I will be goddamned to hell if I will let this go without finding out who murdered David."

Coulter saw the anger and the determination in Sanderson's eyes. "I'm sorry," he apologized. "I know you will. It's—"

"Forget it. But when this is over, write this story, will you? I'd like people to know that David died for his country."

Coulter nodded. "I will. Did David's emails get through? He was sending them over his satellite connection, said he would send to multiple locations to make sure you got them."

"You know, that ended up kind of weird. I gave David a list of our firm's secure websites, and he told me that he would send anything he got to me and to his own firm's secure website in their LA office. We didn't get anything at our offices inside the U.S., and David's office never got his emails either. But our Paris office got them. They called me yesterday and I had them make print and data stick copies and send them via courier, as well as through our firm intranet. We got them an hour ago and I have our tech people working on them."

Coulter reached into his ancient Filson's canvas briefcase, extracted four data sticks. "Here's my set. Keep the originals secure, make me a duplicate set, and have somebody draft an affidavit for me to detail source, origin and custody." He rose and poured himself a third cup of coffee and returned to his seat. "Where do we go from here?" he asked.

"I assume you'd want to write this up, get the story ready for your papers," Sanderson replied. How fast can you get the stories ready?"

"I've been drafting a summary overview since I was in San Jose. "But I think you should leak the contents raw, push them onto the internet."

"Why?" Sanderson asked. "It's an incredible story, you—

"No," Coulter responded. "David told me that this will have far more credibility if you get the source documents out there with some kind of summary. The important thing is to get this out onto the web *now*."

"Why?"

"The emails," Coulter said. "Somebody was able to block the emails that David sent from Costa Rica to his firm and yours in the United States. Which means somebody is building incredibly sophisticated firewalls, using search technology to read into email text and attachments in real time and stop them before delivery if certain subjects or key words or concepts are involved. I don't think we've got a hell of a lot of time left to push this out into the public domain."

Sanderson nodded. "I'll take it to Ben," he replied. "But he's going to want our legal team to go over the documents and the deposition first, and be sure that we can legally prove everything we say. He won't tear the country apart during a crisis unless he's damned sure he's doing the right thing."

"Move *now*," Coulter urged. "While there's time. Point me at the lawyers."

Cable Hollings arrived at the Pentagon that afternoon with his usual pensive expression replace by one of ashen fear.

"We've got samples," he said, when he, Elizabeth Gray, and Karol Horvath were seated in a secure conference room in the Joint Staff offices. "All three attack sites, and from Nevada. The urban warfare training camp was north of Elko was at an abandoned bible college that went bust along with the rest of Nevada's real estate ten years ago. From the size of it, it looked like the Phalanx could run five hundred men through there at a time. It's abandoned."

"How long was the camp open?" Horvath demanded.

"About six months," Hollings replied. "That's what we got from interviewing folks around the base who might know—grocers, bartenders, hookers—anyone who might have serviced the people at the installation. A large group showed up there for the first time in mid-April, and they rotated new groups through every six weeks. So maybe 2000 fighters got trained."

"What about the rest of the people identified in the social network analysis? Can you start arresting them?"

Hollings shook his head, already aching from the stress, and promised himself a couple of Advil, a nap, and perhaps even a shot of bourbon before that day's mid-afternoon status meeting. "Acosta or the White House would shut us down the moment they heard about any attempt to begin arresting the members of the Phalanx. And we've got much worse problems."

"What?" Gray asked sharply.

"The site outside Vegas was located at an abandoned freight terminal. One of the warehouses there contained a machine shop, a big one. Some of the tools had been removed but it's pretty clear what it was—a metallurgical furnace and some pretty expensive precision lathes were left behind. My forensic crew wasn't two feet inside the doors when their radiation detectors started going nuts. I'm having the guys from the Nevada office that did the initial search of the site pulled in for a medical examination to see how much radiation exposure they took. They said they didn't spend a lot of time in the machine shop building, so maybe they will be okay. I hope. Not much good at prayer these days." He puffed out his cheeks and blew out hard, trying to discharge some tension. He looked, Elizabeth thought, all of his years and twenty more.

"I should have seen it coming," he continued. "Anyway, the whole damned machine shop building was hot. My technical guys didn't want to put formal conclusions about precise chemical content into their report—I told them it would be better if the official results came from Los Alamos. But they were worried too."

"Why are they in danger?" Gray asked. "The spent fuel used in the bombs is dirty, but the gamma emitter count was pretty low. With protective gear they were fine."

"That's not right," Hollings replied. "When I said the radiation levels were high, I meant *high*. My boys and girls are telling me that shop didn't just process spent reactor fuel. Somebody was machining seventy percent HEU 235. Bomb grade metal. A loose nuke. Or maybe a couple of them."

There was a long silence. "How fast can Los Alamos do the forensic work?" Horvath finally asked.

"It would take two to four days from the time they receive the samples," Elizabeth responded.

"Really, Major?" Horvath asked. "How do you know that?"

"I grew up in Santa Fe, General," she responded. "My father was a nuclear chemist at Los Alamos."

Later that night Elizabeth Gray looked at Paul Coulter quite skeptically as he came out of the shower and back into their bedroom. "I'm amazed that there are no bullet holes in that ancient hide of yours," she said as he slid into bed.

"So am I. I think they figured that when they hit the plane everyone would be on board. By the time they found out I wasn't on the plane, they knew that Jenkins' deposition had gotten out by being sent to Fairchilds' Paris office. So I don't think they'll come after me again...at least not now. No point."

"Will Giles get the story out?" she asked, worried.

"At least the guts of it. The deposition transcript and the documents that Jenkins turned over, especially the Reed indictment. Giles' legal team is staying up all night to review the documents and fact check the summary I wrote. I told them they should start leaking the documents now."

"But your story—

"It can't be under my byline. I can't be reporter and witness and part of Giles' team."

"No Pulitzer for you," Elizabeth replied. "I'm sorry, Paul, you deserved it. You and Graham. Is Karen Jenkins all right?"

"So far as I know. She had the good sense to keep running, and will lay low in Nicaragua for a while. I don't even have an email address for her, but she's got the email for Graham's dead drop via Paris. She's got a good cover— posing as a recently divorced woman on a long trek through Central America. Changed her looks completely. Quite a look, actually. She'll keep moving until she knows for sure that the story is out and she is safe."

"I liked her." Elizabeth looked at him slyly. "I wondered if you would like her too."

"I did," Paul replied honestly. "But you are stuck with me, Elizabeth. If you run, I'll follow."

"If I run," she said, reaching for him, "I'll run slow."

Chapter Forty-One

Congressional Joint Session
The House of Representatives
The United States Capitol
Washington, D.C.
Monday, October 17
12 noon EDT

The Vice-President gripped the podium in the House of Representatives. "Ten days ago," he began, "in the aftermath of the terrorist attacks on our western cities, the President tasked me with determining who authorized, conducted, and carried out these attacks, and whether further threats confront us." Jackson sipped from a glass of water to ease the perennial rasp in his voice. "Since then, we have assembled a team of over three hundred senior scientists, analysts, investigators, and operatives through the Office of Homeland Intelligence to make that assessment. I am reporting to you today on what we have found.

"The intelligence that we are receiving from our newly restored surveillance systems points to the unmistakable conclusion that the dirty bomb attacks of October 3 are a precursor to a campaign of sustained terror attacks aimed at destroying our economy and our way of life by targeting not just our cities, but also our essential facilities—our ports, our power plants, our communications and computing systems. These attacks were and are being carried out by a new coalition of Islamic terror groups that have bridged their internal divides between the sects of their religion. This coalition has taken the name *Qa'idat al-Jihad*, or 'the Base of Jihad," which pays sick and twisted homage to Al Qaeda, as well as to other Islamic groups long since contained. The members of this coalition include key leaders in the governments of Iran, Alawite Syria, the ISIS Caliphate, the Shia Islamic Republic in Iraq, Gaza, Lebanon, and Somalia." Jackson traced a finger across the touch sensitive screen on his podium. The two large screens arrayed on either side of the dais in the House chamber flared into life and a satellite photo appeared on both screens. "This is the *Deir ez-Zor* province of the Islamic Caliphate, in what was formerly eastern Syria," he said. He zoomed in on the image and the scale enlarged until a complex of buildings and trailers in the high desert emerged into focus. "This is a former Syrian military complex," he continued. "It was converted seven years ago into a munitions manufacturing plant, then abandoned in the Syrian Civil War. In the last five months it began operating again." Jackson displayed a series of images showing trucks, earthmovers, and heavy construction gear moving cargo into the area, improving the access roads, paving a concrete pad. "We learned of this facility through an analysis of electronic intercepts, despite extreme efforts at secrecy by the Caliphate, Shia Iraq, Iran, and the terror groups involved. Our human intelligence sources, which I cannot disclose, shed further light on the purpose of this facility."

Jackson focused the image to the highest possible magnification. Individual images of people crossing through the compound could be seen. They appeared to be wearing radiation suits with helmets.

"Two days ago we raided this facility," Jackson continued. "The brave men and women who undertook this mission included nuclear scientists and technicians as well as combat trained operatives. They found that this facility was designed to handle and machine nuclear materials, including spent fuel. We have tested the chemical characteristics of the spent fuel processed at this site and compared it to the spent fuel used to arm the dirty bombs on our west coast. The characteristics match. The dirty bombs that contaminated Seattle, San Francisco and Los Angeles came were loaded with spent nuclear fuel ground into fine and deadly dust at this bomb factory." Jackson touched the podium screen beneath him and new images filled the large screens behind him. "We destroyed this evil place," he said. A series of photographs showed the buildings and trailers being exploded, set on fire. "We lost six brave men and women. As for the terrorists…those who were not killed in the initial assault are now being interrogated. The information we have obtained causes us great concern. For we have learned in just the past twelve hours that this facility has produced at least ten more dirty bombs packed with ground reactor fuel designed to be deployed with truck bombs like those used on October 3. We also believe that this facility has produced two to four primitive, but potentially viable nuclear weapons capable of ten kiloton blasts. We believe these weapons are in transit to the United States. The President gave the orders one hour ago placing all of our military, homeland security, intelligence, and security forces on world-wide alert at ThreatCon2. There is a significant chance that, unless we can intercept these weapons, we will be under nuclear attack." Jackson paused and turned toward James Robinson, who walked slowly through the House Chamber. "The President," he said.

The Chairman of the Joint Chiefs of Staff, Admiral Jonathan Collins, turned to the service chiefs and directors of the Joint Staff who were seated with him in the E-Ring's tank, the Chairman's conference room. Collins, a bone-thin former naval carrier pilot who had grown up dirt poor in a Maine logging town, gestured at the screen. "Where did all *that* shit come from?"

"Not from us," Karol Horvath replied. "Jackson's stove-piping his own intelligence from his own sources. DIA has nothing about this."

Collins turned his bleak pale blue eyes toward Marine Lt. General Raymond Lowery, the Joint Staff Director for special operations. "Tell me where they got the commandos, Ray," he said. "Did they get SEALS, Rangers, Marine Recon, what?" he demanded.

"Not from us," Lowery said, the skin of his bald head gleaming under the conference room's LED lights. "We supplied no one.

There are a couple of other possibilities. Energy has some fairly sophisticated security and strike teams; they usually recruit from our special ops units when our guys get past our age requirements. Or, more likely, they were contractors from Dark/Star. They probably added science guys from the NEST teams, gave them combat training. But none of it was ours."

"This is nuts," Collins said, leaning forward intently. "What the fuck are they doing?"

James Robinson took his place at the podium in the Chamber of the House of Representatives. Vice President Jackson and Speaker of the House Miranda Cardwell sat behind him, their mutual disdain apparent from their rigid body language and conspicuous silence.

"I come before you today to discharge my duty as President to protect the American people and confront the grave risks we face," Robinson intoned.

"We *will* respond to these attacks with the full force and strength of America's military might. We have a powerful doctrine of retaliation that follows the Word of God as set forth in the book of Deuteronomy and requires us, for our own protection, to take an 'eye for an eye and a tooth for a tooth.'" Robinson looked out at his audience and saw the looks of confusion multiply across the faces of the members of Congress and Senate. "We cannot watch and wait as these weapons are brought into our country and as these attacks accelerate. Ordinary measures will not protect *you*, the American people, for the next warning we might receive could be in the form of a mushroom cloud. I am therefore invoking, effective immediately, the provisions of our National Continuity Plan to deter and defeat these terror attacks." Robinson paused, but there was no applause, only a stunned and wary silence, even from the Republican benches.

"The National Continuity Plan," he continued, "has six major elements. First, because of the damage and disruption to the states of California and Washington, we cannot hold a fair and representative election in less than three weeks without the possibility of massive voter fraud. Moreover, this wave of new attacks may very well be *aimed* at our election process—think of yourselves and your neighbors, lined up to vote at your polling place, the targets of a radioactive bomb! We *cannot* risk holding our elections as scheduled on November 8. Therefore, all federal elections will be postponed until at least next May 1 to provide our wounded sister states time to repair their damage, and for our national government to contain this threat. Present members of Congress and the Administration will hold their positions until new elections can be held next year.

"Second. As of today the National Continuity Authority will be activated. It consists of five hundred senior federal officials who have been trained for emergency management, and will assume the overall direction of our federal departments and agencies. The Continuity Authority will be led by a man who has demonstrated his superb skills and courageous dedication to duty on many occasions: Vice President Jackson."

Jackson nodded gravely from his seat on the dais. The Republican side of the House Chamber rose to their feet but the applause was uncertain, tentative. Speaker Cardwell, a former film actress still famously beautiful in her seventh decade, remained seated and stared stonily at the Republican members, as though selecting her future targets.

"Third. Federal troops from Northern Command and other units will be stationed in our twenty largest cities to protect essential assets and assure public order in the event of yet another cowardly terrorist strike against civilians. I ask every citizen to remember that these troops form the shield that protects all of us, and to cooperate in all ways with these American heroes."

"Fourth. We cannot rely, in these dangerous times, on outmoded and delay-ridden judicial procedures in our clogged federal courts. Terrorists must be identified, detained, and have their crimes swiftly judged and punished. I am therefore announcing the expansion of the Federal Intelligence Court, which will be re-named the Federal Anti-Terrorism Court. Using my authority under the Military Commissions Act, I am making emergency appointments of two hundred fifty new federal trial commissioners who will preside over all matters involving terrorism and sedition on United States soil. No case will take more than six weeks to be decided from the date that initial charges are filed. Appeals will be strictly limited.

"Fifth. In order to detect and deter acts of terrorism, we must surrender—temporarily!—some of the privacy rights we hold dear. Beginning immediately, all citizens will be issued a new national identity card. This card is your friend—it will enable you to travel, to complete credit card and banking transactions, to receive federal and state benefits, and to rest assured that the other passengers on your airplane flight or in your train car are not terrorists seeking to kill you."

"Sixth. There is a group of American patriots, all good Christian men and woman, almost all combat veterans, members of our great and patriotic military family. They have volunteered their time, their hopes, and their honor to serving their country in its time of need. This group of volunteers has come forward in the finest tradition of this country, the tradition that runs from Bunker Hill to Bull Run, from Fredericksburg to Fallujah, to fight for their country. They are being deputized as Special Federal Marshals. Respect them and follow their directions, as you would your neighborhood police officer or fireman, for they too represent the decent and law abiding element in our nation that serves without question."

Robinson paused, mopped his brow. "My friends, I know many of you are in shock. I know many of you are dismayed. But I cannot 'preserve, protect, and defend' the Constitution of the United States when our citizens are being killed and our institutions shattered by terror violence. These measures are temporary. They are designed to prevent the terror attacks that we believe are being plotted and co-ordinated at this very moment. And they will succeed in protecting you. I believe—

James Robinson stopped and gaped in astonishment. Behind him, Speaker Cardwell had risen, nodded to her caucus, and departed the dais. She walked with a determined stride up the aisle, toward the double doors at the end of the center hallway of the House Chamber. As she passed the Democratic Senate delegation Ben Giles rose, took her arm, and marched forward with her. The line of Democrats exiting the House Chamber became a stream, then a river, as the delegation stood, waited to exit, and turned their backs on James Robinson.

Robinson turned to his Vice-President. "What in *Hell?*" he demanded.

Jackson responded calmly. "Turn back to the cameras. Smile. If you are resolute, Mr. President, we will prevail, with God at our backs."

"Listen to me," Ben Giles pleaded. *"Listen to me.* This is Greece in 1967, this is Chile in 1973, this is Argentina under Peron, this is Russia under Putin. This is how a democracy dies."

"We are under *attack*," Grant Dodd replied, voice hot. He was a conservative independent senator from South Dakota who caucused with the Democrats in order to retain his iron grip on the agriculture committee, but made no secret of his disdain for Ben Giles. "We've had three cities damaged, nearly destroyed. Are we supposed to wait for the rest of the country to get hit, maybe with real nuclear weapons, before we take action? This 'Base of Jihad' group is out to kill us. We should back the Administration on this."

"How do you know that?" Giles demanded. "Because Jackson said so, showed a few pictures? None of this intelligence came through the FBI, the CIA, or DOD. I just got off the phone with Admiral Collins, Chairman of the Joint Chiefs, and they are as puzzled as anyone else. This is crap Jackson stovepiped through Homeland Intelligence and Dark/Star. Where's the analysis? Where's the briefing to the Joint Intelligence Oversight Committee? Where's the fucking CIA? Why didn't we use our special forces on these raids instead of Dark/Star mercenaries? None of this makes any sense."

"You can't really believe that Americans would attack their own country," Dodd scoffed.

"Nobody can know what to believe in the absence of evidence. We've had these bastards beating us over the head with the red shirt of terrorism for twenty years now. We stand up now or we surrender our democracy. The choice is that stark, ladies and gentlemen. There will be no going back. There's no democracy that delayed its elections under pressure and ever held them again on time—it took Chile nearly thirty years to crawl past Pinochet and re-establish civilian control of the military. It took Argentina more than forty years to get past the Perons and the Generals. If we go down that road, what will be left of us after that much time? And what will be left of the world? Those countries were weak, peripheral. We are supposed to be the leader of the world, the essential nation. If we become a fascist dictatorship, we are looking at world war."

The doors to the Senate Caucus room were flung open.

"Federal Marshals!" the men barked. They were dressed in black jumpsuits with blue patches on their shoulders. Despite the unfamiliar uniform, they wore the silver five-point star inside a wheel badge of the U.S. Marshal's Service over their left breast. Half carried H&K MP5A5N submachine guns. The other half carried Sig-Sauer P-228s, the very accurate hand weapons of the Federal Sky Marshals.

Two of the Marshals detached themselves from the group and approached Ben Giles. "We need to take you into protective custody, Senator," one said. "Your life is at risk."

"I don't doubt that," Giles responded wryly. He held his hands up to be cuffed. "Fight this, Senators. There *will* be another day."

Within a day half the democratic members of Congress were detained, along with a majority of the Supreme Court. Protests and skirmishes broke out in forty cities across the country, beginning in college towns like Berkeley, Boulder, Madison, Iowa City, Ann Arbor and Tucson, but spreading quickly to larger cities. New York was paralyzed by a general strike led by its Mayor that shut down Wall Street and the Federal Reserve. Banks across the country began to close as they ran out of cash. Looting broke out as strikes shut down airports, harbors, rails and truck terminals. UPS, FedEx, Wal-Mart, and Amazon provided only sporadic deliveries. Homeland Intelligence and the NSA set up fire walls and tried to throttle the Internet but couldn't stay ahead of social networking sites rerouting their servers through the cloud and via darknet sites; army troops began to seize control of server farms across the nation and shut them down. A national strike set for Sunday morning aimed to bring five million people into the streets across the country. They would find boots on the ground waiting to confront them.

Chapter Forty-Two

Coulter stood just behind the skirmish line, on the steps of the World War II monument on the National Mall. He guessed that perhaps three hundred thousand protestors had made it in to Washington by noon that Sunday, despite the government's shut down of airports, train stations, DC Metro, and bus service into the District. Civilian media helicopters and aircraft had been banned from the Washington sky; ground television and webcast crews had been interned as soon as they arrived at the Mall. The day's story would have to be told by citizen witnesses on the ground with cams and cell phones, piece by piece.

Most of the protesters were massed behind him, around the Lincoln and Viet Nam memorials. In front of him, less than a hundred yards away, stood six companies of regular army troops, probably from the 79th Brigade Combat Team at Fort Belvoir, and perhaps six hundred or so black jump suited federal marshals newly deputized from the Phalanx. The federal troops were equipped with urban combat gear: face-shielded helmets, padded chest protectors, arm and leg guards, riot shields and batons, side arms in locked holsters. Gas masks dangled from their necks. Every fourth Army soldier seemed to be carrying a burn gun—a microwave crowd control weapon— or a grenade launcher to propel gas grenades. The Phalanx troopers carried street sweeper shotguns or M-4 carbines, held in ready position. Rows of Strykers, up-armored Humvees, MWRAPs and the M-1117A Guardian Military Police tanks that looked slightly squashed and ridiculous but that carried more firepower than an infantry squad stood behind the troops.

Paul raised his hand-held vidcam to take a wide-angle shot of the government forces. The two lines viewed each other in wary silence; the slogans previously shouted by the protesters—Fascists! Fascists!—died away as the tension rose. Somewhere in the Army position an order was given and the troops raised their tear gas weapons and began to fire, followed by the much larger tear and pepper gas canisters launched by the M-1117s' stubby, nasty little turret guns. The gas grenades and canisters landed all around the World War II Memorial. A roiling cloud of gas spread among the protestors. The Army and Phalanx troops began to beat their riot batons against their shields, a tactic to frighten opponents that was older than the Romans.

Coulter took out the industrial rebreather mask he had bought at a paint store the previous morning and fitted it, with protective goggles, around his face. The improvised gear would protect him for no more than thirty minutes, but he remained where he was and kept filming. Other protestors were not so well equipped. A panicked group of perhaps fifty broke forward toward the Phalanx end of the skirmish line, trying to escape the gas. As they ran forward the Phalanx soldiers surged toward them, batons raised. One young woman, obviously pregnant and carrying a sign saying "Down with Christian Fascism" was struck by one of the lead troopers across the face and knocked to the ground. The black-suited Phalanx soldier slashed at her face twice more, and then struck repeated blows to her pregnant belly.

There was a moment's pause, as though both sides were briefly stunned by the act of brutality. Blood gushed from the woman's head, mouth and vagina. The Phalanx trooper made no effort to help her.

He stepped away and raised his baton but his triumph did not last long. Two hardened anarchists, fully prepared for the day in fatigues, helmets, armor, and military surplus gas masks, appeared as if from nowhere on a dead run. They carried quart plastic bottles of gasoline. They dowsed the Phalanx trooper and, before he could move or react, lit him on fire. He danced with St. Vitus for a moment in the flames, screaming. Before he finished dying the Phalanx had raised their weapons and fired directly into the crowd.

The Colonel commanding the Fort Belvoir regular army troops had a bullhorn. "Stand Down! Stand Down! Cease Fire!" he screamed. About half his own troops paid no attention, and unlocked their weapons.

Paul Coulter opened one eye. The effort cost him as much as he was prepared to bear; he kept the other eye closed. But he kept that one eye open, despite the pain coming from his head and almost all of his body, to watch the sheer beauty of Elizabeth Gray in full body armored ACU, black beret, combat face paint, and complete fucking angry rant. Paul had seen her in that state that only once before in his life but it made a deep and lasting impression.

She had a Fort Belvoir noncom standing at rigid attention, sweating. The Phalanx marshal beside him stood at a disdainful parade rest.

"You stupid fucking morons," Gray shouted, her command voice in full roar. "You idiot excuses for soldiers. This is a fucking *reporter*, you dumb shits. Didn't you have enough fun today killing a PREGNANT WOMAN and her child, then shooting, oh, about a thousand people? Are you insane? Do you know how much trouble this kind of shit causes for the President, for Coordinator Jackson?"

"These bastards burned one of my soldiers, Major," the Phalanx marshal responded.

"I've seen the video. I would have done the same fucking thing to your stupid undisciplined creep." The 'marshal' turned red with anger and was about to respond when Elizabeth hit him in the throat with the rigid heel of her palm and knocked him to the floor. He was scarcely able to breathe; if she had struck a quarter inch lower she would have ruptured his larynx and killed him in less than four minutes. Elizabeth snatched his sidearm and touched the muzzle to his forehead. He could not speak but she had his attention.

"You are alive," she hissed, "only because I don't see fit to kill you now." She turned, his gun in hand. "Corporal."

"Major!"

"If this prick moves in the next twenty minutes, take out his knees and hips. Use his weapon. I want to read an after action report that says he is crippled for life from tragic self-inflicted wounds. Clear?" She handed the nearly distraught Corporal the sidearm she'd snatched away.

The Phalanx officer started to get up but Elizabeth kicked him in the groin so hard that Paul imagined the man's balls had been knocked up into his throat. He writhed in agony, no longer interested in the conversation.

Elizabeth gestured towards Paul. "I am taking this prisoner to DIA to debrief him, Corporal. I expect *no* interference. But if there is *one* more fuckup from you or your unit I will personally assign you to security duty at the oil fields in the Niger delta, where the jungles are filled with poisonous insects and snakes and rebels who shoot at you. Am I *real clear*, Corporal?"

The noncom stiffened even more."Perfectly, Major! Your pass code is 'Daylight'. I am relaying that code to every security officer at this facility. If you have any problems, contact me by sat phone." He gave her the number and his personal security code, which she repeated.

Elizabeth hauled Coulter upright with the Corporal's help. She pulled his arm around her shoulders, slipped her own arm across his back and around his waist. She walked him out of the chain link enclosure into the center of the green grassy field.

Coulter squinted into the now dark sky, eyes dazzled by the harsh stadium lights. His mouth fell open in shock at the sight of the green grass field divided into a thousand chain link cells.

"Fuck," he mumbled. "This is RFK stadium. What did they do to it?"

"Make with the feet, baby," Elizabeth replied quickly, speaking directly into his one good ear. "You need to do about four hundred yards to get your ass out of here."

"No sweat." Coulter moved briskly, then suddenly stopped, bent by a racking cough, and spit blood onto the field. "Something might be busted inside," he said, when he could draw ragged breath again.

"No shit," Elizabeth replied. "Three hundred yards now. I love you. Lean on me."

Raj Gavde finished sewing up a wound in Coulter's face and sat back to review his work in the sun room of his home in Alexandria, a room that he had converted in this last 24 hours to a small illicit infirmary. Gavde had been Coulter's grad school roommate at Columbia, Coulter in journalism and Gavde in medical school. They had bonded playing IM basketball and drinking beer in cheap bars around the campus and on upper Broadway.

"You have some internal bleeding," Raj said. "If you were a lawyer I'd send you back to RFK, 'cause what I'm about to do is malpractice."

"Like?" Elizabeth said anxiously.

"He's got a medium concussion, three broken ribs, and minor internal bleeding," Gavde replied. "But he'll heal, and the internal bleeding should stop. You've got to get Paul out of here, Elizabeth, because word is likely to leak that I'm treating people and I'm going to get busted in the next forty-eight hours." Gavde reached into his pocket, held out four small pills. "The last of my private stash of Oxycontin," he said. "Prescriptions for pain meds are being monitored. The Virginia Medical Association just announced that doctors have to email all painkiller prescriptions in real time to Homeland Security. So make these last.

"For two days Paul should sleep if he can. The third day is going to be tough—but after that he can get by on Naproxen. This is going to take about a week to resolve, I suspect. Paul, you with us? Understand?"

"Wilco," Coulter said fuzzily, then passed out again. He woke again inside a hybrid sedan from the Pentagon car pool that Elizabeth had somehow commandeered.

"Where we goin'?" Coulter mumbled.

"Hush Baby," Elizabeth responded. "You'll be safe...inside the belly of the beast."

Chapter Forty-Three

The Roosevelt Room
The White House
Washington, D.C.
Tuesday, October 25
10:00 A.M. EDT

"I am aware of your instructions, Mr. Vice-President," Admiral Jonathan Collins, the JCS Chairman, said defensively. His bony face took on a high color that his subordinates knew meant that he was barely in control of his temper. "But I question their wisdom. The military believes that the political situation in the country is urgent. Regular Army troops have fired upon and killed American civilians for the first time in nearly one hundred years, and not just in Washington. The death toll across the country from last week-end's protests stands at one thousand eight hundred seventy six, with over six thousand wounded. We cannot continue on this course. The country is being torn apart."

Jackson eyed Collins narrowly. He was flanked by four aides seated just behind him at the head of the conference table. The Chiefs stared back, unmoved.

"Any use of force against the rioters last weekend was provoked, Admiral," Jackson rasped. "I'm sure you watched in horror, as I did, as two of the rioters you seem so bent on protecting poured gasoline on a United States Marshal and burned him alive on the National Mall."

"Sir, that supposed 'Marshal'—who'd been in that position for under a week and never received crowd control training—had just murdered a pregnant woman and her baby with a riot baton. That is exactly my point. We have to stand down the more…blatant aspects of emergency control and focus on the domestic threat posed by any loose nuclear material that has been smuggled into the country. We need to resume the constitutional course."

Jackson gestured to an aide, who touched a key on his laptop and caused a large screen across the room to descend from the ceiling, blocking the view of Remington's *The Rough Rider* that normally graced the chimney breast over the white enameled mantel and black marble fireplace. "Since you and your officers seem unable to discern the real threat facing this country, Admiral Collins, I thought I would show it to you." The screen came to life displaying an aerial view of Azadi Square in downtown Tehran, Iran, in early evening. The Square was densely packed with perhaps a half million people. At the front of the crowd stood army soldiers in desert camouflage and the blue suited officers of Iran's air force and navy. The Islamic Nuclear Guard took pride of place at the very front of the crowd, standing at rigid attention in their emerald green jumpsuits and white silk scarves, waiting for Supreme Ayatollah Kurosh to address the crowd. Kurosh was of the new generation of Mullahs, superficially more willing to keep the Revolutionary Guards and their rabid attack dogs, the Basij Militia, in their barracks and nod toward human rights, buying time to build up Iran's military strength and its nuclear arsenal. He now took the podium and held up his hands to silence the chanting crowd, his dark eyes flashing under the black turban that designated him as a direct descendant of Mohammed.

"When was this?" Collins demanded.

"A little over four hours ago," Jackson replied. "I realize it takes some time for intelligence to make its way through your bureaucracy," he added sarcastically. He resumed playing the transmission, with the verbal content contemporaneously translated into English.

"I am aware," Kurosh began, "that the government of the United States, seeks to use the tragic terrorist attacks on their cities as an excuse to make war on the people of Iran. This is a false claim. We did not attack the United States. Allah, the Merciful and all powerful, did not command us to attack—only Allah knows the time of all things. Yet if we are attacked, we are prepared to repel the forces of evil and take the war to their homeland with nuclear fire if necessary." Kurosh gestured broadly to the troops arrayed below him. "We are ready. Our air force, our army and navy, our missile men, and especially the Islamic Nuclear Guard, are prepared to strike anywhere in the world. Allah will guide their hands and their weapons. Allah will safeguard the Revolution. Allah will protect his people."

Jackson gestured, and the speech was shut off. "That, Admiral Collins," he said coldly, "is where the threat to this country lies. Twenty-four hours ago the President directed that the Chiefs provide an updated report on Iranian war planning. I am here to take that report."

"Mr. Vice-President," Collins replied urgently, "Iran is a tactical and not a strategic threat to this country. Their maximum ballistic missile range is 2,500 kilometers—enough to hit Israel, Europe, and our bases in the Arabian Peninsula. They cannot hit our homeland unless they have already smuggled weapons into the United States."

"What about the *Darius* and the *Khomeini?*" Jackson demanded. "They have two missile boats deployed less than four hundred miles off the Eastern seaboard. And those boats may have nuclear warheads on their missiles."

"Mr. Vice President," the Chief of Naval Operations, Steven Kramer, responded, "I'm a submarine officer. I know those boats. They are converted Chinese surplus *Song*-class vessels, with only four missile tubes per boat. The Iranians do not have a nuclear weapon small enough to be mated to the Chinese missiles designed for these boats."

"What if they are naval equivalent of suicide bombers, Admiral?" Jackson responded. "Carrying weapons they can't launch, but can detonate? A nuclear detonation inside the port of New York, Boston

Harbor, or Chesapeake Bay—we could be decapitated as a country inside of an hour."

Kramer shook his blunt-featured, Teutonic head. "I don't think so. The conversion of these boats from attack to SLBM use drastically altered their sonar characteristics—my boys say they sound like a wheat thresher, even when running on electric propulsion. Their top speed is half of what my attack boats can do. They have no nuclear reactors; they're dependant on being resupplied by an Iranian oiler that doesn't want to venture far from Venezuela. I have the *Santa Fe* and the *Tucson* tracking both boats. The Iranians are staying outside the 24 mile zone. If there's any turn toward one of our ports, or even just the shoreline, we'll know it. The oiler can be taken out by planes from the *Stennis* or the airfield at Guantanamo. If you are inclined toward a preemptive attack, deliver a message to the world declaring a one hundred mile naval exclusion zone and I will take those boats out inside of half an hour. The point will be made."

Jackson considered what Kramer had said, made a note. "That's probably the right first step, Admiral Kramer. But I want to be briefed on the full war plan." He looked expectantly at the JCS Chairman, Jonathan Collins.

Collins gestured to the Marine General who headed J-7, the operational plans directorate, to begin the briefing. A giant map of the Red Sea and the Arabian Peninsula filled the screen. "The Red Sea is a naval deathtrap," the Marine began. "You'll have to go nuclear in the first attack. No warning." He could not quite keep the disgust out of his voice.

Karol Horvath had remained seated in a chair well behind the conference table, waiting to be called on and to brief if the need arose. There was no need; Jackson had again apparently stove-piped his own intelligence. When the meeting was over after four tense hours he rose and stepped to the head of the table, where Jackson was huddled with his military aides.

"Mr. Vice-President? A word?" he asked.

Jackson looked up at him, a mixture of bemusement and caution on his face. "Regarding, General?"

"A personal matter."

Jackson cocked his head and stared for a moment, then curiosity overcame caution. "One minute. It's a busy day for all of us, Karol."

Horvath gestured toward the side of the room. "In private?"

"All right." Jackson gesture his aides away, stepped to the side of the room. "What's this all about?"

"It's about you, Kyle." Jackson stiffened at Horvath's failure to address him by title but Horvath continued too quickly for him to object. "You were the best officer I ever served under. The model special operations officer, the model I have tried to teach to every officer who serves under me. But you cannot go on with this. The Chiefs will not accept a permanent seizure of the government."

"The Chiefs," Jackson said, "are in the process of being replaced."

"They expect that. They will not go."

Jackson's eyes narrowed. "In office or not, I expect them to remain loyal to the Constitution and the Commander in Chief."

"They will. But the problem is that we won't have a lawful Commander in Chief in three months. I can promise you two things. The Chiefs will not abide further deaths of civilians. And they will not let you set up a permanent junta."

"The people are with us."

"Perhaps for now. But Kyle…these things have a way of turning. The gun in the mouth. The meat hook. The noose. I am begging you to stand down while there is still time. To be the hero I know and respect."

Jackson looked at him without expression. "If you fight us, Karol, you will be removed. By whatever means necessary."

"I know that, Mr. Vice-President. There's nothing more to say, then."

Karol Horvath exited the meeting with the Chiefs around seven P.M. For once he looked his age. "Major," he said after his return to the Pentagon, wearily thumbing through the briefing papers he would read that night, "Can you fly a Seahawk helicopter?"

Elizabeth looked puzzled. "Absolutely, sir. It's just a Blackhawk in Navy drag."

"Report here at 0600."

Chapter Forty-Four

"What the *hell* is that?" Elizabeth Gray said into her flight helmet mike as she piloted a Navy MH-60 *Seahawk* helicopter low over the gray water of the Atlantic Ocean about forty miles east of Kitty Hawk, North Carolina.

Karol Horvath, seated in the co-pilot's seat of what was supposed to be a standard Navy VERTREP flight from Norfolk Naval Air Station, permitted himself a chuckle. "That, I hope, is the future of the Navy," he replied. "God knows it cost enough."

The ship below them was painted in dark Navy gray. She had an inverted tumblehome hull, with the sides sloped steeply inward above the waterline. Her deck superstructure was a squat elongated triangle that ended at a flight deck that seemed to barely float above the Atlantic swells. The ship resembled a cross between an F-117 *Nighthawk* and a Civil War-era ironclad, the C.S.S. *Virginia*.

"She's the *John Ericsson*," Horvath continued. "After the *Zumwalt*-class destroyer prototypes failed, the Navy went back to the drawing board, rethought the design from the war-fighting and propulsion aspects, and came up with the *Ericson*. This beast has a trimaran hull and the radar profile, even to long wave radars, of a rowboat. Her electronics are shielded against pulse attacks. Her propulsion comes from a compact nuclear-electric system that only needs to be refueled every four years. She's armed with anti-aircraft interceptors, cruise missiles, 5 inch ERGM guns, and fore and aft rail guns that fire depleted uranium bolts to knock down ship-to-ship missiles. And she drafts just sixteen feet of water, half of the *Arleigh Burke* class destroyers, so she can get in close to shore if she has to."

Gray noted Horvath's obvious pride but said, "Great, but why are we ground pounders here?"

"Two reasons," he replied. "First because she's EMP-shielded. She's not vulnerable to signals interception by plane or satellite. Second, my little brother is her captain, and that makes her a secure site for this meeting."

"But who are we meeting?" Gray persisted.

"The Combatant Commands," Horvath replied.

The Commands' representatives waited in the cramped briefing room adjacent to the *Ericsson's* below water command center, within the zone of the ship designed to be impervious to signals intelligence interception. Captain Mark Horvath, a decade younger than his brother Karol, greeted them at the flight deck, hugged his brother once, and led them below. As Gray and Karol Horvath entered the room, eight men and two women, all deputy commanders or principal aides to the four star generals and admirals who commanded the six regional field commands, Northern, Central, Southern, Pacific, Africa, and SACEUR, the Supreme Allied Command of NATO in Brussels, and the four functional commands, Joint Forces, Special Operations, Strategic, and Logistics, rose to their feet.

"At ease," Horvath said. "Please sit down. I know you've all had a long journey here. The Chairman was very reluctant to ask for this meeting. But the events of the past two weeks compel that we meet and discuss the present situation. The rules today are that there are no ranks, no service fights, everybody speaks freely and the truth about what they and their commanding officer thinks."

"God damn it, Karol," Fred Scott, a Rear Admiral and deputy commander of CENTCOM, exploded out of his chair. "We've got no business meeting like this or having this discussion. Everyone in this room has taken an oath to the Constitution and that is the end of the discussion. We have to support the lawful civilian authority."

"I agree, Fred," Horvath replied mildly. "I would simply place some emphasis on the word, 'lawful.' As things stand after January 20 there will be no 'duly elected President' to serve as Commander in Chief. What do we do then? Whose orders do we follow?"

"The President has invoked the Continuity Authority," Scott replied. "That makes him the lawful commander in chief until the Authority is revoked and things get back to normal."

"Does it?" The voice that broke in belonged to Air Force Major General Roberta Kennedy, a B-52 bomber pilot and the deputy commander of the U.S. Strategic Command at Offutt Air Force Base. "There are specific criteria in the Continuity Act that have to be met before the President can invoke the authority. I don't think they've been met, or that what we've suffered so far, bad as it is, justifies canceling the election. Hell, we had a Presidential election during the Civil War, with half the country in flames."

"There's the threat of Iran," Marine Brigadier Gwen Casey replied. She was the newly promoted senior aide to the Navy Vice-Admiral, Harold Palmer, who helmed the Logistics Command. "Everything we're being told says that the Iranians were behind these attacks. It's the same pattern we've seen from them for a decade. They hide behind their surrogates, Alawite Syria, Hezbollah, the Shi'a government in eastern Iraq. We should be gearing up for war, as the Vice-President directed."

"We have not yet confirmed that they were behind the attacks," Horvath responded. "And the Iranian government specifically denies any involvement."

"What about the spent fuel? I thought that came from their reactor," Casey persisted.

"I'm told it only matched on seven of ten chemical characteristics," Rear Admiral Joseph Washington of PACCOM replied. He was a nuclear engineer and had served as both chief engineer and captain of nuclear submarines. He leaned forward in his chair, focused on Casey. "I'm also having trouble seeing it strategically. The mullahs are never the martyrs. Iran is a nuclear power, but a primitive one. They can't launch a preemptive strike that defeats us or Israel—at least not before we retaliate. We have a combined 384 nuclear warheads aimed at them as of this morning. And the Israelis would probably throw a few megatons just to say Happy Chanukah."

"The Mullahs don't react the same way to the loss of human life that we do," Casey said stubbornly.

"They do if it's their own lives," Washington retorted. "Hell, if they really have a ten kiloton nuke they should have used it, slipped it into the in the Washington yacht basin. They could have killed three fourths of the government, left us paralyzed for months. *A dirty bomb strategy makes no sense for them.* If I'm going to buy into a war with Iran, the forensic characteristics of the bombs have to be a one hundred per cent match. Anything less is just another Iraq WMD scam."

An hour later the argument was unresolved. The room was tight, the air stagnant. The ship was taking heavy sea and her fresh air intakes were closed; they were now functioning below decks on charcoal filters, like a submarine. There was a preliminary vote, on a motion by Brigadier Casey, to decide the scope of JCS Collins' authority to direct the Combatant Commands. JCS authority was denied by a vote of six to four.

"Jack didn't expect you to fall in line and follow his orders as a matter of command," Karol Horvath said. "He can read the statute. I don't think this is the issue."

"That's because you lost the vote," Casey shot back.

"No, General, it's not," Horvath replied patiently. "Jack and I had a front row seat during the DC riots after Ben Giles was imprisoned. The Chiefs will not accept Giles' continued imprisonment."

"Giles was detained for his own safety," Casey shot back. "There were terrorist threats on his life."

"Threats?" Horvath asked stonily. "Have you seen one documented threat against Ben Giles' life in any media, here, Europe, the Middle East, even Al Jazeera? Why is he being held incommunicado? Imprisoned I said and imprisoned I meant."

"I think I had better get involved in this," a quiet weary voice said from the back of the room. Major General Manuel Davis, the deputy commander of Northern Command, rose and stood before them. "You know who I am," he said simply. "That was my Brigade Combat Team on the Mall. When those asshole 'deputized' Federal Marshals' opened fire, my soldiers lost their discipline and helped take 642 American lives. I have never been so ashamed." He paused, focused on Brigadier Casey. "Please tell Admiral Palmer this directly," he said, referring to her commanding officer. "If he's going to openly support Jackson's junta, he'd better keep his pilots on the ground, his sailors on their cargo ships, and his quartermasters off the streets. My command is not going to suffer the loss of any more American lives. Not one. My officers and troops are as sad and disgusted and angry as I am about what happened on the Mall. We will not fire the next shot. We might fire the last one."

He looked at the group. "This comes from my boss. NORTH-COM is not going to support Jackson and the White House unless four criteria are met.

"First. Before we take any military action against Iran we have absolute proof that the Iranians are responsible for the West Coast attacks. Nobody in my command wants to get screwed over like Colin Powell did when Cheney sent him into the United Nations with a load of garbage to sell. If that happens again it will be the end of the military in this country as we know it.

"Second. We must have United Nations approval for any military action against Iran, by a majority vote of the entire General Assembly.

"Third. No American military unit will fire on American civilians again. That includes federalized units of the National Guard and these 'Phalanx' deputized marshals. Period. Local police and state national guards can handle any domestic situation. If the Phalanx takes on my soldiers they will regret it.

"Fourth. Ben Giles will be released—*now*. The Congress will reconvene within sixty days and an emergency Presidential election will be held between Ben Giles and James Robinson within one hundred twenty days."

"Or NOTHCOMM stages a coup d'état?" Casey demanded.

"No, General. No coup d'état. We simply won't obey Jackson."

"We cannot do this," Fred Scott said, pleading. "This violates every principle of civilian authority over the military. If we do this, we become Pakistan or Argentina, with the military always threatening the duly elected government."

"You're back to the same problem, Fred," Karol Horvath replied. "Duly elected. After January 20, who do we take our orders from?" He rose and faced the group. "The Chiefs stand with Northern Command," he announced. "I need to know where others stand."

The Combatant Commands ultimately voted to back the Chiefs and Northern Command, seven to three. Logistics, SOUTHCOM, and CENTCOM dissented. The cold looks that Horvath received from those three departed deputies told him the issue was not resolved; it had been a straw vote, not a consensus. "Roberta," he said, taking the deputy commander of the Strategic Command aside, pulling her into his brother's office. "Scott Air Force Base in Illinois reports to the Logistics Command, to Palmer. It's the largest Air Mobility Command base we have. What can I do to get it under control?"

She shook her head, her red hair tied back into bun, the streaks of gray that marked her as a new and very worried grandmother quite visible. "Karol, I'm not sure whether Doug Petrie—the Scott base commander—agrees with Admiral Palmer about this or not. Is there a specific concern?"

"Yes. The 82nd Airborne at Bragg and the 101st at Fort Campbell. Both are under CENTCOM. Do they still have their own air transports?"

"No, not anymore. Scott controls the disposition of the transports, but they routinely approve and dispatch aircraft on request to either base."

"Roberta, I need General Petrie to keep transport aircraft away from those bases. I want aircraft inspected, disabled, put on report, sabotaged, whatever it takes, but *keep them on the ground.* If Petrie won't do it, I'm going to have to get Collins to replace him, and that may mean an open breach with Palmer."

"Any aircraft from Scott would have to have permission to fly from NORAD, Karol, before they could move in American airspace. Especially now, with emergency flight limitations in effect."

"And how do NORAD and STRATCOM ultimately enforce those restrictions?" Horvath persisted.

Roberta Kennedy's eyes widened. "We'd…we'd have to have our fighters shoot them down."

"Can't do it that way," Horvath replied. "No more dead civilians, and no military casualties, Roberta. We have to keep the lid on this."

"This cannot happen here," Kennedy replied.

"No, it can't. So talk to Petrie and find a way to keep the transports on the ground," Horvath replied.

Chapter Forty-Five

General's Row
Quarters 22B
Joint Base Myer-Henderson Hall
Arlington, Virginia
Wednesday, October 26
10:35 P.M. EDT

Karol Horvath stood in front of his marble fireplace, a small glass of single malt scotch forgotten on the oak mantel. His home was a red-brick Victorian duplex, twelve rooms on each side, with bright white-painted porches and interior halls heavy with the dark oak floors and trim that bespoke elegance when the house was built in 1902. By seniority Horvath was entitled to a bigger house on the Row, but he hardly felt the need. His own children were grown, and he liked the young Rear Admiral who shared the adjacent unit with his four school age children. On warm autumn nights they would invite Horvath to join their touch football games or to shoot hoops in the basketball half court that had been installed in the back yard. There had been no games on this night; a cold wind had blown in from the Atlantic that rattled the dying leaves on the Row's majestic oaks between intermittent gusts of rain.

Horvath turned to Elizabeth Gray.

"Paul can't go," he said flatly.

"He goes or I don't, General," Elizabeth Gray replied, holding her ground. "And Los Alamos wants me to pick up the package in person."

"Do I get a say in this?" Paul Coulter demanded.

Both Gray and Horvath glanced at him dismissively. "No," Horvath replied.

"All right, Major, tell me why Los Alamos is demanding that you be our messenger," he continued.

"Two reasons," she responded. "First, I grew up on The Hill and in Santa Fe. They know me, know my face, and trust me. Second, they are absolutely scared shitless. That means they have found something very serious and very bad. These are people who model nuclear explosions and manufacture plutonium triggers for nuclear weapons. They do not scare easily."

"But why add Paul to this?" Horvath persisted. "He was photographed and DNA sampled on Black Sunday. His doctor removed the data chip they put in his neck, but they'll figure that out pretty soon. They've linked his military records, driver's license, passport, social security account data, federal identification, and every image of him that has ever appeared in the media into his file. They will use TriPlex and make him a data mining priority. He'll be lit up like a Christmas tree, and about as easy to catch."

"Somebody has to witness this," Elizabeth responded stubbornly. "If Los Alamos has found something conclusive we still have to tell the story, make it convincing, and make it real. Otherwise we'll get rolled over. Truth won't matter, fear will. Look at what happened in the 2004 election. The war hero was portrayed as a coward. The coward and the draft dodger were made into men of iron. And people believed it."

"It still doesn't have to be Paul."

"Yes, it does. It's his story. And, to be practical, the odds of getting the information out increases when there are two of us carrying it."

Horvath ran a hand through his steel gray hair, took a poker from the set of cast iron tools on the hearth and poked at the fire. "All right," he said, straightening up to speak. "Paul goes. But he goes on his own, separately. If he makes it to Santa Fe by Sunday night without being followed, good. If not, Elizabeth, you go on to Los Alamos alone."

"Agreed," Elizabeth said reluctantly. "How does Paul go?"

"By ground," Horvath replied. "There are gypsy busses that don't ask questions and don't require retina scans. Paul can also buy cars, drive them and dump them." He turned to Paul. "Stick to secondary roads and small towns. Stay off the interstates. Avoid the big truck stops, off-ramp filling stations, fast food restaurants. They all have cameras now and you never know when the images are being uploaded to Homeland Intelligence. If you leave tomorrow you've got three days. With all the dodging you are going to need to do you are going to be pushed for time. Here."

Horvath passed him a manila envelope. Paul opened it. He found two identities inside: driver's licenses, social security cards aged to look worn and brown, as if carried in a sweaty wallet for years, Visa and Mastercards. New federal identity cards. Faded pictures of people he did not know.

"Both of these identities were prepared by the Defense Intelligence Agency. Oh, the people named were once real enough, but they died in early childhood. We created their social security work histories, school transcripts, credit reports and uploaded them into the relevant databases. Don't use the credit cards; they won't work. We can create fake identifications and inject them into federal databases but we can't fund any domestic undercover operation unless we bring in the FBI. Can you get some cash without triggering the reporting that would come with major bank withdrawals?"

Coulter nodded. "I have somewhere north of twenty thousand dollars in cash. It's dribbled in over the years, a small share of the annual rents from a couple of buildings that my mother's family owns. The checks are always drawn on Credit Suisse and never more than three thousand dollars. I do report the income and pay tax."

Elizabeth cocked an eyebrow at him. "Where?" she demanded.

"Originally, under the bed," Coulter replied sheepishly. "There's a small canister safe under the floorboards. I pulled the cash out a couple of weeks ago in case we couldn't go home. I stashed it with Roy Gruber. At Paulie's Grill."

"You left twenty grand with a bartender?" Elizabeth asked, incredulous.

"More like twenty three grand, I think. A couple checks came in two months ago."

"With a *bartender?*"

"No one more trustworthy," Paul replied

"And you were going to tell me this…when?"

"Hey, I had a concussion," Paul replied defensively.

She was about to return fire when Horvath held up a hand. "Paul, some free advice: don't ever hold out on Elizabeth again; she's smarter than you are." He picked up his long forgotten glass from the mantel. "Major. You go on a regularly scheduled MATS flight to Kirtland AFB in Albuquerque at 0600 Saturday. You're my liaison to a Special Forces intelligence project with the 27th Special Operations Wing at Cannon AFB in Clovis, New Mexico. The next planning meeting doesn't happen until Wednesday 2 November at 1400 hours. In the meantime your cover is a 72 hour leave compassionate leave to visit your mother. You're due in Los Alamos on Monday, 31 October."

Horvath raised his glass and tossed back the scotch. "Don't fuck this up. I want both of you back in one piece."

Los Alamos

Chapter Forty-Six

Coulter's journey west started at a Goodwill store in Alexandria, Virginia at eight A.M. on Thursday morning. He bought five days' worth of second hand clothes, stripped to the skin in a dingy storeroom and dressed hurriedly in jeans, wool socks, black turtleneck and red flannel shirt under a denim barn coat. He filled a duffel bag with the rest of the clothes he'd purchased and dumped his own in a trash bin in the alley behind the building. Coulter then jogged a painful half mile in used hiking boots that were not a perfect fit to the bus station and caught a commuter bus to Richmond, Virginia. By 11:15 that morning he had bought his first car, a clapped out 2008 Mazda hatchback, and headed west.

He would pull the same dodge twice more, alternating dreary stretches on busses with newly purchased junk cars. The local gypsy busses that had sprung up to connect small towns and remote suburbs when gasoline had grown expensive were nothing more than recycled school buses with hard thin seats and little heat, but they were cheap, they ran, and they were of little interest to state police or the increasingly common Dark/Star patrols.

It had been a bleak journey. Indian summer died as he was passing through the Appalachians. The south central Plains from Illinois through Southern Missouri and south into Oklahoma were soaked with cold autumn rains. Coulter stole license plates late at night from parked cars on dark side streets. He avoided telephones, never used a computer, and scrounged food and coffee as best he could from small neighborhood grocery stores, heeding Elizabeth's warning that many of the chain restaurants and fast food joints along the Interstates and major secondary roads had been fitted with surveillance cameras.

Coulter was appalled at how badly the country had been damaged by the Great Recession that never seemed to end. In Washington, the worst effects of the Bust were eased by steady federal payrolls. D.C.'s restaurants remained busy, her shops mostly solvent; houses and apartments had fallen in value but not so much as to cause their owners to abandon them. In the Middle South and the Plains the situation was much worse. Coulter drove through miles of semi-abandoned exurban housing developments, stranded on secondary roads on the far outskirts of Cincinnati, Lexington, and Memphis. The strip malls built to service them were mostly empty, their walls marred with graffiti and gang signs. More than a few had been cheaply remodeled into evangelical mega churches that provided as much, if not more, social support than the governments of these stranded suburbs could afford. The churches spawned day cares, food banks, chore and tool exchanges, Christian bookstores, modest cafes. Too many of the people Paul met seemed as worn as the country itself, clothes sagging with age, ragged children in tow, and angered beyond sense or reason.

The clutch of the second junk car he'd purchased, a 2009 Dodge Caliber, had felt loose when he'd bought the damn thing outside Memphis. Coulter cursed himself for six kinds of fool for failing to have it checked and sure enough, it started giving out just west of Oklahoma City. The sky was black. High winds and rain lashed the car; the temperature was in the forties and falling fast, and by midnight Oklahoma could be having one of her famous ice storms. He had to quit for the night and find new wheels in the morning. He glanced over at his map and decided to head south on U.S. 183; there was a small town, New Cordell, about twenty miles to the south, and he needed to sleep.

Cordell been one of the Oklahoma land rush towns that sprang up over night in the 1890s, after most of Oklahoma was stolen from the Indian Territory. At the town's northern outskirts there were vacant lots with burned over foundations, the homes never rebuilt after the August 2015 tornados that ravaged much of the state west of Oklahoma City. He counted six churches, ranging from steeples to storefronts, before reaching the center of town. He turned right and found himself circling a faded but still handsome town square. An elaborately restored courthouse of prairie brick with white Ionic columns and a metal cupola anchored the west edge of the square, but the neighborhood had not fared so well. A few of the low brick buildings held offices for the sort of lawyer you hope the other guy has, tucked between antique stores, a pawnshop, a dollar store, a bail bondsman, two religious bookstores, an abandoned bank, and a couple of bars.

Coulter found what he was looking for a half block west of the square, a door front between a barbershop and a tiny hardware store with the legend "Oxford Hotel and Rooms" marked in chipped black paint on the frosted glass door. Lights were on. He parked in the angled street space in front of the hotel, found the door open, and mounted the stairs to the second floor. An elderly woman sat behind a hotel counter, with ten key boxes mounted on the wall behind her. Only two keys were out. She stared at a television across the room.

Coulter dropped his bag on the floor in front of the counter, nodded in greeting. "I'd like a room for the night if you've got one," he began, offering a tentative smile.

The woman looked him up and down skeptically. "Doesn't look like we're exactly booming here, does it?" she rasped. "Thirty dollars and bath down the hall, fifty for a private bath."

"Down the hall is fine," Coulter replied. He took out his wallet, laid two twenties on the counter, and passed over a very good fake driver's license that identified him as Edward Shannon of Eau Claire, Wisconsin.

The woman took the extra ten dollars without comment, glanced at the license, chose not to photograph or scan it, passed Coulter a metal key, and turned an ancient paper registration book toward him, gesturing for him sign. "What brings you down here from Wisconsin?" she asked.

"Wanted to get out of the cold weather," Coulter replied, deadpan.

The old woman laughed a deep rich laugh that belied her weathered skin and thin gray hair and suddenly made Coulter imagine a much younger woman, with beehive hair and a tight 1960s skirt and sweater. "Not exactly well informed, were you, soldier?" she finally added.

"No ma'am," he answered, grinning. "Is there a hot meal and a beer within walking distance?"

"Maude's place," she replied. "The South Square Grill. Tell her that Marybeth says not to water your drinks like she does to most strangers."

The South Square Gill was, as promised, centered on the south side of New Cordell's town square, between a Hair Hut and a vacant storefront that had most recently been a hobby shop. It was both cleaner and more occupied than Paul expected. It was the Saturday night before Halloween, now a distinctly unpopular witch holiday in the heart of the Bible Belt. He guessed that many kids in this town would suffer through a prayer service with no opportunity for juvenile mayhem, the sugar-fueled ritual of toilet paper, tomatoes and spray paint that Paul had enjoyed so much during his slightly delinquent childhood.

He entered a dark comfortable room with a full back bar and leatherette booths, a place where middle-aged parents could get away from the kids and have a drink and a quiet meal. Coulter took a place at the bar, asked for and got a shot of Jim Beam with a draft beer back, and looked over a menu heavy on beef and short on greens.

The barmaid, a thick-waisted frizzy blonde with a tired face and reddened eyes took his order in cold silence and finally brought him a cheeseburger, onion rings and a wedge of iceberg lettuce with Thousand Island dressing. Coulter noticed a band of white skin on her ring finger under the bar lights and concluded that the breakup must have been recent; the last thing she would want was inane chatter with a strange man. He opened the Oklahoma City newspaper on the bar and read, squinting in the dim light. The shock of the West Coast attacks had all but frozen business, the already dismal stock markets had lost another third of their value, and even the oil and gas industry was in trouble as people hunkered down and stopped driving.

He had nearly finished his meal and a second beer when the television behind the bar blared into life. "Hush, everybody," the barmaid demanded. "This is important."

The image of Royce Reed filled the screen. He stood silent before the alter of his home church in Sacramento, California, his head bowed. He slowly raised his arms toward the heavens.

"Lord," he intoned. "This is the hour of crisis. Our people lack strength. Three of our cities have been shattered. Our fields lie fallow, our businesses fail. Your people are hungry. Your people are in need."

Reed raised his head, his powerful black eyes burning into the screen. *Trick television,* Paul thought. *He's being enhanced.* Then he noticed that the tavern buzz had dropped to silence. The people around him stared at the screen.

"Worse than all of that, Lord," Reed continued. "Worse than the destruction, worse than the radiation sickness, worse than the hunger, worse than the need. Worse than all of that. We are divided. We riot in the streets. We fail to give support and our faith to your servants, James Robinson and Kyle Jackson. So many seek to return us to the godlessness that has brought us to this hour."

Reed's face shifted, twisted into something very much like rage. "Curse the dividers, Lord Jesus! Curse the unrepentant! Curse the ones who will not follow! Let us unite, let us be strong, let us wage the Your battles!

The bar remained quiet as the television choir broke into Reed's personal anthem, *See Now the Chariots of the Lord!*

When the song ended a sudden chorus of Amen! filled the bar. Paul Coulter, keenly aware of his status as a stranger in a scarred and frightened community, put too much money beside his plate and left as quietly as he could.

In the morning the sleet had stopped. Coulter found that Cordell had lost its last car dealership, new or used. He nursed the Caliber back up to the freeway and drove west on the frontage road as far as he dared, finally spotting a Used Cars! We're Open Sundays! sign a few miles past Clinton. He hurriedly looked over the cars, concluded the haggle and drove off the Big Mike's Elk City Used Cars lot in a fifteen year old Ford Explorer that cost him $1000 cash plus the scrap value that the old Dodge would fetch at the Long Beach metal yards where the Chinese buyers roamed, eager for scrap steel to feed their furnaces. The price was extortionate because the Explorer's engine had a valve knock and would, as Mike himself cheerfully admitted, require a quart of oil every three hundred miles or so. But the shocks seemed decent, the steering tight, the tires passable retreads. Big Mike, having gotten a better cash price than he dared hope, passed Paul the blank federal car sale paperwork with a wink and threw in a half case of motor oil and a gallon of anti-freeze. Coulter wished he knew how to whistle as he got back on the freeway. The morning sunshine had faded and the clouds to the west were again turning an ominous black—but he had just 550 miles, only nine or ten hours even in tough weather, to go.

For a moment Coulter feared that he had made a fatal mistake by jumping back on the freeway for the last twenty miles through east-central New Mexico, wanting to pick up 284 at Clines' Corners and run directly north into Santa Fe. A trio of New Mexico State Police cars and one black-windowed Homeland Security SUV massed on the highway beside him. He focused his stare straight ahead and gradually slowed to a steady three miles an hour less than the speed limit, attempting to figuratively nod the head to their authority and let them pass. They eventually did and he made the exit north, grateful that his lack of caution had not done him in, at least not yet. Coulter's eyes shifted cautiously from the road to the rear view mirror as he took the Old Las Vegas Highway and then Old Santa Fe trail, the back roads into downtown Santa Fe. Snow began to fall and the roads grew slick as the elevation rose towards Santa Fe's seven thousand feet. It was about six P.M. when he finally dumped the Explorer, keys in the ignition and doors unlocked as an invitation to theft, on a side street in the South Capitol neighborhood just below the Santa Fe River. He trudged the last half mile north to the Plaza, glad for the warmth of an old wool hiking sweater and the barn coat. At the corner of Old Santa Fe Trail and West San Francisco Coulter turned through the adobe entrance and ran up the brick stairs into the lobby of the La Fonda Hotel. He almost inhaled the warm lacquered brick floors, white walls and dark heavy beams, as if coming home.

The front desk clerk, a spectacularly pretty young woman with the name "Garza" etched on a brass nameplate pinned over her left breast, looked at him skeptically. His bruises were still vivid; he was dressed in a thrift store barn coat, carried a worn duffel bag, and now had snow frosting his hair. "My car broke down a couple miles back," Paul Coulter said apologetically, which was not too far from the truth. "I can never find a cab in Santa Fe."

"Well, that's certainly true," the clerk replied, thawing a bit. "So how can I—"

"There should be a message," Coulter said quickly. "From my wife? She should have checked in several hours ago. I'm Henry Cooper."

The clerk checked her computer. "I don't—no, you're right, here it is. Can I see some identification?"

Coulter handed her the second of the false driver's licenses he carried, this one from Virginia. She scanned it into her system; the light turned a favorable green.

The desk clerk finally smiled, relieved by his apparently legitimate i.d. and the cost of the room the fictitious Mrs. Cooper had taken. "Your wife is waiting for you in 508. Room service has an order for champagne, with dinner for two to follow. So things are looking up for you, Mr. Cooper. Have a wonderful evening."

Elizabeth greeted him at the door in a pale cream gown of sheer silk. The room she was lit only by candles on the dining table set up at the foot of their bed. Wine had just arrived. A pinion fire danced in the shadows behind her in an adobe kiva. Paul tossed his bag into the room as she slipped into his arms and closed the door behind them.

"The answer, by the way, is yes. I will marry you. So I thought we should have a wedding night," she said, and then they did not talk for a very long time.

Chapter Forty-Seven

They left Santa Fe together at a lazy eleven thirty, fueled by a room service breakfast, happy and quiet. Paul drove Elizabeth's rented but thankfully modern Ford SUV north out of the city on 284, enjoying the sunlight reflected in the first snow of the season but concerned about the thick black line of clouds in the east as they passed the high ridge alongside the Santa Fe Opera, the village of Tesuque in the valley below. He gestured at the sky.

"Looks like a nasty norther," Elizabeth agreed. "But I doubt it will hit

The Hill, much less Santa Fe, before late afternoon at the earliest. We should be on our way by then."

"How will you get back?" Paul asked.

"MATS flight," she responded. "I'll take the meeting at Holloman, then deadhead back to DC on the first available plane, whatever it is."

"Where do I go next?" Paul asked. "And when will I see you?"

"You've got the worst part of it, I'm afraid. Karol thinks we need to take at least one hard version of the Los Alamos data offshore immediately. He's worked out an arrangement for you to deliver a copy to a military attaché at the French Embassy in Mexico City. I don't think it's going to safe for you to fly. You'd best travel by the same rules you followed getting here."

Paul groaned. "In Mexico that's a thousand miles on buses. My ass is too old for this."

"Nothing wrong with your ass and related parts last night, old man," she teased.

"This will cut short wedded bliss, I know it," Coulter replied. "Besides—

"I knew I'd have to trade you in for a newer model," Elizabeth replied, her voice serene. "Just don't miss the turn up to the Hill. Left on 502 in Pojoaque."

Coulter turned as instructed. The previous night's snow was white on the sides of 502 as they began the long climb to the Los Alamos Mesa two thousand feet above. The Rio Grande valley dropped behind them, the river deep in its canyon. The sun was still bright despite the coming storm and flooded the Rio Grande basin with light.

Elizabeth looked away from him, transfixed by the views. "I want to come home," she said softly. "Can we live here, Paul? When all of this is over, when we don't have to run any more, I want to live here. At home."

"Might as well," Coulter agreed. "I'm pretty much cooked in Washington. But what can I do?"

"Lots of opportunities for handsome middle-aged men in Santa Fe," Elizabeth said lightly. "Gigolo, horse groom, real estate sales, investment fraud—

"Writers?"

"Lots of writers, all broke. We'll find a way." Elizabeth grew quiet, seemed to withdraw within herself as they approached the entrance to Los Alamos. "Keep going straight past the airport," she instructed. "Stay on Trinity Drive, it's easier. When you get to Diamond, turn right and head for the North Mesa."

The house on Camino Encantado was a modest old two story split-level, pale blue with white trim, on Los Alamos' North Mesa. The steep hillside behind the house was forested in young ponderosa pines and pinion, marking this as one of the Los Alamos neighborhoods that had suffered from the vast Cerro Grande forest fire that nearly burned the Lab and its surrounding villages to the ground.

Three men and one woman were waiting for them inside the living room, seated on a pair of leather sofas with work papers, plates and cups scattered on a large rustic coffee table in front of them. The man who had opened the front door for them, tall and stooped in his early forties with thinning hair and dressed in fraying corduroys and an old wool sweater said, "I'm Dr. Sanders. These are my colleagues on the forensics team: Saul Baranov, Avram Litsky, and Li Choy Peng, who goes by Linda. We're ah, waiting—I've never done this before. I guess we should ask for your identification or something."

Paul held out his White House Press badge, now revoked. "Paul Coulter. This is Major Elizabeth Gray, United States Army. She's here at the request of your LANL Director, and on orders from the Joint Chiefs of Staff." Elizabeth held out her Army identification for inspection. "Is Dr. Hohauser—

"I'm here, I'm here," a sharp voice said from the kitchen. LANL Director William Hohauser stepped into the living room from a back hallway dusting snow from his shoulders. At sixty he was a still solid man over six feet tall with thick gray blond hair and pale blue eyes in an amused, skeptical face. "Elizabeth." He gathered Gray into a tight embrace. "Relax everybody," he added. "This is Donald Gray's daughter. You can trust her with your life."

"I think we already have," Linda Peng replied softly.

"Yeah, there's that. Saul? You got any more coffee?"

"Take just a minute," Baranov replied, heading for his kitchen.

Coulter tried to place Hohauser's accent: mid-Atlantic, he decided, with a west coast overlay. That checked with the little he knew of his background: a physicist, raised on Long Island, undergrad at Caltech, with master's and doctorate from Berkeley, post doc at the Fermi lab in Illinois, then six years at CERN in Switzerland doing particle physics at the Large Hadron collider. Like most physicists, if

Hohauser got his Nobel it would be for the work he had done before he turned forty and settled into academic and administrative life.

Hohauser finally released Elizabeth, turned toward Paul. "You must be Coulter. The reporter."

"That's right," he responded. "I'm along to tell the story."

"If you live long enough," Hohauser replied. "It's one mother-fucker of a story."

"We started by reviewing Dark/Star's analysis of the radioactive materials left at the sites of the bombings," Hohauser began. "They'd done what we would do with our own samples: spectrographic analysis, physical property analysis, radioactivity and isotope measurements. At first it seemed pretty consistent with our findings. Dark/Star's labs concluded that the uranium in the spent fuel had been mined in the Khorasan Province of Iran. There are a lot of mines there now—something like six per cent of the world's raw uranium production. But the chemical characteristics of uranium ores are pretty similar throughout the Caspian Sea basin—an ore from Kazakhstan to the north, or Turkmenistan to the northeast, can be essentially identical.

"So—we went on to reactor characteristics. They tied the spent fuel to Iran's Bushehr I reactor. It's a pressurized water reactor, originally started by the Germans when the Shah was still in power way back in the 1970s, mothballed after the revolution in 1979. They restarted construction after the Iran-Iraq war ended, retrofitting the containment to a Russian PWR design called a VVER, which uses a modestly enriched U-235—anywhere from 2.5 to 7% enrichment—as fuel. It went on-line five years ago. Like any reactor fuel, you burn it and you're going to get various plutonium isotopes, which would seem to explain the dirtiness of the bombs."

"So the analysis from Dark/Star was accurate?" Paul asked.

"It looked like it," Hohauser responded. "Then we got the second set of samples from the dirty bomb sites, and the samples that the

FBI took in that machine shop in Nevada. And we couldn't replicate the Dark/Star lab's results."

"How did they differ?" Elizabeth asked.

"My guys here are pretty smart." Hohauser gestured at the four scientists still seated around the low table, nervously drinking coffee. "The initial chemical characteristics seemed to pair up. Could have been the same ores. Then all the results went to hell. You see, you take the same fuel, but burn it in different types of reactors, you're going to end up with a different post-fission spent fuel product. Here it wasn't even the same fuel. You see, the Soviets developed another type of reactor, called an RBMK. Chernobyl was an RBMK. They're all shut down now. They were graphite moderated, water cooled, amd use natural refined uranium—essentially cleaned up yellow-cake—in the fuel rods. They produced more plutonium because of the nature of the reaction—one reason the Soviets liked them, they got electricity and about a bomb a month from them. But it results a whole different chemical and isotopic analysis. Clear as night and day. The bombs used on the West Coast were juiced with RBMK generated spent fuel. Iran had no access to, or use for, that type of spent fuel."

"Can you say that in a court? Testify to a reasonable scientific certainty?" Coulter asked.

"This isn't a matter of reasonable scientific certainty. *This is certainty.* Physical chemistry doesn't lie. Everything's off. Chemistry, age—this fuel wasn't burned in Bushehr, it was burned in a different kind of reactor over forty years ago. Somebody in our government has fucked with the evidence in the biggest murder case since 911."

There was silence. Saul Baranov got up to drop another log on the fire, passed again the plate of cold cuts, cheese and rolls, but no one ate.

Elizabeth broke the silence. "What about the samples taken from Nevada?"

"Matched our analyses from Seattle, San Francisco, and Los Angeles. All except for the highly enriched uranium. There was HEU in Nevada, and it came from somewhere else. Not RBMK at all."

"So where did these radioactives come from?" Elizabeth asked impatiently.

"From us," Hohauser replied.

"This is crazy," Elizabeth said vehemently. "I cannot believe that the United States military would provide uranium and plutonium for use in a domestic attack."

"Not saying they did," Hohauser replied. "Neither knowingly nor voluntarily. But I can tell you where this stuff came from. The spent fuel in the dirty bombs was Russian. It was burned in 1984 in the Kurst I reactor in the Kurk Oblast, a small Russian administrative province on the border of the Ukraine. The spent fuel was stored at a reprocessing facility on the northern edge of Chechnya. A sensible place to do plutonium reprocessing if you don't give a shit about the people living there, but not so smart when the local folks rebel and kick your ass out. After Yeltsin started the first Chechen War the rebels figured that the radioactives might be useful. They captured the storage facilities and the reprocessing plant. And so in July 1995 soldiers, scientists and technicians in a joint operation, Russian *Spetnatz* and American Special Forces, were sent in to take back the site, dismantle the reprocessing facility, and evacuate the spent fuel to the United States so that it could cool and eventually be disposed of. The army selected the storage site in the United States. An abandoned ammunition depot, a Superfund site, Tularosa, right here in New Mexico."

"You couldn't—"

"Let me finish. The traces of HEU that the FBI found in Nevada are bomb metal, north of seventy per cent enriched HEU. It can be weaponized in a crude artillery shell device, with probable yield of somewhere between three and six kilotons. We don't know how much metal went through there, but you'd better plan on one to four bombs."

"And where did it come from?" Elizabeth demanded again.

"Again, from us. It was seized in the Spring of 1998 by American Special Forces in a raid on a secret former Soviet weapons fabrication site in southern Turkmenistan. It was called *Golden Talon*—one of the more audacious military actions in United States history. Iran saw an opportunity, to seize a cache of nearly a quarter ton of bomb-grade metal. Turkmenistan, in the post-Soviet chaos, had essentially no functioning military. Clinton sent in a battalion sized Special Forces unit that beat back the Iranian assault, secured the site and held it for three days while technicians from this lab and the Nuclear Regulatory Commission packaged the uranium and trucked it to Ashgabat, where it was flown back to the U.S. in C-5 transport planes. We've held it ever since, to re-blend it and burn it in our naval reactors. As you know, those reactors use a much more enriched fuel than civilian power reactors. The Navy stored some of that fuel at Tularosa—and that's where it was taken.

"You can't know this," Elizabeth protested. "The mission plans and the after action reports would be so deeply classified—

"Who?" Paul cut her off. "Who was the commanding officer?" he demanded

"The Special Operations commander for both missions was the same: Colonel Kyle Hunter Jackson."

"We've emailed the encrypted source and origin data for the nuclear materials to a half-dozen scientific institutes and agencies around the world," Linda Peng explained. "To CERN, to the French National Center for Scientific Research, the British Royal Society, the Japan Atomic Energy Institute, to the Ford Foundation, and to the UN International Atomic Energy Agency in Vienna and Geneva. But we're not sure if anything got off the Hill. Some kind of deep firewall has been thrown up around every data transmission originating here. We need to get it out by courier."

"You didn't answer my question," Gray said, confronting Hohauser. "I still don't know how you got the mission data you claim to have retrieved. All of that would be encrypted inside secured Defense Department systems not accessible from the Internet. We are talking about felony violations of the National Security Act and Patriot Three."

"Can't do shit about the legal side, Elizabeth," Hohauser said dismissively. "We did what we did and we're either going to get a fair trial, or we're not. But once we knew it was our stuff, we had to find out where it originally came from. As to the technical side, Avram figured that out in ten minutes."

Avram Litsky, the shy computer scientist, finally spoke up. "DOD maintains a computer center here," he explained. "Direct links to the Pentagon, not an Internet connection. We simply disabled their security, opened up the servers, and removed the memory cores. Then we froze them in liquid nitrogen. The DRAM chips in the cores retain their data for several minutes when the power is shut off. When you freeze the chips they hold their data for up to three hours. We plugged them into my cryptographic systems and used pattern recognition software to tease out the encryption codes. Once we had the codes, hacking into DOD's data bases was not difficult."

Hohauser had been listening to Litsky's explanation with one ear, the other attached to a cell phone. "Shit," he said abruptly. "Somebody knows you are here. The Hill's being shut down."

Chapter Forty-Eight

"The Lab's swarming with federal agents," Hohauser said. "A mix of Homeland Security investigators and these new federal goons in the black uniforms. My security chief is trying to hold them off, divert them by having them search the Labs," Hohauser responded.

"Can we drive off the Mesa?" Elizabeth demanded.

Hohauser opened his phone again, punched in numbers, queried, listened. "No. 502, 501, the East Jemez Road, and the Pajarito Road have all been blocked."

Elizabeth looked at the light beginning to fail in the dark snow-laden New Mexico sky, and the clock on the wall beside the fireplace. The long discussion had taken more than three hours. "There's an airport here," she said. "Is there an aircraft we can charter?"

"Not that I know of," Hohauser replied. "The Lab maintains a Bell Jet Ranger at the airfield. But my pilot is down in Santa Fe, hospitalized with a bad case of the flu."

"I can fly it," Elizabeth responded. "What are we taking with us?"

"These," Hohauser responded, opening his palms and displaying six fifty gigabyte data sticks. "Copies of the report along with all the raw data. Like the emails we sent out, they're encrypted." He displayed a small air pressured hypodermic. "These data chips have the decryption codes. They are about one millimeter in diameter—smaller than the head of a pin." He stood in front of Coulter, said "I need some skin here, Paul." Coulter opened his barn coat, lifted his turtleneck sweater, and Hohauser swiftly injected him above his right hip, below the bandages that still compressed his ribs. "Elizabeth? You're a lady; I'll let you pick your spot."

"Small of the back, please." She turned, raised her shirt, and accepted the implant.

"Good. When do you want to take off?"

"Sunset is just after six. The moon doesn't set until well after eight. I'd like to wait for a fully dark sky but I don't think we can risk that. Let's go now and I'll take off in the dusk without running lights."

"I agree," Hohauser replied. "Give Saul your keys; let him stash your rental car in the canyon for a couple of days. Everyone else, scatter. Go home, go to a bar. Do your laundry. Anything you might do after work. I'm going to take these people to the airport and hope that being Director and a gifted natural born asshole lets me bluff them through."

The snow had thickened throughout the afternoon and five to six inches of new snow lay on the ground. Hohauser drove quickly in his black LANL-issue SUV, hoping that the security personnel from down the mountain were still engaged in a snipe hunt through the labs. The hardest part came from the terrain; they could not drive directly from the North Mesa to the airport because of Pueblo Canyon, but had to pass through the center of town. On Diamond, at the intersection with Canyon Road, they would drive just north of the Labs themselves.

They were in luck; roadblocks had not yet been set up at Trinity Drive. Hohauser more or less slid through the intersection and headed east, pushing through yellow lights where he could and trying not to draw too much attention. He bluffed his way through a road block at East Park, just shy of the airport, promising that he would check in at the full security station that had been set up on 502 just beyond the Eastgate industrial center on the road to White Rock.

When they reach the airport, a single long runway with a small terminal building, Hohauser drove directly inside the open hanger and pulled up next to a white and blue Bell Jet Ranger with LANL markings. "Incredibly bad security," he said. "We have north of two hundred pounds of plutonium in the Labs on any given day and you can roll into our local airport without waking anyone up. Well, today it works. How are we going to get this bird out of here? It's fully fueled—just under a hundred gallons, call it 3.5 hours. Normally we tow it on the skids."

"Not tonight," Elizabeth said, looking out the open hanger door and judging the sky just dark enough. "Tonight we fly."

Hohauser's face turned grim. He regarded them for a moment and then kissed Elizabeth gently on the cheek. "Go," he said softly. "I'm so sorry for putting you at risk. But we needed someone we could trust."

Elizabeth kissed the older man and then turned to Paul, suddenly all military officer again. "Grab the emergency kit," she commanded as she sprinted to the helicopter. She unshipped the tie down from the rear rotor blades and threw herself into the right hand pilot seat as Paul scrambled behind the copter to the left door. He shoved their kit—a black duffel with maps, thermal blankets, a compass, two liters of water and four MRE rations, two knives, and Elizabeth's small Walther automatic—into the space behind their seats. Elizabeth rushed through the preflight checklist mounted above the windshield, switched on the power, and started the compressor. The jet engine whined as air was compressed; when the temperature grew to one half the 150 Celsius max hot start she dumped fuel into the combustor and the turbine began to howl. When the compressor passed 25% power the main rotor began to turn. Elizabeth waited while the temperatures rose, then gently rolled the throttle forward. The Jet Ranger rose four feet off the floor, vectored right, and sailed out in the blowing night snow.

Paul passed quickly through his normal helicopter ritual—skin shading green, reaching for and filling the airsick bag—then sealed the bag and tossed it out the window. He put on a flight helmet with earphones, activated his mike.

"Honey," Elizabeth said, "you are the only Marine Recon Bronze Star winner in history who gets airsick in helicopters."

"I know," he said ruefully. "But at least it's over quick. You got a plan, or are we heading second star on the right, and straight on 'till morning?"

"Plan," Elizabeth responded. The edge of the Los Alamos Mesa passed below them; the gaping Rio Grande valley opened up, a miles wide gray-black hollow broken only by the scattered lights from ranches and cars near the river.

Elizabeth reduced the rotor speed and the Jet Ranger fell toward the valley floor two thousand feet below. Paul hung on and gritted his teeth; the chopper straightened into level flight scarcely twenty feet above the shallow Rio Grande.

"Plan?" Paul asked again, as breath returned to his lungs.

"Fly low. We're a bogey to any civilian, military, or Homeland Security radar at the border," she replied. "So I'm staying in the river bed. About forty miles north of Albuquerque I want to juke west over the Santa Anna and Las Lunas Pueblos at low altitude with no running lights. When we're about thirty miles south of ABQ we can return to the Rio Grande, skim the river. Then, about halfway between Truth or Consequences and Las Cruces, I want to leave the river and head west again."

"Why?" Paul asked.

"Kirtland AFB is located at the Albuquerque Airport. Holloman Air Force Base is just west of Alamogordo. Holloman has a nasty little Homeland Intelligence team there. With Apache helicopters. And four F-35 jump jets."

"Do the taxpayers know about this unit?"

"No. But if you look at all the nuclear shit we have spread all over New Mexico, from LANL to White Sands, it makes sense from a security perspective. I really don't want to tangle with them."

"What's the end game?"

"Fly south by south west. The border controls and defenses are weak east of Agua Fria along the southwest boot heel of New Mexico. Rough canyon country—lots of ways to stay under the radar until we are across the border. You might want to keep that second air sick bag handy."

"And then?"

"We see how good our hiking boots are and whether the phony passports and Mexican visas will fly."

"Where do we go after that?"

"South. Where your good friend Karen went—someplace between Guatemala and Columbia, with white sand and good surfing."

"I'm with you. I've even still got money."

"Good, baby, good. You know how I hate washing dishes. Hang on. We're going to do some very low flying now. We're getting too close to the Santa Fe airport."

They passed the southern front of the snowstorm between Santa Fe and Albuquerque and the three quarter moon was bright in the sky, brighter than Elizabeth liked but it made flying without running lights at low altitude over the Pueblos to the west more manageable. "There's a valley between Las Cruces, which is on the Rio Grande, and the Cooke mountains to the west," Elizabeth said, her voice scratchy over the chopper's intercom. "When we get close to the boot heel, around Deming, I'm going to swing west to the New Mexico-Arizona border. Agua Prieta in Sonora, Mexico, is just across the border. From there it's easy—if you like Mexican busses. Or we can maybe fly local—down to Cabo San Lucas before crossing back to Mexico City. You really still have cash money?"

"At least twenty thousand left," Paul replied. "Let's take a suite at the Camino Real in Mexico City. I've always wanted to do that."

"Deal," Elizabeth said. Paul could not see her expression; the flying helmet hid her face from him. But he could feel her smile.

"Ok, baby, quiet time," she said. "We're cutting between Las Cruces and Silver City, and I'm going to be clipping the ground at thirty feet or so. This is going to take all I've got."

"Oh shit oh shit oh shit," Elizabeth said, her voice breathy with stress.

"What?" Paul demanded.

"Three lights, behind us. I'm guessing they are Apaches from Holloman. If they're F-35s, that's worse. Either way they are going to overtake us in about four minutes. No radio contact; they're not out here to talk to us. They probably already have missile lock."

Paul peered to his right, checked the map display with the GPS locator that automatically set their position. "We're over the Mexican border. Will they break off?"

"Fuck, no. Easier to apologize to the Mexicans than give up. Hang on; I'm going to drop us into a canyon." Elizabeth palmed the stick and the Jet Ranger lost altitude in a hurry. She turned hard left and slipped the helicopter, now flying on its side, between two large masses of rock into the entrance of a river canyon. The borders of the canyon were tight and flew past Paul like some ghostly 3-D movie; the movie effect actually helped him ignore the fact that a glancing touch against the rotors would tear the chopper apart.

Coulter looked into the rear projection screen of the helicopter's display panel. "They're on us," he said. "Lights are getting bigger, they are following." Suddenly the moonlit night exploded into white light and two red streaks passed on either side of them.

"They're firing Hydras to light us up," Elizabeth said grimly. "They may not be fitted with Sidewinders; if they had them they would have tried to kill us already. So until they get into weapons range with the chain gun we have some kind of duck and hide chance." She suddenly turned the Ranger hard right and barely missed the protruding wall of the canyon. Paul kept his eyes on the rear display;

suddenly one of the trailing lights behind them exploded into a greasy yellow-orange ball of burning jet fuel.

"He must have hit the rocks at the turn into this canyon," Paul said. Adrenalin coursed through him. "I can't see the others," Coulter exclaimed. "Have they broken off?"

"I doubt it. They just went to altitude to hold position and see what we do." Paul watched as Elizabeth flew the ever tighter canyon. A grey ghostly wall loomed ahead.

"Shit."

"What?"

"It's a box canyon," Elizabeth said quickly, already slowing. "We've got to split up. Take the emergency bag and the data sticks. I'm going to try to find a garage for this thing that they can't see. We are…about seven miles west of Agua Prieta. Mexican highway 2 is about two miles south. Head due west, even if you have to climb up canyon walls, and wait for me a mile from here. Don't try to get to the highway before morning; better if you can hold out until sundown tomorrow."

She dropped the helicopter to the canyon floor and Coulter felt the skids lurch on the uneven ground. "Go! We've got to do this! I'll find you—

"No!" Paul shouted. "We go together!"

"No time! If you love me Paul, Goddamnit, *go!*" Elizabeth suddenly shoved him with all her strength through the open door. Paul was holding their survival bag in his right hand; his left had only a loose grip on the cabin door frame. He started to tumble, off balance, through the open door. As he fell Elizabeth gunned the main rotor and shoved the chopper skyward. The last thing Paul saw in the cockpit before he fell away was the helicopter's fuel warning light burning red. The bird was empty, less than two or three minutes of fuel left.

Coulter landed heavily on his back on the stony ground, the wind knocked out of him, as he realized in horror what Elizabeth was going to do. He could manage nothing but a strangled, choked, "No!" as Elizabeth lifted the helicopter and flared it over the end wall of the box canyon, then threw it into a desperate corkscrew turn as a pair of missiles streaked into the cabin. The 30 mike slugs from the Apaches' chain guns tore what was left apart and ignited the remaining fuel into a fireball that briefly flamed up and showered burning fragments of metal and bone into the canyon below.

In the morning Coulter waited and watched from a shallow cave deep in the canyon, its entrance nearly twenty feet above the canyon floor. He was wrapped in a thermal blanket but still shook from the cold of the desert night. Two Apaches had returned about an hour after dawn. Four men emerged. They walked the area where the remnants of the Jet Ranger had fallen to gather the fragments that evidenced the murder they had done. Coulter fought off his nausea and watched them intently, memorizing faces, heights, weights, body proportions, the rhythm of their walks and the manner in which they held their heads. He watched for nearly seven hours. They had removed their name and rank insignia from their uniforms but wore no masks; he felt certain that he could find and identify them in court. If there was no trial he had other plans for them.

When they finally took off it was late afternoon. Coulter waited another half hour to be sure they were gone. After he emerged from his hiding place he took compass headings and built eight small rock cairns to mark the boundary of the site, so that a forensics team could examine it later. He set the cairns at the four cardinal and four intermediate points of the compass rose. It was the only rose he could leave for her.

Six hours later, feet bleeding, he walked into Agua Prieta. At midnight he caught the last bus of the night south to Hermosillo.

Inauguration Day

Chapter Forty-Nine

Hotel 1915
Alajuela, Costa Rica
Monday, January 16
10:45 A.M. CST

From Paul Coulter's journal:
The world now knows.

The data sticks from Los Alamos that I took to Mexico City were picked up, as promised, by a French Army captain designated by Karol Horvath. He took them with a murmured "I am sorry for the loss of your wife. She was a brave officer and a beautiful woman."

I didn't correct him. Elizabeth and I were married in every important sense; I never believed that the temporary lack of clergy or judge had made any difference. Elizabeth was a first and foremost a beautiful woman. If she had been less of an officer she might have lived.

Four days after I delivered the data sticks the UN International Atomic Energy Agency confirmed the Los Alamos findings: both the spent fuel and the seventy per cent enriched U-235 bomb metal had come from 1990s American raids on Chechnya and Turkmenistan, snatched away from potential terrorists more than twenty years before in two Special Forces operations, Sudden Resolve and Golden Talon, both commanded by Colonel Kyle Hunter Jackson.

Our federal government has gone essentially silent. James Robinson, having sold his soul to keep his office, still lives in the White House, now rumored to be a drunken ghost of the cruel and reckless man he once was. By statute, his lease on the joint doesn't end until Friday.

After that, what?

The question is Kyle Jackson. The National Continuity Authority has all but ceased issuing directives. The military commands that had briefly supported him now demand approval of every action by the Joint Chiefs of Staff. But Jackson still seems to hold sway with senior officers in two major commands: CENTCOM and SOUTHCOM, both army-dominated, both most likely to have troops sympathetic to the Phalanx. CENTCOM owns the two most important bases in the American military, Fort Bragg and Fort Campbell, their airborne units the most ferocious warriors. So there is a stalemate: the Joint Chiefs control the logistics and the paratroopers remain on their bases so long as they have no planes, at least for now. The military politics is fluid.

The Air Force and the Navy, thank god, say they have locked up the nukes. The Army hasn't had tactical nuclear munitions since Charlie McConnell signed the Treaty of Warsaw that eliminated them from all NATO and Russian arsenals.

There are two fears now. The first is that Jackson will go south, proclaim a rebellion and fight a war of attrition. The second is that between one and four nuclear weapons, primitive or not, working or not, have never been found.

Yesterday Jackson left Washington by ground and took a mutinous quarter of the Fort Belvoir Combat Brigade with him. The Chiefs had deployed a cordon of F-35s over Washington but decided to let Jackson go, postponing the day they dread, when American military units may square off against each other. I don't blame them; talk should precede civil war.

Rumor has it that Jackson will go to Fort Bragg and on to Charleston, which has historical resonance and a plethora of bases—Beaufort Air Station, Fort Jackson, and Paris Island—that may be loyal to him. The nuclear submarine base at King's Bay, Georgia, is not far away. The Navy says that all subs and nuclear armed surface vessels have confirmed their loyalty, replaced their old nuclear launch codes with ones known only to the JCS. They have gone to sea, but no one will breathe easily until the crisis is over. The King's Bay subs are to be feared when their captains' loyalties are uncertain. It is startling to think that what may hold back a mutinous Kings Bay submarine captain from attacking New York is a Trident commander from Bangor, Washington, with missiles trained on Charleston and Atlanta and Montgomery and New Orleans.

Inauguration Day—January 20—is four days away from today's celebration of Dr. King's birthday. The greatest protest in American history is forming across the West and the North and even much of the South, demanding Ben Giles' release and free elections. The protests will be spearheaded in the cities and the South by African-Americans organizing from their churches and homes. They are the shock troops of protest: they still hold fast the words and dreams of Dr. King, of Malcolm X, of Fannie Lou Hamer, of Thurgood Marshall, of John Lewis. They remember, in a way that white America has forgotten, what struggle is like. They know it in their bones.

At noon on Friday—the hour we no longer have a lawful President—something on the order of ten million people will gather. Another three million citizens who fled the country will swarm the borders and hopefully engage the border guards with talk and not violence. We will ask our soldiers and police to recognize us as brother and sister citizens—and not shoot us.

I hope that a book that Elizabeth gave me is still at our home in Washington. I wish I had it now. It is a privately published collection of Albert Camus' wartime essays. In 1946 Camus wrote:

> I have always believed that if people who placed their hopes in the human condition were mad, those who despaired of events were cowards. Henceforth there will be only one honorable choice: to wager everything on

the belief that in the end words will prove stronger than bullets.

The bus leaves here for Mexico, and then on to Brownsville, Texas, in about an hour. I don't know how this ends. Elizabeth will be with me at the border.

Author's Note

It Can't Happen Here, Sinclair Lewis' 1935 novel, depicts the rise of Senator Buzz Windrip, a Huey Long sort of fascist, to the Presidency in the depths of the Great Depression. Windrip's election was promoted by America's foremost 'radio bishop' and aided by a splintered opposition, a force of bully boys known as the 'Corpos', and secret financing from shadowy wealthy backers. A series of coups subsequently deposed Windrip in favor of General Dewey Haik, a hard-edged militarist. Haik's unjustified war against Mexico leads to the formation of a liberal, democratic underground led by Senator Walt Trowbridge, which launched attacks from Canada and began a civil war.

Seven Days in May, by Fletcher Knebel and Charles W. Bailey II, published in 1962 at the height of the Cold War, imagines an unpopular liberal President, Jordan Lyman, who forges a risky nuclear disarmament treaty with the Soviets over the objections of his generals, particularly the charismatic James Mattoon Scott, the Chairman of the Joint Chiefs of Staff. Scott and most of the Chiefs plot to seize control of the nation's telecommunications network and imprison the President during a national military preparedness exercise. Scott's plot is revealed to President Lyman by Marine Colonel Jiggs Casey, the director of the Joint Staff, who, with the help of the President's closest aides and friends, blocks the South American-style coup.

I've attempted to depict what some of the same historic forces explored by these earlier books might look like in the 21st Century.

The long hardships of the Great Recession have led, as in the 1930s, to the rise of a right-wing populism that overlaps with evangelical Christianity and has a far louder voice over the internet and Fox News than the radio preachers of the 1930s. Knebel and Bailey foresaw the dangers of a military establishment estranged from the civilian government. Our wars in Iraq and Afghanistan have been fought by a relatively small cadre of soldiers, too often out of sight, out of mind, and ill-served as to wages and medical care. The modern NSA has cyber, surveillance, and telecommunications capabilities far beyond anything imagined in 1962. The flood of dark money into our political process has helped the hard right win control of 54 seats in the United States Senate with twenty million fewer citizen's votes than were cast for the minority. The dangers are clear, and they are present.

Every American generation will confront authoritarianism in different ways and for different reasons. This is how I hope it will *not* happen here, in our time.

About the Author

Fredrick Huebner litigated investment and securities cases in Seattle for more than thirty years, and now mediates and arbitrates those types of disputes across the western United States. He is the author of six previous novels: *The Joshua Sequence, The Black Rose, Judgment by Fire (an Edgar Award Nominee), Picture Postcard (Winner of the Washington Governor's Writer's Award), Methods of Execution, and Shades of Justice*. He now writes from Kohala, Hawai'i.

Made in the USA
Middletown, DE
19 May 2015